By AR Bryant

CRAFT BLESSED
A Broken Spirit

Published by Dreamspinner Press
www.dreamspinnerpress.com

AR BRYANT

A Broken Spirit

Published by
DREAMSPINNER PRESS

8219 Woodville Hwy #1245
Woodville, FL 32362 USA
www.dreamspinnerpress.com

A Broken Spirit
© 2025 AR Bryant

Cover Art
© 2025 Aaron Anderson
aaronbydesign55@gmail.com
Cover content is for illustrative purposes only and any person depicted on the cover is a model.

Trade Paperback ISBN: 978-1-641-08800-8
Digital ISBN: 978-1-641-08799-5
Trade Paperback published March 2025
v. 1.0

Content/Trigger Warnings

Mentions of sexual assault of an adult and minor
Mentions of suicide attempts
Mentions of familial neglect
Mentions of sexual slavery
Explicit M/M relations
Mentions of self-harm
Alcohol consumption
Suicidal tendencies
Swearing

To My Grandmother

PROLOGUE

ASYL HAD always wanted to be special.

He was the apple of his mother's eye, his father's pride, and beloved lordling to the servants. For the last thirteen years of his life, Asyl had been groomed to take over his father's business. Well, not all thirteen, truthfully. Ten, perhaps. He was the heir to their family, the only child who made it out of infancy, so a lot rested on his shoulders.

Today was his thirteenth birthday, and the hour grew ever closer to his Awakening. At the exact second that he drew breath in this world, he would be blessed by the Goddess Ilyphari with a Craft. There were nine Crafts he could be blessed with, guiding the rest of his life with a related career he would naturally excel in.

Most, if not all, parents wanted their children to be blessed with an elemental Craft. Harvesters controlled plants, able to encourage them to maturity from a simple seed and will. Gaians could move the earth under their feet with just a thought, shaping the land and finding precious metals and stones. Aquans ruled the oceans and rivers with the ability to breathe underwater, able to locate and call upon underground reservoirs. Ignians were fireproof, able to call upon flames at will—or smother them. Gales could summon the winds ranging from a small breeze to massive storms.

The most coveted of the non-elemental Crafts were the Healers, who were able to pour their Craft into their patients to speed up recovery time. Secondly were Seers, able to see into the future, even if their Visions weren't exactly clear in their meaning. Sympathetics were strong empaths, able to read the emotions of those around them, discerning truth from lies as easily as breathing. The least wanted Craft was to be an Illusionist, able to make fantastical images out of thin air, often working as storytellers or actors.

Though being blessed with any Craft was nothing compared to the excitement of finding one's Fated—the one person made specifically for him that he would find when the time was right. The Fated bond was established at the same time as the Craft blessing, though there were academics who claimed the bond was forged at birth, simply maturing when the child reached thirteen.

Asyl had grown up with stories of how his mother bumped into his father on the street and upon looking at each other, they'd felt the tug of their Fated hearts. Perhaps they'd made their way to the street by the urging of their bond, whispering for them to alter their usual routines. Some people talked as if the tug on their souls was physical, while others just likened it to an awareness.

His parents had been married within a year, as most Fated couples were, and he was born ten months later. It wasn't uncommon for couples to have children quickly and often, and many couples who could afford it ended up with large families. Being an only child was the one thing that Asyl wished he was able to change. He would love to have younger siblings to spoil and look after, taking away the sadness in his mother's eyes.

As it was, he would stand with only his parents on his thirteenth birthday, sans siblings. Awakenings were massive affairs, friends and family invited to join in the anticipation and celebration. The child would be showered with gifts and a feast containing their favorite foods spread out along countless tables. Depending on the season and time of the Awakening, sparklers would be passed around to the children for them to run around with.

Then when it came time for the Awakening itself, Asyl would stand between his parents and tilt his head to the heavens as the revelers counted down the seconds. His Craft Mark would be revealed in the center of his forehead, a few shades darker or lighter than his skin tone, and he would learn his path in life. Of course, his father's political friends were exchanging coins, betting on what Asyl would be blessed with.

At least Asyl had his one childhood friend in attendance. Lady Naias Elrel, who had Awakened as an Aquan eight moonturns ago, was just as eager to see what he would be blessed with. They stood quietly by the buffet tables, despite the other kids running around and adults chatting excitedly to each other. Asyl held Naias's hand tight, his body vibrating with fear and excitement.

The suns were setting, lighting the clouds with pinks, oranges, and purples. His backyard had a warm glow to it, giving all the decorations an orange hue. Tables were adorned with white cloth, held down with platters of his favorite meals. Colorful candies in small glass bowls fit in wherever there was space. His Gale father had set up special torches to keep mosquitoes and wasps from getting close to the backyard. It smelled wonderfully of the forests to the west that they'd visited a couple of years ago. His Harvester mother had outdone herself, cultivating the most beautiful plants and delicious fruits for the party.

After the last two hours, the tables were no longer groaning with food, almost picked entirely clean by Asyl's family and his father's contacts. The second of his first breath was rapidly approaching.

He couldn't wait.

He was terrified.

Asyl eagerly ran over to his parents when his father gestured for him to join them, a smile on his father's handsome face. His mother dipped down and covered his face in greasy kisses, leaving lipstick smudges behind as he giggled and squirmed away from her. His parents took a hand each, and he bounced on the balls of his feet, closing his eyes and tilting his head to the sky, feeling the radiating warmth of the setting sun on his skin.

All around him, the revelers counted down the seconds, and Asyl took a deep breath and held it in anticipation. Would it hurt when his Craft unlocked? If it did, would the pain be only for a second? How would it feel to be a non-elemental? Asyl squeezed his parents' hands tight, the countdown falling into single digits.

Naias had whispered excitedly to him that she'd briefly felt dizzy, suddenly aware of the moisture in the air and how much water the clouds above were carrying. She'd explained that she felt like she was underwater when the days were humid, though she was learning to block out the overwhelming sensations with the help of her tutor.

Father told him he'd felt the currents in the air, all the way up to the highest cloud level. He could feel the vibrations in the air of the larger fowl flying within a couple of miles, and his skin had buzzed with the proximity of insects. He too had training to block out the constant overstimulation his Craft bestowed upon him.

Mother had felt a rush of life. Surrounded then as he was now by shrubbery, flowers, and trees, she had immediately learned which ones were healthy, which ones needed a little bit of help, and which trees were reaching the end of their lifespan. Somehow, she'd instinctively known that she could coax the slightly blighted plants back to perfect health with a song or praise. She hadn't bothered to learn how to block out what her Craft told her, not minding feeling the status of every plant within fifty yards.

Three.

Asyl bit his lip, practically dancing in place. He heard his mother laugh at his excitement, her voice high and bright. His father chuckled, running his thumb over the back of Asyl's fingers.

Two.

Naias shouted out encouragement to him, whooping and hollering. She stirred up the other kids who'd accompanied their families, and Asyl grinned at the cracking adolescent cheers.

One.

Asyl breathed out, his whole body relaxing as he anticipated the rush of his Craft coming to the forefront. He was ready. Elemental Craft or not, he would be the best person he could possibly be. He'd be the son his father wanted. Make his mother proud. Once he was old enough, he'd seek out his Fated and bring him home. Live his life in bliss.

Asyl had always wanted to be special. He opened his eyes, confused after a few seconds had passed. He didn't feel any different. Didn't feel any sort of power welling up inside of him. Hadn't become aware of the wind, water, earth, heat, or flora surrounding him. No one had told him that wishes tended to find loopholes.

His mother dropped his hand as if it had burned her. Asyl turned to her, startled, his eyes wide. Panic started to rise inside of him, and he looked around wildly. Something had to have gone wrong, right? Maybe the hour was incorrect. Minute. Perhaps the Healer transposed a number or two. Even as he frantically cast his mind about for a logical answer, he knew the truth.

His Awakening had failed.

How could his Awakening fail? He'd never heard of something like this before.

"Mother?" Asyl managed to squeak out.

His mother backed away from him, shaking her head as she pressed her hands over her mouth. Tears welled in her eyes, and she shook her head. Her sob echoed through the backyard, breaking the stunned silence that had fallen over everyone.

"What's going on?" Naias demanded. "Where's Asyl's Mark?"

Behind him, his father stepped away, leaving him to stand in the center of the backyard alone. The adults regarded him with something akin to fear on their faces. Parents grabbed their children, stopping them from moving close. Clearly frustrated, Naias started to rush toward him.

"No!" Lady Elrel cried out, grabbing her daughter.

"He'll steal your Craft," Lord Elrel spat.

Asyl took a few steps back, looking between all those who'd been smiling and laughing just moments ago. One of his father's associates clapped his father on the shoulder, an agonized look on his face.

"Do we kill it?" the man asked.

It. What was it? His breath caught when the man looked at him, his eyes sharp and filled with hatred. He... was the it?

"Father?" Asyl implored him, taking a step toward him.

"Stay back," the associate said, his voice colder than Valvinte in winter. "What do you want to do, old friend?"

"Everyone leave," Father said briskly.

The backyard emptied with a dizzying speed. Parents scooped up their confused children or hauled their elder ones away. His grandmother moved forward in the crowd, and for a second, Asyl thought she was heading for him. Instead, she spat on his face and hurried over to her daughter and sat next to her. Stunned, Asyl brought his hand up, lightly touching the spittle running down his cheek.

"No!" Naias shrieked as her mother tried hauling her away. "Tell me what's going on! He's my best friend!"

"The goddess has looked into his soul and found him tainted. She refused to bless him. A Void," Lord Elrel sneered, his impressive mustache curling. He turned to Mother, who was openly yet silently weeping. "My condolences. I hope you're able to carry a *proper* child to term."

His best friend screamed at her father that there had to have been a mistake. Naias tried to rush toward him and was lifted off her feet by her father. Her defiant shouts echoed through the silent backyard, demanding that her father put her down. There clearly had to have been a mistake!

"My friend," the associate began.

"Please leave," Father murmured.

The man simply nodded, casting another frigid glare at Asyl, and followed the rest of the revelers out of the garden. They were alone now. Or rather, as alone as one could get in a manor. Servants stared at him from the deck and many windows. The faces of the maids that had been with him his entire life were ashen, and Asyl could see that one or two of them were crying.

His father's butler, on the other hand, was a different story. He openly glowered at Asyl, as if he hadn't cheerily given him a gift only a half hour ago: a beautiful pocket watch that showed the heavenly bodies, telling him the time with the greatest accuracy Gale inventors could determine.

"What do you wish, sir?" the butler asked.

Father stared down at Asyl, and he stared right back, terrified. He still didn't understand what was happening. What was a Void? He'd never heard of such a thing until now. But that… that wasn't possible. His father told him everything, even if Asyl was too young to fully understand the nuances of his business deals.

"Father, please," Asyl said, his voice trembling.

"Get out," his father snapped. Asyl jerked as if he'd been stabbed. His fingers and toes were growing cold, even as his stomach rebelled and warned him that he was going to vomit, making him break out into a sweat. "Get the *fuck* out of our lives. You are no longer my son."

Tears sprang to his eyes, and Asyl's throat closed. He tried stammering a plea, wanting to change his father's mind. Hadn't he been a good son? He'd done everything his father asked of him, even eating foods he hated, simply because he wanted to please the man. He was good at his studies, though he found it hard to socialize with the others in his classes. He treated the servants well, respected his parents and the adults in his life.

What could there possibly be within him that marked him as tarnished? Unworthy? He'd read novels and watched plays where the villains were Craft Blessed. Surely the Goddess would have seen the corruption within their souls and denied them a Craft. But what had he done?

"Father," Asyl tried again, his vision blurring, "what have I done wrong?"

"You survived," Mother snarled from behind him. "Why did you live when your siblings didn't? Saddling me with a useless, damned child, giving me false hope that I could have a wonderful family. You disgust me."

"You're not wanted," his grandmother sniffed, glowering at him. "Get out before we have Kusinut fetch the police."

Trembling, his legs barely supporting his weight, Asyl stumbled to the garden gate. He put one hand on the white-painted wood and looked back. Father was staring at him, his eyes completely blank. It was the same look he'd had when Asyl's paternal grandfather had died. A shudder ripped down his spine, and Asyl slipped out of the gate.

It swung shut behind him with a finalizing clang, physically and emotionally cutting him off from his family. Fear gripped him as he stared down the darkening street, paralyzing him for just long enough to hear his father try to comfort his grieving mother.

"It's okay, my dear," Asyl heard him say gently. "I know seeing so many friends with kids is hard. But we're still young, and we can keep trying."

CHAPTER 1

GODDESS, DID he hate the rain.

Even with Siora's expert handling of the umbrella, Kende still got plenty wet. He did his best skirting puddles and Craft-powered vehicles or horse-drawn carriages, but his trousers were still soaked halfway to his knees. If it wasn't for his duty to visit the Alenzon apothecaries to ensure their quality, he would have stayed inside by the warm fire with a good book.

Those Healers preferring to work with physical ingredients and enhancing their healing properties with their Craft, rather than training as a physician, would turn to alchemy. Whether it was because their Craft was too weak, they didn't have the stomach for urgent care, or they preferred to have their own business, it didn't matter to him.

What did matter was if the potions, salves, tinctures, and whatever else the Healer created were actually effective. If they were, then Kende verified how potent they were, making sure that the proprietor was truthful about their wares. He refused to let the citizens of his fair city be swindled and purchase falsities with their hard-earned money.

So far, Kende was pleased with every visit he made. He made it a habit to grab random products from the shelves and test the potions near the proprietor. Potions and concentrated tinctures were the easiest for him to test. He either dipped a specifically made testing strip inside the potion or used a dropper with the tincture. If they had healing properties, the strip would turn green.

Salves and ointments were a little trickier, as they were completely mundane. While the test strip did work, it wasn't infallible and took much longer than with their magical counterparts. For that reason, most apothecaries didn't bother mixing or stocking them. Only children needed mundane healing, and most parents would take their child to a doctor rather than hunt through countless apothecaries looking for the cure they needed.

So Kende was completely surprised and pleased when he walked into a far-flung apothecary called Enchanted Waters. The walls of the small front room were covered in shelves, and the floor space was dominated by a large circular display shelf. Kende merely raised a hand in greeting to the shopkeeper, his eyes firmly fixed on the sheer number of products lining the walls.

None of the vials and tins had a single speck of dust on them. The shelves themselves were immaculate, telling him that the stock moved regularly. Even the way everything was arranged made perfect sense. The largest section was marked for general healing. Potions lined the circular display, ranging in strengths for a simple bramble cut to closing surgical wounds. Tinctures sat on the top rack, sold only in one strength to be diluted by the purchaser at will.

There were dedicated sections for burns—either made by exposure to the sun, contact, or heat—along with others for common winter illnesses, prenatal care, sores and rashes, chronic pains, and even sleep aids. It was… an insane amount of stock, and when Kende inspected the prices, he received another shock. The most expensive items were the tinctures, and those only sold for a couple of silver. The weakest potions were a few coppers.

In other words, the alchemist was selling their wares for less than a cooked meal. They'd marked everything as if they should be common household items rather than a luxury. How had he never found this place before? It was far too established for it to have gone unnoticed two seasons ago when he'd last walked these streets. Bursting with questions, Kende did as he always did when he inspected a shop. He grabbed random items from the shelves and walked over to the woman behind the counter.

"Hello," the woman said, smiling brightly at him.

Odd. She wasn't a Healer. Her Craft labeled her as an Aquan. How could an Aquan make these potions? They needed to be charged by a Healer to work properly on a Craft Blessed. Kende didn't understand, but maybe she was simply minding the shop. Either way, he examined her carefully. She seemed familiar to him, though from where was escaping him for the moment. There was also a wariness and deep concern in her blue eyes that he couldn't place.

Was everything in here a sham? That would explain the insanely cheap prices and sudden appearance of the store.

"Hello, miss," Kende replied, forcing a smile. He showed her his inspection permit, letting her take it when she reached out for it. Clearly, she was no naive woman to just glance at it and shrug. She slowly read the permit, seemingly understanding it easily. That could either attest to her schooling or how good of a grifter she was. "I'm here on inspection to ensure quality. Are you new to this location?"

The woman snorted a small laugh and shook her head, her wheat-colored hair spilling over her shoulders. She was dressed surprisingly well. Her clothes were of fine quality, even if they were simple and muted in color. How could she afford such nice fabrics? Surely she couldn't raise enough money in a moonturn to pay rent, let alone splurge on quality frocks. When she handed him the permit back, he caught a whiff of a subtle floral perfume often used by ladies of the minor nobility. Curious.

"No. We just finally got a sign last moonturn," she replied, giving a one-shoulder shrug.

Well, he would see if he'd be shutting the place down today. Kende uncorked the first potion and paused, surprised at the aroma that wafted from the small neck. Out of the corner of his eye, he saw the blond Aquan grin, leaning against the counter and watching him. Potions usually didn't smell. They were little more than water with a natural dye added, and the Healers did the rest with their Craft. This one was… different.

Kende pulled out his small book of testing strips and set them on the counter. He dipped one into the berry-red potion and was a little surprised to see that the strip had been dyed a light pink. The color changed a few heartbeats later, the deep green of a quality potion overtaking the pastel pink. Kende stared at it and turned to locate his secretary.

Siora Thelee had worked with him for the last decade, and she'd seen plenty of charlatans try to set up shop and avoid detection for as long as they could. Her scrunched nose told him that she was thinking what he was. This place seemed far too good to be true. And when things were too good to be true, they tended to not be real.

He handed her the potion, and she sniffed it curiously before she regarded the potion critically, swirling it. There was maybe a bit of detritus in the potion, but if there was, Kende couldn't make it out. Leaving the questionable potion in Siora's capable hands, Kende turned to the others. He dropped a few beads of the tincture on a different test strip and was once again baffled to see the deep green.

He started in on the salves, aware that he'd taken nearly one of everything in his quest of proving the shop a fraud. Every single one he tested gave him the same result. When he pressed the pad of his index finger to the one that claimed to lessen pain, he was startled to feel… well… not feel anything. His whole finger had gone numb. Kende didn't need the test strip to know that this one was legitimate.

"Any questions, Lord Kende?" the woman all but purred.

"Do you make these?" Kende asked, bristling at her amusement.

"Nope. I just mind the shop. Better with people than my brewer is," she said.

Interesting that she called the alchemist a brewer. Kende decided not to push it. Instead, he capped everything and cleared his throat.

"I'd like to see recipes of everything," he told her. "While the test strips say these are good, I'd still like to make sure nothing harmful is in them."

Her playful expression dropped immediately and became guarded. She stood to her full height, which was a half foot shorter than him, and folded her arms tightly across her chest.

"I can't do that," she said firmly. "My brewer is out getting ingredients today, and I won't let someone look at his books without him present."

"All right," Kende conceded, knowing full well he wouldn't be able to push her. She seemed the fiercely loyal type and stubborn as a mule. "Please call upon the Ruvyn manor once he's returned. As much as I'd like to believe these truly are all effective.…"

She scowled at him but nodded. Kende packed up his test strips and accepted the small basket Siora handed him. A minute later, he had all the products he'd used for testing piled up carefully inside. After a moment of hesitation, Kende slipped her a gold coin. While he usually only paid shelf price for what he used to test, he figured she could use the money.

The coin disappeared within a second, and she eyed him curiously. She gave a stiff curtsy, and Kende bowed to her. As he and Siora began to leave, a hooded figure stepped into the shop, dripping wet. Without complaint, the man backed out and held the door open for Siora. She just smiled and opened the umbrella. Kende gave the person his thanks and stepped out onto the street.

"You called?" the person asked as they entered the store.

"Thanks so much for coming. I'm concerned—"

Their conversation was cut off a moment later with the door snicking shut. Kende turned and stared up at the façade, where a brand-new sign had been installed. It was much cleaner and brighter than the rest of the stone structure. There was a second floor. Perhaps she and the brewer slept above to reduce their costs? But why did the potion smell so sweet? He'd have to get Gojko's opinion on the products.

Right now, he wasn't sure if he should get Enchanted Waters shut down or not. Surely the test strips hadn't failed him. Was there something in their products that tricked it? That wouldn't explain the numbing of his hand, though. He still couldn't feel his finger. Well, he supposed he wouldn't be writing much for the rest of the day. Kende rubbed his hands over his face as he turned and began walking.

Another week of visiting apothecaries in this district, and then he'd be done. He could take a couple of weeks or even a moonturn off before plotting his course through another district, this time on the opposite side of Alenzon. Closer to the gentry and elite society. He'd have Siora go out first with the Craft vehicle or have Toemi take her. That way she could verify each apothecary in the district and mark down new ones or update their existing list.

It was menial work, but it kept the citizens safe. Even if his father didn't see the point in it. Hell, his father had grumbled at him that if the common folk were stupid enough to purchase a hoax, they deserved to lose their money. Kende very heartily disagreed. Perhaps it was his Healer nature. Perhaps he just had a gentle heart. He would never know.

As Kende walked, thinking about his next route he'd take tomorrow, grateful that he was finished for the day, he was dimly aware of his hair and shoulders getting soaked. Someone was calling him. Two someones. One lay in front of him and another behind. But wait…. Was the one in front of him real? There wasn't anyone in front of him.

"Kende?" Siora called, breaking him from his stupor.

A shudder ripped through him, and he belatedly realized he'd walked several blocks toward the seedier parts of Alenzon. Siora trotted up to him, the basket from Enchanted Waters swinging in her hand. She quickly covered him with the umbrella, her breath coming in quick gasps.

"Siora," Kende replied, blinking a few times, "is everything okay?"

"You tell me!" she snapped. "You just started walking off, and when I tried to stop you, you started running!"

Kende looked around again, this time more carefully. He could see cloaked figures in dark alleyways. Some had their cloaks over their shoulders, yet their faces were concealed, showing off parts of their bodies. Oh dear. If his father knew he'd been in a disreputable part of the city, the duke would suffer from apoplexy.

Even as he looked around, Kende watched a man strolling down the street with an umbrella pause in front of one of the sex workers. He caught the glint of a coin, and the man disappeared into the alley with her. The sight made his stomach churn. Despite all he did, all the programs he tried to sponsor, he still was unable to get everyone in homes with enough food that they didn't have to return to the streets.

"We need to leave," Siora said urgently.

"Wait," Kende snapped.

He didn't mean to. The idea of leaving right now left him cold with terror. Why? What was wrong here? It didn't seem like there was anything truly wrong, once one disregarded those who had to turn to sex work to feed themselves. Or the homeless curled up in the porticos of closed shops, dozing fitfully in threadbare clothing. Was it the blood that was being washed away by the rain?

But that wouldn't make him want to stay. Something here was calling to him. Kende turned in a circle once more, trying to see if he could get at least a direction. Without thinking about it, he started to walk. This time, Siora kept pace with him, though she had a dark look on her face, glowering at anyone who dared look at them for too long.

They were in danger here. None of these people cared that he was Duke Ruvyn's son. All they saw was a posh man and woman who clearly had money—money that they could use to feed themselves or purchase drugs. Maybe find somewhere warm to sleep for the night that was able to provide hot water for a bath. Neither of them had elemental Crafts. Siora was a Seer, but she wouldn't be able to divine who was a threat just by looking at them.

Kende stretched out his long legs, walking as fast as he dared without leaving Siora behind. He could feel the eyes of the destitute and the starved on him. Men and women both bared their bodies to him, trying to lure in the fancy man. Maybe he should have been concerned at the sheer number of people who seemed to inhabit this neighborhood, but Kende could barely think about anything that wasn't the voice calling him.

It wasn't a voice, really. An urge. A tug. Kende's breath caught. After thirty years, he'd halfway given up on finding his Fated. But now his soul was telling him it was time. Time to claim the man who was the other half of his soul. He fought back the urge to break into a run, well aware he couldn't leave Siora behind, as much as he wanted to. Something was telling him that he couldn't dawdle.

"Kende!" Siora gasped out, half trotting beside him to catch up. "Please slow down."

"I can't," Kende replied, his voice rough, "I can't slow down. He's in trouble, I think."

"Who?" Siora exclaimed.

"I don't know. I just… I have to go to him," Kende said.

He glanced at his assistant. She seemed to process what he said, and her face split into a brilliant grin.

"Your Fated is nearby?" she asked. Siora gave a small, surprised huff. "I'll stop complaining."

Kende knew Siora was one of the few who were eager for him to find his Fated. Siora's husband lived at Ruvyn manor with her, she having been one of the lucky few who found her Fated when she was young. Surprisingly, they didn't have any children, though Kende had never asked why. It seemed insensitive to ask, and he'd not even been out of his teens when she came into his life.

Finally, the compulsion ebbed and Kende stilled in front of an abandoned temple. He stared up at it, taking in the crumbling stone, broken stained glass windows, and overgrown window boxes. He briefly wondered how long it had sat dilapidated and neglected. Years, given how much moss was sprouting from the brick. Kende looked down and hastily took a step back. There was a smear of blood-darkened mud leading from the street into the temple.

The next thing he noticed was that no one else was around. All the sex workers and thieves had fallen back at some point. No homeless slept in the portico, trying to stay dry. Frowning, Kende walked up the few steps to the temple door that had been knocked off one hinge. The remaining one squealed in protest as he pushed inward. Most of the ceiling hadn't caved in yet, leaving the foyer, washrooms, and worship hall completely dry.

Anything of value had long since been either taken with the priests or stolen. There was nothing in the foyer except for damp stone, a musty smell, and faint rustling. Detritus in the form of fallen leaves and discarded paper swirled along the stone floor in small whirlpools. The near stillness of the place made him uneasy.

Why weren't the vagrants using Ilyphari's temple to sleep in? Surely this would be an easy place to curl up in, and it was spacious enough it could hold quite a number of people. Was it because this was once a place of worship? He'd figured since no one was using it, the temple would become fair game. Kende glanced behind him as Siora shook the umbrella free of the rain and collapsed it.

"Why is no one in here?" Siora asked.

"I was wondering that myself," Kende replied.

Maybe he should try to get another fundraiser going. During his walk here, he hadn't seen any other temples. Perhaps he could raise enough money to turn this place into a hostel with temple aspects. Make it somewhere safe for those who didn't have somewhere to stay to sleep. Kende wasn't sure if he would be able to stir the nobility to sympathy, though he knew full well some of his siblings would chip in.

There were never enough hours in the day for him to do everything he wanted. Get those vulnerable off the streets, make sure they were healthy, fed.... It seemed Alenzon itself fought against him whenever he tried suggesting helping those who had no dignity or decency whatsoever. Just the argument made him bristle, but Kende was only the youngest child of Duke Ruvyn. He really didn't have much power or influence.

Maybe he could get his cousin to help.

That was a thought.

He heard movement in the worship hall. The voice calling to him went silent, and Kende's heart crashed against his ribs. Throwing caution to the wind, Kende ran to the open doorway. Due to the heavy rainfall, advanced hour, and dark gray stone, it took Kende's eyes a minute to adjust. Even though his body urged him forward, to run as fast as he could, he pushed the compulsion down. It wouldn't do any good to fall and hurt himself. Sure, he could just heal his injuries, but that wasn't entirely the point.

As his vision slowly adjusted, Kende saw a large statue of the goddess Ilyphari. She was kneeling, her head tilted down as if in supplication, her hands cupped together in her lap. Huh. This wasn't exactly a denomination he was familiar with. Most temples had Ilyphari standing tall with her hands outstretched to the sky, head tilted back as kids did during their Awakening. Some had her posed as a mother, hands cupping her swollen belly in imagery of her being the mother of every living person on the planet.

But cowed? A shiver ran down Kende's spine, and he slowly approached the dais. The ceiling nearby had given in, rain pelting the unprotected floor just inches away from the prone figure. Something snapped in his chest when he saw the heap of fabric, and Kende knew without question that this was his Fated. He... he couldn't be too late. The song was gone, but surely it was because of his proximity. Right?

Surely the goddess wouldn't be so cruel as to lead him to his Fated, only to reach him seconds too late. Trembling, Kende dropped to his knees next to the man. His cloak was still wet, so he hadn't been out of the rain for too long. Kende pushed back the hood, pressing two fingers to his Fated's neck, seeking a heartbeat. Behind him, Siora inhaled sharply.

"Get away from it," she said, her voice shaking.

Blinking once, Kende shook his head, relaxing slightly when he felt the weak, thready pulse beneath his fingers. That wasn't a great sign, but far better than no heartbeat at all. He ever so gently rolled his Fated onto his back, pressing his hand to the man's chest to dive into him. Even as he felt his Craft drain from his reservoir, Kende's mind stayed exactly where it was.

Frowning, Kende pushed harder, succeeding in nearly draining his reservoir completely. That in itself was a major feat. Being unable to dive into another adult to learn what was wrong and needed to be healed only meant that his patient was too close to death to save. He'd failed. What good was it to have such a large reservoir and well to draw upon when he couldn't even save his Fated?

"Kende," Siora shouted.

He felt her hand clamp around his arm, and she tugged fiercely. Startled, Kende blinked a few times to look up at her, trying to clear his mind.

"What?" he said, frowning. "Can't you give me some peace? I can't... I can't heal him."

"Of course you can't heal it!" Siora spat. "It's a fucking Void!"

Kende's head snapped up, and he turned to look at her. He pulled his arm away and cupped his Fated's chilled face. What he'd thought was a Craft Mark was just a smear of blood and dirt. His face was marred with large bruises and old scars. There was a huge cut on his temple, and his lip had been bisected. Even with all the energy he'd poured into his Fated, his wounds showed no sign of improvement.

During all of his time in school, he'd never learned about how to treat Voids. His instructors had assured him that Voids were rare enough that a casual Healer such as he would never encounter one. Why would there be a Void for him to take care of in his family? Gojko had been a family doctor for many years before entering into private practice when Duke Ruvyn employed him. That settled it.

He needed to get his Fated home. Preferably before he died. Since his Fated wasn't reacting to his healing Craft, he decided to do a cursory examination as if he was a preteen. Craft healing didn't work until a child's Awakening, so Kende had learned how to check for broken bones to help take care of his young cousins and niblings. Nothing shifted that wasn't supposed to, which meant he was likely stable enough to move.

"Kende! You need to get away from it," Siora implored.

Kende gathered his Fated into his arms, gently lifting him as he got to his feet. The man winced and groaned, his eyes fluttering open for just a second as he squirmed ever so slightly. Maybe he was putting pressure on a wound that was causing him pain.

"I'm sorry. Just bear with me for a minute. We'll get you patched up," Kende murmured to him.

"You can't be bringing it with us!" Siora said, aghast.

He looked at his assistant with a scowl. Her face was pale, she was holding on to the umbrella so hard her knuckles were white, and her hands were shaking. Kende glowered at her, curling his Fated closer to his chest. Hopefully his warmth would help stimulate his Fated's body and keep him breathing.

"He's my Fated. Of course I'm bringing him back to the manor. He needs help, and Gojko is more experienced than I," Kende said.

It hurt to admit his failings, but he wouldn't risk his Fated's health based on senseless pride. Kende started to walk past her, but Siora stepped in his path, blocking the way to the front door.

"Voids don't get Fated. They're not blessed for a reason, Kende. That's why their Awakening *fails*. The goddess doesn't want them," Siora pleaded with him. "Whatever bond you're feeling with it is false. That's probably why it's in here. It must have defiled this temple with some sort of... sort of Void trickery to lure someone in."

Kende frowned. "I'm taking him back to the manor, Siora. That's final."

"It's a criminal!" Siora snapped.

"He's the victim here!" Kende shouted, finally losing his patience.

"Self-defense!" she shouted back.

His Fated stirred weakly in his arms again, one hand coming up to slap ineffectively against Kende's chest. The man's breathing stuttered, and Kende shook his head. They were wasting precious time.

"If that's how you feel, Siora, you can find yourself another position without a reference," Kende said stonily.

Her lips thinned as she glared at the Void in his arms for a minute. She huffed, throwing her shoulders back and holding her head high as she marched toward the entrance. Taking her silence for assent, Kende followed her from the abandoned temple. Either that, or she'd just walk off. It seemed she was willing to deal with the Void for now. The umbrella snapped open, and she waited impatiently for Kende to step underneath the waxed canvas.

They started to backtrack toward Enchanted Waters, where their Craft vehicle was parked. Kende worried they wouldn't make it. They'd walked for so long, surely they wouldn't make it back in time. Siora looked up at the street signs once they got to an intersection. She frowned and glanced over her shoulder at Kende.

"We're only a block or so from Enchanted Waters," she said.

Curious. Kende shrugged and nodded in the direction of their vehicle. They were moving quickly, Kende utilizing his full stride, making Siora have to trot to keep up. He still wasn't pleased with her, spouting hateful vitriol over someone she didn't even know. The goddess paired her children up deliberately. She wouldn't have bound a criminal to him.

Would she?

He really didn't want to try and redeem a thief or murderer. Nor would he want to expose his family to such a character either. Kende doubted his Fated was in any sort of trouble with the law. Hopefully it wasn't just wishful thinking. By the time they reached the carriage, his Fated was shivering uncontrollably. Kende climbed in first, carefully protecting his Fated's head so as to not whack it against the iron struts.

He sat down on the bench, placing his Fated sideways on his lap, and cast about to locate the towels they'd stocked in the cab. He bundled up his Fated as well as he could while Siora got in and sat behind the steering stick. Kende shifted slightly, wrapping his heavy great cloak around his Fated, trying to trap all his body heat. How long had he been lying on the cold stone, slowly chilling him to the core?

Siora wrapped her long fingers around the steering stick and breathed out slowly, invoking her Craft. Between one breath and the next, Kende felt the combustion engine roar to life. She carefully maneuvered the vehicle into the road, slipping past both horse-drawn and Craft-powered vehicles. His Fated's uncontrollable shivering tapered off, and Kende looked down at him.

The man was looking up at him, his pale blue eyes glazed over and unfocused.

"Hey," Kende murmured ever so gently, reaching down to cup his face. "You're gonna be okay."

For a moment, Kende thought that his Fated was rolling his eyes at him. Until his eyes slid shut completely and his body went limp.

"Siora," Kende said urgently.

"Almost there," she intoned.

Indeed, they were already driving up the drive to his manor. She parked as close to the portico as she could and opened the door for him. The front door opened and his steward, Birgir, stepped out onto the front step, arms folded behind his back. Great. Just exactly who Kende had wanted to avoid. The man was an insufferable gossip and usually reported everything of note back to the duke. If Birgir realized what his Fated was, then Kende knew his father would be here within the hour to throw him back out onto the street.

That wasn't going to happen. Siora preceded Kende out of the carriage and popped open the umbrella once again. Kende tugged his Fated's hood back over his head to help disguise him. Curling his Fated into his chest to hide him completely, Kende carefully carried his soul's twin out of the carriage and up the front steps. Birgir's eyes widened, and the Gale rushed toward him.

"My lord—" he started.

"Not your business, Birgir," Kende said flatly.

"This isn't a charity house, my lord!" Birgir snapped at him.

"It is for this one," Kende replied shortly.

He briefly wondered if his father would be visiting him soon or if the staff would find any and all excuses to come by his chambers tonight. Kende slipped past his steward, pointedly ignoring the hefty man's glare as he stepped into the manor. He ignored the surprised glances from the maids as well, Birgir's indignant demands for answers bouncing off the foyer's wood-paneled walls.

Maybe he should have told Siora not to tell him anything. Too late now. If she told Birgir that the unconscious man was his Fated, he'd be beating his curious and congratulatory siblings, aunts, uncles, and cousins away with a stick. If she told Birgir that his Fated was a Void... well. He knew his assistant's feelings on that matter. He wasn't sure how much of his family had the same sentiments.

To the right was his family's extensive library that nearly ran the whole length of the manor. One of the left doors led to his personal study. The dining hall and ballroom were along the back, with a cozy kitchen tucked in the corner. Stairs wrapped up to the ballroom doors, the balcony giving him a clear view of the entrance hall.

Kende took the stairs two at a time, heading toward his bedchambers. One of the chambermaids squeaked as he approached, quickly retreating inside his room and holding the door open for him. Once he passed over the threshold, she ran around the sleeping area and started lighting all the Ignis wall lamps.

"If Siora hasn't gone to get Gojko, please fetch him," Kende said.

She curtsied and ran out, quietly shutting the door behind her. Kende laid his Fated on his large bed, brushing his hood back again. He shrugged off his great cloak and tossed it to the other side of the bed, not caring how it fell or how long it might take to iron out the creases. His Fated's cloak was in much worse shape, nearly deteriorating as he unclasped it from his shoulders.

A low moan escaped his Fated as Kende slid his arm underneath his shoulders and lifted him. He braced the man to his chest, wiggled the cloak free, and dropped it to the floor. The cloak must have offered some protection against the attack. Some of the long gashes in the fabric didn't have corresponding wounds. His Fated's tunic was made of durable material, in good repair, and splattered with various colors along the stomach and hem. There were a few spots of rust-colored blood. Nowhere near enough to justify him being unconscious.

His Fated clearly had a job. He'd been lucky to find someone who didn't care about some trumped-up fearmongering and hired him. While he wasn't well-versed in every single law of Averia, he was fairly certain that it wasn't illegal to employ a Void. It just came down to the individual viewpoints of the employers and fellow employees. Kende had never thought about it too much before, but was that why his attempts at fundraising for the homeless kept failing? How many Voids were on the streets?

He thought back to the sex workers he saw in the alleys. How almost every one of them had their hoods up. Kende had figured it was because of the rain. Was it more than just trying to stay dry? He couldn't be the only member of the gentry who actually cared, could he?

Kende very gently wiggled the tunic off his Fated's body, not wanting to cut it in any fashion. He could summon one of the girls and have them clean it thoroughly. That way, when his Fated woke, he'd have something comfortable and clean to wear. He folded it loosely and set it on the nightstand, frowning at the intense bruising on his chest and stomach. There were a few spots where the skin had split and bled.

He glanced up at his Fated's face, checking to see if he'd roused again. The man hadn't moved from where Kende had gently laid him back down.

"I have to see the extent of your injuries," Kende told his sleeping Fated. "I promise you, you're completely safe with us."

He didn't get a response, as he expected. Nodding, Kende undid the drawstring to his Fated's parachute pants just as his door opened. He hastily let go and turned around. He'd protect the man's modesty from as many people as he could. Gojko bustled in and frowned, blinking owlishly behind his spectacles at seeing the sight before him.

"When Siora said you needed my help...." He trailed off.

"Close the door," Kende replied, glancing past him.

Sure enough, there were a few maids lingering, getting on their toes to try and peek into the room. Kende moved to block their view of his Fated's bare forehead. Siora slipped into the room and bumped the door shut with her hip. She still had a disapproving frown on her face, folding her arms across her chest.

"My Fated," Kende said in the way of greeting, "but.... Well, I wasn't trained to heal him."

Gojko's brows drew together, and he stepped up beside Kende. His breath caught in his throat, and he glanced at Kende before bending over the prone Void, his fingers dotting across each dark purple-and-black bruise marring his chest.

"You weren't trained to heal a Void?" Gojko inquired. Without waiting for a reply, he looked over his shoulder. "Siora. Warm water and a cloth. He's dirty."

Kende sighed. "My professors basically said that between my rank and having you, there was no need for me to know how to heal a Void, since I wouldn't ever encounter one."

Gojko snorted and muttered a string of curses under his breath. He sighed and glanced up at Kende.

"Remove his pants and shoes, please," Gojko said.

Confused, Kende nodded and walked around his physician and carefully slid his Fated's trousers down. He didn't want to reopen any half-healed wounds by being rough for no real reason. The man's shoes were a curious pattern he hadn't seen before. The upper part of the shoe seemed designed to be easily removed from the sole. For repairs or replacement, he figured. That would help keep footwear costs low.

From his novice estimation, the soles were worn, though nowhere near needing replacing. There was still plenty of tread left. Why was his cloak so threadbare, yet the rest of his clothing was sturdy and obviously well kept? Which was the ruse, the heavy work clothes or the disintegrating cloak? Did it really matter right now?

No. Not really. All that mattered right now was getting him back to full health. Which, speaking of, Kende examined his Fated's legs, wincing. There was a map of heavy bruising here as well, though it seemed localized to his hips and thighs. Who could do this to someone? Gojko grunted, and Kende wrenched his eyes away from the awful bruises to look at what his fellow Healer found.

The man was holding his Fated's wrist and had lifted his arm for easier inspection. Right in the crook of his elbow was a puncture wound with blood crusted around the site. Kende's stomach fell.

"So, he's a Tratane user," Siora sneered from behind him.

"No," Gojko said. "Kende, opinion."

Kende glanced over everything. The bruising, the wounds on his face. How cold he was, sluggish…. Tratane was an upper. He wouldn't be unconscious after injecting himself with a dose.

"They…." Kende trailed off, hesitating briefly. "Did they take his blood?"

Gojko nodded, gently pressing at the site. That got him an agonized whimper from his Fated. The sound tugged at Kende's heart, and he scurried up to the man's head, cupped his jaw, and ran his thumbs over his cheekbones.

"It'll be okay," he murmured. "We just need to figure out how to help you."

"You can help by washing him," Gojko drawled, a smirk playing on his lips.

Kende stood and turned, taking the bowl from Siora. Her face was pale, staring at the sheer damage done to his Fated.

"Still think he's the criminal here?" Kende asked acerbically.

"No," Siora whispered.

"Explain," Gojko snapped.

"Voids are the absence of the goddess's light," Siora said, though there was a slight waver to her words. "They're natural-born criminals...."

"I think my daughter would disagree with you," Gojko growled.

That was news to Kende. He stared at his physician, startled at this revelation. Gojko had a Void daughter? He knew about the girl he had who was also a Healer. As far as he could remember, she left Averia completely and was employed somewhere in their eastern bordering kingdom, Zothua.

"But—" Siora started.

"If you continue in that ridiculous vein, you can leave," Gojko told her.

Since the door didn't open, Kende assumed she was staying. He wet the cloth and gently dabbed at the muck on his Fated's face. The water dirtied at an alarming rate, nearly black with grime by the time just his face was cleaned. Siora must have anticipated this, as she quietly placed another bowl of water on the nightstand. She gently gathered his Fated's clothes and cracked the door open to instruct the loitering chambermaids to take care of them.

"So how do you heal a Void?" Kende asked softly. "I poured so much energy into him, but I still couldn't dive into him for a diagnosis and prompt his body to heal."

"You can't," Gojko said simply, tending to the wounds on his Fated's face. "For all intents and purposes, you have to treat Voids as if they never had their Awakening."

"Kids don't take your energy, though," Kende said, frowning.

"No. You can drain your reservoir and well down to your soul and still not affect their bodies as if they were Craft Blessed," Gojko explained. "Your Fated will always have to use mundane ways to heal."

Kende thought back to Enchanted Waters, where they sold an expansive range of mundane products. Was the apothecary popular with

Void clientele? It was possible, considering how close they were to the seedier neighborhood of Alenzon. Maybe that's why everything was so cheap.

"So, we can't get him to full health tonight," Kende said softly.

"No. I don't think his life is in danger, despite his heart acting as if he's in the middle of a race," Gojko said. "Where did you find him?"

"An abandoned temple," Kende replied, shrugging awkwardly as he washed his Fated's chest. "I heard him calling for me."

"Curious," Gojko murmured, slowly finishing his examination. "Maybe he was accosted by some zealots who believe that Voids are essentially evil incarnate."

"But why take his blood?" Kende asked.

"Maybe some sort of messed-up ritual," Gojko said, shrugging. "Maybe they were just trying to make sure he would die."

Kende sighed, setting the bowl of grimy water aside and sitting on the edge of his bed. He reached out, brushing the long black hair away from the man's face. His Fated's head tilted toward his touch, a soft sigh passing from his lips. Gojko watched the exchange, his head cocked.

"Interesting," he murmured. "I've never heard of a Void having a Fated. I think I'm going to have to delve into the archives at the academy. See if there's any mentions. Do you know his name? That way you can tell his family he's safe."

Kende shook his head, his cheeks flushing. "No. He's barely been able to even open his eyes. He's got a job somewhere, based on the clothes he had on. I just hope he doesn't lose it solely for having the misfortune of being attacked."

Gojko nodded, looking a little forlorn. He smirked and caught Kende's eye. "Well, then you could move him in and pamper him to death."

"I have faith in your abilities as a Healer to help me keep my Fated hearty and hale," Kende teased.

Siora returned to his side and handed him a pair of soft pajamas. Kende quickly got to his feet and dressed his Fated, finally tucking him under the covers. The man would sleep here, and Kende would take the couch across the room. It was more than comfortable enough, so Kende had absolutely no qualms about sleeping on it. Gojko finally declared himself content after using an antibacterial salve on his Fated's open wounds and applying a sickeningly sweet ointment to his bruises.

He hoped that his Fated woke soon. Then they could sit in the lounge area of his bedchamber and learn all about each other. What his Fated's dreams were, where he worked, what his favorite food was, if he liked to read…. He wanted to know absolutely everything he could learn about his heart's twin. Kende cupped his face and pressed their foreheads together, careful of his Fated's wound, willing him to heal quickly.

He wasn't sure what he'd do if the man destined to be his rejected him outright.

Chapter 2

Warm.

He was warm. He hadn't thought he would be again after being chased over half of the abandoned district of Alenzon and then thrown down on the frigid church floor. He could still see the men hovering above him, feel their hands on his shoulders and ankles, holding him down. Hear their laughing taunts. The sharp prick of the giant needle they'd shoved into his arm. Then sweet oblivion.

He must be dead, right? They'd intended to exsanguinate him for some reason he wasn't privy to know or understand. Asyl flexed his fingers and toes, relieved to feel all of them responsive. He needed them to be able to work. His fingers at least. Toes were debatable. It was quiet, dark, and comfortable. He was able to open his eyes just slightly to see a soft glow come from the direction of the foot of the bed, but not much else.

Not dead, then. Someone's home. Maybe a church or hostel? Asyl didn't know. He probably should care, but he couldn't get the energy to summon even a spark of fear. Exhaustion pulled at him, and Asyl curled up on his side, falling back into the darkness.

There was a heated discussion going on around him the next time Asyl surfaced. Not exactly a fight per se, but voices were raised, tense. It sounded like the argument was between a man and a woman. It was brighter this time. He was so damn tired. His arms and legs were heavy and slow to respond. Even his eyelids didn't want to cooperate. Why was he so much more exhausted this time than before? Was he being drugged?

Asyl must have made a noise or shifted slightly to alert the others in the room. The voices stopped, and something cool was pressed to his lips, sending a jolt of pain down his jaw. He felt something roll down his lower lip and chin. A soft cloth caught whatever it was, keeping him clean. Asyl's arm obeyed his demand to push the hand away, but only succeeded in raising his hand an inch off the mattress before it thumped back down.

In all the years he'd spent on the streets, Asyl had never felt so delirious and drained. As much as he tried getting his limbs to act the way he wanted them to, he just lay on the mattress like a cat napping in a sunbeam. The pressure returned to his lips, this time gentler, though Asyl still twitched at the pain. He tried tilting his head away. A soft hand guided him back.

Whatever they were dosing him with, he didn't want to drink it. Until a few drops got past his slowly weakening efforts. Just water. Plain water, nothing added or diluted. Asyl parted his lips a little more, seeking another drink. Whomever was assisting him was taking their time, making sure he didn't choke on too much at once. Not even the slightest coppery tang making its way into each mouthful made it any less heavenly.

The container was moved away before something else, something cooler, replaced it. This time the mixture had a taste past the growing copper tang from his bleeding lip. It was a mundane healing tincture, mixed with a sedative and pain reliever. He could taste the individual herbs that had been distilled and refined in its creation. From what he could distinguish, the tincture was of a fantastic quality.

Where in the hell was he?

Hospitals didn't use tinctures of this quality, and private citizens usually didn't have the funds to purchase them. Did Naias find him? Goddess, he hoped not. His best friend had been through far too much to find him damn near dead. He'd even lost his purchases of that day, having dropped the basket once he realized the thugs meant to do more than just beat him. Would she ever know what happened? Surely, she'd look… right?

Once the tincture was drunk, he was given some more water. Or… broth? Definitely bone broth. Whomever was caring for him knew what he needed to recover. Neither liquid had been given to him in excess that would be uncomfortable. Just enough to satiate his body's needs and help give it the energy he needed to heal.

Honestly, it was a relief, being in the hands of someone capable. Not many people knew how to take care of a Void. Poorly trained or ignorant Healers relied heavily on their Craft to heal him the few times one had tried to assist with minor cuts or burns. It didn't work, and instead Asyl would have to retreat home and treat his wounds with the tinctures and salves he made. If he was lucky enough to make it home. He hadn't been this time, having been chased away from his store.

The men who attacked him knew he was a Void. He'd been targeted for that alone, for whatever goddess-forsaken reason. Asyl knew that deep in his bones.

Being pinned down, seeing his blood siphoned from his veins…. Asyl shuddered at the memory. Whomever was next to him must have misinterpreted his shiver, as a moment later the pressure on his chest doubled. They rubbed his core vigorously before rubbing his arms and legs. Heat spread through him, and Asyl settled further in the blankets. That felt nice. He felt his body react to the stimulation and couldn't be bothered to care what the person taking care of him thought.

It had been so long since he'd been consensually touched, anyway. Naias tried giving him some form of comfort in the way of irregular hugs, but she was the only Craft Blessed who didn't flinch and cringe away upon seeing his naked forehead. His obvious difference made it hard and dangerous to find a bedfellow. Either they'd be disgusted by him or weirdly obsessed. Asyl learned to live without being touched. Especially after Tillet.

The rubbing stopped, and he heard a small rumble of laughter. That clued him in that he was near a man, or potentially at his mercy. That knowledge chilled him more than reliving his beating. At least he would have only died with the exsanguination. If he was in the hands of another power-hungry man…. Asyl would rather take his own life than let that happen again.

His fear kept him semiconscious for longer than the observers likely expected. He dimly heard them asking him questions and talking directly to him, though he couldn't quite understand what they were saying. Sometimes he was able to muster the energy to make a small noise in lieu of a reply. Someone kept gently touching his jaw and hand. Asyl did his best to tamp down any craving he had about soaking in that attention.

Eventually the questions stopped coming, and he finally drifted back into oblivion.

WORN OUT, Asyl slowly opened his eyes. He felt like he could keep sleeping for another day or so, but he was already massively behind on work. Naias would torment him if they ran out of anything while he lazed about in bed. How long had he been sleeping? Asyl had no idea what day it was. He blinked a few times, clearing his vision and freezing at realizing he wasn't at home.

None of what happened had been a dream. Where was he? What day? Was Naias even aware he was alive? If he hadn't been able to talk— at least coherently—to whomever was taking care of him, she likely didn't know where he was. The room was dim, only the fireplace on the opposite wall was lit, though he could see several wall-mounted lamps.

A fireplace in a bedroom?

Where was he?

Asyl did his best to not move or draw attention as he looked around carefully. He was indeed in what seemed like one of the fancier hotel rooms. The wallpaper was a dark red with a chocolate-brown wainscoting, Ignis lamps mounted on the walls. It was spacious, with room enough to have a few bookshelves and chairs in addition to the fireplace. There looked to be a privacy screen folded away that separated the sitting area from the bed. The bed itself had insanely soft sheets, and the most comfortable mattress Asyl could just melt into.

Except Asyl couldn't help but notice there were a few paintings on the wall depicting… men. Not powerful portraits with swords and horses, or in the middle of unleashing an elemental Craft, but men depicted in sensual poses. That wasn't anything he'd see in a hotel. Maybe a brothel. Oh Goddess, had he been kidnapped and sold? Had they just been waiting for him to get healthy before forcing him into a contract to repay them?

Fear coursed through him, and he quickly sat up, much to his head's disagreement. Asyl groaned, holding his head in his hands for a moment as the world spun before he took stock of himself. Most of his injuries seemed to be healing remarkably well. Granted, if they were using the same quality salves as the tincture, that wasn't too much of a surprise. Except, no brothel would pay that high of a fee for someone who might bring them a good income.

Asyl threw back the silk covers, staring down in fascination at the beige pajamas he'd been dressed in. He could feel the soft cotton against his skin, not chafing anywhere sensitive. Goddess knew his work pants did quite often. Heavy canvas and sweaty skin weren't exactly compatible. Slipping his feet from between the sheets, Asyl slowly stood, looking around again. Now that he was taking his time, he could see more details in the dim light.

His work clothes were folded and had been placed on top of a dresser. Asyl lifted his tunic, baffled at the color. It had been cleaned thoroughly, all the splashed potion stains washed out. When was the last time he'd seen the nice pale green? It looked like someone had even sewn the slashes too. Fairly expertly, since he could barely see the mended string. There wasn't even a hint of blood in the tunic, yet he knew this was his, not a replacement.

Quickly looking around to make sure he was alone, Asyl shucked the borrowed pajamas and hastily pulled on his work clothes. They were rougher than what he'd been given, but he couldn't very well leave his clothing behind. He'd paid good money for them.

Where were his cloak and boots? Asyl looked around, dismay filling him as he wondered if whoever had found him had taken them on purpose. Hidden them from him so he'd feel that he couldn't leave.

If they thought he wouldn't run barefoot, they were mistaken.

The door between the dresser and bookshelf opened. Asyl skittered back, balling his hands into fists. If they expected him to be docile, they were in for a massively rude awakening. A man stepped inside, his hair glowing golden in the firelight. He was looking at some papers in his hand, chewing on his lower lip. The man was slightly taller than him, broader in the shoulders and sturdy-looking. What Asyl could see of his arms showed nicely toned muscles.

Fuck, he was gorgeous.

But so had been the last bastard whose home he'd been in. Asyl tamped down the sudden urge to nestle into him and never leave his side. He'd been fine not being touched these last four years; he could go even longer without someone else in his life. Yet even as he did his best to convince himself that he didn't want to be anywhere near the blond, his... everything wanted to give into the sudden, strong pull.

The blond's eyes raised toward the bed, and he stopped in his tracks, seeing it empty. A brief look of panic crossed his face until he noticed Asyl slowly shrinking into the shadows. Their eyes locked, and Asyl felt a shock course through him, rooting him to the spot. Oh shit. Oh fuck. Why did he have to be so handsome? That's all this was. Just carnal attraction. It didn't mean anything. Couldn't mean anything. Not for a filthy Void.

"You're finally awake," the man's deep voice rumbled.

Asyl shuddered, trying to control the flush rising to his cheeks. He took another step back, finding himself bumping against the wall. At least the man didn't immediately pursue him and pin him, forcing him to fight. Instead, he stayed exactly where he was, his shoulders relaxed and expression soft. Just a ploy to try and catch him off guard.

"How are you feeling?" the man asked, a warm smile curving his lips.

Very kissable lips.

Why was he even thinking like this? Why was his body craving this man's attention as much as he needed air? Nothing good came out of such an attraction. Besides, it had been so long since he'd even viewed another man romantically, much less sexually. It didn't stop his body from warming and a flush coming over his cheeks. The man's low voice wasn't helping much either.

The blond tossed the papers he had in his hands onto a nearby chair, and Asyl got a glimpse of the tight black vest he wore over a short-sleeved shirt. He inhaled sharply, seeing the royal crest embroidered at the hem of his vest in shimmering red thread. Gold hair, forest-green eyes, tall. Healer Craft Mark. Asyl's legs gave out, and he collapsed to the floor.

Oh shit.

He was in Lord Kende Ruvyn's house?

The blond rushed over, looking startled, and knelt in front of him, grabbing his shoulders. His touch was gentle, as to be expected from any Healer. Yet his skin tingled wherever Lord Kende put his hands. After everything that had happened in his life, his body was actually responding to another's touch. Asyl didn't want to examine that too closely. Didn't want to give any weight to the traitorous urges. He needed to get out of here.

"M-my lord," Asyl managed to stammer, "I apologize for disturbing you."

Lord Kende looked confused, and he sat back, his hands leaving Asyl's shoulders, taking the warmth with him. Asyl missed the warmth and comfort immediately, then chastised himself. There was no point in craving his touch. A Void had no business even being in his presence. He could barely even lift his gaze past the man's chin.

"You haven't. I brought you here," Lord Kende said. "It's all right. Just breathe. You've been out for a week, fighting an infection and blood loss."

A week?

Asyl inhaled sharply, staring wide-eyed up at the duke's youngest son. He'd been putting the man out for so long. With how the room looked, Asyl had no doubt that this was Lord Kende's personal bedroom. Full-body tremors shook him, and Lord Kende reached out again, cupping his face. Asyl jerked, barely stopping himself from pulling away as to hopefully not insult the man.

"It's all right. You're okay," he said with a gentle smile. "I'm glad to see you're up."

Lord Kende took his hand and pulled him to his feet, leading him away from the wall toward the sitting area. Heart beating wildly, Asyl stared up at the man. He felt unsteady and light-headed, unable to figure out why he was having such a reaction around Lord Kende. This couldn't be his normal anxiety.

"How?" Asyl managed to say weakly.

"I found you in bad shape," Lord Kende said, not releasing his hand. Instead, he slowly rubbed his thumb across his palm. "I brought you here so you could heal."

"You… you know what I am," Asyl said slowly.

Lord Kende nodded. "It doesn't bother me that you're a Void."

Asyl couldn't help but flinch at the term, finally dropping his gaze. Lord Kende tilted his head back up, smiling softly at him, his eyes gentle. He didn't want to even try to interpret that look, but he had a feeling he knew what it was. Asyl closed his eyes so he didn't have to see what he was expected to do in payment. There would only be one reason a lord would take the time to let him recover. In his own bed at that.

At least the rug was soft when he dropped to his knees. Lord Kende made a small, startled noise. Pushing conscious thought from his mind and escaping back to the comforts of his shop that he'd likely never see again, Asyl reached up to work the man's belt. His hands were caught, and Lord Kende knelt in front of him.

"What are you doing?" he asked gently.

"I…. Isn't this why you brought me here?" Asyl asked, refusing to meet the lord's eyes.

"Not at all," Lord Kende replied sharply. "I brought you here because you're my Fated."

Fated. Oh, that was a joke. Asyl couldn't help the sneer and bitter laugh that exploded from his lips. He yanked his wrists from the man's soft grasp, scrambling to his feet and away from him. There was no way in hell he'd ever believe that outrageous lie again.

"Just because I'm a Void, you think I'm stupid?" Asyl demanded. "Voids don't get Fated. We get attacked for no damn reason and struggle to do anything worthwhile, let alone *live*, because everything depends on your stupid Craft!"

Lord Kende looked surprised at the outburst; then what looked like hurt crossed his face. He got to his feet and approached Asyl, who quickly backed away. This time he headed toward the fireplace, refusing to be pushed up against a wall again. The heat against his back made it easier to judge how far away he was. Lord Kende hadn't lost that gentle bewildered look. As if he couldn't understand the truth of the situation.

"I don't think you're stupid," Lord Kende said, his voice returning to that soft tone. Placating. "My family's physician confirmed that the stains on your tunic were from potions. High-quality ones at that. Do you make them?"

"Why do you care?" Asyl growled, not feeling charitable at all. "There's no place for me in your society."

"That's not fair to you," Lord Kende said, taking a step toward him.

Asyl hopped backward, glancing around. He could dart around the couch to the door and run away. There was more than enough room to sidestep the lord. Except he had no idea where he was in the house or if there was a guard outside the door. Fuck, he was trapped.

"It doesn't matter what happens to me," Asyl snapped. "I'm a Void. Worth less than the dirt on your shoes. I know my place. It's not my fault you can't accept that."

Asyl would have expected anger from the other man. Instead, all he saw was sadness in his expression. He could feel a foreign energy gathering in his body, and he knew he could run fast so long as he trusted it. In fact, his body positively thrummed with energy even as his palm itched.

Tearing his eyes away from Lord Kende's, Asyl darted past him to the door and flung it open.

"Wait!" Lord Kende exclaimed.

He ignored him. Asyl darted from the room, quickly taking in his surroundings. A maid looked startled as she spun to see what the ruckus was. What looked like the front door was downstairs to his right. Without breaking his stride, Asyl sprinted down the large staircase and rushed to those heavy oak doors. It took him a minute to open them, and he hated how his arms were already trembling.

Glancing behind him, he saw Lord Kende rushing to the top of the staircase, gripping the rail. Asyl couldn't help his snarl at seeing the startled look on his face.

Glowering at the man, Asyl flipped him off.

Turning, Asyl ran from the mansion into the wall of rain. Now he was glad he was barefoot. The soles on his shoes were starting to get thin enough he wouldn't have as good of a grip on the wet concrete. He ran down the drive and onto the street, taking off in a random direction. It didn't matter which way he went. Either way would get him home... eventually.

Gasping for air, Asyl got several blocks away before he slid into an alley and collapsed. His whole body trembled from the exertion, and he took a minute to just breathe. They may have given him a hearty broth when he was conscious enough to drink, but that was no substitute for real food. His feet burned from running on the rough concrete. Asyl gingerly stood and hobbled through the alley, looking for street markers. Dismay filled him when he finally found one.

He had half the damn city to walk through to get home and no money to request a carriage ride. Not that any self-respecting carriage would even let him in. Despite the fact that he was beyond soaked, he was a Void. There were many things he'd never be able to do just because of how people perceived him. He had resigned himself to be a pariah the moment he left his parents' backyard.

Sometimes Asyl wondered if he had any siblings. If he did, and they were born shortly after his disowning, they'd be right about the age to receive their Craft. The idea made his eyes sting, and a lump formed in his throat. He'd been a good kid, hadn't he? He'd always obeyed his parents, treated everyone with kindness, and rarely got angry. So why had he been abandoned by the goddess? What was it about him that was so undesirable?

Asyl choked back a sob, hugging himself as he trudged through the streets toward home. It didn't matter. He'd never see his parents again, and he'd never know his siblings, if he had any. Naias put herself at risk daily even associating with him. If her family knew she was speaking to him, let alone selling his silly concoctions, they'd disown her in a heartbeat. Then she wouldn't have the trust fund her parents had set up for her, and they'd really be in trouble.

The only reason their shop even worked at all was because of her trust fund. It didn't matter if they lost money most moonturns. She'd bought the building years ago, so they only needed to worry about property taxes twice a year. They'd only been short for that once, and Naias pulled money from her fund to cover it. Granted, that had been closer to the beginning of their shop's lifetime. Just knowing they had that safety net was nice.

He owed Naias so much. The least he could do for her was to not make trouble and keep his head down. Goddess knew he didn't want to cause her grief. A whole week. Naias was going to kill him once he got home. Maybe she'd take pity on him. He'd seen the heavy bruising spanning most of his body. Speaking of, where was he? His feet ached something terrible, so he must have walked a ways already.

The more distance he put between him and Lord Kende, the more his chest ached. His throat tightened, and his belly would empty if it had anything in it. Hell, his body felt vaguely feverish, and he couldn't help but keep thinking about the blond. About his gentle smile, kind eyes, and slow movements. As if Asyl was a spooked gelding that he didn't trust to not bolt. Well, that part had been true at least.

Looking around, Asyl found the signs at the nearest crossroad and sighed with relief. Two more blocks. The rain hadn't let up, and he was chilled to the bone, but he was close to home. He didn't know what time it was with the clouds obscuring the sky. Sometime at night, he knew that much. Being in familiar territory helped him relax more, and Asyl spotted a few of the sex workers he knew, trying to entice the few who braved the rain for a quick fuck.

Finally, he could see the gable of his home, and his shoulders slumped. Gingerly, Asyl stepped down the back stairs and fell heavily into the back door. Whatever energy he'd felt earlier was completely gone, leaving him bereft. If Naias wasn't here, he'd slide down the door and curl up into a ball. At least there was a slight overhang that would keep him mostly dry.

It took Naias a minute, but the lock clicked and the door swung inward. He barely stood in time and heard a litany of curses as he was pulled inside. Oh, thank the goddess it was warm. Sitting quietly on the bench she shoved him onto, Asyl sat as still as his shivering body would allow. Naias quickly stripped him of his sodden clothes and hung them on the fire grate to dry. She bustled around him, wrapping him up in a thick blanket, attacking his shoulder-length hair with a towel.

The entire time, she berated him about how worried she was while he'd been off gallivanting around and seducing men with his eyes. Asyl knew she didn't believe that's what happened, but her teasing fantasy was her way of coping with the fear and anxiety she'd suffered this last week. When his teeth no longer chattered, Naias had him drink warm tea before rushing off again.

Naias came bustling back a minute later, thrusting a hearty sandwich into his hands. Asyl gratefully wolfed it down, barely tasting the seasoned roast beef and herb butter. Naias sat next to him on the bench, tears in her eyes. Full and comfortable, Asyl finally took a deep breath and straightened to look at her with a soft smile.

Home in the workroom, herbs, both distilled and raw, lined the walls in countless shelves, filling the air with a heady scent. Boxes of vials, bottles, and pots for their products, along with twine and paper so he could scrawl what each item was and attach it to the container, were stacked almost haphazardly in the corner. His distilling apparatus, the sizable cauldron that stood empty, and his large workbench with his tomes that contained his recipes for everything they sold were well used and bulky, taking up what little floor space remained.

When Asyl had shown Naias how to make the mundane concoctions so she could help prep, she'd been uncomfortable and had nearly ended up spoiling the batch. Ever since then, she refused to do anything, leaving it to Asyl. Especially when it came to the potions that invoked the consumer's Craft. She'd gone so far as to not even approach the workroom door if he was making a potion.

Slowly, he told her what had happened. How he'd been attacked viciously by three men. One had a knife that had cut him, another a rod to hit his legs so he'd have a hard time running. The third had the exsanguination implements and an evil grin on his face. Even recounting it to Naias, in a room where he knew he was safe, caused Asyl to shudder. The other two had grabbed him after he'd fallen, let the third have some fun softening him up with his fists before pinning him down and draining him.

Naias sat there horrified, tears running down her face and her lower lip quivering. She cleared her throat and wiped the tears from her eyes, taking a breath to try and steady herself. Once she was able to listen again, Asyl told her about how he'd woken up a few hours ago at Lord Kende's place, and his declaration that he was the man's Fated.

Hearing that, she scowled as she rubbed his back.

"Never heard of a Void being Fated to a Craft Blessed," she said, "but I didn't think Lord Kende was one to take advantage of someone else."

Asyl shrugged. "Never really talked to or heard about him before. Just knew enough to know who he was."

Naias smiled. "That's because you're a lucky bitch and you don't have to go to galas and all that bullshit. Honestly, I think the life you have now is perfect for you. You would have been so bored going to all the events I do. Plus, you don't have your parents nagging you to try to actively seek out your Fated. If they're my Fated, then we'll find each other when we're ready."

Asyl smiled at her rant, letting her pull his feet up so she could inspect his soles. She got up and walked to the front to grab something. When she returned, she spread a numbing salve on the bottoms of his feet.

"I had Rojir look for you," Naias said, rubbing her eyes with the back of her hands again. "He found your basket, but it had been pilfered of the rarer herbs. Even with all his contacts on the streets, no one had seen you without it."

"I'll have to call for him and thank him," Asyl replied, smiling gently. "I don't know if he would have ever found me anyways, being in the temple."

Naias shook her head. "I wish I could say I don't understand it, but…." She sighed gustily. "People are disgusting when it comes to superstitions and prejudice. Have you thought about going to the police?"

"Why would they care, Nai?" Asyl asked wearily. "I'm just a Void. They'd just laugh me out of the building if I went and claimed attempted murder."

She scowled, her pretty features drawing tight together. Asyl knew full well his best friend didn't share the sentiments that the rest of the gentry had. She actually thought for herself instead of blindly following the teachings of the church, believing that Voids were little better than devils. Maybe it was because she'd known him before his Awakening failed. Asyl's mind flinched away from the thought. He hated missing his parents. They clearly didn't miss him.

"Think I'll be able to stand tomorrow?" he asked, trying to change the subject.

"Tomorrow, you stay in bed. Our shelves are getting thin, but they're not bare yet," she replied. "Our reputation is getting better all the time, so we're getting more customers. But I've been telling everyone who's been coming in and complaining at the lack of product that you've been sick, and that gets them to back off."

"You're wonderful, Naias," Asyl said with a smile.

"You know it," she said, grinning at him. "Let's get you to bed."

She wrapped his feet in loose bandages, and leaning against her, he headed up the narrow, rickety stairs to his apartment. As soon as he was in his tiny room, Asyl threw back the covers on his twin bed and slid between the sheets with a bone-deep sigh. Naias kissed his forehead, tucked him in as tight as she could, and left the room, leaving the door slightly ajar.

It was good to be home.

CHAPTER 3

KENDE STARED out the window, wishing that the rain would let up. It had been a full moonturn since he'd seen his Fated, and every day it made his heart ache. He knew the man was still out there somewhere. Now that they'd connected, however briefly, he could feel him. It was faint, and sometimes he'd catch a whiff of some herb or hear humming.

At first he thought he was going crazy, but after confiding in Gojko, the portly man just smiled and told him he was hearing his Fated when he was content. Kende hoped that his nameless Fated was safe and warm wherever he was.

Maybe it was time to make a bigger effort to try and find him. Kende had continued his visits to apothecaries around Alenzon and had started quietly asking about a Void that made potions. Because of his rank, none of the proprietors had actually laughed in his face, but their expressions told him enough. None of them believed that a Void could make potions or would even employ one to help.

Had he been wrong about the man's profession? The way he'd been so defensive about it made Kende think that, no, he'd been on to something. But why would a Healer need a Void to help make potions or mundane salves? There really was only one answer.

They wouldn't.

The thought struck him out of the blue, and Kende straightened from where he'd been leaning against the window frame. Out of every single apothecary in the city, there was one that wasn't run by a Healer. And she'd even told him that she wasn't the one who made the items she sold. At the time of their visit, she'd told him that their brewer was out. Had the brewer been out or collapsed at the feet of a statue in an abandoned temple?

Then there were the peculiar potions. How were they made with actual ingredients, but no less effective than a Craft-charged potion? In fact, they might even be more effective. He'd sifted through the basket of products he'd used for testing and had Gojko use some of them on his unconscious Fated. Even Gojko had been surprised at the quality of the salves and ointments.

He had to get to Enchanted Waters. Kende turned from the window and left the library, calling for Siora. He wanted to know if his theory held up or if it was all wishful thinking.

When she arrived and he explained, Siora shrugged. That was good enough for him. It had taken a long time, almost the full moonturn, for Siora to believe that the Void was his Fated. Maybe it was his deteriorating mood and long bouts of antisocial behavior that had finally convinced her. Getting her to be friendly toward his Fated would be another fight.

Siora had finally confided in him about a fortnight ago that she and her Fated had met only briefly and hadn't realized what they were feeling until they'd parted without knowing who the other was. It had taken them a long time to come together again, and she didn't even have the weak connection that Kende seemed to have.

That confused him. How could he and a Void have an instant, stronger connection than two Craft Blessed? According to all of the texts, a bond couldn't exist between them due to the very nature of a Void. It didn't make sense, and there was no going and talking to a priest about it. They'd be biased against his Fated the moment he told them he was a Void.

Armed with his aide and a pair of peculiar shoes, Kende set out. This time they took the horse-drawn carriage. He didn't want his Fated to feel left out and unable to do anything if they brought the Craft-powered vehicle. Kende wanted to make sure the man felt as comfortable as he could make him during their courtship. Because it would be a courtship this time. No easy Fated connection, both sides knowing instinctively who their heart's twin was. Kende was going to have to work for his Fated. He didn't mind the thought. He'd be worth it.

The ride across town made him nervous with every street they passed by. More nervous than his first ball or the first time he'd tumbled into bed with another man. Did his Fated have experience in bed? He assumed so. The way he'd dropped to his knees so easily....

What had happened to him that he'd so readily resigned to sexual acts? Kende had seen the blank look, his eyes slowly unfocusing. His bafflement at being rejected, and then the swift refusal at the idea of being Fated told Kende that the Void hadn't led an easy life. He wanted to sweep him off his feet, hold him close, and try to show him how precious he was.

Just as long as his instincts were right and he was able to see his Fated again. It wouldn't take that long to show the Void they belonged together. They held half of each other's hearts. The Void belonged to him as much as he belonged to the Void. Sure, they'd have fights, Kende wasn't stupid enough to believe everything would be perfect, but their bond would be unbreakable once it was forged.

The carriage driver, Toemi, stopped in front of Enchanted Waters. Having an Aquan shopkeeper, that name was most definitely a little bit of humor from the two inside. The more Kende thought about it, the more he was sure his theory was correct. Siora stood a few paces behind him as they entered. There were a couple of other patrons, and Kende quietly browsed while he waited.

Even after all this time, the shelves still weren't quite fully stocked like they had been the first time he passed through. That was curious. Was the store just that popular, or were they having a hard time making the products? Maybe a little bit of both. But it had been a moonturn. Surely his Fated would have been able to get everything caught up.

Kende hoped that the man was all right. Now that his anxiety was easing, he realized that he knew exactly where his Fated was. The Void was in the back room, moving around. So, he'd made it back safely. That was a huge relief. Kende hoped that the other man could feel their tenuous bond, Void or no. Kende was a fairly skilled Healer. Maybe the strength of his Craft would be enough to bleed over.

Once the other two patrons left, Kende approached the cashier. The Aquan took one look at him and her usual cheerful smile dropped off her face. She stood up from her languid pose and squared her shoulders, her lips setting in a hard line. The chilly reception he'd gotten last time was nothing compared to the glacier he was facing down this time.

"May I help you, my lord?" she nearly spat.

Siora hmphed behind him, "Sir, if this is the company your Fated keeps, maybe it's best to walk away."

Kende sighed and shook his head. "I believe our friend has the right to be cautious. If how my Fated acted during our brief time together is any indication of how he's been treated in the past, I'd be cautious too."

At his words, he saw the woman's expression soften slightly.

"You really do think he's your Fated," she said slowly.

Kende smiled. "Yes, miss. I know he's in the room behind you working on something. Can I get the name of his benefactor?"

The woman snorted. "I'm hardly his benefactor. He's skilled, and if it wasn't for the fact he doesn't have a mark, I wouldn't need to be here."

"I was impressed by the quality of this shop when I was here for inspections," Kende replied. "He must have worked hard to perfect his recipes."

"He did," the woman replied proudly and finally smiled. "Naias Elrel."

"An Elrel," Kende said and blinked before grinning. "Yes, I do see the family resemblance now. You've got your father's eyes and your mother's ethereal beauty."

Lady Naias flushed and glanced toward the door behind her. She sighed heavily and turned back to face him.

"Look… I don't need to tell you that he's been hurt before," she said.

Kende held up a hand and smiled at her. "I figured. Please don't tell me anything about it. I would rather hear what happened from him whenever he's ready to talk about it. If he's ever ready to talk about it. I just want him to be happy and know he's safe. Whomever attacked him… they're probably still roaming free."

Lady Naias looked pained as she smiled and nodded. "All right. Everything I've heard about you socially has been positive, so I'm willing to take a chance that you're not a total prick. Your lady stays out here, though."

"Sir," Siora squawked in protest.

"I agree to your terms, Lady Naias," Kende said.

"Well then, Lord Kende, good luck. He's making mundane tinctures today, and I believe he's currently distilling, so he should have some down time to get acquainted with you," Lady Naias said.

With another smile at her, Kende slipped around the counter and quietly opened the door. Indeed, the man was sitting at a desk with a multilayered contraption of glass and fire. It was percolating, and he had his head in one hand, blinking slowly at the text he had opened on the table.

The room itself was magnificent. So many herbs and spices in close proximity should have been chaos on the senses but instead just smelled like the heavily spiced kitchens during a grand feast. It was at a comfortable temperature and completely dry. A large cauldron stood on an Ignis Plate, currently empty and clearly cleaned. One wall had boxes piled against it, small labels on each one, detailing what was inside.

Bottles, vials, pots, twine, paper, wax.... Then there were the herbs braided together, hanging from the ceiling and hooks on the walls.

It was a chaotic order, but one that Kende felt oddly familiar with. In fact, this entire room made him feel cozy and safe. No wonder his Fated adored it here. Kende took the opportunity of not being seen to admire his Fated.

His black hair was shiny in the low light, just brushing over his shoulders as he leaned over his book. Those intense pale blue eyes were sleepy, narrow, and slightly slanted skyward. His cheekbones were high, offering an ethereal look to him when paired with his heart-shaped face. A cute dainty nose tilted upward. Perfect for kissing. Speaking of, his Fated's lips were slightly parted as he studied, not quite pure red. There was a bit of brown in there as well.

Kende set the shoes he was carrying on a nearby box to free his hands. He kept his footsteps light as he approached and stood a few feet away from the desk. His Fated looked exhausted, with dark bags under his eyes. Had he relapsed and caught a fever? It was warm enough in here that Kende wasn't able to feel any unnatural heat coming off his Fated.

"Are you not sleeping well?" Kende asked.

In hindsight, he should have expected the man to panic. His Fated jumped to his feet, knocking over the stool he'd been sitting on with a crash, and stumbled backward toward the door behind him. That likely led to the outside. Kende didn't want him to vanish again, a bolt of panic rushing through him. He held up his hands in a gesture to show he meant no harm. His Fated was wearing the pale green tunic they'd washed and mended for him. It was already lightly stained again. That made him smile faintly.

"How the fuck did you find me?" the man snapped.

Kende's smile widened. "This is the only apothecary not run by a Healer, and you had potion stains on your tunic. Why would a Healer need a Void to make their potions for them?"

"To help keep stock," the man retorted, his eyes darting around nervously.

"Possibly. But everyone I asked was incredibly insulted that I even suggested they have a Void employed," Kende said and shrugged. "Personally, I think they're missing out. You make some of the best products in the city."

At that, his Fated flushed and ducked his head. Was he not used to getting any sort of praise? He really hoped Lady Naias told him how brilliant he was as often as she could. Kende slowly took a step forward as if his Fated was a spooked colt and felt some relief when he didn't back away.

"Can I at least know your name before you kick me out?" Kende teased with a smile.

He was rewarded with a small smile as his Fated looked up at him. His winter-pale blue eyes sparkled with amusement in the low light.

"Asyl," he supplied.

A sense of rightness settled over Kende, and he sighed, closing his eyes briefly. He looked around the workroom at all the ingredients, carefully labeled and sorted. This was where his Fated had been for years and years, working away in anonymity without the larger population knowing how wonderful he was. It seemed a shame to him.

"Well. You already know who I am. But to you, I'm just Kende," he said and walked a bit closer to his Fated.

Much to his delight, Asyl didn't move. Instead, he tilted his head before looking incredibly confused. He began tugging at the hem of his tunic, betraying that the stains were from his hands rather than being splashed. Out of all the nervous habits Kende witnessed, he thought this one was the cutest.

"You're still thinking we're Fated?" Asyl asked, frowning.

"Do you hum sometimes when you work?" Kende asked.

Asyl's head snapped up in surprise, and he stared at Kende. He nodded and tugged at the hem of his shirt again. Stepping forward once more, Kende was finally within reach of his Fated. He slowly took Asyl's hands in his, running his thumb over the man's thin, scarred fingers. So many small cuts littered his hands, and calluses roughened his palms. The hands of someone who had to work for a living.

"Do you have a family name?" Kende asked.

He felt Asyl begin to pull away and gave a small token resistance before letting him go. Asyl hugged himself tight, hanging his head before shrugging.

"I've forgotten it," he said, and Kende knew that was a lie. "It doesn't matter. They don't want anything to do with me anyways. I'm damned, or something to that effect."

Kende sighed. He reached out and unfolded Asyl's arms so he could hold the man's hand. He brought it up to his lips and kissed the back of his hand, right on the mole that sat perfectly in the center. Slowly, he felt Asyl relax. Kende gently tugged the man toward him, placing his other hand on his hip. They weren't that far apart in height, only a handful of inches. Asyl looked up at him, confusion plain on his face.

"I still don't understand why you're drawn to me," he said.

Kende shrugged. "Who knows. But it's for a reason. And I can tell you I wouldn't change the fact that you're a Void for the world." Asyl tried pulling away at that, but Kende kept a hold on his hand this time. "I really wouldn't. Think about it. You've worked hard here to make these potions. If you had a Craft, this store wouldn't exist, and some of the best potions and mundane medicines wouldn't be readily available for your neighbors."

Asyl stilled at that, throwing him a curious look. "You really believe that?"

He nodded. "Yes. Also, no one with a Craft would dare flip me off in my own home."

Kende watched as his Fated flushed a dark red up to his ears. Cute. What wasn't cute was how badly someone had hurt his man—the fact he reacted so violently to his status and how wary he was of the idea that someone like him could have an admirer. All that in addition to how he seemed to not be used to compliments. Well, that meant he'd have to give out plenty when they were deserved.

Positive reinforcement.

Carefully, Kende crooked his finger under Asyl's chin as he moved in close, tilting his head up. He saw the man's lips part and smiled. The split on his lip was fully healed, leaving only a faint scar behind. Kende wanted to spend the time to get to know every single blemish on Asyl's body. But for now, he could content himself with learning one.

"May I kiss you?" he asked. "Nothing too intense." That flush returned, and Asyl made a small noise in the back of his throat. Kende couldn't help but snicker. "I'm not going to assume. Can you give me a definitive answer?"

"Yes," Asyl breathed.

Oh, that sound went straight to his dick. Later. Once Asyl was ready and knew he wasn't under any obligation whatsoever to say yes. Kende tilted his head and bent down, brushing their lips together. Asyl sighed and gently grabbed his doublet, getting on his toes to press up into the kiss. The puffy scar on his lip felt slightly different, but Kende paid it no mind.

He let Asyl lead, only having intended a quick peck, but he wasn't complaining with the languid, searching kiss he was receiving. Kende slipped his hand from his Fated's chin to cup the back of his head, not putting any pressure in his touch. Asyl needed to know he was free to move away whenever he wanted to. He hadn't expected the soft, almost needy whimper that came from Asyl.

Goddess. A simple kiss got that much of a reaction? Asyl pulled back, seemingly startled by himself, and blinked rapidly. Kende didn't let it bother him. He was just overjoyed by having Asyl in his arms in the first place. After a minute of his Fated staring at him in disbelief, Kende breathed out a small laugh.

"Hey," he said softly.

"Hi," Asyl whispered. "I…. Um."

He jerked away, and Kende let him back off even as Asyl's tongue darted out to wet his lips. When neither of them moved for a minute, Kende tilted his head. He felt far out of his depth here, not sure what to do next. He'd never had such a hesitant lover before. Shy, yes. But clearly warring with himself out of past fears and trauma? Kende took in a slow, deep breath.

"I brought you something," Kende said gently, trying to deflect or break the tension.

His Fated blinked once and took another small step back to put a little more distance between them. Kende turned to retrieve the shoes, trying to show Asyl that he trusted him. That he wasn't a threat or wouldn't stare him down and force his subjugation. He would be as vulnerable as his Fated, even though he didn't fully understand his fears.

Kende picked up the shoes, smiling a little. Siora had taken them to a cobbler who had eagerly inspected the design and even replaced the soles with a minimal fee. The opportunity to learn something new had been half of the payment, the Gaian had told him. Now his Fated's shoes had good, sturdy, quality leather to last him for a long time.

He approached slowly again and held them out once he was at arm's length.

"These were getting repaired when you woke," Kende explained gently. "Sorry it took me so long to return them to you."

Asyl reached out with trembling hands and looked down at his feet. Kende was helpless to follow his gaze and smiled faintly at the stockings he saw in lieu of any sort of footwear. A small pang of realization hit him then. Did his Fated only have one pair of shoes? Had he been effectively trapped at home while Kende took ten years to figure out where his Fated was?

He felt a quick flash of shame. Kende should have put the clues together quicker. Was this why the store was still fairly empty? To his untrained eye, there appeared to be more than enough back here to keep the shop stocked, but he didn't know Asyl's alchemy. Because it was alchemy, not simply brewing. Kende was still curious how it worked, but that would be a discussion for later. Much later.

For a minute, neither of them moved. Asyl stood silently, his brows drawing together sharply a few times as he seemingly tried to process what was happening. Was this really such a foreign concept? Kende took another step closer and gently grasped his shoulders. He didn't want to try and have Asyl feel trapped, but he felt like he needed the physical comfort.

A second later, Asyl fled upstairs, dropping the shoes.

Trying to not take it personally, Kende slowly followed, hoping that Asyl wasn't too upset. The stairs were narrow and steep, forcing him to slow down. Kende could feel his Fated's anxiety rising to a near overwhelming level. That wasn't good. He didn't question how he could already feel Asyl's emotions. He was just glad he could.

Following the ragged gasping, Kende found his way through the simple barebones kitchen into a cozy little bedroom. There wasn't much to it, the bed small and the rest of the furniture cramped together to try and get as much in as possible. Asyl deserved better. Kende was proud of what his Fated had already accomplished, but he wanted to pamper the man before him.

He had a feeling that wouldn't be too appreciated. Not right now at least. Kende would work his way up to large gestures of his affections. Right now, he had to be careful just in case he drove his Fated away instead. There had to be a way where he could spoil his Fated without stepping on his toes and his pride.

Asyl sat on the edge of his bed, head in his hands as he curled in on himself, his breath heavy. Kende knelt before him, placing a hand on his knee. Worry tugged at him when his Fated didn't even respond to his touch.

"You're having a panic attack," Kende said softly. "Try to regulate your breathing. You can do this. Follow my lead."

Gently, he guided Asyl into a breathing pattern, and slowly, the man began to relax. His body slumped forward, and Kende caught him, cradling Asyl to him. He gently rocked him, nuzzling the side of his head.

"Can I do anything to help?" Kende asked. He felt Asyl shrug. Kende slowly rubbed his back, squeezing him tight. "I'll always be here for you. I want you to be happy. Even if you never want to see me again."

There were a few heartbeats of silence before Asyl tilted his head, resting his cheek on Kende's shoulder to look up at him. The makings of a mischievous smile toyed at the edges of his Fated's lips.

"Maybe if you were a better kisser," Asyl teased him.

Kende snorted. "Oh, it's like that, is it? Well, then. When you're ready, I'll make sure I kiss you so hard you'll forget your name."

"Already forgot half of it. Shouldn't be too hard to forget the rest," Asyl murmured.

"Oh, I doubt that bit," Kende replied. "You've got a lovely name."

Asyl made a small noise and flushed, burying his face in Kende's neck.

"My lord?" he heard Siora call from the workroom.

Kende groaned and pulled away after making sure Asyl was steady enough on his own.

"Do you get any time off?" Kende asked.

"I got a week off a moonturn ago," Asyl said.

Kende smiled. "Time off that doesn't include recuperating. As much as I didn't mind you in my bed, I would have rather you been conscious for a good majority of it."

Asyl flushed and ducked his head. His bare feet shuffled against the wooden floorboards, and he finally said, "I take Sundays off."

"Then would you like to come over officially? I swear Birgir has damn near popped a stitch demanding I tell him who you are," Kende said.

"I... um. Well, I suppose it's better than what I usually do," Asyl muttered.

"And what do you usually do?" Kende asked.

"Um. Nothing different than when I'm working. Maybe a bit more—Oh Goddess, the distillery apparatus!" Asyl cried and jumped to his feet.

He pushed past Kende and rushed downstairs. Siora gave a small scream of surprise, and Kende chuckled. That would teach her to poke her nose in while he was with his Fated and trying to earn his trust. Kende wasn't going to abandon him like his parents did, nor hurt him like whomever had done in the past.

This wasn't going to be a normal Fated love story. Kende was fine with that. He got to his feet and ambled downstairs. Siora was watching Asyl as he checked over the apparatus, swirling the glass bottle and inspecting the mixture with a critical eye. Apparently whatever he was looking for was fine, and he relaxed, gingerly putting the bottle back into the contraption before fiddling with something else.

"Sir," Siora said softly when he approached, "you're needed at the house. Your sister has arrived."

Goddess help him. A thought struck him, and Kende looked away from his Fated to gaze at Siora.

"Which one?" he asked.

"Jaclyn."

As obnoxious as his sister was, it was her husband that he wanted to talk to right now. Usually he accompanied her wherever she went, so theoretically he'd be at home too. Macik was a detective with the Alenzon police. If Kende could talk to him and see if he could help bring the men who attacked Asyl to justice….

Kende moved forward, waiting for Asyl to put down the glass he had lifted. He was decanting the distilled liquid into labeled dark glass bottles. Asyl tapped the funnel on the last one, quickly corked it, and set the items aside. With a light touch on his shoulder, Kende turned his Fated toward him. Asyl looked up at him and shot Siora a panicked look.

"Ignore her," Kende said gently. Asyl swallowed hard and nodded, dropping his eyes to the ground. Sighing, Kende tilted his head up. "I want to ask, and it's okay if your answer is no. But do you remember who attacked you a moonturn ago?"

Asyl shuddered and nodded. "Yeah."

"If my brother-in-law thinks he can do something, would you be willing to talk with him and give him descriptions about what happened?" Kende asked.

He felt his Fated shiver, and his eyes closed. Kende gently rubbed his upper arm, letting Asyl debate internally about what he wanted to do. Eventually the man shrugged, avoiding his gaze. He almost seemed to deflate from whatever conclusion he'd drawn up for himself.

"I doubt they'd be willing to help a Void," he said softly. "They weren't interested before."

Before?

Kende frowned. "The police have a duty to every citizen. Every single one. That includes you and any other Voids that are living in Alenzon. You deserve to feel safe as much as anyone else here. If my brother believes they can do something to find these men who attacked you, I can sit with you to ensure that you're taken seriously. That shouldn't have to be the case, but I will."

Asyl sighed and shrugged. "If you think it's best."

"I want you to be happy. I want you to be safe. If they targeted you specifically because you're a Void, then that's something our police need to be looking out for," Kende replied, running his hand through Asyl's soft hair.

"The only reason you care is because you think I'm your Fated," Asyl said with an edge to his voice.

"I would care even if you weren't and you were a random person I found in need at the temple," Kende replied sharply. "No one deserves to be beaten up so severely as you were. Your assailants deserve to have charges pressed against them."

Asyl frowned at him, but he didn't pull away either. Hoping that was a good sign, Kende gently drew his Fated to him, wrapping his arms around him and tucking Asyl's head under his chin. It took a minute before he felt the man's arms loosely curl around his waist. Siora gave them another minute longer before politely clearing her throat. Kende groaned, though he didn't move away.

Instead, he looked down and cupped Asyl's face, tilting his head up. They were still pressed fairly close together, and his Fated just looked at him, his face flushed.

"I can send a carriage for you on Sunday," Kende said.

"No," Asyl replied. "I can walk."

He wanted to protest and insist that he make sure that Asyl got between their places safely. The gesture wouldn't be welcome and might ruin what little trust they were slowly forming. Instead, he bent down and pressed their foreheads together.

"Come over whenever you want," he said. "Even if I'm not awake, someone will be to let you in." Asyl nodded and made that same affirmative noise that he had made earlier. Kende found himself smiling. "May I have another kiss?"

This time Asyl didn't respond. All he did was tilt his head and press their lips together. His Fated seemed even more nervous with unfamiliar company around, pulling away after a fairly chaste kiss. Kende let Asyl slip from his arms, smiling at him.

"I'll see you Sunday," Kende murmured and backed away.

The last thing he wanted to do right now was leave. While he had no fantasies whatsoever that they could solve their differences today, Kende wanted to spend more time with his Fated. If Asyl's lingering grip on him was any indication, he wanted him to stay as well.

He shot Siora an exasperated look, and she politely ignored his frustration. In the main shop, Kende made sure to have a friendly farewell with Lady Naias, even though he had to keep it brief, as she was helping other customers. He was recognized by some of the patrons and politely turned down inquiries about his projects and petitions for future ones. Kende noticed a few of the customers shrank away, holding their cloaks close to them, hoods up even though they were out of the rain.

Eventually they returned home, and Birgir gleefully told him where his sister was. Jaclyn was waiting for him in the parlor, lap desk set up and working on one of her never-ending survey projects. Beside her was Macik, her Sympathetic husband. He had some files he was reviewing, writing down notes in the notepad he carried with him everywhere. Kende took a seat on the chair opposite of the couch they were working on and waited for them both to get to a point where they could pause in their work.

Jaclyn was his eldest sister and the one he got along with the least. She shared his emerald green eyes, but she had the brown hair of their father, whereas he was blond. Currently, the thick curls she'd inherited from their mother were pulled into a loose knot at the nape of her neck, though a few tendrils had escaped to frame her sharply featured face. Today she wore a deep red tunic under a white sash, tied at her hip to accompany her pure white breeches. She had her riding boots on, so perhaps she'd come straight from an event or was planning on riding with Macik after their meeting.

Speaking of her husband, Macik had a soft face and kind blue eyes. He was incredibly easy to talk to, though Kende was quite jealous of how easily he was able to style his brown hair. He kept it short on the sides, only slightly longer on top. His outfit was similar to Jaclyn's, though his breeches were brown, and he wore more practical walking shoes. The lines on his forehead and around his mouth were a bit deeper since the last time they'd seen each other. Kende wondered if he was working on a difficult case.

Eventually, Jaclyn gave a put-on sigh and slapped her quill down, sitting back into the couch and folding her arms tight across her chest. Kende simply raised an eyebrow at her and didn't move. If she wanted to start off their conversation like this, he would simply wait for her to snipe first.

"Brother," his sister said, her voice carrying a bit of impatience, "we've been here for quite some time."

"I was occupied across the city. If you'd called ahead, I would have been able to meet you here sooner and made sure we both would have been able to utilize our time effectively," Kende replied. "What can I do for you?"

"I need you to organize one of your charity affairs," Jaclyn said. "You know how to plan those. I've got the space already set up for next week."

Next week?

"For how many people?" Kende said cautiously.

"At least two thousand," Jaclyn replied.

Kende did his best to not outright laugh at her. He managed to turn it into a small choking noise.

"Two thousand people in a *week*? If you want people to attend, you need to give them at least a moonturn's notice," Kende scolded her. "That way they can make sure their schedules are free, and if they're not, adjust their schedules so they can attend. Pushing something like this last minute won't garner any favors and either stress out those you want to attend, or they'll disregard it completely."

Not to mention getting catering, security, any sort of donation for a charity auction, guest speakers, or any other number of small things that needed to be seen to would be impossible.

"So what, I just wasted my time getting the hall booked?" Jaclyn snapped.

"See if they can push it out a moonturn. If they can, then you and I will work *together* to make your charity event. Including finding designers for the invitations, what you want the space to look like, and catering if you want there to be food. Which I highly suggest there be," Kende said.

Jaclyn huffed, "If I wanted to do that, I wouldn't be asking you. *You* handle it."

Kende closed his eyes and counted to five before giving her a hard look. "If you want me to plan a benefit for one of your charities, then you will help me. I can't read your mind. I don't know what you want. You haven't even told me what the charity is for."

"It's for our smaller clinics in the poorer parts of the city. They need help with building repairs and new equipment," Jaclyn replied with a thin smile.

"That's a wonderful cause," Kende replied, nodding. "I still need a moonturn minimum."

She huffed. "Fine. I'll finish this report, and then we'll leave and head to the hall to see if they can reschedule."

"While you're doing that, Macik, can I talk to you?" Kende asked and stood.

His brother-in-law stared at him for a few seconds before he shrugged and nodded. The two men retreated to his study near the parlor. Kende shut the door pointedly and sighed heavily, then rounded the desk and sat in the plush chair. Macik plopped into one of the smaller ones meant for guests.

"What's up?" Macik asked.

"What's the department's policy when it comes to assault on Voids?" Kende asked.

Macik blinked once but didn't demand an explanation. Instead, he replied, "There's no special policy, really. We keep mundane salves and healing items on hand at the station just in case we need them, since we can use them on children as well, but otherwise it *should* be business as usual."

"So, if a Void was attacked and left for dead," Kende said slowly.

"It will be treated as an attempted murder case," Macik said. "Is everything all right?"

Kende sighed. "I met a Void. He was horribly bruised and had lost a lot of blood. I wasn't sure where to go, so I brought him here, and Gojko and I took care of him. He hasn't told me anything really about the attack, but I know it was bad based on his wounds. I think he would have died if I didn't find him when I did."

Macik nodded slowly. "A hospital shouldn't refuse treatment to anyone, regardless of their personal beliefs when it comes to Voids. They take care of children, so they would have the items needed on hand to help them. But I understand your caution. There's still far too much prejudice concerning Voids."

"That's why I wanted to talk to you first before encouraging my friend to go to the police and make a formal report," Kende said.

"Your friend," Macik said with a twinkle in his eyes. "Try that again."

Of course the damn man would read into that statement. Even if he wasn't a trained detective, he would have been able to feel the depth of Kende's emotions toward Asyl. Sympathetics were notoriously hard to lie or omit details to. White lies usually weren't successful either.

Kende felt his lips twitch in a small smile, and he rubbed the back of his neck. "He's my Fated."

"A Void as your Fated," Macik said and whistled slowly. "No wonder you didn't want to say that in front of Jaclyn. I love her dearly, but I think she'd go off if she heard that."

"Well, she and the rest of the family will have to come to terms with it eventually when I introduce him and later marry him," Kende said and shrugged. "But the later she finds out, the better."

"I most certainly won't tell her," Macik said with a snort. "You have fun with the introduction plan. Whenever your Void feels comfortable talking about it, send for me. I'll come by with my partner, and we can take his official statement."

"Thanks," Kende said and rose from behind his desk.

"This Void," Macik said as he got to his feet, "you really think he's your Fated."

"Yes. I'm drawn to him, I can sometimes smell where he's at or hear him humming, I knew where he was when I was near him, and I want to spoil him rotten and ensure he's happy," Kende said. "I think I can still tell he's at work now that I spent some time with him this morning. Our bond must have grown a bit."

Macik smiled. "I'm a little surprised he's not here already."

"He's been hurt before, so I'm taking it slow," Kende said. "I'm guessing he used to be in a relationship, and it ended badly."

"That's a shame," Macik murmured, "but if anyone can help, it's you. You've always loved your partners fairly and treated them well even after they left. He'll come 'round."

Kende regarded Macik with a bit of surprise. He'd always thought no one in the family ever really paid attention to his prior lovers. The animosity between his family and partner always seemed to be there whenever he attended a family event with them, despite Kende's best efforts. Perhaps Macik had always watched from afar, too nervous to break away from the expected norm and talk to Kende and his lover.

It had gotten to the point where Kende had eventually stopped dating altogether. He'd gotten the impression that the last few men he'd let into his life viewed him as a convenient stopgap for loneliness before they found their Fated. Hell, his last lover had found his Fated while they'd been vacationing in Valvinte. Kende had come home alone and arranged for his lover's clothes to be shipped to the new house he shared with his Fated.

Kende tilted his head and smiled faintly at his brother-in-law. Maybe at the next gathering, he'd find and chat with Macik, family be damned. It's not like they didn't already view him as a failure. He was already a huge disappointment to his father. What was one more transgression?

With that in mind, Kende left the office with Macik. Jaclyn glanced up from her work and sighed noisily before packing everything away. Her personal attendant quickly took her bag and desk from her, standing off to the side only to follow a few paces back when the three walked to the front door. If it was possible, the rain was coming down even harder. Jaclyn let out another sigh and raised her hand. The droplets turned to steam before they touched her, her assistant, or Macik.

Once the three were in the waiting buggy, Macik sent Kende a pointed look. Kende gave a small nod in return, and the Craft vehicle trundled out of his driveway and down the street toward their house. Groaning and finally relaxing, Kende slumped against the wall, grateful when one of the servants shut the front door to block out the chill.

"She is quite the force of nature," Birgir observed, sounding smug.

"That's a polite way of putting it," Kende replied with a snort.

"Sir. If I may make an observation," his steward said slowly. When Kende gave him a nod, he said, "You seem much more at ease. Did you find what you were looking for?"

"Yes, Birgir," Kende said and smiled softly, "but that's all the gossip you get."

He walked to his library, smiling at the harrumph of protest his steward made behind him.

CHAPTER 4

ASYL STILL couldn't really concentrate two days later. He'd done his best to put the lord out of his mind for the past moonturn, trying to ignore the urge to wander back across Alenzon to Ruvyn manor. He hadn't been able to sleep well, his chest aching, and feeling as if he'd been forgetting something important. Something he needed to do. Or rather, be with some*one*. His body ached for Lord Kende as if he was the air he needed while he drowned.

Then when Lord Kende came by again... he'd been nearly paralyzed with fear, convinced the man would just pick him up and haul him away. Disregard everything he'd built these last four years, scraping anything and everything he could together to open and maintain Enchanted Waters. While he hadn't had much more than the clothes on his back nine years ago, that's exactly what happened with Tillet.

But Lord Kende wasn't Tillet, Asyl tried reminding himself often. Instead, the man had been the picture of politeness, charm, and understanding. Who even asked their partner for permission to kiss them? Apparently, Lord Kende did. He'd clearly sensed and seen that Asyl was terrified and had done his best to allay the dread that choked him. The gentle offer of sending his carriage, and not fighting him when Asyl said no.... It confused him.

He wanted to tell Naias everything, but he had no idea how to even broach the subject with her. She was wary of the lord, though she'd seemingly softened slightly after meeting him. According to her, Lord Kende was quite charismatic and had a kind demeanor. But then again, Tillet had been kind at first. Before he found his real Fated and Asyl was nothing better than—

Asyl shook his head savagely, shoving the memories to the back of his mind. He didn't want to think about it. There was no reason to, really. What happened, happened. He suffered five years for his stupid teenage hopes, and he knew better now. It didn't matter what his body wanted. Not when it had betrayed him so many times over the course of seven years. It didn't matter that it felt like he was waking up from a dream.

Suddenly wanting things, having desires, wishing he could be by Lord Kende's side was infuriating. Just about as irritating as being able to feel exactly where the man was in Alenzon. That hadn't been there before. Just as he'd felt Lord Kende's frustration at being interrupted and having to leave. The cautious excitement with Asyl agreeing to meet him again. The fear for his safety.

Not worrying about himself and his well-being. No, Lord Kende was concerned about a worthless Void. It baffled Asyl. Sure, Tillet used the excuse of Asyl's safety to keep him locked up in his home, but this concern was quite different. Maybe because Lord Kende had expressed his worries but trusted Asyl could take care of himself? He didn't know. All this was so confusing, and Asyl's mood fluctuated wildly. The only solace he could find was throwing himself into his work.

That still didn't stop his mind from churning. Last night, before she left, Naias had reminded Asyl to go to Ruvyn manor to hear Lord Kende out. Asyl had just scowled at her until she giggled, kissed his forehead, and darted away before he could smack her. Of course his best friend, ever the romantic, would want Asyl to have a Fated and live happily.

But live amongst the gentry again? The thought made his skin break out into a cold sweat. If Lord Kende announced him, if the others found out who Asyl was... he'd cost his supposed Fated his entire livelihood. There might even be a chance he'd be disowned. He'd probably even ruin his parents' business and reputation as well.

The concern of costing Lord Kende his family almost eclipsed the pure panic at the idea of going to another man's house. He didn't think Lord Kende would prevent him from leaving. Yet the last time he'd thought that, he lost five years of his life.

He wasn't ready, Asyl told himself. Sure, he'd escaped four years ago, but the thought that he might be in the exact same position again made his hands shake. If it wasn't... if Lord Kende really did want an equal rather than a pet... maybe it could work. He didn't want his autonomy taken away again. To be isolated from everyone, unable to brew his potions and run his shop.... Asyl closed his eyes and slowly rocked on his feet above the quiet shop.

Maybe he should write to Rojir. The man had lived on the streets for nearly thirty years now. He'd seen it all. Maybe he would have some advice about what the hell was going on. Was there something the gentry had to force a bond? If anyone knew, it would be Rojir. Asyl had never heard of such a thing, but who knew? Ignian inventors came up with new things all the time. Maybe some Sympathetic found out how to echo the Fated courtship.

And yet his lips still tingled when he thought about Lord Kende kissing him, and his body shivered upon remembering the way the blond touched him. He'd been completely polite, not once pressuring him or had any sort of wandering hand intent on groping him when he was vulnerable. No, Lord Kende had been a perfect gentleman, keeping his hands on Asyl's hips or waist. He'd… brought Asyl's shoes back. Maybe that wasn't such a big deal, but they were the only pair he had. The fact that the soles had been replaced didn't escape his notice either.

The more he thought about it, the more he considered wandering toward the manor.

Truthfully, there really weren't any comparisons between Lord Kende and Tillet. Asyl knew rationally, he didn't have much to fear from the duke's youngest. The physical changes to his body after meeting Lord Kende were the biggest signs that yes, he was being truthful. That they were Fated to each other. Even if Asyl hadn't felt the initial tug, he had to admit, that's what he was feeling now.

Which had been completely absent the entire time he'd been with Tillet. He'd just been so desperate to be seen. Desperate to be loved and cherished. No longer having to sleep on the streets, curled up underneath some flimsy newspaper or cardboard for warmth. Not having to worry about being arrested for loitering or indecency if he propositioned the wrong john. He'd fallen for Tillet's bullshit so quickly; he didn't even realize what was happening until it was too late.

If being able to vaguely feel Lord Kende's emotions, know where he was over a distance, have sensitized physical reactions on contact…. If that was all a part of the Fated bond, then no wonder the Craft Blessed were desperate to find their Fated. Asyl could easily see the appeal, as much as he was scared of it. It was almost like an addiction.

He wished dearly that Naias would find her Fated soon. Even though her finding her Fated would likely be the end of Enchanted Waters, Asyl still wanted her to find happiness. Naias was beyond special and had a large heart, having immediately taken him in right after he'd escaped Tillet and nursed him back to full health. She'd weathered his nightmares and wretched screams that threatened to wake the entire neighborhood. Naias would be a wonderful, patient mother once she found her Fated.

She deserved to be spoiled by her Fated, whomever he turned out to be. Asyl knew she wished she had more opportunities to wear her nicer clothing, rather than commissioning plain, boring frocks so as to not intimidate their customers. Naias had a great head for business too, though she knew when her opinion wasn't needed. Never once had she tried to take over Enchanted Waters, his recipes, business plan, or his workspace.

Quite the opposite, really. She'd been delighted when he told her that he wanted to keep the prices of everything as low as they could after he explained why. Enchanted Waters was the only apothecary in the area, skirting the edges of the abandoned city blocks most of Alenzon's Voids called home. Asyl made as many salves and ointments as he could to help them relieve their aches and pains.

Many Voids barely had two coppers to rub together. They tried to scrape out a living in a society that hated them for no reason other than not receiving a Craft on their Awakening. While Voids usually tried to band together, to pool their resources and keep each other safe, it often wasn't enough. One day of being unable to attract any customers could mean no dinner.

Asyl remembered many days when he'd gone hungry.

That's why he sold so cheaply.

Hell, sometimes he'd given his fellow Voids mundane medicines for free. Naias had been present for one of those conversations. It was well past closing, and they were enjoying a late dinner together when a Void had knocked on their back door. She'd been nearly rigid with pain and half starved. Naias had immediately gotten her something warm to drink and gave her the rest of her meal. Asyl had retrieved a few pots of salve for chemical burns and given them to her without a thought.

Sometimes Asyl saw her during his trips to the herbalist. While the burns she'd suffered on almost half of her body were obvious, the scarring wasn't as bad as it could have been. That was what kept Asyl going after three years of running Enchanted Waters, of having just barely enough money to scrape by and wearing clothes down to nothing before purchasing new ones. Sure, he could charge exorbitant amounts for his medicines, but that wasn't the point.

He could help his fellow Voids, so he would. And sitting at his work desk, his mind running in circles, wasn't helping him or them. Whatever Lord Kende was or wasn't to him didn't mean anything at this moment.

He couldn't abandon those who had supported him on the streets, the Voids he'd grown up with who had tried to protect him from the harsh realities of the world. He owed them. If all he could do to help was make sure they had cheap but effective medicine, then that's what he'd do.

Asyl consulted the inventory list, sighing at what was low in stock. He'd been distracted for a good part of this last moonturn, so he hadn't put out as much as he normally did. They were heading into winter, so of course their cold remedies were starting to sell at a faster pace. Maybe he could get ahead if he spent today making a couple of batches. Generic healing for scrapes, cuts, and bruises was always needed, and those were easy to make. Some sort of rash was going around if the inventory count was correct for their salves, and it always was. Naias was the one who tallied everything.

Well. That was definitely a day's worth of work. Asyl rolled out a second cauldron, hefted it onto his spare Ignis Plate, and pulled the dust cover off. He crouched and fiddled with the controls, getting both plates fired up. While those heated to their highest temperature, Asyl drew from the purified water Naias provided him, filling both cauldrons almost completely full.

Humming, he wandered to his herb wall and found the plants for the generic health potion, quickly calculating how much he needed. He tied their stems together with a bit of twine and double-checked his math. Once he was satisfied, Asyl tossed the bundle into the first cauldron. It made quite a satisfying *plunk* when it hit the water.

Right now, what he produced would be the weakest variant—and the cheapest. Once he siphoned about a third off to fill a batch of those, he'd put in more herbs to bump it up a grade until he got his highest potency. The cold medicine would be done the same way. Asyl got that one started as well, setting the extra herbs he'd need on a table to either side of the cauldrons.

While those steeped, Asyl counted out all the bottles he needed: clear glass for the generic and dark amber for the cold medication. He lined them up in neat rows on the tables, then grabbed a funnel and ladle for each potion and set them aside as well. Now that was all set up, Asyl retrieved their tags and twine and sat at his workbench. Carefully, he wrote down the names and their strength on the blank side. The other side was embossed with the shop's logo to draw customers back.

That had been something Naias suggested. Asyl was forever grateful she had all her tradesman knowledge from her parents. If the worst happened, or rather when Naias left him, he might be able to survive on his own. Maybe he could figure out some temporary dye so he could draw a Healer mark on his forehead. Were there laws against Voids impersonating a Crafted? He'd have to look that up at the library. Asyl stopped humming, staring down at his cramped handwriting.

What even was his life anymore?

Sitting in a back workroom, barely seeing the sun, and just making medicines day in and day out? He didn't even have any hobbies anymore. What did he do for fun? Once, he'd liked reading. Now he only read when it came to research on a new potion, tincture, ointment, or salve. He was pathetic. There was nothing inside him to attract anyone, and it's not like he cared anymore.

What could Lord Kende possibly see in him?

Asyl slumped back in his seat, sighing. Yeah, he was a real catch. Damaged goods. A sad, pathetic man who was getting to the point where he was too scared to go outside. His job demanded that he did, so he could purchase herbs of the best quality he could find. Maybe he could work directly with his supplier and they could deliver instead. He'd likely have to purchase in larger quantities, but even that wasn't a bad idea. They could just stock up on herbs. At least it would stop him from being randomly mugged.

Gathering the labels, Asyl got to his feet and grabbed the twine and shears. He quietly attached the labels to the first round of potions before checking the boiling mixture. It was just about ready. Asyl attached the rest, and that brought him to his first decanting. He dropped the funnel into each bottle and filled them up carefully. After dumping in the next bundle to enhance the potion, Asyl turned his attention to the second cauldron.

Corking took a little while, but his absolute favorite part was dipping the tops into wax to seal it. He had a three-wick tallow candle burner that heated a fairly large ceramic container. The ceramic heated evenly all over, keeping the wax at the perfect temperature. The container held plenty of wax for his work needs—almost enough to seal four complete batches of potions if he was ambitious enough.

Asyl found himself humming again as he pressed the shop's logo into the cooling beeswax on the top of the cork. This really was therapeutic. Something about seeing the store logo stamped into smooth blue wax was soothing. Leaving the potions to boil for a longer length of time, Asyl started working on the salve. He thought he heard something click, but when he paused, Asyl didn't hear anything in the shop.

Warmth suffused his chest, spreading down his arms and making his fingers tingle. His lingering anxiety eased, much like how Lord Kende had helped him through his panic attack. Maybe he should have at least sent him a message letting him know that he'd be staying home after all. Or maybe Asyl could have invited him over here to keep him company while he worked. That would have been nice.

Shrugging, he scooped out a large chunk of beeswax, following up with some oil and plant butter, dropping them into his mixer. His arm would most definitely be tired after this. Asyl began humming again as he located the long metal stirring whisk and began incorporating the base. He'd make a good number of pots for the rash and save the rest of the base for whatever sold during the week for quick, small batches.

Soft singing floated from behind him, gentle enough that it didn't draw Asyl from his humming or concentration of mixing. Curious. He hadn't thought that the melodies he hummed had words, but they must have, because the lyrics sounded right. Where would he have heard a song like this before? It had to have been when he was still loved and cherished by his family.

His parents had been fairly rich, and his or his parents' birthdays often came with a minstrel or a full-on band to entertain the party. That was the most likely explanation, even if he didn't remember the details. Slowly, the words formed more in his mind, and he began singing the song with the other voice. He hadn't sung in, what, at least seven years? About the time he realized what a prick his ex was.

He switched from that song to another that softly bloomed in the back of his mind. He'd heard it quite often as a child when his mother used to sing to him. The other voice took a minute before it echoed him, this time a little stronger, and not as quiet. Deeper than his, the other voice resonated quite well, enhancing his voice rather than overtaking it. They sounded fairly good to his ears.

Asyl's arms were tired by the time he deemed the base thoroughly mixed. He set the large bowl aside and dropped the already gathered ingredients into his polished marble mortar. It and the pestle had been a gift from Naias to help reduce the amount of product lost in the porous stone set he'd been using. In all fairness, his previous pair had been the cheapest he'd been able to find, and the quality of his salves had only increased with her gift.

Tapping the pestle against the rim briefly to the song, Asyl began crushing the berries and acorns, sitting back in the chair and cradling the mortar in his arms to get the best leverage. The last notes faded away, and Asyl sighed, not really knowing any other songs. There hadn't been much time in his life to sit still and listen to music. Behind him, the voice picked up again, softer, and Asyl simply listened as he evened out the mixture into something akin to a paste.

It almost sounded like a love song. Granted, most of the songs he knew were. They were the most popular and requested at a party, after all. Asyl found himself listening more to the tune than the actual words. He got to his feet and turned to check on the potions. He mixed them both with their respective ladles, pleased to see the darkening liquid bubbling away merrily. It wouldn't be long before he'd be ready to decant the next batch.

Asyl turned back, scooped out the amount of base he needed for the salve, dumped it into a large glass bowl, and placed a fine mesh sieve on top of it. He knew the melody of the next song and hummed along with the singing voice as he returned his attention to the potions. He filled the next batch of potions, corking, sealing, and branding them with brisk efficiency. He tossed in the last bundle of herbs to each cauldron, and with the final strength set up to boil, Asyl returned to his salve.

He took his time with the sieve, making sure all the berry seeds had been removed with as little liquid lost as possible. Asyl used a smaller whisk to fully integrate the compound, constantly making sure he wasn't missing any of the base hiding alongside the bottom and sides of the bowl. He stood and turned to retrieve the small porcelain pots from his stack of crates and froze.

Sitting on one of the boxes was Lorde Kende. He was dressed in a simple white button-down and a black vest with matching black trousers. His coat and greatcoat were draped on some of the higher piled boxes. The lady that was usually with him didn't appear to be around. Immediately, Asyl felt his anxiety start to rise, and he tugged at the hem of his tunic even as his heart stuttered and he yearned to walk into the man's arms.

"Lord Kende," Asyl said.

The blond raised an eyebrow at the formality but just smiled faintly. "It was getting late, and I was worried."

"How did you get in?" Asyl asked.

"I swung by Lady Elrel's place and got a key," he said, handing it over. If he was offended by the speed in which Asyl snatched it back, he didn't look it. "She wanted to know you were all right, though she couldn't join me."

Asyl stared at him but finally gave a faint nod, placing the spare key on his workstation. He moved to the smaller crates that held the containers he needed, trying to keep his breathing even as he counted out the pots for this batch. Somehow, he managed to not drop them despite his shaking hands. Neither of them spoke as Asyl sat at the bench and quietly filled the wells, making sure they weren't messy once he evened off the top, scraping off as much excess as he could.

Silence grew between them, and Lord Kende didn't try to fill the air with mindless chatter. Asyl wasn't sure if he was glad of that or not, though the silence wasn't exactly oppressive. Instead, he kept his head down, capping the pots once he was finished, just barely able to fill the last one with the dregs in the bowl. He filled out more labels. These were square with four holes instead of one on a rectangle. Their logo filled the square but faded enough that Asyl's handwriting stood out.

He wound the twine in a cross pattern on the pots, threading it through each hole in the label. It took a little extra time, but this seemed to be the best way to get the labels on their product. Once he had finished, Asyl got to his feet and found a cloth that had been soaked in beeswax to cover the bowl of the remaining salve base. It stuck eagerly to the bowl, and Asyl knew it would keep for a while.

When Asyl returned his attention to the cauldrons, he mixed the potions and frowned, seeing that they still weren't the right color. Had something gone wrong? His math was correct. He knew it was, though at the moment he doubted himself. Despite making potions for three years, he struggled with his confidence.

Determined to not have to talk to Lord Kende and tamping down his urge to stay close, Asyl picked up the inventory sheet. He needed to update the numbers with what he'd made today. He gathered the weakest healing potions in his arms and walked to the shop floor. First in, first out, though his potions wouldn't and couldn't spoil once capped. Asyl moved what stock remained to the front and set the newly brewed potions in the back.

Asyl took a slow, deep breath before returning to his workroom. Lord Kende hadn't followed him out to hover or force him into a conversation. The man had stayed on his perch, quietly watching Asyl with a soft smile on his face. Asyl had the sudden urge to wiggle close and press a kiss to the corner of his mouth. It was getting harder to push his errant thoughts away.

Even by the time he'd finished stocking the store with what he'd already decanted, the strength of the potions still wasn't right. Asyl fished up the bushels of herbs and counted them, making sure once again that his math was correct. It was. Apparently it just needed more time. Scowling, Asyl stirred both cauldrons and walked to the other side of the room to open the back door.

He hadn't been aware of how sweaty and hot he'd been until the cold air hit his body. It was already evening. Even though it was raining, there were enough breaks in the clouds that he could see the sky turning orange. Asyl stood in the threshold for a few minutes until he began to shiver. He retreated inside, noticing that Lord Kende still hadn't moved from his spot on one of his boxes.

"You've seen me. I'm well. You know where the door is," Asyl finally said flatly.

Maybe if he left, Asyl could get himself back under control. Could get the urges out of his head and return to normal. The moment he wished to go back to how things were, even his mind rebelled at the thought. He hadn't been happy a moonturn ago, just going through the motions of life. Eating and sleeping when needed and working all the rest of his time.

Even the small bouts of joy at being able to help the Voids of Alenzon didn't hide the truth that Asyl was beginning to see. The truth that he hadn't wanted to see until Lord Kende essentially shoved it in his face whether he was ready or not.

He hadn't been happy.

Not for a very long time.

Lord Kende frowned and got to his feet. Even now, he looked more confused than frustrated or angry at Asyl's dismissal. Asyl could *feel* his confusion and hurt at being rejected. The Healer took a step to approach him, and Asyl backed up, bumping into the outside door. Lord Kende stopped, seemingly aware that his advance wasn't welcome.

"I don't understand. Did I do something wrong?" Lord Kende asked.

Asyl stared at him for a minute and looked away. Truth was, he really hadn't, and Asyl knew it, deep down. Lord Kende had been a perfect gentleman, giving up his bed to make sure Asyl healed from his assault. He probably would have made sure Asyl got home safe if he'd been allowed to help when he woke.

Then earlier in the week, he'd gently helped Asyl come down from his panic attack, not pushing Asyl into the bed he'd been sitting on and trying to stake his claim like Asyl had somewhat expected. Every time Asyl expected the worst from him, Lord Kende surprised him again and again, showing him affection rather than a heavy hand. And that was much more dangerous.

"Please leave," Asyl said weakly.

Otherwise, he'd never be able to let Lord Kende go.

He turned and walked to the cauldrons, checking on the potions. They still weren't ready. In fact, they weren't boiling nearly as much as he would expect. Kneeling down, Asyl checked the Plates and sighed when he saw they had shorted out again, growing cold. He grabbed a rubber mallet, whacked the edges a few times, and fiddled with the dials. Damn it. These two were worn out, and he really needed to replace them.

Just like he needed to make sure the roof was fine, needed to check why his oven upstairs wouldn't work half the time, and figure out which window was the one letting in cold air…. There were too many things that needed his attention. While they had a decent amount in savings, mostly thanks to Naias and her inheritance, it wasn't enough that he could justify taking any out to replace specialty Ignis items like these. They cost one year of property taxes just to purchase a *used* one. A new one was roughly three times that. The shop did well, but not that well. They had to make do.

Once the burners caught, Asyl stood and stirred the potions again, not wanting the herbs at the bottoms to get burned. That was a quick way to spoil the rest of the batch, and he'd like to at least break even on the herbs and supplies he purchased. Slapping the dirt from his knees, Asyl turned to look at Lord Kende, who hadn't moved from where he was standing.

"I talked with my contact at the police," Lord Kende said, very clearly not leaving anytime soon. "They would welcome you to come in and talk about the attack last moonturn. Macik was upset that you didn't feel safe to come forward and be taken seriously."

Asyl scowled and immediately went on the defensive. He folded his arms tight across his chest and hunched slightly. A quiet voice in the back of his mind told him that Lord Kende had only followed up on what Asyl had agreed to two days ago, yet he couldn't help but feel that the blond was overstepping and trying to control him. There was no way in hell he wanted to talk to the police, family connection or not. He just wanted to be left alone…. Didn't he?

No.

He was safer alone.

Voids weren't blessed with Fated. He smothered the voice in the back of his mind, not wanting to listen to reason right now. Feeling Lord Kende's emotions, where he was in the city, always wanting to be by his side and in his arms… all of it had to be some sort of Craft trickery. There would never be a happy ending for him. He felt a rush of foreign energy, not unlike what he'd felt when he woke in Lord Kende's bed two days ago, and his left palm began to itch. The sensation fueled his doubt and anger, turning it into a raging inferno.

"Wouldn't you know who they are? You're probably the one who sent them," Asyl accused.

Lord Kende's jaw dropped, and he shook his head, his eyes widening in alarm. "Absolutely not! I don't ever want to see you hurt—"

"It was pretty convenient timing," Asyl interrupted with a sneer, unable to stop his harsh words, despite the soft voice in his mind beginning to shout at his sudden vehemence. "Any longer and I probably would have been dead. But no, somehow you found me in an abandoned building off the beaten path and had enough time to get me to your place to patch me up."

"We find our Fated when we're ready," Lord Kende protested.

"*Your* Fated," Asyl retorted harshly, "for you Craft Blessed, sure. For us Voids, we get nothing. How many times do I need to repeat myself? Voids get *nothing*! And I'm not some stupid idiot who will get my hopes up again!"

CHAPTER 5

AGAIN?

Asyl didn't seem to realize that he'd just dropped a massive proverbial bomb between them. Kende felt his chest constrict at the idea that someone had lied to his Fated and hurt him so thoroughly. No wonder Asyl was carefully guarding his heart, and not trusting him quickly. Not that he could really blame him. Kende took a few steps forward, and Asyl danced back, glowering at him.

They'd been fine together two days ago, with the exception of the panic attack that Asyl had suffered. Kende shouldn't have stayed away for so long. If he'd come back the next day, maybe he could have built on their tenuous relationship and strengthened it. Kende had just worried that Asyl would react... well... like this, if he'd pursued more aggressively.

But that still didn't explain the sudden change in Asyl's perspective. Kende had been able to feel Asyl's reluctance to go near him or acknowledge their bond. He'd felt the quivering energy kept carefully controlled, knowing it was the tug of their bond. Asyl's hesitation. His fear. Then a foreign surge of energy with the most bizarre signature that Kende had never felt before in all his time learning at the university.

Even if Asyl didn't want to acknowledge it, just being around each other strengthened their bond. He could read his nervous Fated easier with every breath they took in the same room, could feel the ball of pain and anger lodged firmly in Asyl's chest beside his heart.

"Someone told you that you were their Fated," Kende said, keeping his voice gentle with an effort. He wasn't mad at Asyl in any way. Rather, his anger was directed toward whomever had hurt the man before him. "What happened?"

"Why do you care?" Asyl snapped, his hands clenched into fists. "You're a lord. You can get whatever you want, so go find some other Void and try to placate *him* into bed."

"I don't *want* any other Void. I don't want any other Craft Blessed. I want you," Kende pleaded.

Asyl snorted derisively and shook his head, putting the cauldrons between them. The heat they were giving off was making him sweat even though he'd already taken off his coats. Weren't cellars supposed to be chilly? He looked at his Fated through a haze coming off the two potions, easily seeing the fear on his face and feeling it in his heart. Kende didn't know what to do. How could he convince Asyl this wasn't a farce, even though he knew that Asyl knew it wasn't?

"I've been hearing you humming these last few days while I've been working," Kende finally said. "Apparently, I would start humming along with you. Siora figured out what songs they were and got me the lyrics for them."

"So?" Asyl said.

At least he wasn't yelling or completely hostile anymore. His shoulders were starting to relax, much to Kende's relief. That wary, terrified look hadn't eased much, but his breathing was evening out.

"Once Fated make contact with each other, they're connected to a degree," Kende said. "There's some kind of sympathetic link, and we can feel some part of each other's emotions. I feel you when you're content and happy. That's when you start humming. Your work makes you happy."

He noticed Asyl's eyes darting to the workbench. Kende didn't dare take his eyes off his Fated. There was no way he was going to let Asyl think he was here for any other reason but him. Something told him that this was a pivotal moment in securing his Fated's trust. If he could get Asyl to acknowledge their bond, understand that they were meant to be together, they could work on his Fated's fears together.

"I don't know what the one who hurt you said to convince you, and I know you don't really have any reason to trust me," Kende said gently, "but please believe me when I say my only goal is to see you smile."

Asyl stared at him. He didn't move from where he was, his gaze almost dead. His eyes were flat, barely holding any emotion as he likely relived the harm he'd gone through. That terrified Kende to the core. Whatever hurt there was there, it was deeper than what he could feel. How much had Asyl gone through? He knew deep down his Fated would be a kind, passionate man. They just had to get there first.

One of the potions hissed, and Asyl blinked, rushing forward. He knelt and reached for the Ignis Plate before inhaling sharply, and snatched his hand back when he touched the dial. Holding his hand to his chest, Asyl got to his feet and nudged the dials with the toe of his shoe instead. The Plate clicked, turning off.

Kende watched his Fated as he quickly checked the potions, turning the second Plate off as well. He was holding the ladles oddly, not using his index finger or thumb or letting them touch anything. Kende blinked, realizing that Asyl had burned himself. He didn't crowd the man, knowing that it wouldn't be appreciated. It wasn't like Kende could use his Craft to heal him anyways. Instead, he just watched as Asyl poured the rest of the potions into their containers.

He felt Asyl's growing frustration as he fumbled with the corks, trying to get them into the narrow necks of the bottles. Kende's heart ached, seeing the irritation on his Fated's face. While he never thought that Asyl would be the type to throw something, he was sure there were plenty of ways to self-sabotage an alchemist's den.

That's when he moved forward. He quietly corked and handed the bottles to Asyl so he only had to dip them into the wax. Kende grabbed the stamp to impress the design on the top of the cork. Asyl didn't fight about him working alongside him, his anger and frustration softening. Maybe he realized that Kende really was only trying to help. It took a few minutes, but the frantic sealing was complete, and now Asyl was trying to tie on the labels.

"Go put on a salve or ointment," Kende said gently, taking the ball of twine from him. "I can do this."

Asyl stared at him for a few seconds, his eyes searching for something. Kende had nothing to hide, so he just regarded his Fated gently. Finally, Asyl gave a curt nod and turned away. Kende quickly tied the twine, making sure they were neatly done. He wasn't anywhere near as fast as Asyl was, but then again, he didn't have the experience Asyl did.

Just as he finished the last one, Asyl returned and glanced at the knot before seemingly accepting his work. He didn't need to say anything. The soft, relieved sigh told him everything. Kende rounded the tables and moved close to his Fated. While Asyl didn't move away immediately, his body tensed back up, and he looked at Kende sharply. Ignoring his glare, Kende lifted Asyl's burned hand and kissed the two injured fingers that he'd wrapped in small strips of cloth.

"How bad is it?" he asked.

Asyl shrugged. "Probably won't blister."

"Good," Kende murmured.

Whenever he touched Asyl, Kende felt a sense of rightness wash over him. This time was no exception. His body and soul relaxed with his Fated at his side, the urges to be close currently satiated. All it took was a gentle tug for Asyl to shuffle forward into his embrace. Kende wrapped his arms around him, holding him loosely, just like he did last time, resting his hands on his Fated's waist. Oddly enough, he couldn't sense that foreign energy anymore. Asyl hadn't, or rather couldn't, use it—Kende would have felt the transfer of power.

He felt Asyl's hand come up to rest on his chest. There was a brief moment when his body was rigid, tense, close to shoving Kende away. Something warred in his mind as his Fated shook for a good minute. He must have reached a decision as he slowly melted into Kende, nestling into him. Kende felt peace flow through his Fated, the quivering energy he'd sensed earlier finally quieting.

"Whenever you're ready to talk about what happened, I'm here. For the attack last moonturn, and for whatever ass who told you they were your Fated," Kende said softly. "Preying on you like that... that's absolutely abhorrent behavior."

"I brought it on myself," Asyl said tonelessly.

"Somehow I doubt that," Kende replied, nuzzling the side of his Fated's head and brushing his lips over the curve of Asyl's ear.

"I was desperate," Asyl said. "I wanted to believe that I meant something to someone."

"There's nothing wrong with that," Kende said, squeezing Asyl briefly.

His Fated began to tremble in his arms again. This time, it wasn't him fighting himself, trying to not give in to the want of being close. This was the deep pain and fear that Asyl kept a stranglehold on, not allowing himself the opportunity to heal. Kende pulled Asyl tighter to his chest, running a hand through his hair to try and offer some comfort.

"My parents made me leave with nothing but what I was wearing not even an hour after my Awakening failed. Do you know what it's like to be on the streets at thirteen as a Void?" Asyl asked.

Kende closed his eyes and shook his head mutely. He had no idea. Even if he'd been homeless as a child, he still had his Craft, and he would have been able to offer it for coin or have a university take him in. Asyl hadn't even had that to protect himself or try and get an apprenticeship somewhere.

"I swear they were waiting."

"Who?" Kende whispered.

Asyl shrugged. "Just people. They saw a homeless Void child and...." He trailed off for a good while. Kende didn't bother trying to guess what happened. He had a feeling and desperately hoped he was wrong. "I did a lot of things to get money or food. I don't think it was even a moonturn before I'd given up everything I had to give in order to eat."

Kende dragged in a shaky breath, hugging Asyl fiercely to him. His eyes burned with tears he was trying to hold back, and he realized that there was an uncomfortable patch soaking through his vest and shirt. Asyl had every reason to cry. To have his safety torn away from him at such a young age, and then to be taken advantage of so soon after. It was disgusting. Asyl deserved better. He hadn't deserved the pain he'd endured for being who he was. Alenzon had failed her most vulnerable citizens—her Void children who were rejected by their families.

But that wasn't the whole story. There was still the person who'd convinced Asyl they were Fated. Several minutes passed, and his feisty alchemist just trembled in his arms. Clearly there needed to be some prodding done if he was going to get the full story. Kende hated needing to open the wound, however slightly, but he knew he needed to understand.

"Who told you that you were their Fated?" Kende asked softly.

"Nine years ago," Asyl began after sniffing slightly, "I was tired and ready to give up. Did you know that Rose Bridge is perfect to jump off of? It's high enough, and the water is shallow with plenty of rocks below during the summer." This time a shudder ran through Kende. He'd been so close to having never known Asyl not once, but twice. "That's when *he* ran up. I probably should have realized then that he just saw a desperate person and could manipulate me easily. All it took was some sweet words and soft touches before I believed him. I hadn't had anyone touch me innocently or care about me in the last four years.

"He took me to his place. Said that it was our home now. He took care of me for the next few moonturns. Didn't pressure me into bed. Made sure I was eating and sleeping well. Gave me nice enough clothes to wear so I wasn't in rags anymore. He wasn't ashamed to show me affection when we went outside."

"What changed?" Kende asked when Asyl paused for a few minutes.

Asyl shrugged. "He got what he wanted. I went to bed with him. Then I couldn't leave the house anymore. He said he wanted to protect me, and to do so, it was best if I stayed indoors. I was happy enough, I guess, even though I was confused. He gave me books, and I started research on potions and alchemy, since it fascinated me. He even let me experiment in very small doses.

"But that changed when he met his real Fated. I didn't understand what happened then. Suddenly I was spending too much money on my research, and he barely touched me anymore unless it was for sex. His Fated didn't want to get rid of me, though. They both liked how I looked, and apparently, I was a nice lay for the both of them. I woke up one day and found I was chained naked to their bed. That's when I realized how much I'd been lied to."

"How did you get away?" Kende asked.

"I didn't."

Those two words sent a chill down Kende's spine. He kissed the top of Asyl's head, rocking him as his Fated gave a small, choked sob. Finally, he felt Asyl's arms wrap around his hips, clutching desperately to the back of his vest. He tightened his arms in response, wanting his Fated to know that he was safe.

"Did someone set you free?"

Asyl nodded. "By then, he was well known for the pet at his parties. He'd come in before the party once preparations were complete, tie me to the headboard, and have his way with me. Sometimes he'd make sure I couldn't close my legs or mouth either." A violent shudder ripped through Asyl. "It took me moonturns to get the taste of urine out of my mouth. They all thought it was funny, and not a single one of his friends or his Fated's friends cared about me as a person. All they saw was the fact I was a Void.

"Except for one guy. He was so nice. I don't know how, but he managed to drug the whole party, and they all passed out after about four hours. He picked the locks, wrapped me up in a blanket, and just walked out with me in his arms."

"Then he left you," Kende supplied.

"I ran away. He gave me clothes and food. The moment I saw an opening, I ran," Asyl said.

"I can't blame you one bit there," Kende replied, squeezing Asyl again. "I take it you've never seen him since."

Asyl shook his head. "By pure chance I ran into Naias, and she was overjoyed to see me again after so many years. I told her I liked brewing, and we came up with this place."

Kende took a deep, slow breath and loosened his death hold on Asyl. Apparently, the man thought he was being dismissed, or was embarrassed about his outburst, as he tried scurrying away. That wasn't going to happen. Not again. Kende caught his arm and reached out to cup Asyl's face, tilting his head up. Sure enough, Asyl's eyes were red and puffy, and he was sniffling intermittently.

For once he didn't ask for permission. Instead, he dipped down and kissed Asyl, earning himself a small squeak. Kende kept it light, delighted when he felt Asyl return the kiss. He wanted to throw his Fated over his shoulder and take him back to the manor where he could pamper the smaller man to pieces. If he thought that would help. If he knew it wouldn't push Asyl away.

"You're supposed to be disgusted with me and leave," Asyl managed to say against his lips.

"I am disgusted," Kende said, ignoring Asyl's wince, "but not at you. I'm disgusted and horrified that someone could do such awful things to you. It pisses me off that it wasn't just one person, but many who treated you like nothing just because you're a Void. That's not okay. I want to find whoever did this to you and burn their house down around them."

"That's not very lordlike of you," Asyl said in an odd tone.

It sounded like he was trying to fight back laughter and a sob at the same time. Kende just smiled, pressing their foreheads together.

"What's the point in having a duke for a father if I can't do some arson every once in a while?" Kende teased. "Besides, my brother is an Ignis. I'm sure he'd love to burn something to the ground without letting anything else catch on fire."

Asyl's shoulders shook as he tried to stifle his laughing even as his eyes filled with tears, looking up at him. Kende nuzzled the side of his head before crouching. His Fated wasn't much shorter than him, but he was quite a bit lighter, and Kende had no problems picking him up. A flash of excitement ran through him when Asyl gasped and wrapped his legs around Kende's hips and his arms around his neck. The amount of trust Asyl was giving him right now meant a lot.

Kende sat down where he'd perched a while back, and Asyl settled right into his lap. The man was still looking up at him, head resting on his collarbone. There was the smallest glint of hope in his eyes. Kende really wanted that to be for him. Or because of him. Or rather, both. He ran his hands up and down Asyl's back, squeezing him periodically. Kende could feel Asyl's apprehension slowly slipping away.

A small hum escaped from Asyl, his eyes drifting closed. When was the last time someone sat with Asyl and just showed him some general affection? Kende smiled and kissed his forehead, where his Craft Mark would have been. How could he show Asyl how much he cared without overstepping too much? His eyes drifted over to the cauldrons and the Ignis Plates. Even he could tell they weren't working well. The energy output was fading, and the Craft reservoir that kept them functional was running low.

Maybe he could get Asyl new plates. Surely he couldn't get upset about something that would only help his business. Kende hoped not. Then Asyl would be able to make more of his fantastic potions. He looked at the ones on the small tables next to the cauldrons and a thought struck him. His sister had managed to move the charity date out by two moonturns.

"Out of curiosity, how many full-strength generic healing potions would you be able to make in two moonturns?" Kende asked.

Asyl's eyes slowly opened, and he sat up, his hands sliding down to rest on Kende's shoulders just by his fingertips. Kende smiled at him, fighting back the urge to lean in and kiss him. He did his best to push down his growing excitement. Asyl had to agree to his plan first, if it was viable or cost-effective.

"Depends on what stock I need to make for the shop," Asyl finally said, "but probably easily a hundred. The problem is the cost. Some of those herbs are expensive, and if I was going to make a whole cauldron of full-strength potions, I'd need to use more than if I was brewing a normal varied-strength batch."

"I can sponsor that," Kende murmured.

"Why?" Asyl asked, frowning.

Kende could briefly see the mistrust sliding into his features and the wariness building back up. He smiled and gave Asyl a small hug, quickly kissing his forehead. The gesture seemed to surprise Asyl, as he inhaled sharply, blinking a few times at him.

"My sister wants to run a charity for some needy clinics in the area. I was thinking maybe we could raffle off ten at a time. The wealthy will bid for them, and then they'd go to various clinics," Kende explained with a smile. "I'll pay for the ingredients. You don't need to get me a list or anything. I'll either go with you, or you can send me the bill."

"You…." Asyl trailed off and frowned. He seemed more confused than anything. "You're running a charity? People actually do those?"

Kende nodded. "I've run quite a few. I've not been sure how to raise money for this one past a typical dinner, but raffling potions sounds like something that would be beneficial outside of just funds. Plus, it would be immediate instead of having to wait for the money, and then ordering what they needed."

Asyl relaxed and shimmied a little closer, settling more firmly in his lap. His Fated dropped his gaze and leaned forward, thumping his forehead against the man's shoulder. Kende rubbed his back again, wondering what was going through his mind. He could feel the maelstrom whirling inside of his Fated. Wariness, hope, excitement, and doubt all tugged on Asyl while he contemplated Kende's offer.

"Do you really think they'd be happy with potions made by a Void?" Asyl finally asked.

"They're the best ones in the city," Kende replied with a small shrug. "Doesn't matter who made them. At least in my mind."

"Even if they're made by a worthless alchemist?" Asyl muttered.

"You're not worthless," Kende countered. "Look at what you built with Naias. You were strong enough to hold out through a horrifically abusive relationship. Worthless people are the ones who take advantage of others and use them for their own gain."

"Not like me," Asyl said.

"Not like you. You have value because you're honest and you've chosen to help heal others to the best of your ability despite everything that's happened. That's remarkable," Kende told him. "You're quite the wonderful man."

Asyl sat back, looking at him, once again searching for some answer Kende wasn't sure he'd be able to provide. He just smiled faintly at his Fated, waiting for him to make a move.

"I'd like to help," Asyl finally whispered. "Will you come shopping with me? I don't know if they'll sell me such a large amount."

"Just say when," Kende replied.

His Fated echoed his smile and licked his lips in a brief display of his anxiety. Asyl leaned in, tilted his head, and pressed their lips together. It was languid, more searching than heated or loving. Testing the waters, seeing where each other's boundaries were. Kende kept completely still outside of returning the kiss, not wanting to accidentally spook Asyl.

Slowly, almost as if he was reluctant to stop, Asyl broke the kiss and sat back. Kende kept his eyes closed for a second more before sighing contentedly and smiling at his Fated.

"Will you come back to the manor with me? I'd like to give you a nice dinner," Kende said. "Then I'll arrange for you to come home. You probably haven't eaten all day, if I know your type."

Asyl stared at him in surprise before flushing. He finally nodded, much to Kende's delight. His Fated shifted to his knees, clambered off him, and walked to the back of the workroom. There, he pulled down what was essentially just a short cape with a hood. That could be something he could gift to Asyl too. Surely he could find a cloak that would fit his Fated and wouldn't be too extravagant, but nice enough to keep the rain off him.

Maybe he could get Naias to enchant it. Kende pulled on both of his coats and held out his hand, smiling at Asyl's blush. His scarred fingers trembled as he reached out and took it, raising a tentative gaze up at him. Asyl moved in close and pulled the hood down low when they left the front of Enchanted Waters. He locked up, and Kende opened the Craft carriage door for him.

The hope he saw in Asyl's eyes earlier seemed to be growing as he stared at Kende, and he vowed not to squash it.

CHAPTER 6

DINNER TURNED into the rest of the evening and several hours into the night.

When they arrived back at Lord Kende's manor, the steward took their coats without a word. Even the lady who followed Lord Kende around everywhere didn't seem to scowl at his presence. Had something changed since their last encounters? Asyl had no idea how to really act around the servants that Lord Kende employed. Outside of the steward and assistant, the others gave him warm smiles whenever they made eye contact.

That alone simply confused him. Without his cloak to hide his forehead, everyone here surely knew he was a Void. And yet no one treated him differently or tried to dissuade Lord Kende from hosting him. One of the maids even grinned at him, and Asyl thought he briefly recognized her from the last time he was here. His cheeks flamed at the memory. What must he have seemed like to Lord Kende's employees? Certainly some kind of madman.

The blond ushered him into a dining chair and kissed his cheek before taking his place on the opposite side of the table. Asyl had flushed at that but hadn't said anything to the contrary, keeping his eyes down at the plate that was set before him. Lord Kende was free with his affection even in front of his staff, which made his heart thud. Yet he couldn't help the anxiety welling inside him from what had happened before.

They were served a simple yet hearty meal: strips of chicken served in a rich bone broth with thick, chewy noodles and vegetables, fresh oven-warm bread slathered in butter and honey, and some sort of berry pie with the flakiest crust that basically melted in his mouth. How Lord Kende stayed fit was beyond him. It wasn't as if Asyl starved and was unable to purchase food anymore, so he really didn't have any reason to be as enamored as he was. Spending his formative years on the streets had skewed his behavior, and he tended to eat as if he never knew where his next meal was coming from.

Lord Kende didn't say anything about what Asyl was sure were bad manners. Instead, he just watched with a soft smile on his face whenever Asyl glanced up at him. At least he wasn't repulsed. Was there anything that would unnerve the man? Completely stuffed, Asyl had slumped in the chair and sighed happily, finally at ease in someone else's home for the first time in eight years. Instead of rushing him out, Lord Kende got them a cup of what he called coffee and sipped it. It was bitter, but with the pie's sweetness lingering on his tongue, it wasn't too bad.

Neither of them forced a conversation. Lord Kende seemed content to let him bliss out from stuffing himself. Asyl could feel his happiness at having him at his table. In his home. He'd felt the rush of excitement earlier when he'd started asking about potions, but still wasn't quite sure what that was directed toward. Having Asyl be useful? An excuse to keep him in his life? He didn't know, and for once, Asyl found that he didn't entirely care why Lord Kende had gotten excited.

Once Asyl felt like he could actually move, Kende led him over to the library and let him have free rein. He felt as if he'd been given everything he ever wanted in life. There were so many books he had no way to get his hands on, restricted only to Healers. Of course, all the books were beautifully bound in leather and printed on actual paper. Asyl darted between bookshelves, cooing at all the volumes, curious about the ones he'd never even seen before. There were plenty more bookshelves filled with fiction, history, poems, geography… anything, really. All Asyl had eyes for were the medical texts.

Kende had finally broken the ice by pulling down a few of the books Asyl was desperately interested in, wanting to leaf through them but too terrified to touch. They walked to a long table that was tucked away in a quiet corner, and Lord Kende got him a sheaf of blank paper along with a blue feather pen and inkwell without prompting. Time passed as they pored through the books, Asyl figuring out a new formula to encourage bones to heal faster than a generic health potion. That sounded exciting, though he wasn't sure how he could test it effectively or humanely.

The two focused on narrowing down the formula and making it as potent as possible with the least amount of ingredients. It was plenty fun and engaging, bouncing his ideas off Kende. The two would pull books away from each other, flipping to pages and pointing to passages in order to prove their points. Once, Kende tapped Asyl's nose with the tip of the pen, making him squeak and rub the ink off furiously.

He didn't remember the last time he'd laughed so much while doing research. Kende was a soft, steady presence that kept him at ease. Asyl's vision was blurring by the time they decided to stop trying to refine the potion. He gave a wide yawn, stretching upward and cracking his back in a few spots. Kende hummed with an amused note, eyeing him softly. It was late, far later than what Asyl had thought it was, and most definitely a long walk home.

"Stay?" Kende asked gently. "I'll sleep on the couch in my room, and you can take my bed."

Asyl looked at him, hesitant to accept immediately. Despite everything Lord Kende had shown him, despite all the gentle words and affirmations, Asyl still worried that he was being played and that Kende would turn on him like Tillet did. But Kende wasn't like that. He had a reputation for being a good man, and nothing screamed predator to him.

Still, he worried.

His concerns must have shown on his face, as Lord Kende's expression softened and he reached across the table, folding their hands together. He could probably feel his hesitation, Asyl corrected. Just as how Asyl could feel Kende's worry about his safety and fear of being rejected again.

"It's late. By the time you walk home, it'll nearly be morning, and you won't have slept much at all. If you want to be in your own bed, let me call my driver to take you," Kende said.

That reassured Asyl more than anything else. The fact that Lord Kende was willing to not only back off, but get him home safely? A soft smile spread across his lips as he felt a warmth bloom in his chest.

"I don't have anything to sleep in," Asyl protested weakly.

"Oh, I'm sure I can rustle up something," Kende replied, tilting his head.

"Well. I'm sure your bed is much comfier than mine," Asyl said, feeling a light blush tinge his cheeks.

Kende stood and held out his hand. Asyl's blush darkened as he took it, rising to his feet. They walked toward the master bedroom, twining their fingers together. Sure, they weren't in public, but even being seen by Kende's staff made him shy. He remembered how fast the maids gossiped. Asyl pushed in close and kept his gaze down to avoid acknowledging anyone else. Kende seemed amused at his reaction but didn't tease him or comment. It wasn't as if they'd spent all evening together.

Once they were in the large master bedroom, Kende dug out a pair of soft pajama pants with a tie drawstring and an equally soft V-neck shirt for him. He gathered his own outfit and left to go into the en suite bathroom to give him space. Smiling, Asyl quietly changed, enjoying the feel of the soft cotton on his skin. Much nicer than his coarser linens. Clothing quality was most definitely something he missed from his time with his parents.

While Asyl was neatly folding his clothes, he heard Lord Kende knock on the door between the bed and bathroom.

"I'm decent," Asyl said, ducking his head.

Lord Kende emerged, shirtless, wearing only a pair of silk pants. The man wasn't ripped, but he was nicely toned. Clearly, he took care of himself between his charity planning and Healer work. Or maybe it was his Healer duties that kept him in shape. Goddess, his skin was damn near flawless, and his nipples were a lovely pink. Wait. Since when did he notice things like that? Usually he avoided looking at another man's body. He hadn't ever been interested. Even before Tillet.

Blushing furiously now, Asyl quickly brushed past Kende into the bathroom and shut the door, desperate to get a barrier between them. He slumped against the wall, looking down at his half-hard cock, trying not to breathe too heavily. Why? Why was this happening? Every time Lord Kende gave him a lingering kiss, his body reacted. Was this how he was supposed to react with Tillet? Why he'd always been annoyed that it had taken a while to get Asyl hard?

He craved Kende's touch whenever they were together and missed him when they were apart even by a few feet. It felt like the urge inside of him wouldn't be happy with their proximity until Asyl was nearly crawling inside of Kende's skin. Was this how Kende felt all the time? Or was this a normal reaction to seeing someone attractive? He didn't know, and it scared him. Scared him more than being locked up.

It had to be the Fated bond. There wasn't any other rational explanation he could think of. How a Void had a bond, he had no idea. Even accepting the idea that yes, they were Fated, was mind-boggling to Asyl. He just didn't know why the goddess who had abandoned him so thoroughly over thirteen years ago decided to bind him to a duke's son.

Shaking his head, Asyl relieved himself before washing up and shyly opening the door. He felt almost silly poking his head around it to locate Kende before coming out of the bathroom, leaving his small safety net and facing the nobleman. He could feel Lord Kende's slight amusement and contentment.

The bed had been turned down for him, and the partition he saw last time he was here was stretched out between the bed and the sitting area. On the other side, Lord Kende was setting up a bed on the couch, just like he'd promised. It surprised him a little that Kende was the one making up the couch and not a maid. Asyl bit his lower lip, tugging on the hem of his borrowed shirt without thinking about it.

"K-Kende?" he asked softly.

When the man looked at him and smiled, a jolt ran down his spine, settling in his gut. Asyl felt his cheeks redden again and internally cursed his body.

"Is everything all right?" the blond asked.

"I...." Asyl trailed off, unable to help himself from staring at him. "Yeah. Um. Good night."

He got a warm smile, and Kende nodded. "Good night, Asyl. I'll turn off the lamps over here once I'm finished setting up. You can dampen the ones over there."

Nodding, Asyl quickly extinguished all the lamps on his side of the partition, leaving the one next to the bed for last. He slid between the sheets, marveling at how comfortable the mattress was. He hadn't been able to appreciate it the last time he was here. Goddess, maybe once he got the roof and oven fixed, he should look into replacing his ratty mattress.

In the dim light, Asyl wiggled and rolled to get the sheets around him, effectively cocooning himself. He snuggled into the pillow and smiled at the warmth surrounding him and the happiness he could sense coming from Kende. Oh Goddess, he could get used to this very quickly. If Kende truly was serious about them being Fated, which Asyl was starting to believe he was.

He wondered how many other Voids had a Fated out there. Had they been cheated for years due to the priests' fearmongering? That was a frustrating thought. What if there was more that Voids were missing out on? If it was missed that they could have Fated, then maybe it took a special kind of potion to accelerate their healing? That was something he could research. Being able to heal a Void quickly would be beneficial for everyone.

Yeah, that would be good.

He'd work on a formula tomorrow. Maybe try working with a full-strength potion and start incorporating ingredients from salves or tinctures to see if that would work. Perhaps if he used less of the water Naias drew for him and more of the herbs that had healing properties.... Small cuts on his arms wouldn't be too much to actually put himself in harm's way, but still enough for a potion to heal. He'd have to let Naias know he was working on something new so she'd keep checking in with him through the day.

The last thing he wanted to do was accidentally poison himself and die trying to help the Void community. Goddess, he was so *comfortable*. He felt like he was floating, and nothing ached. The door opening caught his attention, and Asyl cracked an eye open to see someone walking into the bedroom. That felt odd. Didn't Lord Kende's people usually knock before they came in? Unless his steward didn't. But Birgir was hefty, whereas this man was fit.

The man's head turned, and Asyl felt his gut clench, his tongue going numb. What was Tillet doing here? How did he get in? Was he friends with Lord Kende? Naias would have known, wouldn't she? She knew Kende socially, and knew who Tillet was, so she would have warned Asyl. Right?

Asyl couldn't move, paralyzed with fear, his heart pounding in his ears. The man stalked toward the bed and sneered down at him.

"Did you really think I wouldn't find you again, Void?" the man snarled at him.

Squirming, Asyl tried to break free of his cocoon of blankets, nearly pitching himself off the bed in his haste to escape. His arms were still trapped in the folds, and he thrashed as panic started to take control of his rationale.

"Go the fuck away!" Asyl snapped. "I'm not going back to you!"

"Like you have a choice? Did you really think Lord Kende would welcome a little whore with open arms and suddenly you're a darling in high society again? You're nothing more than a worthless cum bucket," Tillet taunted. "You're just here to warm his bed."

Asyl finally managed to get his arms free just as Tillet jumped on him, pinning him to the bed. Shouting, Asyl clawed at the man's face, doing his best to kick him in the nuts. No, no, he didn't believe that Kende would sell him out. He'd seemed genuinely horrified at what had happened to him.

Was one of his staff trying to get rid of him? They all seemed really nice. How could they betray their lord like this? How was Kende still asleep? Asyl opened his mouth to scream as loud as he could.

Fingers wrapped around his neck and squeezed. Asyl squirmed harder, trying to throw the man off him, gasping for air as his heart beat frantically. No. No, not like this. He didn't want to go back. He would die before going back.

"Asyl," Kende's voice came to him faintly.

Was he just now waking up? Asyl tried to cry out, only managing to make a garbled noise.

"It's all right, Asyl," Lord Kende said.

How was it all right? Oh Goddess, the lord really had sold him out. Why? Had this really all been an insanely elaborate ruse? Please no. He just wanted to be left alone. If he couldn't be happy, he at least wanted to be content. He couldn't help the sob that choked him or stop the tears streaming down his face.

Why couldn't he just be left alone?

CHAPTER 7

SLEEPING ON a couch was awkward. Even having one as nice as his, it wasn't deep enough to lie on his back, and Kende wasn't a side sleeper. He woke frequently, unable to truly fall into a deep sleep. Then there was the near constant shifting from Asyl on his bed. Maybe his Fated couldn't sleep right now in an unfamiliar area.

Or he was just a bit anxious from his history. What happened to him still pissed Kende off when he thought about it too much. Being tied to a bed and raped whenever his captor felt like it. He could feel Asyl's unease and fear through their bond, despite his Fated being asleep. Kende hated that he was so upset in his sleep that he could feel it clearly.

Asyl cried out, thrashing now. Jolting awake, Kende threw off his blanket and jumped to his feet. He turned on a lamp, grateful for the Ignis technology easing the way. Hurrying over to his bed, Kende put the lamp on his nightstand to see what might be affecting his Fated. Asyl's face was skewed in pain, his breath coming quickly as he rolled from side to side, trying to get free from the sheets he was wrapped up in.

"Asyl," he crooned gently, tugging at the blankets. Maybe he was panicking from being restrained? He really didn't know what was causing his distress. Instead he tried to keep his voice gentle as he said, "It's all right, Asyl."

He got back a tortured whimper in reply. Kende managed to get his Fated free of the blankets, yet Asyl still thrashed from side to side, his scarred fingers clenched into fists. Kende ever so gently shushed him, cupping his love's face.

"Sweetheart," Kende murmured, "you're having a nightmare. You're safe with me."

Asyl jerked awake, his glazed eyes wild. He didn't seem to recognize that he was awake and safe. His Fated whined, tears streaking down his face as he rolled from side to side, blindly batting at someone only he could see. Kende lurched for the call bell, hoping that maybe Gojko would know what to do. It took Siora a minute to get to his room, a robe tied around her.

"Sir?" she asked, eyes darting between the two.

"I need you to get Gojko," Kende told her.

Siora nodded and ran out to get the other Healer. Kende lifted Asyl in his arms, concerned with the blank look persisting in his eyes. Maybe some cold air would help shock his system and get him to fully wake. Kende carried him to the door to his balcony, listening to Asyl's labored breathing and quiet moans. He tilted his head and gently kissed the curve of Asyl's neck, awkwardly shifting his Fated so he could open the outside door.

The cold air quickly revived his Fated. Asyl breathed in sharply, and he fell still in his arms. Kende carefully placed him on the padded bench and sat on a nearby chair, not wanting to crowd him. Without his support, Asyl seemed to curl in on himself, staring down at the floor. It wasn't long before he began shivering, and Kende hoped it was from the cold. He couldn't feel anything through their bond, and that worried him even more than the dead stare.

Kende looked up as Gojko slipped out onto the balcony, holding a large steaming mug in his hand.

"What happened?" Gojko asked.

"Nightmare," Kende replied simply, shrugging.

Asyl shook his head and pulled his legs to his chest, his breath starting to come fast again. Kende's resolve broke and he crossed over, taking Asyl's hand from his lap so he could hold it gently. He shushed him, leaning in and pressing his face into Asyl's hair. Gojko knelt in front of Asyl, pushing the warm mug to his upper arm.

"Please drink," Gojko said gently. "It's chamomile."

At his request, Asyl finally raised his eyes to look at him, blinking slowly. He nodded meekly and took the mug, raised it to his lips. Kende reached out, stabilizing the cup as it shook alarmingly in the man's grasp.

"Can you tell me about it?" Gojko asked. "Talking helps."

For a long while, Asyl sipped the herbal tea, just staring down at the floor. Gojko and Kende waited patiently, both lightly touching him to offer comfort. Siora brought them both some blankets to bundle up and ward off the chill. Finally, once the tea was nearly gone, Asyl looked up at Kende. The pain in his eyes nearly took his breath away, his chest aching for his Fated.

"Tillet was here," he said, his voice rough. "He was trying to kill me."

Tillet. The name wasn't familiar to Kende, and he frowned, trying to recall everything Asyl had told him earlier. None of what his Fated had told him had included names, even with the one who'd held him against his will, though that was the most likely culprit. Who else in his life would affect Asyl so severely outside of his parents? And likely the first man who'd pinned Asyl for money. Except Asyl probably didn't know that man's name.

"Is that the one who chained you to a bed?" Kende asked gently.

Gojko's hand spasmed, and he looked at Kende sharply. He wasn't upset at what he'd said, rather at the topic. Nor was he angry that Asyl's torture was being spoken about. No, if Kende knew his fellow Healer, Gojko would want to know everything about this Tillet and go after the man who chained Asyl to chase his own pleasure.

Asyl nodded numbly, staring into the remnants of his tea. A small growl escaped Kende, and he slid closer to his Fated, tucking Asyl's trembling body into his side, hugging him close. He could feel the beginning of Asyl's emotions thawing, though he was pleasantly surprised that it was safety rather than fear coming through their bond.

"No one can get in here during the night unless it's my family," Kende told him. "No random man can get in here, and as far as I know, it's not common knowledge that you'd come here."

"If you know his full name and description, I can give it to security. That way Tillet won't ever be able to get in or get close to you while you're with Kende," Gojko said.

"I can even assign someone to you," Kende offered, placing a kiss to the top of Asyl's head. "That way you won't ever have to worry about him."

Asyl looked up at him, finally meeting his eyes. He slowly began to relax into him, sipping at the last bit of the cooling tea. In a halting voice, he described Tillet Gaten, a tall Ignis man with brown hair and blue eyes. Gojko squeezed Asyl's knee, thanked him, and returned inside. If Kende didn't know any better, he'd think that Gojko would only tell his private security. Macik would likely be by in the morning and want more information.

"Do you feel any better?" Kende asked.

"Cold," Asyl murmured.

Smiling, Kende wrapped his arms around Asyl's shoulder and under his knees. His Fated squeaked when he was picked up, clutching at him with one hand, tucking the mug into his lap. Kende quickly retreated inside, pushing the door shut with his hip and kicking it closed. Immediately, the warmth of the room enveloped them, and his Fated sighed with relief.

Kende sat Asyl on the edge of his bed, smoothed out the blankets, and pulled them back. With a little prodding, Asyl set the mug on the nightstand, shrugged the blanket off his shoulders, and slid under the covers. He looked sleepy, his eyes taking longer to open every time he blinked. His poor Fated was worn out.

Without thinking or really asking, Kende turned off the lamps and made his way to the other side of his bed. He climbed in, scooting close to Asyl. The man's skin was cold to the touch, but Kende didn't care. He wrapped his arms around Asyl and pulled him close, pressing his chest into his Fated's back.

"Kende," Asyl protested very weakly.

"I'm not going to sleep separate from you," Kende told him. "I want you to know that if someone comes in here, I'll be right here to protect you."

His Fated whimpered but nodded, the brief spike of fear melting away. Tremors ran through Asyl as his body warmed until he finally fell still, slowly relaxing. Kende kept him close through it all, humming softly while he waited. He wasn't going to sleep until Asyl did.

"I've never actually just slept in someone's bed before," Asyl admitted quietly, "even with Tillet. He expected sex every night before sleeping."

"Then he missed out on something wonderful," Kende murmured. "There's not much better than just being close to a lover."

"I wouldn't know," Asyl said.

"I know," Kende replied, tilting his head and kissing Asyl's temple, "but you'll learn. I want to show you."

As he brushed his lips down Asyl's temple toward his cheek, his Fated squirmed. Pulling away, hoping he hadn't overstepped, Kende caught a soft giggle coming from Asyl.

"What?" he asked, smiling.

"Your stubble tickles," Asyl told him.

"Oh, does it?" Kende said with a wide smile.

He squeezed Asyl, getting himself a squeal from his Fated as he pressed his face into his neck. Kende slipped his hands under the sheets, trying to tickle his sides, and was delighted when Asyl writhed and began laughing. His laugh was bright, making Kende immediately want to hear more of it. Grinning, Kende nuzzled into his Fated's neck, letting his stubble rasp over his skin. Asyl gasped sharply, his body going taut in his arms.

Oh.

That gasp had been made in arousal.

They both fell still, Asyl breathing hard from Kende's tickling.

"Kende," Asyl whispered.

Kende hummed softly and nuzzled his neck again, making Asyl sigh, the quietest of moans coming from him. Fuck. His cock began to harden, and Kende kissed his Fated where he'd scratched with his stubble. There wasn't anything he wanted more than to roll on top of Asyl and show him the difference between a fuck and making love. But that's not what his Fated needed. Doing something like that would just prove to Asyl that no one actually slept in bed with another without any sort of sex.

Even still, he wasn't going to pull away and make Asyl think he did something wrong.

"One day, when you're ready," Kende replied, his lips moving against Asyl's ear, "I'll love on you for hours."

Asyl shivered in his arms and said, "What if I'm never ready?"

"Then we'll just sleep, and I'll pamper you however you want," Kende replied.

His Fated hummed softly, and after a moment, spun in his arms and burrowed into Kende's chest. Holding him tight, Kende finally closed his eyes and let himself relax. They lay together for a long time, neither of them moving away. Asyl's breath evened out, signaling that he'd fallen asleep, and Kende followed him shortly after.

JUST AS Kende predicted, Macik was at breakfast. It was later in the morning than usual, since Asyl had slept in and Kende refused to eat without him. His Fated was exhausted from his late-night panic attack, taking a while to wake up. Kende wasn't going to leave his bed until Asyl was aware of where he was and knew he was still safe.

Asyl seemed quite a bit calmer around Kende, leaning into his touch whenever Kende reached for him. While he was doing his best to not overwhelm his Fated with constant affection, Kende was infinitely pleased with the change. He offered Asyl a new outfit that he'd had made for him. The tunic and leggings were a plain beige and low quality compared to what Kende wore, but Asyl had blushed a deep red and regarded the clothes reverently.

It wasn't like Kende didn't want the absolute best for his Fated. He knew that if he gave Asyl clothes of the highest quality, he'd end up losing an argument to get the man to keep them. Getting him something that was more middle-of-the-road still made Asyl feel special, but not to the point of embarrassment or inferiority. In theory. In practice, his Fated's reaction was even better when Asyl got on his toes and tilted his head up, silently requesting a kiss.

Kende only hoped that Asyl wasn't offering affection because of his gifts.

He bent down and pressed a soft kiss to Asyl's lips, feeling only happiness through their bond. There was no hesitation, no wariness in his eyes. The trust that Asyl had given him delighted him, and Kende wanted to do nothing to betray that trust.

The gentle ease between them faded once Siora came in to pester Kende to attend breakfast and tensed further when Asyl spotted both Gojko and Macik. The change saddened Kende, and he hoped that one day maybe Asyl wouldn't mind seeing his brother-in-law or mentor. Breakfast was a stack of perfectly golden pancakes with a whole spread of toppings including fruits, nuts, and whipped cream. Asyl had been entranced by the variety and ate heartily, much to Kende's delight.

After an hour, the table was cleared, and Macik leaned forward, clasping his hands.

"You likely know why I'm here, don't you," Macik said.

Asyl shrugged, staring at the table and refusing to look up at him.

Macik frowned at his reticence. "I want to tell you that if you or any other Void are a victim of a crime, we're here to help. If you have to ask for me specifically, that's fine. I'd rather you come to me with issues than not at all."

"You're only here because of Kende," Asyl muttered.

Kende closed his eyes at the pain and disbelief in his Fated's voice that echoed how he felt through their bond. He was hoping they'd gotten past all this. Except now it seemed like whenever they were around anyone else, Asyl reverted to his solitary and guarded ways. At least they were making progress when it was just them.

"In a way, yes. Kende is my brother-in-law, so I'm able to come here when needed," Macik said. "However, if I didn't want to help, I wouldn't have come or said I would look into what happened to you."

Asyl raised his eyes to Kende, and he smiled ever so gently, trying to encourage his Fated to speak. Tugging at the hem of his shirt, Asyl finally nodded and turned his gaze over to Macik.

"What do you want to know?" he asked quietly.

"Can you tell me what happened between you and Tillet, and how long ago everything occurred?" Macik asked, pulling out a spiral-bound notebook.

After taking a deep breath, Asyl spoke of his time in Tillet's home. His detached recounting drove a hole in Kende's chest, and after a look at Gojko, he knew his mentor wasn't unaffected either. Consulting his bond only told him that Asyl was rebuilding his walls, closing himself back off. A small gasp behind him told him that Siora had been lurking in the doorway. When Asyl got to his rescue, Macik frowned a little.

"Do you know anything about this man?" Macik asked.

Asyl shook his head. "I barely remember what he looks like. Tall, I think? Light hair…. I might remember him if I see him, but I wasn't really paying attention when it was all happening."

"Understandable," Macik said gently. "Do you remember Tillet's Fated's name?"

"No," Asyl replied. "He was careful to not mention his name at all."

"All right. Now tell me about the men who attacked you the night Kende found you," Macik requested.

Asyl sat back in the chair and furrowed his brow, thinking. His eyes darted to Kende briefly, and he recalled his Fated's accusation yesterday—that he'd hired the thugs who attacked and nearly killed Asyl. Hopefully now his Fated knew that he would never willingly put him in danger. Finally, Asyl let out a breath.

"One was bald, about as tall as Kende, and had brown eyes. The other two were twins. They were taller, one with really long black hair, the other's short, and green eyes," Asyl said. "They came prepared. Their brandishing of weapons is what made me bolt in the first place. They were just faster than me."

"Do you have any reason to believe you were targeted because you're a Void?" Macik asked.

Asyl nodded. "They were telling me how worthless I was and that I was better off dead rather than leeching from society." Asyl snorted, and Kende knew exactly what his Fated was thinking. He could feel the bitterness. Society rarely helped Voids. "Before I passed out, they were talking about how to find and drain other Voids."

Macik growled faintly and sighed. "Do you know any other Voids?"

"Yes," Asyl said, looking up at the detective. "I reached out to them once I was home, and they all said that they'd be careful and spread the warning to their contacts to ensure they would be safe too."

Macik nodded. "Could I get their names and addresses?"

Kende could see Asyl tense, and distrust warred with worry on his face. Obviously his Fated wanted to help his fellows, but he wasn't sure that Macik could be trusted. Kende leaned forward and reached out to grab his hand. Asyl immediately squeezed, holding him tight. The maelstrom inside his Fated ebbed slightly.

"We don't want anyone hurt," Kende said. "No Voids are going to be arrested just because some gang is potentially targeting a whole demographic."

Finally, Asyl nodded and looked up at Macik. He rattled off a list of names and last known addresses, which were crossroads instead of homes for the men, and ducked his head once he was done. After thanking him, Macik got to his feet and quietly left the manor.

"I want to go home," Asyl said quietly.

"All right," Kende replied. "Will you let Toemi take you home? It's raining, and you don't have a proper winter cloak."

Asyl tugged on the hem of his shirt before nodding. Kende walked his Fated to the front door and, ignoring Birgir, kissed Asyl gently on his temple. He helped Asyl get into the carriage and nodded to his driver. The horse whinnied and trotted off with her handler's tongue clicks, heading out to the street.

He turned to see Birgir scowling at him.

"My lord," his butler drawled, "far be it from me to tell you what to do—"

"Then don't," Kende replied sharply. "I'm not interested in hearing any anti-Void nonsense. Asyl is always welcome here, as is Lady Naias Elrel."

Birgir opened his mouth before seemingly deciding against whatever he was going to say. Instead, his steward nodded tersely and bowed. Kende walked past him to Siora, who was waiting for him quietly in the entry hall.

"What's on the agenda today, sir?" she asked.

"Do I have anything planned?" Kende replied. When Siora shook her head, Kende smiled. "Well then, I think we should replace our friend's ruined cape so the rain can stay off him. Then I'd like to talk to some Ignis crafters for boiler plates."

"Boiler plates?" Siora asked.

"The two Asyl have are temperamental and spotty," Kende said. "He struggled with making his potions yesterday, and those are his livelihood. I want to help him be able to support himself."

"That's a nice act of charity," Siora commented. "Do you think he'll accept it?"

"If he complains, I'll just tell him that it's my thanks for helping with Jaclyn's party," Kende replied, shrugging.

Siora snorted and shook her head at that. She wandered off with the promise she'd be back before it was time to leave. Kende finished getting dressed, shrugged on his great overcoat, and waited in the portico. Just as she returned, the carriage arrived, the horse's coat shiny with the perpetual rain that plagued their city in autumn. The mare tossed her head and came to a stop in front of Kende and Siora. Birgir rushed forward and opened the carriage door as Siora unfurled an umbrella.

As much as Kende truly didn't mind getting a bit wet going from door to door, his status dictated that he shouldn't have to worry about such mundane issues. It always seemed a little overkill to him, especially since the ocean was nearby. The weather was perpetually temperamental and prone to change within five minutes. Kende sat back on the bench as Siora joined him with a small smile on her face.

"Where to, my lord?" Toemi asked through the small hatch by the man's seat.

"The Ignis Heating store," Kende said.

If his driver was surprised, he didn't say anything. Instead the man shut the door and snapped the reins to goad his mare into a trot down the street. Siora sat quietly on the other side of him, pulling out a book and reading it. Kende closed his eyes and consulted his bond. While he wasn't entirely aware of where exactly his Fated was, he knew that

Toemi would have told him if Asyl got off before he got home. He could still feel the anxiety in him, though it slowly was overtaken by joy. A minute later, he heard humming. His Fated was brewing his potions.

The ride took about twenty minutes, far to the outskirts of town, where if the Ignis inventors ended up with an item that exploded during testing, it would do minimal damage. Before Siora could get the umbrella out, Kende hopped out of the carriage and walked into the store.

A bell rang from overhead, signaling his entrance. He heard shuffling in the back, but Kende didn't mind having to wait. Instead, he wandered the sparse store, looking at what was on display. There were burner plates along with the lamps that he had in his manor. Small ovens, large ovens, heating elements for a bath or a mattress. If he hadn't been here with Asyl in mind, Kende would have loved to chat with the inventor about the bath-heating elements. For now, he supposed he'd have to handle the maids boiling the water and pouring it into his tub, since none of those he had employed were an Ignis themselves.

For now.

How nice would it be to turn on one of those elements and heat the bath while getting undressed? Or to be able to free up his maid's time in not having to spend so long trying to draw a bath for him? Being able to control how warm it was, so if he and Asyl decided to bathe together, they could take as long as they wanted without the water going frigid....

"Can I help you, my lord?" a timid voice asked.

Looking over, Kende smiled kindly at the small redhead walking around the checkout counter. She had a heavy apron on and was currently shaking off thick heat-resistant gloves. The Craft Mark on her forehead showed her as an Ignis, though she seemed fairly baby-faced. Maybe she was relatively new here.

"Yes, I'm looking at your Ignis plates," Kende said, returning to the stand showing off the devices.

"Oh yes, sir. What do you want to know about them?" she asked, bouncing on the balls of her feet.

"How expensive are they?" Kende asked. "I have a friend who has two, and they're malfunctioning. What's their shelf life?"

"Usually they work for about five years before needing to be serviced. Depending on who repairs them, they can wear out after ten years, but there's a few that are still working over thirty years later. We currently don't have any used ones in stock, though I will say the newer models take repairs a lot better than the older ones," the redhead explained with a perpetual smile and upward lilt to her voice. She really seemed to love her inventions, and Kende was grateful for the enthusiasm.

"How much is it to repair?" Kende asked.

"That changes between stores. We repair Plates for one platinum each," she said.

One platinum? That meant nothing to Kende, but he'd also seen how much Asyl sold his potions and mundane tinctures for. On top of ingredient costs and however much the building rent price went for, when would his Fated be able to afford that? Unless Lady Naias had bought the building out fully, but Kende suspected she hadn't.

"All right, how much is a new one, then?" he inquired, a little worried about the price.

"Five platinum."

Behind him, Siora gave a low whistle. Yeah, that was a lot. Kende closed his eyes briefly and nodded, deciding on what he wanted to do. He had no idea how old Asyl's Plates were or how many times they'd been serviced. This way, he knew for sure his Fated would be getting the best item that would last him for years. Maybe by then, Asyl would be content to let him pay for things. Or resigned. His soon-to-be-lover was quite proud and strove to be self-sufficient.

"How many do you have?" Kende asked.

Siora made a small noise and sighed. "Sir. Do you really think Asyl will accept without complaint?"

"I look forward to fielding his frustration," Kende replied with a smile.

The redhead giggled and blushed when the two looked at her. She cleared her throat and said, "We currently have three on hand."

"Perfect. I'll take all three of them. Can you deliver?" Kende asked.

"Of course we can, sir! Where to? Do you need them today?" the Ignis gal asked, hurrying back behind the counter.

"Enchanted Waters, and if you can deliver them today, that would be fantastic. If not, tomorrow will work," Kende told her.

The girl nodded, scribbling on a pad of paper with a graphite rod. She smiled up at them and held out her hand when Siora extended hers. Coins clinked as they passed hands, and the redhead counted them quickly before nodding.

"We will get them to Enchanted Waters as soon as possible," she said.

After thanking her, Kende turned and left the store. Siora ran after him, managing to get the umbrella open before he could get too far away from the building. They stepped into the carriage, and Kende instructed his driver to head to the tailor that he used. Siora smiled at him but said nothing as she opened her book again.

He truly hoped Asyl would take his gifts as what they were. Gifts. Something to spoil his Fated during their courtship. While he didn't want to take away all of Asyl's independence, he really did want to fold his Fated into his arms and have him relax for the rest of his life. Goddess, all the pain Asyl had already suffered in his short years…. The man wasn't yet thirty, and he had already suffered through so much trauma. Kende wasn't sure how to approach his Fated and persuade him to move in and get married.

Oh hell.

There would need to be an introduction gala to announce Asyl as his Fated, and to have the nobility and gentry get to know him. Then there was the possibility of royalty showing up, due to his father being the king's brother. Crown Prince Yolotzin would likely be in attendance at minimum, so long as he was in the kingdom. They had a good relationship, as they played a lot together as youths, and he knew that his cousin would be delighted that he finally found his Fated.

But the gala would truly be the proverbial tip of the iceberg. There was still an engagement party, the wedding ceremony, and the subsequent reception party that would be publicly held. That didn't include all the familial duties. He'd have to bring Asyl to his parents' mansion and have a formal dinner with them first. Then they'd host a smaller party where the rest of Kende's siblings and their partners along with his niblings, aunts, uncles, grandparents, and cousins could say hello.

All the calls to the nobles' houses who would want to meet the Void who stole Kende's heart.

Would his shy alchemist Fated be able to handle it? He had an idea that Asyl already came from high society and likely had the proper manners beat into him as a child. It might just take a bit to have him remember and then build on what he knew. Did Asyl remember how to dance? By thirteen, Kende already knew the simpler stately dances, but he was in a higher caste than Asyl might have been. He really needed to talk to his Fated about all of this.

There were hundreds of parties in their future. Hundreds of people that they'd need to meet and schmooze to keep their support in any further charity events. Kende was already a little bit of a black sheep in his family, still unmarried after thirty and having been blessed with a non-elemental Craft. Oh well. Now that he knew who his Fated was, that was one "issue" taken care of. Now it was a matter of easing Asyl into his world.

Goddess, this was going to be an uphill battle.

The carriage stopped in front of his tailor, and Kende hopped out. This was going to be another fight, he was sure. Siora followed, not even scolding him about using an umbrella. Apparently she'd already given up on that futile task for today. Kende walked inside and smiled at Maerie, the Illusionist who ran the shop.

"My lord," she said warmly, "how can I help you?"

"I need a cloak made for someone a few inches shorter than me," Kende said, "good quality, durable, and simple. No extra embroidery and a common color."

The woman frowned at that, brushing her brown curls out of her face. "My lord, that's quite an unusual request."

"I'm aware," Kende said and smiled, "but my friend's cloak is in tatters, and he needs a new one."

"Then surely he deserves only the best quality and a beautiful cloak," Maerie said, even as she stood to walk over to the hundreds of fabric bolts she had. "What is his coloring?"

"Black hair, blue eyes," Kende replied. "But no, something simple, please. I don't want him to protest, and he likes to walk the city at any time, so anonymity is the way to go. That way he's not a target to get mugged."

Maerie frowned. "Does he live in a bad area?"

"Not exactly," Siora interjected, "but he lives across town and often insists on walking to or from the manor unless Lord Kende can convince him to take the carriage."

"I like him already." Maerie chuckled, her fingers dancing over all the fabric.

"Then you must come to Jaclyn's charity event in two moonturns. I'm going to try and convince him to attend," Kende replied. "Of course, I might bring him by before that for a new outfit."

The woman smiled at him and walked over to the several shades of blue she had in stock. She hummed and rocked from side to side for a moment before turning around.

"What color are his eyes again?" she asked.

"A very pale blue," Kende said, smiling softly.

Maerie grunted and returned to her colors before pulling out a deep blue bolt.

"I would like it to match his eyes, but that would be too flashy. This should complement his eyes instead and draw out their color. I'll oil the underside and line the inside with fur, so that way he'll stay warm and dry. I'll add a deep hood to this as well. Give me a few days to complete this, all right?" Maerie conceded with a smile.

"Thank you," Kende said.

Siora moved over to one of Maerie's assistants and handed her a gold piece. The rest would be given to her upon completion. Pleased that Asyl would be dry and warm during the upcoming winter moonturns, Kende turned to leave. Maybe he should visit his Fated in two days to make sure he had his new Plates delivered and hopefully set up. With any luck, Asyl would just sigh and thank him. Though, knowing the man, Asyl would probably glare at him and get snappy.

He was looking forward to it.

CHAPTER 8

THREE FUCKING Ignis Plates. An Ignis redhead named Keyna arrived with another Ignis man who looked like a mountain. Asyl had basically all but fled upon seeing them, letting Naias figure it out. No one wanted to know that a Void was making potions and tinctures. Instead, he sat on the stairs up toward his quarters. Naias and the redhead hit it off immediately and laughed with each other as the large man got the Plates set up and calibrated. These were permanent installations, unlike his old ones, which were heavy but portable.

Asyl knew damn well who'd sent him the Plates. He'd felt sparks of joy and excitement from the man as he'd traveled across the city several times these last few days. This had to have been what he was doing. Even though Kende told him he didn't want to take away his brewing, the man still found ways to interfere…. Maybe that was too mean. Kende was giving him one hell of a gift to help with his business and didn't seem to want anything in return.

Except to be his Fated.

Everything he'd been told about him not having the capacity to have a Fated was being proved wrong. Clearly, Voids were able to have a destined lover, though it relied on the one who was Craft Blessed to find them, and hopefully not be prejudiced against having a Void as their Fated. Though maybe those who were paired with a Void had the temperament and mindset to not care. Kende clearly didn't care that he was a Void. Maybe it was their bond that gave him an insight into what the Craft Blessed felt.

Outside of his insight into how Kende felt, Asyl found that he seriously missed the man while they were separated. It was a deep ache in his gut, almost physically painful, as if his body was urging him to return to Kende's side. When they were together, he wanted to climb him like a tree or drop to his knees. *That* reaction was something he didn't quite understand. Maybe it was because Kende was his Fated that he wanted to give him everything and his body was craving intimacy.

During his time with Tillet, not once did Asyl have that sort of urge, nor did he react to any of the men that had taken him to bed.

For once, he was starting to believe that he wasn't going to be alone for the rest of his life, even though he'd tried to push Kende away a few times. He desperately wanted to believe that Kende was right and that they were made for each other. Kende was perfectly kind, had seemingly large amounts of patience, and was willing to wait. Willing to wait for Asyl to be ready for him, willing to give him space when he needed it, and willing to let him go. That was something Tillet would never have done.

Naias found him on the stairs, curled up and hugging his legs tightly.

"Everything all right?" she asked.

"I think I'm starting to really believe that he's my Fated," Asyl said.

A brilliant smile broke out on her face, and she pulled Asyl to his feet, down the stairs into the back room, and began bouncing happily. He couldn't help but laugh as he tripped over his own feet, grabbing at her to keep his balance.

"Finally!" she exclaimed. "You're so lucky. Lord Kende is such a wonderful man. Are you going to make potions for his charity?"

"Yeah. I think that's why he got me the new Plates," Asyl replied with a small smile.

Naias giggled for the first time in moonturns, squeezing his hands. "Well now you're down a cauldron."

"That I am. I think I'm going to go purchase one while it's currently not pouring down," Asyl said.

A bell rang from the front, and Naias immediately dropped his hands and ran to the store. She came back a minute later with a sly smile and handed him a bouquet of roses set in a glass vase with a ribbon tied around the neck. Asyl flushed, took the flowers from her, and cradled them close to his chest. He supposed the Ignis Plates weren't enough of a gift.

Still, it was nice and a bit romantic to have fresh flowers delivered. Asyl brought the roses up and breathed in their fragrance, delighted that it wasn't overbearing. He walked over to his work desk and cleared off a corner, stacking his notes in a haphazard pile. The vase fit perfectly, the flowers adding a nice spot of red, pink, and white amongst all the green from his herbs.

Naias giggled and gave him a bone-crushing hug before she was called away again. It was nice seeing her so excited about something again. For a while, she'd been almost bored from the minutiae of everyday life. Work here, go home, deal with gentry duties, rinse and repeat. Naias needed a vacation. Maybe he could ask Kende for someone who could watch the shop while she was gone. Yeah, next time he saw him, Asyl would ask.

IT TOOK Kende another two days to come back. Asyl hadn't thought of going to visit him, mostly because he was too excited to play with the new Plates, though he thought of him often. The potions boiled quickly, almost to the point where Asyl had to rush to keep up or set everything out in advance so he could just stir and monitor the liquid. He couldn't make his tinctures or salves while he waited for the potions to brew like he used to. Even the full-strength potions would be quick to make now.

Asyl didn't have the ingredients to make the health potions Kende wanted for the charity, so he stuck to his usual three-tiered potions to keep the store stocked. Maybe he could take Kende with him to the market when he went to get the ingredients. He'd already done all the math and adjusted it for the new Plates and their effectiveness. Instead of the predicted hundred, Asyl could probably make about four times that. The thought was heady, and all Asyl could think of was how much they'd be able to raise.

The knowledge made him immensely happy, and he was humming when he heard the door that led to the shop open behind him. He heard a soft chuckle and knew that his Fated had joined him.

"You're excited," Kende said.

"How can I not be?" Asyl replied and jumped up from his workbench, leaving the half-mixed burn salve behind.

He trotted over to Kende and threw his arms up for a hug. The smile that lit Kende's face was magical, and the blond squeezed him tight, burying his face in Asyl's neck. He felt the man inhale deep and held Kende tighter. It took a few minutes for them to part, just enjoying being in each other's arms. The pain in his chest that he'd been growing accustomed to finally eased, and his heart thrummed at being so close to its twin.

"I expected you to fight with me," Kende admitted with a sheepish grin as he took a step back. "I'll gladly take this type of greeting, though."

Asyl snorted, looking up at him. "As if you haven't known exactly how thrilled I've been with the new Plates. I don't think I've ever been so excited for an acquisition for the shop before. Besides, I've been hearing you laughing these past few days as you've been wandering what feels like the entire city. I know you've been to a bakery and a flower shop recently… which. Thank you for the roses."

Kende's smile grew. "You're welcome. I've been trying to find a place that can supply us centerpieces and a cake for the charity event, and the roses caught my eye. So far, I've gotten the bakery on board."

"You'll find an adequate florist, I'm sure," Asyl said.

"I will," Kende assured him. Asyl tilted his head, and Kende leaned down to give him a chaste kiss. "You said you can hear me?"

Asyl nodded. "Yeah. I know what it means. I'm… starting to believe that we're Fated."

Kende just smiled, his eyes warm, and pressed their foreheads together for a while. Asyl let out a slow, contented sigh and wiggled closer, wrapping his lanky arms around his Fated's neck. This time when they parted, Asyl gently took the man's hand in his.

"So, the Plates are working well?" Kende asked, as if he really needed to.

"Very much so. They're incredibly good and end up boiling the potions quickly, which will be great for your charity," Asyl said. "Thank you. The two older ones were definitely on the way out, and I couldn't really afford to repair them or get new ones."

"That's fortunate. Did the Ignis crew take your old ones?" Kende asked.

Asyl shook his head. "They're too outdated. Not even worth repairing, from what the lady said."

"Well then, I'm glad I decided to get you some new ones," Kende said.

"I'll try to pay you back," Asyl said, knowing full well his Fated would dismiss it.

True to form, Kende rolled his eyes and smiled softly. "No you won't. It was a gift. Besides, the price is outrageous. Maybe it was the place I went to, but even Siora was shocked."

"Yeah, that's why I always got secondhand ones," Asyl said and shrugged. "But now that you're here, I was wondering if you'd want to visit my suppliers with me. I need to get started on the healing potions sooner than later."

Kende nodded. "Of course. I'll gladly be your pack mule, unless you want to take the carriage."

"We can walk. Or are your lordly legs too feeble?" Asyl teased.

Laughing, Kende took a step back, tugging on Asyl's hand to lead him toward the front of the store. Usually Asyl left through the back, not wanting to show himself to the customers. This time he stuck with Kende, gazing around his shop. They were finally fully stocked, and there were several customers browsing. Siora stood off to the side, a package under one arm and a tincture in her other hand with a thoughtful look on her face.

"Oh. Maybe we should take your carriage," Asyl murmured, seeing the rain.

Kende shook his head. Siora replaced the tincture, hearing him, and walked over. She handed him the thick blue bundle that she had been carrying. Curious, Asyl took it and shook out the bundle. It was a heavy hooded cloak, fur lined with a midnight-blue shell. The fur itself was a nice salt-and-pepper color, helping break up what would be a solid block of color. This must have cost so much, despite looking incredibly simple.

"But," Asyl protested weakly, holding the heavy cloak, unable to take his eyes off it.

"You need a new one, since we kind of ruined your old one," Kende explained and smiled at him.

"That's the weakest argument," Asyl said and laughed. "Really?"

"Really. But I'd love to take you to Maerie and get you a new outfit for the charity if you'll let me," Kende said.

"You want me to go?" Asyl asked, fear gripping his stomach.

"Of course. It's only fair since you're helping," Kende replied and shrugged. "I may want to show you off too."

Chuckling, Asyl swirled the cloak over his shoulders. The weight settled firmly on his body, comforting him, and the hood was deep enough to protect him from the wind. It was so insanely soft, and Asyl held it shut, delighted to feel himself warming quickly. Kende seemed amused by his reaction, taking his own heavy cloak from Siora. Not entirely waiting for his Fated, Asyl darted out of the store, barely feeling how cold it was.

He was practically bouncing from the excitement of his new gifts. Of Kende thoroughly spoiling him in ways that weren't obtrusive. He was delighted that Kende respected his need to work and even encouraged it. The fact that Kende wanted to show him off made his cheeks flush. Kende didn't want to hide him. Didn't want to treat him as a secret lover. His friends, family, and society would know they were Fated.

"Ready?" Kende asked, laughing when he joined him on the sidewalk.

Asyl twirled and nodded before heading toward the market. After a few blocks, Kende reached out and twined their fingers together. His heart felt light as he shifted closer to his Fated and squeezed his hand in return. Now he really hoped that Naias would find her own Fated soon. If it made him so giddy and he was a Void, how much stronger would it be for a Craft Blessed?

Maybe that's why Kende was so intense about him.

Despite the rain, the walk was quite lovely. A lot of the late-autumn and early winter plants were blooming, rain dripping off their leaves and petals. Wind chimes rang from the porticos of the businesses they passed, and swirling designs marked the sidewalk, revealed only by the rain. Horse- and Craft-drawn carriages passed them in the street, rolling slow enough to not douse them with water.

Though, really, the best part about their walk was having Kende at his side.

The sound of chatter intensified the closer they got to the market. No matter what the weather was, it was always open, ready to sell to those who needed herbs, berries, fruits, and vegetables for one reason or another. Asyl glanced at Kende, who appeared delighted, taking in the busy market with a broad smile on his face. They wandered for a while, since the herbalist wouldn't close for hours yet. Kende seemed enchanted by his surroundings, slowly moving to each stall and making notes.

Asyl enjoyed watching his Fated take special interest in the booths, inspecting the fruits and vegetables. Probably for quality, or maybe seeing if he wanted his servants to purchase from the market rather than wherever he got his current foodstuffs. Kende returned his attention to Asyl and smiled, walking up to his side. When Asyl tilted his head up, Kende dropped a gentle kiss on his lips and took his hand again. He could get used to Kende's soft, small affections.

If anyone around recognized Kende, no one approached or hailed him. The two of them were left in relative peace until Asyl got to his herb supplier. They entered the storefront and went back to the greenhouse without stopping to chat with the lady behind the counter. She and Asyl knew each other well enough, she wasn't going to stop him.

It was warm inside the hothouse, and Asyl pushed the hood back, immediately flushed. Ignis heaters stood in each corner, keeping the encroaching winter chill away. Rows and rows of herbs grew in an almost chaotic manner, and the air was scented with a sweet perfume. This almost felt like a second home to him. The cracked windows that let out some of the heat allowed the sounds of the market and rain to drift inside.

The Harvester who was in charge of the large greenhouse rushed over from where she'd been kneeling and clasped Asyl's hands in her dirt-stained ones. She gave him a quick kiss on the cheek before letting him go. Kende stepped back, watching them with an amused smile, and followed the two deeper into the greenhouse.

"My dear Asyl," the woman said, "has there been a problem with your last shipment?"

"Not at all, Heina," Asyl replied with a brilliant smile. "Actually, I'd like to purchase a large amount of herbs for my healing potions. I've been requested to donate as many potions as I can to a charity that will support smaller clinics in the area."

"Oh, that's wonderful news," Heina cooed, turning to grab her ledger.

They bent over her stock list, and Asyl gave her the amounts he needed. Many bushels would need to be delivered, as Asyl wouldn't be able to carry the quantity home, even with Kende's help. While he could feel his Fated's curiosity, Kende politely stood back, instead inspecting all the medicinal herbs on sale. Because these potions were destined for charity, Heina tried working out a discount for Asyl.

"What is the full amount?" Kende finally asked, walking over after the two couldn't reach an agreement.

Asyl was refusing to let her give a discount, while the Harvester insisted that she did it for the overall health of Alenzon. The two were just stubborn enough that they'd talked in circles, neither of them wanting to give in.

"Three platinum," Heina replied, blinking owlishly at him.

Asyl winced even as Kende nodded. "For the amounts given, that makes quite a bit of sense. We want the finest quality potions for the charity, and Asyl makes the best in the city."

Heina slowly smiled even as Asyl flushed. She drew herself up and straightened her shoulders, obviously taking pride in that statement.

True, his potions wouldn't be as good quality as they were without her herbs, so he didn't begrudge her pride. Kende reached into his pocket and pulled out his coin purse.

Asyl glanced away, embarrassed that he wasn't able to pay for the components outright. Even though Kende had already said he'd cover the cost, it still felt odd to watch the man count out the coins needed. Heina took the money, regarding the two before slowly smiling.

"Lord Kende," she finally acknowledged him, "what's your interest here?"

"I'm hosting the charity," Kende said, looking at Asyl with one eyebrow raised, silently asking if he could tell her. Blushing, Asyl slowly nodded, and Kende's smile grew. "Asyl's also my Fated. But that's not known publicly or privately yet beyond a few people."

Heina's face brightened. She looked between the two of them, taking in Asyl's reddened cheeks and Kende's soft smile before breaking out into a massive grin and throwing her arms around Asyl's neck. Asyl laughed even as she squeezed the stuffing out of him, returning her embrace.

"Oh, my dear Asyl, I'm so happy for you," she squealed, hugging him tight to her. "It's such a delight being with your Fated. You'll be so happy, and I have no doubt that Lord Kende will take very good care of you."

"He will take great care of me as well, I'm sure," Kende said gently.

Catching his eye, Kende gave Asyl a sweet smile, and he could only duck his head in return. Heina pulled away, gripping his upper arms, and leaned in, pecking his cheek. One of her assistants called for the Harvester, and she bustled away, taking her ledger and the platinum with her. Asyl looked up at Kende, hating how warm his cheeks felt.

"You're really not ashamed that we're Fated," Asyl said.

"Why would I be ashamed? You're amazing," Kende replied, dropping his voice. "I have nothing but the utmost respect for you."

Kende cupped his face and tilted Asyl's head up, kissing him slowly. Sighing happily, Asyl melted into him, returning the languid kiss. Kende's arms slipped around his waist, holding him close until they parted and walked toward the front of the greenhouse. Asyl twined their fingers together, waving farewell at Heina as they left.

Excitement thrummed through him at the promise of a large delivery. He still needed to hit up the supplier he used for his glass bottles, wax, paper, and twine. Tugging on Kende's hand, Asyl took him to the two shops he needed to visit to put in his order. Both discussions mirrored the one he had with Heina, though Kende omitted their Fated status, solely based on the lack of privacy.

Carrying several balls of twine and a couple blocks of wax in a small basket he was borrowing from his supplier, Asyl headed back to his home with Kende by his side. While Kende had offered to carry the paper, Asyl ended up taking the delivery option. They needed to be embossed anyways, and that would take time. Besides, Asyl enjoyed being able to hold Kende's hand on the walk back.

Despite Siora and his carriage waiting for him when they returned, Kende helped Asyl put away the balls of twine and cut down the wax blocks into easily meltable chunks. They curled up on Asyl's dwindling boxed containers and exchanged small kisses as they just relaxed into each other. Once the store grew quiet, Asyl followed Kende into the carriage with Siora for a nice evening at his manor, blushing furiously at Naias's whistle.

THE NEXT two moonturns passed in a blur of activity. Asyl spent his days steadily brewing potions not only for his shop, but for the charity. Pretty much every evening he spent with Kende at his home. Sometimes the man would come get him himself with Siora and his Craft-powered carriage. Other days, he'd send Toemi with his horse-drawn carriage to pick Asyl up. On the days it didn't rain, Kende simply sent a note to Asyl, inviting him over.

Just the knowledge that Kende knew he liked to walk and wasn't insistent on ferrying him around constantly made him happy. Asyl would grab his heavy cloak that Kende gave him, swaddling himself in the thick fabric, nearly bouncing as he walked across the city. No way would Tillet have let Asyl walk so far under his own power at any point in their relationship. It was a nice show of trust and independence that Kende just gave him without a second thought.

Dinner was always a delightful meal, and Asyl was expanding his palate with exotic or expensive meats, spices, and fruits. He even got to try han-han meat, which Kende told him was a large, vibrant blue desert bird that Zothuan ranchers raised. It was gamey, yet the meat was moist and tender. Asyl immediately adored it, though he was adamant that Kende would not spend far too much on the meat. Having it at special events would be more than enough.

Many nights, the two ended up in the library doing research, though sometimes they sat in the back garden's gazebo to enjoy the freezing rain with warm mugs of coffee, tea, or cocoa. Kende had an Ignis heater in the middle of the structure to keep them warm. It was delightfully romantic, and Asyl found himself relaxing further with Kende and looking forward to seeing his Fated at the end of every night.

Even though Asyl knew Kende wanted him to spend the night, or better yet move in, Asyl refused outside a couple of times. He needed to know that Kende would respect his wishes, despite already knowing in his heart that he would. Not once did Asyl simply leave without being thoroughly kissed, though, generally leaving him with an ache in his gut and a tightness in his trousers.

How his body reacted to Kende was only growing stronger, to the point where Asyl nearly wanted to give in completely. He knew that Kende would gladly take him in and support him outside of his business. Kende would make sure he ate healthily and well, providing him with warm and nice clothes, and have him sleep in the comfiest bed he'd ever slept in. He wanted to sleep with his Fated every night and be able to cuddle into the man's warm body as he fell asleep. To be able to kiss him whenever he could.

It was such an ideal future that should have tempted Asyl to the point where he wouldn't be able to say no. Except he still refused to give in to the urge to let Kende fully into his life. To give the man power over him. Asyl knew Kende was nothing like Tillet. Hell, Kende was angry over what Tillet had done to him and paled whenever it was mentioned during a visit from Macik.

Much to Macik's growing frustration, he wasn't getting very far in tracking Asyl's assailant down. Tillet had seemingly gone to ground sometime during the last season, taking his Fated with him. Macik had tried to squeeze more information out of Asyl, if he knew about any bolt-holes that Tillet owned. None of them voiced their concerns that Tillet might have grabbed a new victim. Asyl really didn't want to think about it.

Knowing his Fated was angry with how he'd been treated in the past made his heart flutter and his resolve crack. Maybe after the charity, Asyl would bring up moving in with the man. He still wanted to run Enchanted Waters and brew there. Or maybe he'd come spend the whole weekend with Kende rather than keep moving back and forth. They'd work it out.

Eventually.

Kende took him to a tailor about a week before the charity. Despite Asyl's protests, Kende wanted him to attend, telling him that because of his massive donation, he deserved to be there. That he deserved to hear how much his potions were appreciated. Finally, Asyl had given in with a small smile, knowing he wasn't going to win this one. At least he'd gotten kissed with his surrender.

The tailor took a long time to get his measurements, and Asyl's skin crawled with how much the woman's male assistant had to touch him while he was in his smallclothes. Even with Kende there, Asyl had felt sick by the time he was able to dress himself. He left the clothes themselves up to his Fated, not wanting to be present for much longer and darting outside to hide with Toemi.

Afterward, he quickly retreated to his home, unceremoniously shutting Kende out. When Kende visited the next day, his Fated held him close, and Asyl explained how he'd felt disgusting while the assistant was touching him, despite him being completely chaste and professional. Kende just held him gently, kissing his neck and rocking him as Asyl worked through his panic and unresolved trauma.

Goddess, he wanted to be with his Fated every second of the day, but how could he when high society would look down on his panic? He couldn't bring Kende with him to every fitting whenever he needed something new. Asyl knew without a doubt that Kende would accompany him without complaint and would reassure him every time that he would stand by him. Even though they hadn't said anything yet, Asyl knew with his whole heart that Kende loved him.

At least he'd be spending the night before the charity with Kende. So they didn't have to plan a time to pick Asyl up, Kende liked to say. They both knew better. It was just an excuse to cuddle up in the man's bed and sleep together. At the end of the two moonturns, Asyl had gotten into the habit of sleeping without his shirt on as well, enjoying the feel of Kende's warm chest against his bare back and his breath on his neck.

Moving in sounded like bliss.

CHAPTER 9

"THANK YOU all for attending. Please enjoy the silent auction in the back with products provided by our local small businesses," Kende said, wrapping up his speech.

He dropped down from the platform, sighing in relief. As many times as he spoke in public, he swore he'd never get used to it. So far, the charity seemed like it was doing well. Every chair had sold, dinner had gone without a hitch, and now it was the entertainment and auction portion of the night. The dance floor opened up, and lords drew their ladies out to swing around.

Kende dodged the partiers, looking around for his Fated. There were so many people here that he couldn't get an accurate ping on him. As much as he had wanted to keep Asyl by his side the entire night, that wasn't fair to either of them. He hadn't introduced Asyl to the gentry, nor as his Fated, so subjecting his love to the rumor mill wasn't fair to him. Though, with how beautiful Maerie's clothes were, Kende barely wanted to look at anything but his Fated.

Asyl had been dressed in a soft blue long loose-sleeved shirt, the hem dropping down further in the back to cover his ass. A black sleeveless vest went over that, and he had on a pair of matching black form-fitting breeches. His ankle-high soft soled boots matched the blue of his shirt and were completely waterproof. His black hair had been braided back from his face, showing off his lovely bone structure and clear skin.

Once Asyl had realized what Kende's stylist was planning, he'd panicked, not wanting his Void status to be displayed so blatantly. In order to combat that, Kende had found and purchased a silver circlet that didn't leave an open spot for the Craft Mark. Instead, in the center of the forehead was an inlaid sapphire, and both of the temples had a teardrop dangling off a short chain. They were close enough to his shirt color that it complemented the outfit wonderfully.

When Kende found out Asyl's earlobes were pierced, he got a pair of silver earrings that were sapphire studs with a dangling teardrop fastened to the backing. They matched the circlet perfectly. Kende had convinced Asyl to forgo any sort of scarf to show off the corresponding necklace. It was a simple silver chain with a pair of round sapphires bracketing a third sapphire in a teardrop cut, settling in the hollow of his throat.

In short, Asyl was positively edible. His skin nearly glowed with a health that hadn't been present before two moonturns ago. The subtle makeup that Siora had applied to him only enhanced his natural beauty and how good his complexion was. Kende only wished they were out to the gentry so he could have Asyl on his arm and show him off.

Next to his Fated, Kende almost felt dull. Even dressed in his emerald-green waistcoat over a brown vest and beige shirt with matching brown breeches, he felt inadequate. He'd never been in the habit of wearing jewelry, so his hands and neck were unadorned. Briefly, Kende wondered if he should step up his mundane sense of style to at least try to emulate a bit of his Fated's beauty.

Truthfully, though, it was a delight to dress Asyl and watch his Fated's eyes widen in surprise and joy at how gorgeous he was. Kende still smiled at the memory of Asyl's gasp and how he'd slapped his hands over his mouth with tears gathering in his eyes when he got his first glimpse of tonight's outfit. Siora had scolded him not to cry and ruin his makeup. It didn't entirely work, and Asyl had laughed as a few tears fell to his cheeks.

Naias swung past Kende in the arms of Lord Harthan, a man that Kende preferred to not associate with. Her long-sleeved, high-topped deep blue frock swirled around her ankles, showing off her black slippers. She, too, was ornamented in sapphire jewelry, though her headpiece was meant to enhance her Aquan Craft Mark rather than hide the fact she didn't have one. Some sort of shimmering blush had been applied to her elfin cheeks, easily drawing the eye.

"Lord Kende," Naias said happily, slipping away from the man who had convinced her to dance to give him a curtsy.

"Lady Naias," Kende said, smiling at the woman and bowing at her in return. "I trust you're finding the evening enjoyable."

"Very much so," Naias replied, though her smile faded slightly. "Do you think you could convince Asyl to dance with me?"

"I think you'd have better luck with that, my lady," Kende replied, chuckling, "though I can try. Is everything all right?"

Naias glanced around, her smile dropping completely. Apparently she didn't see what was concerning her as she shook her head, her ruby-red lips parting back into a brilliant grin. Naias gathered the hem of her skirt and curtsied to Kende before returning her attention to the well-dressed man she'd ignored for the last minute.

Interesting.

Kende was aware of Lord Harthan and his reputation, and he watched the man critically for a minute. He didn't think he'd be a good match for Naias, Fated or not. It didn't seem like either of them felt the tug, and perhaps it was just Naias wanting to dance that she'd accepted his offer. Harthan was a notorious womanizer. Maybe he should leave a note with Siora or the front guards to make sure Naias didn't leave with him.

She was an adult, though. If she wanted to leave with Harthan, who was he to discourage her? Harthan gave Kende a stiff bow and held out his arm for Naias, then led her back onto the floor. He waited for a minute longer, trying to knock back the protective instinct that was slowly extending to Naias as well. Especially since she meant so much to Asyl.

Macik and Jaclyn were the next to intercept him. His sister wore a stunning red shimmering gown that in the right light, seemed to glow orange and yellow. It had a plunging neckline, almost to the point of indecency, and a slit up both sides to her hip. Well, if she wanted to wear it and Macik didn't protest, what was Kende to say to his big sister?

"Lady Jaclyn," Kende greeted her with a now forced smile. "Macik."

"Little brother," Jaclyn said, her voice tight as usual, "you've outdone yourself. The charity is wonderful, even if the food was a little subpar."

"So far there've been no complaints, so your opinion seems to be in the minority," Kende replied, dropping his smile completely. "How may I help?"

"Just wanted to thank you for putting this on for me," Jaclyn said. "I appreciate the effort you've made. Hopefully I won't need to dip too much into my own allowance to make up for what I promised the clinics."

"I think you'll be quite surprised with how much the silent auction will bring in," Kende said stonily. "Don't despair quite yet, sister. We will find out how much we brought in tomorrow once everything has been tallied."

"*Perhaps* we should trust Lord Kende as he trusts us to do our duties," Macik suggested calmly to his wife. "This is what he does for a living. He'd know best."

Jaclyn sighed. "Yes, you're right. The professional host would know the best way to maximize a charity event."

Kende bit down on the inside of his cheek and forced himself to smile faintly at his sister. Of course she wouldn't appreciate what he was doing, only see him as some frivolous child who didn't know what to do with his life.

Not that he'd admit she was right in any capacity.

There weren't a ton of options for a Healer. Going into alchemy or becoming a physician seemed to be his only choices. His Craft really was wasted on his charity work, but Kende held no desire to follow in the footsteps of his fellow Healers. Neither would he step on Asyl's toes and ask to help out in Enchanted Waters.

No, he'd stay a professional host, despite Jaclyn's obvious disgust with what he did. At least he still helped a lot of people with the money he raised. Macik didn't need to know Kende well to understand the insult his sister gave him. Nor did the man seem to need his Sympathetic Craft to know that her words stung, given the frown on his face.

"My dear," Macik said sweetly, "why don't we look over the silent auction items? The potions there are quite intriguing with their robust color, and I'd like to see who supplied them. It would be nice to have some on hand at the station. If one alchemist made all of them, maybe they could sell in bulk to the force."

"What a wonderful idea," Jaclyn said, her face brightening. "Perhaps we could talk to this Healer about making potions available to several different emergency personnel or jobs with a high injury rate."

The two walked toward the tables in the back, and Kende let out a low breath, closing his eyes briefly. Of course they'd assume Asyl was a Healer. Who else would brew potions and pursue alchemy? Obviously, it *had* to be a Healer. Kende was starting to really hate the expectations society placed on each Craft Blessed. Asyl deserved to be an alchemist as much as any Healer.

At least Macik seemed to appreciate what he'd done today. He should warn Asyl that he might have bulk order requests soon so he could let Heina know to expand her stock. While Kende knew Harvesters were able to grow specific plants on demand, he wasn't sure if the quality would be the same, or if it would be more expensive, as it used her Craft.

It didn't take long at all for him to be accosted again, and unfortunately it wasn't by his Asyl.

"Lord Ruyvn," a woman hailed, a smile on her haggard face.

Kende turned to see Lady Ilfa Seni walk up to him. She was dressed in a baby-blue slinky dress with an oversized black cardigan that fell to her hips. The color palette resembled Asyl so similarly that Kende briefly stopped to stare at her, surprised. He managed to smile the moment she got closer, hoping she didn't take his gawking for any sort of interest.

"Lady Seni," Kende said, bowing to her. Hers was one of the older families that demanded respect and prestige. The Seni line was very old money, with some ancestors that had married into the royal family. In some way, they were likely related, though Kende didn't want to think about that fact whatsoever. He wasn't a fan of Ilfa, though her husband was quite a bit more palatable. "How are you this evening?"

"Well enough, Lord Ruvyn," Ilfa said, curtsying. The motion drew his eye down toward her stomach, and Kende wondered if she was pregnant again. She and her husband had started having children later in life, and it seemed they weren't wasting any time filling their nursery with offspring. "I regret that I'm unable to sample the wine you've selected, with my condition."

So, she was. Kende bowed to her with a smile. "May I congratulate you on your next child. Have you any news on your newest addition?"

"Not much," Ilfa said proudly. "My Healer believes it's a girl."

"Well, little Lady Airol will be delighted to have a sister, I'm sure," Kende said, already glancing around to see if he could locate Lord Seni. Pregnant women were not his forte, especially when it was Lady Seni. "Is there anything I can help you with? Surely Lord Seni wouldn't leave you to attend alone."

"Oh no, he's here with the twins," Ilfa replied, waving her hand dismissively. "I had to slip away from him to come talk to you. I was wondering if you'd be interested in helping me set up a new charity."

"I already run and manage a great number of charities, Lady Seni," Kende said. "Perhaps I already have one established for the cause you have in mind."

"You don't," Ilfa said, her fake levity disappearing immediately. Her face dropped to a deadly expression that made Kende shudder. "I would like to organize a force that catalogs and incarcerates Voids with a specialized branch of law enforcement."

A cold jolt ran down Kende's spine, settling in his gut. What the fuck?

"I don't understand," Kende said, taking an unconscious step back.

Ilfa made a derisive noise. "Voids. You know them. They're the scum of our world, criminals, vagrants, and troublemakers. They need to be locked up if not eliminated for the safety of our Craft Blessed children. Surely your priest has spoken of these devils."

"I will *not* support that," Kende replied harshly. Not even if Asyl wasn't his Fated. There would be no way in any event he'd entertain the thought of what she was suggesting. "Voids are essential members of our society."

"By harming us, you mean? I suppose they make enough work for Healers and Sympathetics and might be good villains for Illusionist plays. But other than that, they're a drain on our resources. They can't contribute to our society in any wholesome way, so they must be eliminated," Ilfa said, her voice cold. "Hopefully the rumors of bloodless Voids being found in the slums is true. Less mouths to feed."

Goddess above, Kende thought, *she really believes she's serious.* Shaking his head, Kende stepped away from her, openly looking for Lord Seni now. There was no arguing with her. No way to tell her how much she was wrong without potentially risking Asyl's safety.

"I believe you need to see a mind Healer. Such thoughts are not becoming of a gentle lady, much less a mother. What if one of your children ends up becoming a Void?" Kende challenged.

An odd look crossed her face, and she ended up rolling her eyes. "Naturally, we'd take care of it."

That sent another chill down his spine.

"Mom!" a boy's voice cried out.

Ilfa was grabbed around the waist by an adolescent boy who couldn't be any older than twelve. He appeared to be close to his Awakening, and Kende feverishly hoped that he would be assigned a Craft. The boy's twin came over more sedately, next to Lord Seni. Arik and Alyn. Those were their names, if Kende was remembering correctly. All of their children's names started with the same letter, despite it probably causing quite a bit of confusion.

"Lord Seni," Kende said, forcing a calmness that he wasn't feeling.

"Lord Ruvyn," Lairne replied, grimacing slightly. "I hope my wife didn't cause you much stress."

"She was just telling me about her newest classification idea," Kende said.

Lairne winced and sighed. "My dear, I thought we discussed this. Leave the Void matter be."

Ilfa turned to him and sniffed, turning her nose up. "Something must be done. Crime is on the rise, and so is the population of Voids. Clearly, the problem presents itself."

"Correlation is not causation," one of the twins said. "Isn't that what we're taught? We can't assume one group is guilty without hard evidence."

Kende smiled faintly at the boy's rebuke, even as his mother snorted in quite an unladylike manner.

"Please go back to the table, my dear. Let me talk to Lord Ruvyn," Lairne said. Sighing heavily, Ilfa nodded and turned, running her hand absently over her stomach as she left. "I deeply apologize, my lord."

"It's all right. Please tell me she's not seriously looking into this venture. Criminalizing a portion of our population based on pure conjecture...." Kende trailed off, frowning.

"Unfortunately, she is," Lairne replied. "Ever since.... Well. She first got the idea nearly thirteen years ago, and it's gotten worse the older our twins have gotten."

Thirteen years? Kende glanced at the twins that hovered next to their father, and a horrible thought bloomed in the back of his mind. The shape of their eyes was familiar, and the way Arik smiled up at him. That was an expression he'd seen many times these last few moonturns.

"Alyn isn't your firstborn," Kende said.

Lairne's shoulders slumped. "No. We didn't know Ilfa was pregnant at the time our first son had his Awakening. It failed, and we disowned him the moment it became apparent he was a Void. It seems that triggered her war to make an extensive list and monitor all Voids. I don't know if she wants to find our son if he's still alive, or if it's more nefarious than that."

"Considering how she was talking about locking them up, I would suggest the latter," Kende said dryly.

That and her barely disguised glee at hearing that Voids might be dying in the streets. How would Asyl feel about such a measure? To be treated as a criminal, even though he worked to make the city a healthier place. Kende inhaled sharply, and Lairne winced at the sound.

"Your firstborn," Kende said, looking at Lord Seni with a critical eye. Yes, the resemblance was there if he looked objectively. Not to mention the name…. "It wouldn't happen to be Asyl, would it?"

Lairne's head snapped up, and he stared at Kende in shock for a moment before he nodded emphatically. "He is, yes. I regret making him leave every day. He would be a wonderful older brother, Void or no. Asyl was always such a kind soul and wanted nothing more than younger siblings."

He could tell him. Tell him about Enchanted Waters. It wouldn't take much in the end. Just tell him that Asyl was the one who made the potions so Lairne could look at the label and see if he wanted to go see his son. Kende worried that might be a misstep. If Asyl didn't want to see his family, Kende would be backing him into a corner. Plus, it might put Naias at risk, even though Kende believed Lairne truly was contrite about disowning Asyl.

But at the same time… he knew that Asyl was constantly pained about being disowned, thinking that he had no one who cared about him. It wasn't true, though Asyl had a hard time believing it. If he could get Asyl to see that his father truly cared about him, then maybe some of his old hurts would heal.

"Follow me," Kende said.

Lairne nodded and gestured for the twins to accompany him as well. Kende led him down the back hallway to the staging room. They'd used it to hold all the crates of potions that Asyl had made for the charity. Once the potions had been auctioned off, they'd be repacked with a slip stating where their new homes would be. Asyl had been so excited about how many he'd been able to make.

"Stay here. Let me track him down," Kende said.

The man simply nodded and took in a slow breath, leaning up against one of the crates. His two boys looked like they wanted to come with Kende, but they started investigating the back room instead. Before he left, one of the twins found a fairly rigid bit of hay and started smacking his brother with it. Kende smiled as he shut the door and consulted his bond.

Asyl was nervous, though not overwhelmingly so. He seemed fairly content, which put Kende at ease. At least his Fated wasn't overwhelmed.

Kende slipped back into the party and dodged the more intent guests who wanted his attention for one reason or another.

After a couple of minutes, he found his Fated by the open bar, sipping some sort of bubbling drink. It wasn't sparkling wine; he knew that much. Asyl didn't really imbibe alcohol, preferring juices and milk instead. Goddess above, he was stunning tonight.

"Lord Kende," Asyl said once he got close.

"Asyl," Kende replied, smiling, "you look ravishing as always."

Asyl snorted, though his was much lighter and more jovial than his mother's. "I've had to beat off several men and women with a stick tonight. Horny bunch you've got here."

"I can't say I blame them. I'm delighted you're coming home with me tonight," Kende said, lowering his voice.

A shiver ran through Asyl, and a discreet glance down showed Kende that his Fated was most definitely enjoying that idea. He'd noticed the shift in Asyl's attitude toward him during the last two moonturns. His Fated was more open to being touched and kissed. It gave him hope that Asyl would one day consent to make love.

"You're tormenting me," Asyl said with a sigh, "reminding me about that big, soft bed of yours while we have to stay here until the silent auction and revelry is done."

"Ah, but allow me to take your mind off tonight's pleasures by introducing you to someone. Rather, a reintroduction, but that's neither here nor there," Kende said and smiled.

He was quite enjoying their flirty conversation and was delighted that Asyl was playing along. It gave him hope that even if it wasn't tonight, he'd be able to seduce Asyl properly soon. He wanted to know how Asyl would call his name once he was inside of his Fated's smaller body. But that was a thought for later.

Resisting the urge to hold Asyl's hand, he led his love through the crowd to the back room where he'd stashed Lord Lairne.

"And why are you bringing me back here, good sir?" Asyl all but purred.

Kende blinked and grinned at his Fated, turning to hold his hand now they were alone. He walked backward, letting his eyes roam freely over Asyl's body. The man flushed as his breath caught and pupils dilated. Kende almost regretted what he was going to do now instead of pushing Asyl against the wall and kissing him blind.

Why not do both? Kende tugged Asyl to him, his Fated letting out a giggle, grinning up at him. He spun him around, cupped his face, and when Asyl tilted his head up, Kende kissed him. Asyl hummed happily, sliding his arms around Kende's waist, pushing up into him, joy radiating from him in waves. His Fated broke the kiss when he was backed against the door and smiled at him.

"Turn the handle," Kende murmured.

Asyl shivered and let go of Kende long enough to unlatch the door. They separated just as one of the twins smacked the other hard enough to let out a yelp. Asyl's face dropped, and the delight he'd just been exuding vanished. He turned to see who was in the room, carefully taking a few more steps in. Kende followed, shutting the door and standing off to the side.

Alyn saw him first, sucking on the back of his hand where Kende could see the outlines of a nasty welt appearing. His eyes lit up on seeing Asyl, and he grinned.

"Oh," Alyn said, blinking a few times. "He looks so much like Airol."

Lairne looked up from the paper he'd found somewhere in the room, and his gaze softened, seeing his true firstborn son. Asyl stood so still, Kende wasn't sure he was still breathing. He moved forward and gently rested his hand on the small of Asyl's back, ushering him forward. His Fated resisted slightly, his eyes never leaving Lord Seni.

What worried Kende the most was not being able to feel his Fated's emotions. Asyl refused to let Kende get him any closer than halfway across the room. The twins approached eagerly, both smiling at their brother. Asyl barely glanced at them, his focus entirely on the man before him. Arik looked up at Kende, appearing confused.

"Asyl," Kende murmured. He gripped his Fated's shoulder gently. "Sweet?"

"Lord Seni," Asyl said flatly.

"Son," Lairne replied, his voice soft.

"You don't get to call me that!" Asyl snapped.

White-hot rage exploded from Asyl, and Kende nearly staggered back from the sheer intensity of it. Where his Fated had been numb moments ago, now Kende was nearly overwhelmed by the emotions coming through his bond. Lairne looked pained, and he took one step closer to Asyl.

"We never should have abandoned you," Lairne said. "I can't imagine how scared you were."

"No, you couldn't," Asyl snarled at him.

The twins backed away then, Alyn observing quietly. Arik clung to his twin, his eyes wide as he watched the confrontation.

"I…." Lairne trailed off, his hands coming up and tugging his vest down. At least Kende knew where Asyl's nervous habit came from. He wouldn't point that out to his Fated, though. Not right now. "I'm so sorry."

"Sorry doesn't erase the past," Asyl spat. "You didn't care for the last thirteen years, so why do you suddenly care *now*? Why are you trying to get back into my life? Is it because I've done something that benefits others?"

Lairne blanched. "No! I just found out that you're still alive. I didn't know you were here."

"Well now you've seen me, so now you can pretend I don't exist anymore," Asyl said.

"That's the last thing I want to do!" Lairne exclaimed. "Come back home, Asyl. You've got siblings that I know you'd be wonderful with."

"I'm not some toy you can take out of the basement when it's convenient for you to use! I have my own life, my own responsibilities, and my own community to take care of," Asyl shouted. "Why would I *ever* go back to the place that ruined my childhood?"

Lairne inhaled sharply and blinked a few times. He rubbed his thumb with his other hand, and he took another step forward. Asyl scrambled back, much like how he'd done when Kende had first started to court him. The thought saddened him.

"What is it that you do?" Lairne asked softly. "I bet you've got a lot of friends in your community. You were always so social."

Asyl sneered at him. "Stop acting as if I mean anything to you. It's embarrassing."

"You do mean something to me!" Lairne protested. "You're my son, and that will never change. We should have never punished you by making you leave."

He took the couple of steps that he needed to grasp Asyl's shoulders. Neither Lairne nor Kende expected Asyl to shove the man away from him.

"*Punished?*" Asyl shouted. "Being punished for not being Blessed would have been sent to my room without being able to have my Awakening cake. Being *punished* would have been being spanked for whatever reason the goddess chose to not bless me. Being disowned isn't a punishment for something I had absolutely no control over since my birth."

"Disowning you was a lapse of judgment—"

"You have no idea what your lapse of judgment gave me," Asyl laughed, though it rang hollow and flat. "I learned how to please a man for money on my third day so I could eat and was raped on the tenth. Do you know what it's like being taken dry and unprepared? No, of course you don't. Because you had parents that loved you unconditionally, no matter what your fucking Craft was.

"I was unlucky to be born to ones whose love depended on what I was blessed by, and I suffered because of it. Not only did your lapse of judgment cost me my childhood, but it also opened me up to a world of abuse."

Lairne's face had gone completely white with a slight green tint, his eyes wide. His hand came up as if to pull Asyl into a hug even as his throat worked to keep his dinner down.

"Is there anything I can do?" Lairne asked softly. "Are you safe now? How can I help?"

"You can help by staying out of my life," Asyl snapped.

With that, Asyl spun toward the front door, his face set in a hard expression, though Kende could see the pain behind his eyes clear as day. Lairne stood there, face aghast as if he'd been slapped. Perhaps metaphorically, he had been. The twins were looking between their brother and dad, clearly upset, but not sure what to do.

Kende stepped in front of his Fated, reaching out and drawing the man close to him. Asyl didn't relax in his arms like he usually did. Instead, he stayed rigid, the overwhelming rage simmering down to a dull roar. His sweetheart was still so angry. Asyl slowly looked at him and swallowed hard before glaring at Kende.

"How dare you," Asyl hissed. "You know how badly my parents hurt me."

"I know," Kende replied softly. "I thought maybe it would be helpful to get some closure. You've always wanted siblings and a family."

"You were my family," Asyl said slowly, "you and Naias. You were all I needed."

Kende's heart plummeted when he understood the subtle meaning behind his Fated's choice of words. He tightened his grip on Asyl, shaking his head.

"I am your Fated, not your family," Kende said gently.

"A real Fated wouldn't have ambushed me like this," Asyl snapped. "Get the fuck out of my way."

"Asyl," Kende pleaded.

"Go away!" Asyl shouted at him. "I don't want to see your traitorous face again! I should have known this was all too good to be true. If I'd known that not only one but *two* Craft Blessed wanted to control my life, I would have jumped without a thought."

Pain exploded through Kende's chest, and his grip went lax as he stared down in shock at his Fated. Asyl shoved him away and stormed out of the room. He felt like he couldn't breathe. Kende wondered if this was what people meant by saying their heart was torn in two. He slumped against the wall and stared down at his shoes.

What had he just done?

"Dad," Arik asked weakly, "are you going to disown us if we're Voids?"

"No," Lairne said quickly, shaking his head. He dropped to his knees and pulled his sons into a tight hug. "I'll never let any of you go."

"You let Asyl go," Alyn said flatly, "so why should we expect any better?"

"I won't make the same mistake twice," Lairne told him.

"But Mother hates Voids!" Arik said, tears gathering in his eyes. "She'll lock us up!"

"If your Awakening fails, we'll deal with it then. Right now, we focus on what we have," Lairne coaxed them, shakily getting to his feet.

"If you're a Void, come to my manor," Kende found himself saying. He knew Asyl wasn't anywhere near him anymore, his Fated's anger still burning bright. "Asyl may not have the funds or space to take care of you, but I can. Actually, tell all the kids in your classes that if they're disowned, they can come to me. It's the least I can do."

Now that he'd potentially just lost Asyl completely.

"Kende?" Naias's voice called out.

Kende cursed under his breath and closed his eyes. He didn't have the energy for the conversation that was about to come. Somehow he managed to stand up straight as Naias came into the room. Her eyes were filled with worry as she entered, though her blue eyes hardened the moment she saw Lairne.

"You didn't," she snarled. With a swish of her skirts, Naias slammed the door shut and rounded on Kende. "How *dare* you! How could you do this to him? No wonder he's distraught!"

"I… I thought perhaps it would help," Kende said softly. "I know how lonely Asyl gets."

"That was not your choice to make!" Naias snapped. "You weren't there when he escaped Tillet. You didn't hear his wretched screams and sobbing through his nightmares. How hard he worked to pull himself together and make something of himself! I was there for all of it. Asyl doesn't need the man who threw him onto the streets for some stupid religious belief in his life!"

Kende swallowed hard, the pain throbbing deeper in his bones, bringing tears to his eyes. It hurt so bad, and underneath the anger he felt from his Fated, he could feel his agony. He'd hurt Asyl. Sure, it had started with good intentions, but it had backfired to epic proportions. He raised a hand to rub at his chest, expecting to feel physical pain, as if he had a bruise.

"What can I do?" Kende asked through numb lips.

"Whatever he told you, abide by it," Naias said coldly. "I can guess what it is. I don't ever want to see you in Enchanted Waters again." He didn't see her hand swing back, and his head rocked with the force of her slap. A sharp coppery taste flooded his mouth. "Now I have to go pick up the pieces again because you idiots can't stop seeing him as anything but a helpless toy."

"Little Nai," Lairne intervened gently. Naias's back went rigid, and her flinty gaze focused on the man as she slowly turned in place. "You've been taking care of him?"

"Only for the last four years," Naias spat. "Take that information however you want."

She spun on her heel and marched out of the room, slamming the door behind her. As if her departure cut his strings, Kende fell back against the wall again and slid down. He tried desperately to consult his bond with Asyl but could only feel the distant pain. With a shock of horror, Kende realized he couldn't tell where his Fated was anymore.

He pressed his face into his hands as he tried to choke back his tears.

He'd lost Asyl.

CHAPTER 10

ASYL LAY on his bed above Enchanted Waters, curled into a tight ball on his side. He'd thrown up earlier today, and now his stomach was cramping. That was a familiar feeling. Asyl had gone hungry on the streets many times before he'd gotten good enough to reliably bring in enough money. Then when Tillet decided he hadn't performed well enough, or if he just got too drunk to remember, the man wouldn't feed him.

Right now, the tearing pain was welcome. It was better than the sharp stabbing he felt all over. He'd been in agony leaving Kende behind and running home in the heavy rains. Each step had made it worse, his whole body fighting against him running away from his Fated. No, not his Fated. From Kende. Lord Kende. When Asyl had gotten home, he'd promptly vomited everything he'd eaten at the charity and collapsed into bed, feverish and sweaty.

Naias had come home sometime later, frustratingly completely dry. She'd pulled the moisture from his body and clothes since she couldn't convince Asyl to head down the stairs and sit in front of the fire. Asyl had just wanted her to leave. He'd ignored her utterly as he felt his whole body go numb and all coherent thoughts escaped him.

That night, he'd dreamed of Tillet again. Naias must have made up the tiny spare bedroom and sat up there, as she rushed to Asyl's side within seconds after his screaming began. He could barely look up at her and buried his face in his pillow. Asyl had forced himself to relax, pretending he'd fallen back asleep until she left him.

He pretended to be asleep every time she came to check in on him. Naias brought him food that he never touched, and he even chucked a bowl of stew out the window when it made his stomach roll. At least the bowl had been wood and not fine china. Much cheaper. A minute later, the glass vase of roses followed the bowl. The delicate glass shattered with a soul-crushing ring, the roses scattering across the courtyard.

Kende had a bouquet delivered every Monday after he spent the weekend with him for the last two moonturns. Asyl always put the freshest one on his worktable, moving the previous one to the front desk, and the one on the front desk to his nightstand. He'd have to ask Naias to throw out the other bouquets when he saw her next.

Despite telling himself he wasn't going to, that he needed a clean break from Lord Kende, Asyl consulted the bond that he was so used to feeling.

It leapt at his touch like a wilted flower desperate for a hot summer's rain. Even though it had only been a few days, their connection had been nearly starved. Asyl could only get an impression of intense loneliness before he let the bond go. He'd be fine, Asyl told himself. The man had plenty of family, servants, and friends. There wasn't any reason for him to feel alone.

Asyl knew Naias was worried out of her mind for him. He heard it in her voice when she begged for him to eat. To get up. To move. To please, do something! Asyl couldn't bring himself to care. The pain tore at every part of him, though the worst was over his heart. It felt as if his ribs were being cracked open and someone was slashing his heart apart.

What had been worse was when he'd packed up every piece of clothing and jewelry Lord Kende had given him. Everything the man had done to dote on him. Asyl had sobbed the entire time, unable to stop, his whole body fighting against him as he threw each piece to the floor. He'd had to. There was nothing he wanted less than Lord Kende feeling as if Asyl owed him something.

Asyl had left a note on top telling Naias to return them to the man and have him arrange for Keyna to come by and remove the Plates. He'd barely had the energy to get unsteadily to his feet, throw back the covers, and collapse into bed. The next time he surfaced, a new bowl of stew was on his nightstand, the old untouched one taken away, and the pile had vanished.

Someone new was coming into his bedroom. Only Naias came up here. Lord Kende did, once. But that was moonturns ago now. Besides, that wasn't how he walked. The gait was completely different. Asyl didn't bother rolling over to look at who was approaching him. If it was someone sent to kill him, he'd welcome it. The agony wasn't worth living anymore. Besides, maybe it would hurt Naias for a while, but she'd finally be rid of a huge burden.

The bed dipped by his legs. Asyl had curled up into a ball on his increasingly uncomfortable mattress. He kept his eyes shut, unable to stop the tremble that coursed through him with the next wave of pain that blacked out conscious thought. A small moan escaped him, tears gathering in the corners of his eyes. When would this end?

"Goddess, you really are one stubborn fuck, aren't you?" a harsh voice asked.

Asyl blinked a few times, trying to clear his vision. He rolled onto his back to see Rojir sitting at the foot of his bed. The man who'd taken Asyl under his wing when he'd been thrown out. Rojir had tried to protect him from the ugliness of the streets, but it was obvious to him that he'd needed to help provide for the community. Rojir had taught him how to please another man and how to be safe about it. He'd been Asyl's closest friend while he'd been on the streets.

"Rojir," Asyl whispered.

"Yeah, kiddo," Rojir said with a sigh.

He reached out, clapping Asyl's thigh. The man looked even more weary than when Asyl had last seen him about a moonturn ago, bringing news about another one of the urchins he took care of going missing. His long brown hair was liberally streaked with gray and fell down to his mid-back in an untamed mane. Was there more gray in his hair now? No, it had to be the lighting.

"You've been running Lady Naias ragged," Rojir teased him lightly. "Poor girl is about at her wit's end. Says it's worse than when you got away from Tillet."

"At least I didn't think he loved me," Asyl muttered.

Asyl curled back up on his side again, ignoring his mentor shaking his head with a disapproving frown.

"You know better than that," Rojir said firmly. "I saw how the lordling looked at you. How excited he was when he'd come through the store on his way to just see you. He got you thoughtful gifts and didn't push you to abandon everything you have to move in with him."

"Easy," Asyl muttered.

"For some, sure. I got the impression he respected what you do here," Rojir said.

"You got that just from seeing him a few times?" Asyl challenged.

"It was more than a few," Rojir rebuked. He reached up and pinched Asyl's ear, making him squeak and clap his hand over it. "I saw you two at the market. Walking around the deserted areas where our community is. You pointing out landmarks. How he'd listen and smile every time he looked at you. Everyone noticed it. We all noticed how happy he makes you."

"Made me," Asyl protested.

"Do you remember the first time I got you drunk?" Rojir asked.

Asyl blinked, looking at him, confused about the segue. How could he forget? He'd been starving, unable to get any customers for the last couple of days. Asyl had stubbornly refused food from Rojir or his then-boyfriend, Mato. He wanted to contribute. But all the men he'd managed to draw in had either refused him because he was too young, or they had recognized him as Lairne's disgrace. Even then, when he'd been a filthy homeless Void, they hadn't wanted to take advantage of his situation for five minutes of pleasure.

Yet none of them had lifted a hand to help. They'd just left, shaking their heads with faces pale. Asyl had gotten desperate then, not wanting to acquiesce to Mato's insistence to eat what they shared. He'd wandered further than he should. Far away from safety and the other Void sex workers who could keep an eye on him. Perhaps one of them saw him leaving and had run to Rojir or Mato. It hadn't been quick enough.

Asyl had found a man willing to pay him more than the going rate. Eager to bring in a couple of silver to help Rojir, Asyl hadn't thought about the rules he'd been taught. He'd been preoccupied with getting something warm to eat and maybe bringing home some fresh bread for once. The man hadn't been considerate, and in the end wasn't satisfied with what Asyl had been willing to give. Asyl could still remember how much it hurt, having his hair pulled as he was yanked off the man and thrown down to the rough cobblestone.

How he'd screamed and cried through the man taking his pleasure without regard to Asyl's comfort. As if that hadn't been bad enough, the man had decreed that he hadn't been satisfied, despite clearly having enjoyed what he'd done, and had turned away with his money to leave Asyl bleeding in the alley. That's when Rojir had arrived, shoved the man around, and gotten a gold instead of a couple silver.

Damages, Rojir called it. Then Rojir had gently replaced Asyl's clothes, despite him jerking away and crying, half out of his mind with pain and fear. He'd picked him up and carried him back to the safety of familiar streets and a tight community. Asyl had been left with Mato, who spent the entire hour Rojir was gone alternating between chastising Asyl for being stupid and being glad that he'd not been hurt worse. At the time, Asyl couldn't imagine how much worse it could have been.

Rojir had returned with bandages, a numbing salve that barely worked, and a bottle of gin. Between the two, they got Asyl to eat a little bit while Rojir attended to his wounds. Then the man had given Asyl his first swig of alcohol. It had been awful, his throat burning, and he'd nearly retched everything up. The second mouthful had been easier, and before Asyl knew it, everything was spinning and nothing really hurt anymore.

Asyl didn't really remember much after that. He had vague impressions of him crying even more, and Rojir cradling him close on the nest of blankets they had in an abandoned house that they called home. The next day, he'd barely been able to open his eyes, his head hurt so bad. Mato had sat with him for the next few days while he healed, claiming that the gold Rojir got from the man could stretch long enough for the two of them to not work for a couple of days.

"Yes," Asyl finally said.

"You want to know the main thing you said while you were crying in my arms?" Rojir prompted.

Asyl rolled his eyes, shifting to lie on his back and regard the older man carefully. "What?"

"You wanted your dad," Rojir said.

Frowning, Asyl shook his head. "Why does that matter?"

"Because deep down, the thing you wanted most was to go home," Rojir said.

Asyl snorted.

"Of course I did. I was a lordling and used to the comforts of money who got thrown out. Why wouldn't I want to go back?" Asyl asked.

"But you never once cried about missing comforts," Rojir replied. "You jabbered on about how much you missed your father. Reading with him, learning the family business, running around the backyard and having fun when he used his Craft to fly you off the earth for a little bit. Not once did you talk about soft clothes, warm meals, or having someone to take care of you. You simply wanted your dad."

"That's changed," Asyl said flatly.

"Has it?" Rojir asked. "I went to him, you know. The next morning, when I left Mato to watch you. I did my best to clean up as much as possible and went to the Seni house. After I told him what happened, he seemed distraught and admitted that he knew you were selling your body. That he was ashamed. Not of you, but of himself. That his actions had driven you to whoring. You really want to know how Mato and I could take care of you without worrying about money?"

"He gave you some," Asyl muttered.

"See, you're still smart," Rojir teased, smiling at him. "Yes. He gave me a small pouch of gold and asked that I not tell you. He wasn't sure how to handle what had happened, and how to bring you home. Though I will say, it was on his mind."

"Then why didn't he come for me?" Asyl asked quietly.

"Lady Ilfa," Rojir said simply, shrugging. "I'd gone back to Lord Seni about a moonturn later demanding the exact same answer. That's when I saw your mother's belly and the vile rhetoric she was spouting off about Voids when she caught sight of me. I knew then that you'd never be able to go home. Lord Seni provided me with some more coin and did again every moonturn until you were kidnapped."

"Why didn't you ever tell me?" Asyl asked.

"It would have just hurt you," Rojir said, shrugging. "Your father loved you and hated the fact that you were on the streets, yet he couldn't figure out a way to bring you back without his wife's rage. He entrusted your safety to me, and I failed when you disappeared."

"I was going to jump off Rose Bridge," Asyl said.

Rojir closed his eyes and squeezed Asyl's thigh tight for a minute. He sniffed, looking down at his lap, and nodded, accepting the truth of his words, and the truth that it hadn't happened. Therefore, there was no use dwelling on it. Asyl supposed he'd never told any of his street family what he'd been planning even after he came back. They would have stopped him.

"He tried looking for you when I told him you'd been gone for a few days. He'd tried getting a few of the police interested in finding you, but no amount of gold would persuade them. I was there with him at the station, trying to convince them that you wouldn't just wander off. They didn't care," Rojir said.

"That's why I never went to them about what Tillet did," Asyl muttered. He shook his head and looked up at him. "Kende doesn't understand it."

"You are very much like your father," Rojir said after a long moment.

"How so?" Asyl asked.

"What business has the Seni line been in charge of for about as long as Alenzon has been around?" Rojir asked.

"Produce imports," Asyl said, frowning now.

"Providing nourishment to his community. And once you were healthy, what did you do? Open an apothecary right near your old haunts and sell your hard work for a pittance. Just to make sure we're healthy. You could have sold to the middle class to make sure their children are healthy working out of Lady Naias's home, but you didn't. You came back to us," Rojir said.

"Why would I help those that threw me out?" Asyl asked. "You all are the ones who took care of me when I needed it the most."

"And then you stagnated," Rojir said.

Asyl pushed himself into a sitting position and glared at Rojir, pain radiating through him once he started moving. Even still, he sat on the bed, leaning against the wall, and scowled at his old mentor.

"If I knew the law would have been on my side, I would have adopted you," Rojir said gently. "Your father provided enough money at one point that if I'd saved all of it, I probably could have bribed enough officials to get the paperwork signed. Perhaps that would have been Lord Seni's excuse to bring you home, but at that point, I don't think it would have helped you."

Adopted him? Asyl felt tears burning in his eyes, and he scrubbed at his face, trying to not get too emotional about the thought. Rojir had wanted him enough that he'd considered the option. He sniffed and pulled in a gasping breath before he was able to get ahold of his emotions again.

"I love you so much," Rojir said, "but once you were able to breathe, you sat down and stopped moving. Changing nothing, just existing rather than living."

Asyl said nothing, staring at the bedspread between him and where Rojir sat. He hunched his shoulders and wrapped his arms around his legs, resting his cheek on his knees.

"What's your point?" Asyl asked.

"You're scared of committing to Lord Kende," Rojir said, as if it was that simple. "So you're using every excuse you can think of to push him away."

"Did Nai tell you what he did?"

"That he got you and your father in the same room?" Rojir asked, grinning. "She was angry about it too at first, but honestly I probably would have done the same thing Lord Kende did."

Asyl glared at him. "He should have asked me if I wanted to go."

Rojir laughed. "You never would have said yes! He saw an opportunity to reunite you with your family and took it. All he knew was how much you missed your family and how much you wanted siblings, and he wanted to try and help."

"I can't be with someone who wants to control me," Asyl spat.

"Is that what you think he did? Wanted to control you?" Rojir asked, sighing. "You know better than that. If he was going to control you, he would have gotten you to move in with him moonturns ago, had you stop brewing, and wouldn't have let you leave the charity. You're just scared."

"And you're a jerk," Asyl retorted. "Kende fucked up, and I can't trust him."

Rojir just smiled, unperturbed by Asyl's near open hostility.

"Not every major change in your life needs to be something awful. Surely being an alchemist isn't too bad. Lord Kende adores you. He's not Tillet," Rojir said. A shudder rippled through Asyl, and he tried not to retch as his stomach cramped. Rojir's face fell, and he reached out, pulling Asyl into his arms and lap, hugging him tight. Asyl shivered from the cold, wiggling to get closer to try and absorb some body heat from Rojir. "He hasn't given up on you."

"How do you know?" Asyl asked, frowning.

"That pain you're feeling. It's because you've rejected the bond. Rejected the one person that the goddess made just for you. If Lord Kende had rejected you as well, then the break would have been clean. As it is, since you were the one to push him away, you're taking the brunt of the pain," Rojir said.

"Will it go away?" Asyl asked wearily.

"No. Not unless you go to him, or he rejects you," Rojir said, "and I doubt he'll give up on you."

Asyl pressed his face into Rojir's shoulder and sniffed, feeling the overwhelming urge to cry again. He was in so much pain, he wanted to have any sort of relief he could.

"Is he hurting?" Asyl asked.

"Yes," Rojir said, sighing heavily, "nowhere near as bad as you are, though."

"How do you know all of this?" Asyl asked.

"My aunt rejected her Fated. She was married to the man of her dreams and didn't want anything to do with her Fated. It took him about a month to understand that she was happy and accept that she wasn't going to divorce her husband. It's incredibly rare for a Fated couple to not work out, but it does happen," Rojir explained.

"If I go to him… if I accept him. Then I won't be here anymore. I wanted to move in with him before and… I don't know what'll happen to Enchanted Waters," Asyl said.

"You need to stop worrying about us and do what makes you happy," Rojir said gently. "We'll survive. Besides, we can always make the trek to you if we're that desperate. Raise your prices and start living your life."

The man pressed his lips to Asyl's bare forehead and squeezed him tight.

"I miss him," Asyl finally admitted, his voice cracking.

"Then go. Eat some of the tasty stew Lady Naias has made to get your strength back, and then go see him," Rojir said.

Asyl sniffed a few times and nodded. He wasn't strong enough to hold the heavy wooden bowl, and Rojir assisted without a single complaint. Asyl almost felt like he was thirteen again, cocooned in Rojir's safe lap, protected from the rest of the world. The warmth eased his pain some as Asyl thought about how he'd get to Ruvyn manor.

There wasn't really an easy way to get Toemi to come pick him up. Sure, he could probably pay a messenger to run to Ruvyn manor, but it wasn't guaranteed that Toemi was even there. Asyl regretted having Naias return the gifts. The rain had reflected his mood the last few days and hadn't let up on the deluge. Since Kende had gotten him that really nice cloak, Asyl hadn't bothered replacing the one that he'd lost.

After Asyl sat in Rojir's lap for a while after finishing the stew, the man nudged him.

"Well?" the man prompted.

"I don't have a good cloak anymore. I had Nai return everything Kende bought me," Asyl admitted, blushing.

"As if," Naias said, stomping up the stairs. Asyl jumped and scrabbled for the sheets, covering his nudity. He hadn't bothered with clothing for the last couple of days since he hadn't really intended to go anywhere. Naias snorted inelegantly at his haste and shook her head. "Please, I've seen your bare ass and penis. Who do you think kept you clean four years ago?"

Asyl flushed. "Naias...."

His best friend vanished from the open doorway and rustled with something in the guest room. A minute later, she came back with a familiar-looking bundle of clothing. Asyl gaped at her when she tossed them at him, frantically grabbing them before they fell to the floor.

"Obviously, I didn't send them back. I realized what we said was a mistake when you went a whole day in complete agony," Naias said, her face falling, "but I didn't want to write to Lord Kende without you knowing and risk upsetting you more. So I wrote to Rojir."

Asyl picked out the blue shirt he'd worn at the charity event and a pair of fawn-colored breeches. His shoes were across the room, and he tossed the heavy cloak Kende gave him onto his pillows. He shrugged into the shirt, realizing that he'd already lost some weight these last three days.

"Now, after you're done kissing and making up," Naias said, folding her arms across her chest and glowering at him, "you need to get your happy ass back here and start working on all of the private orders we've been getting for your health potions. Apparently someone cut their hand fairly badly while you and Lord Kende were indisposed, and since high society isn't fond of Healers doing anything but sitting in their clinics...."

She trailed off and rolled her eyes. Asyl could see past the bravado she was putting on. Her eyes were rimmed with a red tinge, and she was sniffing a little bit. He grabbed Rojir's shoulder and climbed out of bed, waiting until he was sure his legs wouldn't fold out from under him before letting go.

"So they cracked open a potion and drank it?" Asyl prompted.

"And were shocked it took so little, tasted good, and was incredibly potent," Naias finished, nodding with a smile. "So now, of course, the fire brigade, police stations, larger clinics, and private Healers want their pound of flesh. You should see the stack of cards for your orders."

"It's quite impressive," Rojir said with a laugh.

Asyl turned his head to regard his... his second father. He overbalanced, standing on one leg as he wiggled on the breeches and began to pitch forward. Rojir's hand snapped out, and he grabbed Asyl's elbow, steadying him.

"How much did we raise?" Asyl asked softly.

Naias turned to his dresser, where a letter was sitting on the top. The seal had been cracked already, as Naias easily opened the envelope. She drew herself up to her full height and daintily cleared her throat, making Asyl laugh.

"All four hundred potions, retail price of one gold, were auctioned to raise over a thousand for twenty different clinics," she pronounced.

"It seems even if you never go back to Lord Kende, your life has changed," Rojir observed. "Why not take the risk and go be with your Fated?"

Asyl stared down at his bare feet, silently lacing up the placket over his crotch. A thousand gold, or ten platinum when converted, was a small fortune. His potions had sold at almost three times what they were worth. That was… humbling in a way. And quite exciting, if he acknowledged the zing that curled through his stomach.

None of them spoke until he was done, and Asyl ran his hand over one soft sleeve of the blue shirt he was wearing.

"I will," he finally said, "if he'll take me back."

"He will," Rojir said gently.

Not responding to him, Asyl pulled on a pair of thick woolen socks and stamped his feet into his boots. He grabbed his heavy cloak and swirled it onto his shoulders. Taking a deep breath, Asyl turned to regard his best friend and dad. He held out his arms to them.

"Well?" he asked.

"He didn't put on any smallclothes," Naias said offhandedly to Rojir, though her eyes didn't leave Asyl.

"Easy access," Rojir replied, grinning.

Asyl gagged. "I don't ever want to hear you two talk about Kende's designs on my sex again."

The other two burst out laughing, and Asyl rolled his eyes before smiling at them. He walked over to Naias and gave her a big hug. She squeezed him tight, humming happily. Rojir got to his feet and put a hand on Asyl's shoulder.

"Go get your Fated, son," Rojir said calmly. "Remember to keep an eye on your surroundings when you go across town."

"Thanks, Dad," Asyl replied, smiling up at him.

With that, he turned and trotted out of his room, determined to see Kende today and finally stop fighting their bond. Somehow, their bond must have realized his intent. While his chest still ached, it was nowhere near as bad as it used to be. Asyl flipped the hood of his cloak up and set out at a brisk pace. It would take about two hours, so he had plenty of time to think.

Think about what he truly wanted out of his bond with Kende. He had to admit to himself that yes, they were Fated. Asyl had just been too scared to allow himself to acknowledge that. Too scared that Kende might end up like Tillet. That he'd be prevented from brewing and running Enchanted Waters. That he'd have to stop talking to Naias and Rojir.

But Kende had never once shown the signs that he would isolate Asyl and abuse him. Quite the opposite. Asyl had no idea how expensive the Plates were that had been permanently installed in his workroom, but they were obviously new. Kende had encouraged Asyl's curiosity and had even engaged with him when he'd started poring through his medical tomes... medical tomes that Asyl should never have had access to.

Kende had never once pressured him to move in. Never once pressured him for something so suggestive as a kiss. He often asked for permission or made his intent known but let Asyl close the last inch as a sign of his consent. Even when they were out, walking somewhere rather than taking the carriage, Kende still wanted to hold his hand.

Logically, Asyl knew he had absolutely nothing to fear.

Comparatively, Kende was nothing like Tillet.

Yet his mind still shied away from committing. Even now, he felt a bit of trepidation in the hollow of his gut telling him to run. Only the pain in his chest urged him to walk a little faster toward his Fated. He wanted this, he told the reluctant part of his brain. Kende would love him with his whole heart, and Asyl would never be alone again.

He wanted to share his life with Kende. Help out with any other charities that Kende hosted. Conduct research at night, debating what the medical texts were trying to say and whether his theories would work. He wanted to sleep in the same bed at night, being held and knowing he would be safe. Even if Kende's prick did get the wrong idea from time to time, though that didn't seem like that much of a huge deal anymore.

Gravel crunched underneath Asyl's feet, pulling him from his thoughts. He looked up to see that he'd started up the pathway to Ruvyn manor. The pain in his chest was almost gone. He was so close to his

Fated. To Kende. Excitement pulled at him, and Asyl lengthened his stride. Not long now! He'd see Kende in just a couple of minutes.

Breathing a little heavy, Asyl rapped on the front door. He started bouncing on his toes, suddenly incredibly impatient. His happiness vanished the moment Birgir opened the door, scowling at him. He inhaled sharply and offered the grumpy steward a weak smile.

"I'm here to see Kende," Asyl said.

Birgir sniffed down his nose at him. Even though the man was a tiny bit shorter than Asyl, he could still stand in such a way that showed his obvious contempt. It made him feel tiny. Unwanted. Asyl's shoulders hunched a little, and his tongue felt numb.

"You're not welcome here," Birgir said.

"Is that what Kende said or your beliefs?" Asyl challenged.

"Master Kende has tired of you. Leave."

With that, the portly man all but slammed the door in Asyl's face. Blinking a few times, Asyl stared at the front door, just inches away from his nose. Rojir had said that Kende hadn't given up on him. Was it possible he could have been wrong? Maybe that's why he'd started to feel better on his walk over. Maybe Kende really had given up on him.

Horror gripped his stomach, and Asyl felt a rising tide of panic at the thought that Kende would abandon him. Just the thought made him want to cry. Breathing hard, Asyl closed his eyes and felt for the bond in his chest. It was there. Weakened due to neglect, but still viable. Birgir was lying. Of course he was. But how to get around him?

Asyl stepped backward off the portico and stared up at the windows, trying to catch any sort of movement. There wasn't any. He had no idea how else to get inside. The servants' quarters would be inaccessible to him, and Asyl wouldn't be surprised if Birgir had instructed the rest of the staff to throw Asyl out on sight. He didn't even know any of Kende's friends or family!

Wait.

No, he did know someone.

Asyl turned and trotted down the long driveway. Which precinct would Macik work at? The closest one was just over a mile away. He could at least start there and work his way outward. Maybe he'd get lucky and one of the officers would tell him where Macik worked. Briefly, Asyl wished he had Naias with him as his spokesperson. Guardian. Whatever

Craft Blessed thought Voids needed. As if they were invalids and unable to take care of themselves.

Snorting to himself, Asyl shook his head at the direction of his thoughts. Hadn't Naias told him how much the police wanted his potions? Clearly, they underestimated Voids, and Asyl would gladly disabuse them of their beliefs as soon as he could. Just as soon as he got back to Kende and got to hold the man again.

His chest was aching by the time Asyl walked up the short staircase to the precinct. While he was intending on going back to Kende, putting distance between them still wasn't easy. Maybe it would be as soon as they finalized their bond. He should have asked Rojir what that entailed. Hopefully Kende would take pity on him and tell him before sealing their bond.

Asyl pushed the hood of his cloak back and approached the front desk. A bored-looking officer with a Gaian mark eyed him. The boredom turned to wariness, and he frowned up at Asyl as he approached. Behind him was an open door that led to the bullpen, where officers sat at their desks. Some were interviewing citizens, while others were working on whatever paperwork they needed to do. It was all a huge cluster of activity that made Asyl's head spin.

"What do you want?" the man said flatly. "We're not a charity."

"I'm here to see Detective Macik," Asyl said, pitching his voice a little louder to have it carry.

At his announcement, the officer sat up a little straighter and openly glared at him.

"Detective Macik has better things to do than listen to whatever tiny thought you've got rattling around in there," the man snarled at him.

Asyl rolled his shoulders back and folded his arms across his chest. He returned the officer's baleful stare and wrinkled his nose at him.

"Detective Macik has personally told me that if I needed assistance to call upon him," Asyl said.

"Oh, right, sure. And who do you think you are, demanding that privilege?" the Gaian sneered.

"Lord Asyl Seni. Now, do you want to feel my father's wrath when he learns that I've been denied my basic right to protection?" Asyl said sharply.

After learning what he had from Rojir, he felt pretty sure that Lairne wouldn't mind Asyl's proclamation too much. Technically, he wasn't really a lord either, having lost that title when he was disowned. Briefly, he wondered if he'd get the title back after accepting his role as Kende's Fated.

The Gaian stammered, obviously confused as to what to do. He was faced with a lordling who was also a Void. Clearly, he couldn't figure out how he should treat Asyl.

"I thought I heard your voice," Macik said from the open doorway, grinning at him. "My brother's Fated. What can I do for you?"

Asyl looked at him and sagged in relief. The Gaian got to his feet and began stammering, his brows knitting together briefly.

"Wait. Voids can't be Fated," the man finally said.

"I beg to differ," Asyl grumbled.

"Come on, grumpy," Macik said, laughing.

He held out his arm and guided Asyl out the front door. For a moment, Asyl thought that he was being dismissed just like that. He planted his feet and looked at him with wide eyes.

"Not here," Macik mumbled.

The man guided him around the building to a stable. A pair of horses were hitched up to a curricle that Macik stepped up into. He waved him up. Frowning, Asyl clambered up, grateful that the vehicle had been stored underneath cover so the seat of his pants didn't get soaked. He pulled his hood up as Macik snapped the reins.

"Macik?" Asyl asked.

"You'd best be going to my brother's place and begging him to take you back," Macik said flatly.

Asyl couldn't help but flush. "How's he been?"

"Sleeping a lot," Macik replied and sighed heavily. "He's been in a pretty good amount of pain, so he's been sedating himself."

Asyl jerked upright and looked at him in horror.

"Rojir said that I'd be handling the brunt of the pain," Asyl said and groaned. "He came by and talked some sense into me. But Birgir wouldn't let me in, so I took a chance and came here to look for you."

"And Pivane had to be manning the desk," Macik grumbled. "Fucking Birgir. You just let me do the talking when we get there."

"Can you get me in?" Asyl asked, hating the panic in his voice. "I just...."

He cleared his throat, not wanting to burst into tears again. Macik glanced at him, a sympathetic look on his face. His smile was sad, and he nodded.

"I'll get you in. He feels wretched about what he did," Macik said.

"He shouldn't," Asyl said. "I freaked out and made a big deal out of something small."

Macik smiled. "I appreciate the fact that you take some accountability for what happened."

They stayed silent for a long moment. Macik hadn't roused the horses to move any faster than a sedate walk, guaranteeing them time to talk. The detective took a deep breath, rallying for what he was going to say next. Asyl had a feeling he didn't want to hear it.

"We're still having a hard time tracking down T—"

"I don't want to talk about him," Asyl interrupted harshly. "I want to focus on my future."

"Of course," Macik murmured.

He stopped the curricle at the portico of Ruvyn manor and sat back with a sigh. Without another word he hopped off and headed up the stairs that Asyl had left not an hour ago. He stood behind Macik as the man knocked. It took a minute for Birgir to open the door.

The man hesitated, looking between the two of them. Birgir finally frowned, holding himself rigid, moving the door slightly as if he couldn't decide whether to shut it in their faces.

"You know, Birgir, it's a criminal offense to prevent someone from seeing their Fated," Macik said with a volatile sweetness.

"That would have to imply that Voids get Fated," Birgir groused.

"Oh, stop regurgitating whatever the priest said at your temple," Macik replied flatly.

He advanced on the steward, and the man automatically took a few steps back. Asyl darted over the threshold and shut the heavy door behind him. Macik looked at Asyl from the corner of his eye and jerked his head toward the stairs. Taking the hint, Asyl hurried to the other end of the hall.

"You can't just let that thing in here!" Birgir protested loudly.

"That *thing*, as you so put it, is your master's Fated. Do you want me to take you down to the precinct on obstruction charges?" Macik asked loftily.

Asyl ignored the argument that Birgir started to spit out, knowing the man would never be happy with him here. There was no point in trying to persuade him. Maybe once he saw how happy he could make Kende, Birgir would back off. As long as Kende forgave him. The two of them had plenty to talk about, and neither of them were completely blameless.

His steps slowed as he approached Kende's door. His bond told him that Kende was inside, though it was still fairly dull. His heart wasn't sharing the sentiment, thudding loudly and rapidly in his chest. Asyl hated how his hand shook as he gripped the knob. Closing his eyes, he took a deep breath and opened the door.

Despite being about midday, the room was almost completely dark. It was a bit musty, as if the chambermaids hadn't been in to air it out recently. The hearth was long since cold, not even embers burning low in the ash. Only one Ignis lamp was currently lit, burning low to cast the dimmest light. The desolation pained Asyl as he quietly shut the door behind him. He located a lump on the bed and heard the slow, rhythmic breathing of his Fated sleeping.

A nearly uncontrollable urge to go to him overtook Asyl. He didn't bother trying to curb his needs this time. Toeing off his shoes, Asyl unlatched his cloak and padded over to the partition. He hung his cloak to dry and walked over to the bed. There was plenty of room for him, as Kende was curled up on his side. Asyl slid beneath the covers, his body feeling as if it would vibrate apart if he didn't get into Kende's arms within the next minute.

Asyl squirmed close to his Fated, reaching out to tentatively touch his bare shoulder. Almost as if he'd been waiting, Kende rolled over, though he still appeared to be asleep. Biting his lip, Asyl slid in close, burrowing into his chest and getting one of Kende's arms to drape over his shoulders. It took only a heartbeat longer for Kende to inhale deeply and hold him tight to his chest in a near-crushing hug.

Elation filled him, making his head spin as the pain he'd been holding for the last few days vanished. Asyl clung to his Fated, throwing one leg over Kende's hip, trying to keep him as close as possible. A desperate whimper tore from his throat as he wrapped his arms around Kende's neck.

"Asyl," Kende said, his voice thick with sleep.

"I'm here," Asyl whispered. "I'm so sorry. Please forgive me."

"Nothing to forgive," Kende replied, nuzzling into Asyl's neck. "I broke your trust."

"Over something that I truly do want," Asyl said, tangling one hand in Kende's soft blond hair. "I shouldn't have yelled at you. I shouldn't have rejected you, and I had no idea I was causing you so much pain."

Kende was silent for a long time, though the intensity of his grip hadn't slackened. A shudder ran through his Fated, and the man tilted his head to kiss Asyl's jaw. That caused an echoing shiver to shoot down Asyl's spine. The fact that Kende hadn't prompted more worried him. Asyl very gently pushed on his chest, and Kende let go immediately.

He missed the warmth instantly, and Asyl ducked his head to try and meet Kende's eyes.

"Kende," he said gently, "do you want me to go?"

"No," Kende replied, though he made no effort to reach out for Asyl again. "I just don't know what to do. I don't want to upset you."

Shit. Asyl closed his eyes and slid his arms around Kende's neck to snuggle in close again. It took his Fated a minute to embrace him once more. He wasn't sure how to face this new side of Kende, insecure and doubting his every intention. Asyl hated it. He wanted his Fated back, but he'd put him here through all the times he'd been reluctant, and then when he'd been confronted at the charity event.

"I've been scared," Asyl said finally. He dropped his head so his cheek rested on the top of Kende's head. "I know you'll never intentionally hurt me, but sometimes I get overwhelmed and feel as if I'm backed into a corner and it's all I can do to get away. That's my problem, not yours. You've done nothing but encourage and support me. It's not your fault it took me until now to see that."

"Your father," Kende said slowly, "he seemed truly contrite about what happened."

"I know," Asyl murmured. "Rojir told me that he'd gone to my father while I was on the streets. Apparently he knew where I was up to the point where Tillet kidnapped me."

"He likely thought you were dead," Kende said. "He must have been so happy to hear you'd survived."

"And then I yelled at him." Asyl chuckled weakly. "I didn't know he'd wanted me back only moonturns after he disowned me. I thought he thought I'd be so excited to come back that I'd agree to do whatever he wanted me to."

Silence fell in the chamber once again. He waited for his Fated to speak, reveling in his warmth and affection. Sure, they hadn't done much more than embrace and exchange a few chaste kisses. What could he do to help get Kende's confidence back? Asyl missed the man's easy strength like he'd miss a tooth.

"Kende?" Asyl asked quietly, "do you want this?"

His Fated tensed and squeezed Asyl briefly before his strong arms relaxed. He knew that Kende wouldn't offer any resistance if he tried to get away.

"I do," Kende said, "but if you don't, I'll release you. I don't want you to be in pain."

"I want you," Asyl said firmly. He smiled when Kende lifted his head to look at him. "I do. I really do. I need someone to push me and stand beside me to make sure I keep my head."

"Asyl…."

"You're mine," Asyl finally said with a low growl, "my Fated."

He gasped as Kende rolled on top of him, the man's lips pressing against his own. It wasn't elegant, but desperate. Asyl submitted to him easily, returning the frantic kiss, opening himself to his Fated. His head spun with the relief he could feel so strongly from Kende. His fears were easing away, leaving behind bliss instead.

His hip felt as if it was going numb, and Asyl wiggled beneath Kende even as the man's tongue slid alongside his. Asyl spread his legs, and Kende fit between them perfectly. They slotted together, two halves of the same whole. He missed Kende's lips the moment he pulled away, despite both of them gasping for air.

"Every inch of me," Kende said, "everything that I am, everything that I will be, is yours."

"And I yours," Asyl whispered, "though I'm not sure what I'm bringing into this relationship."

Kende snorted. "Really? You're a smart businessman with passion and intimate knowledge of those who are unhoused and can give insight on Voids. Not to mention gorgeous."

Asyl flushed and smiled up at him. "Is that enough?"

"You are enough," Kende murmured.

Grinning, Asyl arched up and placed a soft, lingering kiss on his lips. A brief spike of fear rolled through him, making him inhale sharply. Kende pulled away slightly, eyeing him carefully.

"How do we...." Asyl trailed off and blushed, looking up at him. "How do we seal the bond?"

"Were you never taught about the Fated bond?" Kende asked, frowning.

"There wasn't a point until my Awakening, and then after that...." Asyl shrugged and sighed. "I was looking forward to learning all about it."

"Well," Kende said slowly, "usually it's sealed with a mutual orgasm. Sex."

Asyl flushed hot at his Fated's words and swallowed hard as longstanding fears pricked him. Immediately he denied that he would ever be able to have sex with Kende. Just the thought of spreading his legs and letting Kende inside him made his throat close, until his Fated shifted slightly and Asyl realized that half of his fear had already happened. Kende was between his thighs, watching him carefully. When had he done that? Asyl bit his lower lip and looked up at his Fated.

"Does... does it have to be penetrative?" Asyl asked weakly. "I don't know if I can handle that."

Kende lowered himself, pressing Asyl into the mattress with his delightful weight. Asyl groaned weakly, wrapping his arms around Kende's shoulders as one of the man's arms snaked underneath his body. He could feel Kende's worry radiating through their strengthening bond as they held each other for a long minute.

"I don't know. I've only ever heard it talked about as penetrating sex, but... all the texts just say mutual orgasm," Kende said, tilting his head and kissing Asyl's cheek.

"We could try frotting," Asyl said, feeling his face burn red at the suggestion. What was he becoming, wanting to rub up against his Fated until they both came? A partner. A lover. His self-doubts and fears felt as if they were easing with the anticipation of sealing his bond. Excitement began to tug at him. "Maybe that would work?"

"It would be a pleasurable experiment," Kende replied, his tone understandably cautious. "Do you truly want to try?"

"Yes," Asyl said firmly, nodding. "I want you, Kende. You're a kind and generous man, and I need that to learn how to open up again. The gifts you've given me, and how you've held yourself back, always waiting for me to be ready... I can't say I'll ever want you inside of me, and I don't want to try the other way around. But this...."

He canted his hips upward, easily rubbing against his Fated's body. Kende let out a low groan, and his eyes slid closed. He pressed his arm into the mattress beside Asyl's head and leaned down. Asyl arched up, capturing his lips in a greedy kiss. Kende's arm slid out from underneath him, and as he thoroughly distracted Asyl with his tongue, he began playing with the hem of Asyl's shirt.

Slowly, always making sure that Asyl could tell him to stop, he hitched the shirt up, bunching it at Asyl's throat. His hips pressed down harder, rubbing and grinding against him. Sparks exploded behind his closed lids, and Asyl moaned into his mouth, meeting each thrust with a timely buck, clashing their bodies harder together. He'd never been pleasured this way or brought pleasure to another just by frotting. Bolts of lust and delight surged inside of him, lighting his mind and making him harder than he'd ever been.

Asyl had to break the kiss, tilting his head back as he cried out with the next rub. The soft cotton that Kende had commissioned the pants to be made of was starting to get too rough on his sensitized skin. What he didn't anticipate was Kende kissing and mouthing at his throat, finally biting the curve of his neck, drawing out a heartfelt sigh that evolved into a moan.

Once, he would have been terrified of this. Terrified of having another man on top of him, pressing down into him. Scared that he'd be reduced to a sex doll once more. As it was, all Asyl could think about was how right it felt to have Kende in his arms. How soothing it was, even as his skin felt as if it was burning.

The man's hand plucked at his nipple, and for a brief moment, Asyl couldn't think about anything outside of what his lover was doing. His lover. His Fated. Happiness welled inside him, bringing hot tears to his eyes. He'd never be abandoned again. Never be alone again. Asyl grabbed Kende's face by the jaw and pulled him back up for another kiss.

He could feel his Fated's delight in Asyl taking an active role. How proud Kende was of him to be able to even do this much. How much Kende wanted this too. Asyl could feel their bond strengthening quickly, becoming more and more sensitive to Kende's emotions. Right now, all he could feel was his Fated's love for him, and just beneath that, the heady lust at being able to explore Asyl's body.

Kende's hand slipped between them and tugged at the strings of Asyl's placket. He wiggled, managing to get one big toe in the hem of Kende's pants and try to pull them down. The man broke their kiss, though he didn't move away, and laughed.

"Want you bare," Asyl groaned. "I need to feel it."

His Fated moaned and finally got the placket to open. Asyl sighed in relief as his prick sprung free from the restraints, lying heavy and ready on his stomach. Precum was already beading at the head, dripping onto his belly. Kende's hand wrapped around his sensitive sex, and Asyl squeaked, bucking up against his Fated's hips. He slapped his hands to his mouth, and Kende chuckled.

"Let me hear," Kende murmured as he ducked and kissed Asyl's throat.

"It's embarrassing," Asyl protested.

"Only because you're unused to it," Kende replied.

He pulled away, much to Asyl's dismay, sitting back on his haunches. Biting his lip, Asyl watched as the man slowly pulled his pajama pants down. He had a thin trail of blond curls bisecting his stomach, erupting in a nest of neat curls at the top of his cock. Which, speaking of....

Asyl flushed, slowly reaching out and touching the tip of Kende's dick with his finger. His Fated was thick, uncut, and precum was leaking from the tip. The skin was velvety soft, and Asyl shivered, pumping it slowly. Kende stretched back over him, a low groan in his throat. Asyl blinked once, surprised at himself for even wanting to touch another man. He hadn't thought about it. Just that it felt right. Felt good. He wanted to bring his Fated pleasure.

Kende tilted his head, nibbling along Asyl's jaw as his big hand came down and wrapped around both of their pricks. Asyl adjusted his grip so that their fingers intertwined as they slowly moved together. He couldn't help but arch and buck into each pump of their fists and was encouraged by Kende pushing down toward him as well. Each grind and stroke was met with another spark of white heat that drove Asyl's mind further from active thought.

Pleasure flooded through him, through the bond, and echoed back into him, driving him higher than he'd ever been before. Nothing had ever felt like this. He was floating, aware of the heat that rushed through him, through his Fated. All Asyl could do was squirm toward that warmth and reach out for it. The tips of his fingers brushed against the heat, and it broke.

Asyl let out a choked sob as he came, feeling hot splashes against his fingers and abdomen. His head spun at a dizzying rate as the bond solidified, even as he spasmed and shuddered underneath Kende's hand. The man slowly stopped, panting hard above him. Asyl's legs slid from Kende's hips, and his free arm that he'd hooked around Kende's neck at some point hit the pillow beside him.

His Fated let go of their spent cocks and slowly lay down next to him. Asyl gasped, his lip trembling, and realized he was crying. A mix of horror and shame coursed through him, and he tried to roll away from his Fated. Kende stopped him with a gentle hand to his shoulder. Gentle kisses to his cheeks, right on the tear streaks, told Asyl that his Fated had noticed. Asyl began to shiver, and another, quieter, sob wrenched free from his throat.

"Talk to me," Kende murmured, kissing his forehead this time.

Asyl could feel his worry and concern. He leaned into the man's touch and scooted closer to his Fated, reaching out for him. Without another word, Kende pulled him into his arms while Asyl buried his face into the man's neck and cried. How could he put his feelings into words? How could he explain that he'd somehow expected sex with Kende to not be pleasurable?

How good it had felt for the first time? How it didn't feel like his body had betrayed him with a release. That he didn't feel disgusting and hating that he'd just orgasmed. There wasn't any way for Kende to understand that he'd hated any form of sex for years. But it was Kende. Maybe he could understand? Asyl sniffed a little, managing to pull himself out of his thoughts. He hadn't been touched against his will like that for four years.

Kende was still holding him close, apparently not caring about the snot and tears that lingered on his chest from Asyl's breakdown. He pulled in a shaky, uneven breath and squeezed Kende briefly before looking up at him.

"I just.…. Never knew it could be like that," Asyl said softly.

Compassion bloomed in his Fated's face and through their bond. Kende tilted his head up and dropped a gentle kiss on his lips.

"I'm sorry it was ever anything but," Kende replied. "No regrets?"

It was almost second nature to pull at the bond to feel the quiet worry that Kende was feeling. Asyl just smiled up at him and shook his head. Kende's shoulders relaxed, and he gathered Asyl in his arms, ignoring the sticky cum drying on Asyl's belly. After a few minutes, his Fated grunted and rolled away. A jolt of fear that he'd be abandoned shot through Asyl's spine, and he pushed himself up onto his elbows.

Kende lit one of the nearby Ignis lamps to brighten the room a little more and smiled at him. Pure warmth and love flowed through their bond, and Asyl began to relax, knowing Kende was openly sending him such reassurance.

"Just going to get a wet cloth for us to clean up," Kende murmured.

Asyl nodded. He wasn't entirely sure he could stand right now anyway. Between his three-day fast, the long trek across Alenzon, and that orgasm, his knees might not be able to hold him. He tracked Kende as he walked into the bathroom, shamelessly looking at his lover's body. Not too muscular, not too boney. Just absolutely perfect.

He wondered if Kende had the same opinion of his body. Asyl never thought he was desirable. Too pasty… thin…. Clearly his Fated didn't mind. Not if the smile on Kende's face and the heat in his eyes were anything to go by when he emerged with a small towel. Kende walked over to him and gently wiped the evidence of their coupling away. He bent and placed a gentle kiss on Asyl's forehead and retreated to the bathroom once more with the cloth.

Asyl tugged off his shirt, balled it up, and tossed it toward his cloak, which had left quite the puddle beneath it. He kicked off his pants and did the same with them. No point in hiding his body or being shy about baring himself to his Fated anymore. Asyl curled up on his side, watching the en suite door, just to see his Fated that much sooner.

As he returned, Kende paused midstep and reached back to dampen the Ignis lamp in the bathroom. Doing so cast a shadow on the inside of his thigh, revealing a multitude of uneven bumps. What were those? Asyl rolled onto his elbow so he could see it better, blinking to make sure it wasn't just a trick of the light.

Were those scars?

Concern and anger flowed through him. Who had dared to hurt his Fated? To make him feel so wretched he needed to cut himself? Or had someone else done so? Kende must have picked up on his hastily dampened emotions as he turned to look at him.

"What are those?" Asyl asked slowly.

Kende glanced down at where Asyl was pointing. His Fated's cheeks flushed, and he sighed, walking over to the bed. He turned up the flow for the second Ignis lamp, flooding the sleeping area of the room with light. Kende slid back onto the mattress, and for a moment, Asyl thought that he was being ignored. His Fated lay down and parted his legs, tucking one toward his buttocks, the other bending and resting the heel of his ankle on his folded leg.

For a minute, Asyl just looked at the man's shapely legs. Sure, he'd seen him in close cut breeches plenty of times, but his tanned skin had always been hidden. Kende walked a lot, if his muscles were anything to go by. He admired the curve of his thigh, and how the low light made his skin glow like wildfire honey.

That was, until he saw how extensive the scars were. Dozens of small paler lines on the inside of his thighs, near his groin, all white with age. Asyl's breath caught, understanding. He reached out, lightly touching the small bumps that littered his Fated's skin from crotch to midthigh. Probably just about where the hem of his shorts hung.

Asyl dragged in a few breaths, feeling as if his chest was on fire while his eyes burned. He blinked rapidly, trying to stop his world from blurring. Who in the hell had hurt his Fated, this infuriatingly kind man, to the point where he felt like he had to cut himself open? He couldn't feel anything through his bond with Kende, and he ripped his eyes away from the scarring to look at him.

"You haven't met any of my blood family yet," Kende said with a sigh, "and that's on purpose. It's not that I'm ashamed of you or that I want you to be a secret. Quite the opposite, in fact. I want to be able to hold and kiss you at charity events and any galas I end up throwing, because I'm proud of you and everything you've accomplished. I want to show off how smart and compassionate you are, and how you truly just want to help other people. But I really don't know how my parents and siblings will receive you. I know it's cowardly, but I would be devastated if they hurt you.

"My parents and blood siblings are all blessed with elemental Crafts. There was a bet every Awakening what the kid would be blessed with, though the money would end up going to a charity or institution of my sibling's choosing. I'm the youngest, and there were a lot of people who assumed I'd end up as an Aquan or a Gale. Not Gaian or Ignis, which most of my siblings are. You know, the 'strong' elements." Asyl snorted at that, and Kende gave him a crooked smile before it dropped.

"Having a child Awaken with a non-elemental Craft wasn't something they'd ever considered."

"And you Awoke as a Healer," Asyl said softly. "Why wouldn't they be proud of that? Or think that maybe your family needed to be balanced out with some healing?"

"That's a nice way of looking at it. My parents didn't see it that way. Not only was their kid gay and looked at the world differently than they did, but now he was a Healer."

"Your parents are homophobic?" Asyl asked quietly.

"They've… warmed up to the idea. I think it startled them more than anything when at eight I proudly declared my best friend was going to be my husband," Kende laughed.

"What happened to him?" Asyl asked.

"He went to Bhyvine and found his Fated there. Even after both of our Awakenings, we were close, and we experimented a lot with each other."

"He never noticed…." Asyl trailed off, lightly touching the scars again.

Kende sighed and reached out for him. Asyl eagerly curled up next to him, resting his head on Kende's chest. The quiet intimacy after bonding was nice, and Asyl found he could easily picture a repeat. Quite a few repeats, if he was honest with himself. He reached down and gently cupped his lover's thigh, making sure he was touching those horrible small scars. Kende stretched out his bent knee, shifting to get a little more comfortable.

"No, he never noticed. I always managed to hide them from him. He was too focused on getting off, rather than taking the time to truly appreciate his partner's body and get to know what makes them feel cared for and loved," Kende said.

"But you stopped," Asyl said. "None of these are new, and you wouldn't show me if you had fresh cuts."

"I did stop. Only because I took it too far," Kende said, grimacing. Asyl waited quietly, just watching. He could hear Kende's heartbeat rise with his anxiety of telling him. No consulting of the bond needed this time. If he wanted to stop, Asyl wouldn't push it. He was about to say so when Kende continued. "I think I was nineteen. My family would make disparaging remarks about me, to my face and behind my back. They often called me worthless and said that my Craft wasn't one a nobleman should have. It made me weak, and my options as a leader had been cut down to basically nothing. My siblings tended to agree.

"So, after my Awakening celebration, they began to bully me endlessly. They'd take my toys, clothes, food, anything really, and tell me to use my Craft to get it back. They always sparred with each other to practice with their Craft, and so they had this connection with each other I didn't have. Of course, when they got hurt practicing, I wasn't ever good enough to help them, and I should just leave them alone."

Asyl scoffed. "They wanted you to use your Craft, but not when they were actually injured."

"Pretty much. It was a power dynamic with them. Or rather, it is a power dynamic with them. Some of my siblings still don't respect me and what I do simply because I'm a Healer. But as a kid, I didn't know how to cope with the feelings of inadequacy."

"So you started cutting."

Kende breathed in slowly and nodded. "Yeah. It seemed to help. It would focus my attention on physical pain, and for a while, the pain in my heart wouldn't be so bad. It was my sister's twenty-first birthday when everything kind of snapped. It hadn't really been much different than other birthdays. My older siblings had their families, and I was relegated to the children's table as usual."

Asyl popped up at that, staring down at him. "You were a teenager and they still had you sitting with the littles?"

Kende nodded. "Yeah. That's how little they respected my Craft. I tried to not make a big deal out of it. I still try not to." Asyl's jaw dropped, and Kende nodded. "Yeah, they still want me to sit with the kids. Ultimately, I think that's what drove me over the edge. I took my shaving razor that night and slit my wrists."

Asyl lunged for his lover's arm, panic coursing through him. How had he not seen any markings on Kende's body? He'd touched his wrists several times, seen them up close as Kende cupped his face. He would have noticed. Right? Kende let him have his arm, and Asyl inspected his skin. There was no scar. No blemish that he could see.

"Wounds healed by Craft usually don't leave a mark," Kende said, "but if you look closely, there's a small seam."

Only when he pointed it out did Asyl see the thinnest line of discolored skin that denoted a scar. Asyl shook his head, looking at his Fated. If he'd slit his wrists.... He felt a wave of love and reassurance come through their bond, and Kende smiled faintly at him as Asyl's anxiety eased.

"Siora found me. She'd been assigned as my assistant the previous week and wanted to review the upcoming week before she retired for the day. Theoretically, I should have been up, and she was so new I didn't think about her being there. Turns out she'd had a Vision of a person with bleeding hands and was fairly sensitive to the way my family treated me.

"Of course she raised the alarm, called a Healer, and I was patched up."

"And your family was likely horrified and disgusted with what you did," Asyl supplied. "Probably saw it as another sign of weakness, even though they're the ones who pushed you to it."

"Some of them, yes. It shocked my parents and most of my family into realizing how badly their behavior affected me. I have a sister and brother who still say that I did it for attention and wanted to take the evening away from my sister to make it all about me."

Asyl snarled, "Tell me who and I'll show them what I think about that."

Kende blinked at him and started laughing. He wrapped a hand around Asyl's neck and pulled him down for a kiss. Asyl went more than willingly, wrapping his arms around his Fated and nestling into his side again.

"Thank you. I know what happened to me is nothing compared to what you endured, but I want you to know that I understand in a way. I know what it's like to crave the idea that if you'd just finished it, you wouldn't have to deal with anything anymore, and life would be so much easier for everyone else since they didn't want you anyways," Kende said.

Tears pricked Asyl's eyes again, and he nodded. "The Healer that saved you. Do you still talk to them?"

"Gojko kicked my ass when I woke up. He told me if I pulled a stunt like that again, he'd heal me just enough so that I was conscious, and then I could patch myself up the rest of the way."

"I'm glad he helped you straighten things out," Asyl murmured.

Kende made a small noise in the back of his throat and just gazed at him. Gently pulling away from him, Asyl sat up and quietly ran his fingers over all the scars he saw on his Fated's leg. His heart's twin knew what it was like to be hated and seen as worthless. Not that Asyl wished it on anyone, but in a way, it was nice knowing that Kende had struggled, too, and wasn't some noble paragon who never had any issues growing up.

Without really thinking about it, Asyl curled down and placed soft kisses over as many scars as he could. He heard Kende inhale deeply, and the man shifted slightly beneath him. Was his skin more sensitive with the scarring? They'd never know if this area had been a hot spot, considering no one had touched the undamaged skin. Still, Kende's marks deserved to be shown affection, and to be seen as what they were. A triumph over what he'd overcome.

"Asyl," Kende murmured.

Looking up at the man, Asyl sat up straight. His lover's gaze was soft, yet his eyes held a heat that he still wasn't quite used to seeing directed toward him. Kende reached out, his hand slowly sliding into his hair, and he scratched gently at Asyl's scalp. Sliding up toward his Fated's head, Asyl diverted and slipped his hands along Kende's chest instead, splaying his fingers.

Kende's chest was firm, and his stomach had the smallest give to it. His blond hair was so fine and light against his skin it was hard to see the fuzz from a distance. Up close, Asyl could see and feel the hair spanning across his chest, trailing down to his groin. Asyl couldn't help the small amount of jealousy at feeling his Fated's pelt. No matter what he did, body hair wasn't something that Asyl could grow very well.

The tips of his fingers found Kende's nipples, and he brushed the small nubs with the lightest touch. A low moan escaped from Kende, yet he made no effort to grab at Asyl. He truly appreciated his Fated allowing him to take his time and explore his body without having to be concerned he was going to be pawed at. Finally, Asyl leaned down and brushed their lips together, unsurprised when the man held him tight to return the kiss.

His lover opened his mouth, and Asyl squirmed closer, partially lying on top of Kende now as he slipped his tongue inside. A full-body shudder traveled down Asyl's spine, and his cock began to fill once again. Kende groaned, and he wrapped his arms around Asyl, not entirely pinning him to his chest, but rather just holding him close.

When they finally parted for air, Kende rolled them over, earning himself a giggle from Asyl. He blinked at his Fated and smiled, enjoying the familiar pressure. Kende leaned down and kissed the tip of his nose, love and affection coming through strongly via their newly cemented bond. Asyl squirmed until he could drape his legs over Kende's, settling more comfortably on the bed.

"What now?" Asyl asked softly, "I've got my shop to worry about, and that'll take up so much time. Especially factoring in travel. It would be easier if I stayed there."

"Well, I know I want you around more than just evenings and nights," Kende said. "How well do you dance?"

Asyl sighed, ignoring the sudden subject change. "It's been so long since I've learned. I doubt I can remember, especially if there's been anything new implemented. Besides, I know all the lead role steps. I have a feeling that I'd need to learn the followers if I'm dancing with you."

Kende snorted but didn't contradict him. "But your parents did teach you before they had you leave."

"Yes. Why?" Asyl asked, blinking up at him.

"I want you by my side," Kende told him, "every day. I want to wake up with you in my arms after spending the nights curled up together. Move in with me. Let me adorn you with the clothes and jewels you wear so beautifully."

Asyl inhaled sharply. "What about your family? If they reacted so poorly to you being a Healer, what would they think of me?"

"I don't care," Kende said and sighed. "They've already made their decisions about me, and they won't change. If they can't be happy for me because I found my Fated, then that's their problem, not mine."

"They won't disown you?" Asyl asked quietly.

"Hell, if they do, I think half of the city would protest, solely based on all the charities and programs I run. Besides, all I would ask is that you'd let me move in with you instead, and I'd gladly learn how to run the front of the shop from Naias to help you out and free up more of her time," Kende said.

"You'd give up all of this. The manor, the clothes, the food, and the position… just to be with me if it came down to it?" Asyl asked, staring up at Kende.

"You are my world, Asyl. I want you in it. The rest is just details," Kende said.

Asyl cupped his Fated's face and pulled him down to draw him into a slow kiss. They exchanged a contented sigh and smiled at each other. All around him, his lover hummed with delight, though Asyl could feel a quiet tremor of anxiety from Kende.

"All right. But why do I need to know how to dance?" Asyl asked.

"Well, the short answer is because I'd have to throw an introduction gala, and you'd be expected to dance," Kende said.

"And the long answer?" Asyl asked hesitantly.

"You and I would be expected to be present at quite a few events. Not all require dancing, but many do. Your introduction gala, firstly. Initially I was thinking about maybe having your introduction also be an engagement party, but...."

Engagement? Asyl's breath caught, and he stared up at his Fated. The man tilted his head, looking at him calmly, as if he hadn't just declared the two of them being legally bound for the rest of their lives. Though hesitating at that seemed a little silly considering what they'd done not even an hour ago. They'd sealed their lives together more thoroughly and permanently than a pair of rings and a piece of paper could.

"But?" Asyl prompted softly.

"I'm prideful. I want to dress you in the most beautiful outfits, and if they're separate, then I get to spoil you some more," Kende said and grinned. "Got to look your best when the prince comes by."

"The prince?" Asyl squawked. "Why would he be interested?"

Kende laughed. "He's my cousin, that's why. We played together all the time when we were kids. Plus, he'd be thrilled to see that I finally met my Fated. Maybe he won't have me accompany him on his diplomatic trips like he keeps threatening."

"It'd be nice to see the world, though," Asyl said wistfully.

"I'd be honored to take you," Kende murmured and kissed him gently.

"So. Um. When did you want to do this introduction? I'm hardly unknown with the gentry. They just pretend that I don't exist or think I died," Asyl said.

Kende rolled his eyes. "Of course they would. It'll have to be a moonturn, at least. That way I have time to set up the party. Food, clothes, orchestra, decorations.... Would you like to help? It's your party, ultimately. I'd like it if you invited any of your friends too, even if they're not gentry."

"Sure," Asyl replied, smiling up at him, "though I've got my store to run still."

"Oh, right. Do you want to keep that location, or would you want to move your store closer? Of course, you're welcome to borrow Toemi every day. Siora and I can take the Craft vehicle when we need to run places," Kende offered.

Asyl blinked up at him in wonder. Offering him use of his carriage for whenever he wanted to go somewhere was one hell of a gift. But to move? That would sever the ties he had with his Void community. Despite what Rojir said, to leave and not look back, that they'd find him if they needed him… he still worried. What if someone was sick and too weak to make the trip? Or if they sent a friend and passed away while waiting?

He bit his lip and ducked his head.

"I don't know," Asyl finally said. "You know there's a reason I have Enchanted Waters where it is. I want to help the people who took care of me."

"What if we visit every other week with a good amount of inventory?" Kende offered. "We could even set up a hub somewhere that they know where to come to in order to get some help. I'm sure you've got someone who could help you coordinate."

"Rojir would," Asyl said, finally raising his eyes to look at his Fated again. "He's got a steady address. Though I don't know how legal it is, so I don't want to bring too much attention to it."

Kende watched him with gentle eyes for a minute. Asyl simply watched him quietly, knowing his Fated was thinking. He didn't want to interrupt, glad to present his Fated with a challenge that he would likely solve without too much pain. Asyl realized he'd forgotten how nice it was to have someone else help him. To be able to delegate.

"What about the temple that I found you in?" Kende asked. "It's only a couple of blocks from Enchanted Waters, and it's already abandoned, so we won't have to worry about evicting someone. We could even renovate some of the rooms so they've got some beds in them. Make it halfway into a hostel or resting area."

Asyl stared up at him, and a slow smile stretched over his face. He didn't remember much about the temple that Kende had found him in. His last memory was the hard blow to the side of his face and his knees buckling. Hitting the ground and feeling like he was being dragged somewhere. He'd resurfaced to see them draining his blood, but he hadn't really known where he was at that point.

Until something had spooked them, and they'd run. Was that Kende stumbling into the temple and scaring them off? Asyl didn't think that

Kende had set the men onto him anymore. He hadn't for moonturns now. Wiggling closer, Asyl flung his arms around Kende's neck, squeezing his man tight to him.

"Is that a yes?" Kende asked, laughing.

"It won't be too much work for you, will it?" Asyl asked softly.

"I think I'll enjoy putting it together. With your and Rojir's help, it'll probably be fairly simple. Besides, we can get the building's ownership and renovated while we set up to move Enchanted Waters and get you settled in here."

Then he could have an excuse to give Rojir money. His second dad had always turned him down so many times before, unless Asyl could somehow twist Rojir's help into something billable. Now he would just be able to get him the coin he needed to make sure everyone would be all right. Maybe actually get the house he currently squatted in legally. Purchase clothes and shoes that fit properly. Warm food in his belly.

It was a little too much to think about. Tears gathered in his eyes, and Asyl quickly blinked them away, gasping softly. Kende paused, his lazy delight turning into concern. He cupped Asyl's face and leaned in, kissed his forehead ever so gently. As if he was going to fall apart with any more affection.

"Asyl?" Kende asked.

"I just," he said and took a shaky breath, "it's all so overwhelming, realizing how open the world is to you and that I'd never have had a chance to do anything you're offering. How many people we can help…."

"That's what the introduction gala is for. People will know you'll be marrying into the family, and anywhere you want to do business will know that. They can't discriminate against you because you're a Void. They'd be denying my husband and potentially snubbing the Ruvyn family and perhaps by association, lose any royal connections they have. Hopefully that'll make them realize that you're no different than me and they'll relax their prejudice," Kende said.

"I think that's a bit optimistic," Asyl said and sighed. "But that would be nice."

Kende hummed and leaned down, kissing him slowly, barely putting more pressure on his lips other than to feel them. He rested their foreheads together and relaxed in the bed, cuddling into him. Asyl wiggled close, enjoying the warmth and security that Kende offered him. He doubted his Fated even realized how much his suggestions meant to Asyl.

Kende had never had to struggle to stay alive and not know if he was safe where he was sleeping that night. The fact that he was willing to back the unhoused Void community publicly was huge. Not only would it tell the gentry that Kende cared enough to make sure they were taken care of, but it might also prompt a few other families to pitch in. Asyl wondered if maybe he could request his father's assistance.

He knew there was always a certain amount of produce lost during transit. Too much bruised flesh, making it unappealing for sales.... If they were already tossing the food away, why not see if they could give it away, or at least sell it at a massively reduced price? That would bring some lost costs back to the company.

Maybe they could even have Maerie come by once a month and see about making simple clothes out of her cheaper fabrics. He knew Kende knew a cobbler well enough that he'd pushed a rush order for him. That was before Asyl took off halfway across Alenzon without his shoes, though. Would the cobbler be kindhearted enough to maybe offer his services at a massive discount as well? Or perhaps at least sell at cost. It was something to think about and bring up to Kende... later....

His mind had begun drifting when he heard a quick rap on the door. Asyl startled awake, blinking a few times. Kende rolled onto his back from his side to look over at the door, kicking a sheet over the two of them. The door opened, and Siora poked her head in. Asyl met her eyes as she took in the situation before her. Despite her seemingly being all right with their relationship, seeing them in bed together was quite different.

All she did was smile faintly, though a small blush spread across her cheeks.

"Your sister is requesting your presence," she said.

"I'd rather not talk to Jaclyn today," Kende groaned.

"It's Maielle," Siora replied.

Kende perked up, pushing himself to his elbows, a small smile on his face. Asyl missed the heat and pressure immediately. Allowing himself to be pouty, Asyl wrapped his arms around Kende's chest and pulled him back down and buried his face in the man's neck. His Fated chuckled and relaxed back on top of him, sliding one arm underneath Asyl's neck to hold him close.

"Give me and Asyl some time to get decent. We'll meet her in the library," Kende told his assistant.

Siora just nodded and left, humming her amusement. Once they were alone again, Kende kissed the top of his head and held him for a while longer. Slowly, Asyl relaxed his grip and tilted his head back to look up at him. Kende dropped a kiss on his lips and moved away with a heavy sigh. It was a little soothing, knowing that Kende wanted to stay as much as Asyl did.

Kende pulled open his closet and started hunting through it before emerging to look at him.

"I got some plain clothes commissioned for you," Kende said with a smile.

He waved Asyl over to the large closet. Surprised, Asyl scooted off the bed and followed him to a corner, where clothes that clearly weren't what Kende usually wore hung. The tunics and vests were blues and purples instead of greens and browns. Asyl turned and looked up at his Fated, feeling fairly overwhelmed again. Kende smiled and leaned down, kissing him lightly.

"Really?" Asyl asked.

"Really," Kende murmured, hugging him close.

Asyl returned to the clothes and reached out, lightly touching the tunics. They were soft and of a higher quality than Asyl would ever have been able to purchase. He tugged down an indigo tunic and a black pair of leggings. Kende showed him the small drawer where he could find smallclothes and socks. After that, he left to give Asyl his privacy. As if he hadn't seen everything the goddess had given Asyl at this point.

After quickly getting dressed, Asyl trotted out of the closet, smiling brightly at Kende, who was waiting for him with a hairbrush in hand. His Fated didn't hand it over, instead insisting that he brush out Asyl's hair for him. It felt nice, standing quietly and feeling Kende's gentle hands in his hair. Feeling the prongs lightly slide across his scalp, taming the hair he'd ignored for the last few days.

Finally they left Kende's suite and walked hand in hand down the stairs to the library. Inside were Siora and a brunette with a Gaian Craft Mark who sat happily chatting away. Something about a party? The brunette looked up and squeed, hopping to her feet. She rushed over to the two and flung her arms around Kende's neck, her toes barely reaching the ground as she leaned against him. The blond laughed, wrapping his arm around the woman, supporting her better, yet never letting Asyl's hand go.

"Hey, sis," Kende said with a brilliant smile. "Let me introduce you to my Fated, Asyl. Asyl, this is my sister Maielle."

"Good to meet you," Asyl said pleasantly.

Maielle let go of Kende, dropping to her feet and staring at him for a second. Asyl's stomach clenched in worry, wondering if she was one of the family members that wouldn't support their relationship. Though how she'd reacted upon seeing him and Kende's lack of worry through their bond helped ease his own worries. He didn't have to wait long before Maielle's smile returned in full force.

"You finally met your Fated!" she exclaimed, and to Asyl's surprise, pulled him into a bone-crushing hug. "Oh, it's so good to meet you! You seem like such a sweetheart!"

Her energy overwhelmed Asyl, and he went silent, wide-eyed, and just stared at her as she gushed over him. Maielle pulled the two of them to the couches where Siora sat with an amused expression. Chuckling, Kende sat on the couch and gently drew Asyl into his lap, holding him close. Maielle beamed at them, plopping down next to Siora and squirming slightly.

"So," she drawled and grinned, "when's the introduction gala?"

"We haven't decided yet," Kende said and smiled. "Macik knows about us, but no one else does. What can I do for you?"

The woman smiled and detailed an idea for a summer ball she had, wanting to invite all her friends with their partners and children. Siora pulled out her notepad that she seemed to always have with her and began taking notes. Asyl listened with half an ear, dropping his head to Kende's chest. Hearing his Fated's steady heartbeat kept his anxiety from rising again, and he enjoyed the rumble of his love's voice from time to time.

Once the bare essentials were written down, the subject changed. To his introduction gala. Asyl perked up, knowing that Kende would want his input for this. They talked flowers, food, what kind of music they wanted, guest list....

"Do you have any Void friends?" Maielle asked Asyl.

He nodded. "Yeah. I've written to them recently. They're doing all right. Staying careful and not going out late or alone."

"Invite them," Kende said.

Asyl inhaled sharply and looked over at his Fated. "What?"

"They're your friends. I was serious in what I said before. They should be able to celebrate this day with you as well," Kende said.

"Besides, I want to meet Rojir. You say he's kept you safe and pushed you to come back to me. I'd like to thank him personally."

"Are you sure? What about your family?" Asyl asked.

"You're part of our family," Maielle chastised with a smile. "Why should it only be Kende's friends and family at the gala?"

"Your friends deserve to know you're happy as much as mine," Kende reassured him.

"They don't have the clothes for this kind of gala," Asyl protested. "They'll be mocked and tormented by the gentry."

Maielle slowly smiled. "You let me worry about that. I'll tell Kende where they can go to get some clothes specifically for your introduction gala."

Asyl nodded. "All right. Rojir at least. Maybe a couple of others."

"Send them letters," Kende said with a smile. "Just let me know who accepts."

"What about Lord Seni?" Siora asked. Asyl stiffened, and a hint of worry came through their bond. "Beside the fact that he's your biological father, he's part of the gentry. It would send quite the message if he wasn't invited but the other minor families were."

"That's up to you," Kende said gently, rubbing his back. "Yes, it would be a slight, and it might drag your father through some drama and controversy, but your comfort comes before that."

"I want to know my siblings," Asyl said before he could think about it too much. "I always dreamed of having brothers and sisters."

"Then we'll invite your father and the twins," Kende said. "That way you can get to know two of your brothers."

"And Lady Seni?" Siora asked.

Kende scowled. "Taking into account what she said to me at the charity, I don't feel entirely safe inviting her. I'm sure we can heavily suggest that only Lairne, Arik, and Alyn should attend without outright telling her to stay away."

"What did she say?" Asyl asked.

"A lot of anti-Void nonsense that's not worth repeating," Kende replied.

Maielle hissed angrily. "She definitely doesn't deserve to attend, then."

Asyl nodded in agreement. For a minute, he'd hoped that maybe his mother would regret disowning him as well. Considering that his maternal grandmother had *spit* on him after his Awakening failed, maybe he shouldn't have been too surprised that his mother hated who he was.

He pushed his deteriorating thoughts away, stretched up and placed a kiss along Kende's jaw. Afterward, the conversation turned back to the more minute details, and the initial guest list was drafted up. By the time Maielle hopped to her feet, declaring that she was going to head to Maerie's, Asyl's head was spinning. There was so much more that came to planning a charity than he thought.

"I'd like to get you an assistant," Kende said, resting his cheek on the top of Asyl's head. "They'll help you with letters, managing whatever you need, and make sure you get to your engagements on time. With all the changes with Enchanted Waters, setting up the weekly or biweekly temple visits, and your gala, you're going to be very busy."

Asyl simply nodded, breathing deep and wondering what the heck he was getting into. Siora left them without a comment, consulting her to-do list that was already quite long. His Fated gently kissed the top of his head, and the two sat on the couch, lazily talking about the party and what the two wanted in their future.

He couldn't wait.

CHAPTER 11

"LORD KENDE," Birgir said in an insufferable tone, "you have a visitor."

With that, the man sniffed and looked down his nose at him before turning and leaving. That was definitely a reaction. Birgir was upset about something… again. He really needed to confront his steward and make sure the man knew he'd have to either get over his issue with Voids or find another position somewhere else.

As much as he didn't want Birgir to leave, solely based on how well he ran the house, Kende wasn't going to let him insult Asyl's friends. Macik had told him that it took threats of imprisonment to get Birgir to let Asyl in after he'd turned him away once. That alone had made him sit his steward down and inform him that one more insult toward a Void would get him punted onto the street without a reference.

He'd leveled the same threat against Siora. At least his assistant had finally seen Asyl for who he truly was and was much more comfortable around him. The demonization that she'd regarded Asyl with at first was finally gone, and she even smiled a little more. Or maybe that was because she was happy that Kende had finally bonded to him.

He turned his attention inward for a moment, locating their bond and tugging on it gently. His Fated was at Enchanted Waters and was quietly happy. Nothing had happened to make him overly happy, just the lingering effects from the morning, when they woke in each other's arms and kissed for a few minutes before Asyl had to leave.

But now he had to return to his visitor. Frowning, Kende stood from his desk, abandoning the contract he'd been looking over. He and Asyl had taken a long time to locate a building his Fated liked for his apothecary. It was larger than his current building, with a larger back room, while the storefront only got a nominal increase. Asyl had quite a few requests for his potions that he was already trying to fulfill, so the extra space was quite attractive.

He'd hired Asyl his own assistant this last week, after seeing his love's eyes glaze over at all the paper Naias had cheerfully handed him.

It ranged from property taxes, to the store's accounting ledger, to all the requests that had only grown, and to his herb supplier reaching out. The sheer panic that had erupted through their bond had gotten Kende to summon Siora to put out the feelers immediately.

Lanil was a wonderful lady and also a Seer. With any luck, she could help guide Asyl if she had any Visions that needed his attention. That wasn't entirely how their Craft worked, though often Seers had Visions that coincided with their current employment or those they spent enough time around. It wasn't an exact science, and even though Averia was known for her Seers, there was still plenty they didn't know about their Craft.

Right now, his Fated was packing up anything he cared to bring over from Enchanted Waters, though it wasn't much past a handful of books and notes. Many of his older clothes he packed would be moved to his new shop as soon as it was furnished properly. There they would be employed as rags or used as more of a smock—something that was completely fine getting ruined.

Kende enjoyed spoiling Asyl.

His Fated was quite enchanted with flowing clothes, Kende found. He eagerly worked with Maerie to come up with gorgeous sweeping tunics and tops that danced in the breeze. As long as Asyl was happy, that's all Kende truly cared about. While he wouldn't bankrupt himself purchasing Asyl a whole closet full of clothing, he definitely had paid Maerie's property tax for the next couple of years.

Soon, Enchanted Waters would move closer, and he'd see his Fated more during the days. Not right next to the manor, as Asyl insisted that if they moved too far, they'd lose the poorer clientele who would be too embarrassed to visit the temple during the weekends. But at least Asyl's day wouldn't be spent walking if he decided to not take Toemi's carriage for one reason or another.

Everything was looking up, and Kende was delighted to be working on several projects at once. Asyl had agreed to the introduction gala, along with the engagement party. While the family dinner was usually before any public event, Kende was breaking tradition to have the gala first. That way he couldn't be pressured to keep Asyl a secret. Expectations would be discussed, and while Asyl couldn't exactly fail the interview, it was possible for many of Kende's family to shun his Fated.

His fully bonded and realized Fated. The three days of overwhelming pain seemed like such a distant memory now. He'd been elated and relieved when Asyl came to him with a sincere apology and wish to do better by both of them. How could Kende have denied him after he'd walked across Alenzon nearly half out of his mind with pain?

Learning that Asyl wanted to try and reconnect with his biological father again had been a pleasant surprise. Sure, he had his adoptive Void dad now, and having both of them at the introduction gala would most certainly be interesting. As much as he wanted to, he wouldn't be able to get Rojir to attend the family dinner. That honor would lie on Lady Naias's shoulders.

Hopefully, Asyl's mother didn't make things worse. If the rumors were true, she was becoming quite the fanatic, and that made him nervous. Would she attend the general gala? Kende hoped Lord Seni would leave her at the house, using her pregnancy as an excuse, and bring the twins as directed in the invitation. Asyl deserved to know his siblings, and they needed to form their own opinions about having a Void for a brother. At least the twins seemed ready and willing to get to know their elder brother.

Someone was sniffling in the entry hall. Kende closed the door to his study and quickened his pace to the front doors. There was a young man standing there with tear-stained cheeks and reddened eyes. He didn't have a Craft Mark, and if Kende had to guess based on his tears, the boy's Awakening had failed in a sense.

Voids weren't a failure, and Kende refused to think of his Fated like that. The Void in front of him was fairly short, dressed well, with a shock of bright red curls styled in an undercut. It wasn't raining today, in one of the rare days where autumn was actually sunny, so he at least wasn't soaked.

"L-L-Lord Kende," the boy sniffed, trying to draw himself upright and invoke his proper manners.

"Yes," Kende said, trying a disarming smile. "What's wrong?"

"My parents, sir," the boy said, shaking, "they… they don't want me."

"You're a Void," Kende said gently.

A small nod and the teenager dropped his head. "My friend Arik said that Void kids were welcome here if their families dis-disowned them."

A sob tore through the boy's throat, and he clapped a hand over his mouth. He hugged himself as tightly as he could, as if it could disguise his shaking and terror. Kende's heart ached. At least the boy had made his way here instead of having to figure out how to live on the streets.

"You're more than welcome here," Kende said in the same soft tone, holding out his hand to the boy. "What's your name?"

"Olire Ebornazine," the redhead said, taking his hand.

"Good to meet you, Olire. My Fated is at his shop currently, but he'll be back tonight. You can talk with him, and he'll help you adjust to being a Void and what it means. My expectations for you while you live under my roof are that you finish schooling and figure out what you want to do with your life. You've got endless possibilities, and you're not restricted to any field dictated by your Craft."

The boy nodded, though his eyes still seemed a little glazed. Maybe he hadn't quite registered what Kende had said, and that was fine. He was probably still in a good amount of shock. There'd be time to remind the boy of his rules, that he'd just realized he needed to make sure he gave the Void children the best opportunity to succeed that he could.

"Have you eaten?" Kende asked. Olire shook his head. "Come with me."

Kende put a hand on the redhead's shoulder and guided him over to the kitchens. There, he left the boy in his cook's very capable hands. He had plenty that he needed to work on, including checking if he had any response from Ilyphari's priests about whether he could take over the abandoned temple near Enchanted Waters. They weren't using it, but of course they didn't want to give it up. Not even to help the most vulnerable.

After about a half hour, Olire wandered back into his study with two large mugs of tea. One he handed to Kende, and the other he cradled to his chest as he curled up on the couch. The look of pure agony on his face made Kende want to comfort the boy and tell him everything would be all right.

If only life was that easy.

He worked in silence, writing out what would be needed for the move to the new Enchanted Waters building. Keyna would be the most logical choice to transport and install the Ignis plates to make sure they weren't damaged. The last thing Kende needed was for his Fated to move and then have the plates stop working. He drafted a letter to Naias to ask her about what was needed for the storefront and what they could reuse so they could keep their upfront costs down. While Kende was footing most of the bill initially, he still wanted to be smart about what they had on hand.

Siora stood from her desk as Kende handed her the letter and left the office, likely to summon a page so Naias could respond quickly. Once he got that, he could figure out what else they needed, based on the blueprints he and Asyl had agreed on. While his Fated was distracted, maybe he could purchase a nice new working desk and chair for him.

He'd already asked the contractors to make specialized shelves for Asyl to store all his supplies with a rolling ladder that had a basket attachment so he didn't need to balance the glass vials while climbing. That kind of special build was quite a bit extra, but Kende was considering it a housewarming gift of sorts. He knew it would pay for itself ten times over as soon as Enchanted Waters opened her doors again.

Kende lost track of time, scribbling away until he heard Asyl's voice in the hallway, likely arguing with Birgir over one thing or another while handing off his cloak to a footman. It took only a moment for his love to trot in, a delighted smile on his face.

"Good day?" Kende asked, sitting back.

Asyl nodded. "I've almost finished packing up. Lanil is great at helping out. She's gotten a lot of my notes sorted and pared down a lot of my books that I don't really need anymore. We're donating the older ones to a Healer college to see if they can use them. For study or starting a fire. Their call."

"That's wonderful," Kende said, getting to his feet and wrapping Asyl in a tight hug.

"Who's the boy?" Asyl whispered into his ear even as he squeezed Kende.

Remembering his charge, Kende led his Fated over to Olire. The boy had curled up on the couch and was now blinking blearily up at the two of them. Apparently he'd fallen asleep at some point while Kende was working, mug of tea completely forgotten on the floor.

"Asyl, this is Olire. He's just been kicked out by his family for being a Void," Kende said.

Asyl inhaled sharply and immediately sat down next to the redhead.

"Hey," he said gently, "how're you holding up?"

"I don't understand how they can just pretend I don't exist," Olire whimpered. "What did I do wrong?"

"You didn't do *anything* wrong. That took me a long time to realize. For one reason or another, the goddess has decided that you don't need a Craft. Maybe what you're meant to do can't be done by someone who does have a Craft, or a Craft would hinder your calling. I don't know. But what I do know is that it's not your fault," Asyl said, taking the boy's hand and squeezing. "I don't have all the answers. I wish I did. Then I'd know why my parents threw me out too."

"So what do I do now? Lord Kende wants me to finish school, but how can I even look at everyone tomorrow?" Olire asked, tears spilling onto his cheeks.

"Your true friends will stay by you," Asyl said firmly. "They're who matter. Anyone who doesn't want to associate with you anymore simply because you're a Void isn't worth your time or energy. If any instructors give you grief, you let me know, and Kende and I will speak to them personally."

Kende smiled at his Fated's vehemence. Clearly, he wanted Olire to finish school and have the opportunities that Asyl should have had. He'd make sure that was possible. Not only for Olire, but any other Void children that ended up on his doorstep. Hopefully the rumor mill would be effective enough to get to all the different schools and no more children would sleep on the streets. A thought struck him, and he turned toward his assistant's desk.

He needed Siora, but the woman was oddly absent. Lanil was quietly standing near the door of his study, watching Asyl with Olire, a small smile on her face. She didn't have any reservations against Voids, which was one of the main reasons Kende hired her rather than another assistant who had much more experience. He'd curled his lip learning that he'd be helping a Void, and Kende had dismissed the man immediately. The shock on his face had been priceless.

"Have you seen Siora?" Kende asked her.

"No, my lord," Lanil replied with a small wince. "Last I saw her, she was heading to the library."

The library? Maybe she wanted to research something to help with one of their projects. Kende nodded his thanks to her and crossed the hallway over to his favorite room. Sure enough, Siora stood inside near the sitting area, her face deathly pale. Her whole body was trembling, and her eyes were wide, staring at nothing. He knew that look, and fear gripped his stomach briefly. Kende hadn't seen her in the middle of a Vision in a long time.

Kende approached her, gently touched her shoulder. It took her a few minutes to inhale sharply, blink rapidly, and stagger. He helped steady her as she got her balance back, and Siora shook her head, rubbing the back of her neck with a grimace. Her eyes refocused as she turned to look at him, and she hugged herself tight. Siora leaned into him, seeking comfort from his presence. If a Vision was particularly vivid, Seers tended to need to be around people afterward.

"What did you see?" Kende asked.

Siora trembled for a minute, closing her eyes as if she wished he hadn't asked. He waited patiently, and finally she took a deep breath and nodded, deciding on what to do. She wasn't required to share her Visions unless they affected him directly. Maybe this one didn't, but Kende wanted to make sure she was all right. Whatever it was, she was still shaking and upset.

"I was standing on the edge of a large dirt cliff," she began, her voice flat. "At first, I thought it wasn't much of a fall, though it gave way to rocks and brambles. The more I looked, I realized that they were bodies. I was standing at the precipice of a mass grave. Then I saw a boy with red hair. The one who just came in, Olire. It was him, and he was dead. When I looked further, I saw...."

She trailed off, choking back a sob, and clapped her hand over her mouth. Kende waited with barely leashed patience, wanting to know what else she saw. Tears gathered in her eyes, and Siora took a shaking breath, visibly pulling herself back together.

"I saw Asyl. Dead," she finally said. Kende inhaled sharply, staring at her as a chill ran down his spine. "All around me were the bodies of Voids, dumped in a pit to be buried and forgotten."

"Okay," Kende said slowly, trying to think through the haze that settled in his mind.

Siora shuddered and wiped away the tears that threatened to spill. While she hadn't been Asyl's biggest fan when he first came into their lives, she certainly enjoyed his company now. It helped that Kende was far happier with Asyl than he had been for the years he'd been alone.

"Kende, what if this gala puts him in danger and he's killed? I keep hearing more and more hatred towards Voids these days when I'm out running errands. There are so many posters calling for their registration and containment. Putting Asyl in the spotlight like this could focus their attention and make him a target," Siora said, her voice gaining in volume.

"My dear," Kende tried soothing her, rubbing her upper arms, "what if introducing him actually protected him? His going missing would be a bigger issue than if he remained anonymous. Besides, my cousin wants to meet him, and my family deserves to know I finally found my Fated."

"Why would I get a Vision of his death if he was protected with the gala?" Siora asked.

"Maybe as a warning that he is in danger and that we can't be flippant about his safety," Kende said and shrugged. "You told me your Visions can't always be taken literally."

Siora chewed on her lower lip, closing her eyes for a minute before nodding. She cleared her throat and stood up straight, rolling her shoulders back.

"What do you want to do?" she asked.

"Assign a security detail to Asyl. He's to go nowhere without a guard present. They shouldn't interfere with what he's doing unless it's actively dangerous, but just be there to keep an eye on things. Maybe assign one to Olire as well. He'll be vulnerable going to school and dealing with the kids there, and I don't want someone to grab him to get to Asyl," Kende instructed.

"Sir," Siora said.

She bowed and left the library with her head held high. Kende stood for a while longer, staring out the window where Siora had been just moments ago. He'd do everything in his power to keep Asyl safe. Should he get someone to help Rojir too? Asyl had told him how important the man was to him, but Kende doubted that Rojir would appreciate someone hovering. It would probably make his community work harder.

Kende sighed heavily, leaving the library as well. There wasn't much else he could do right now. As he walked back across the hall, Birgir approached him. Kende paused, though he really wasn't in the mood to get into a fight with his steward. Birgir said nothing to him, regarding him with a disapproving frown, and handed him a thick letter.

Saluting his steward with the missive, Kende spun on his heel and entered his office. Asyl and Olire were still talking, heads together as if they didn't want anyone with a Craft to know what they were talking about. He couldn't imagine the terror Siora felt, seeing the two on the couch dead and tossed aside as if they were nothing. Even the idea made him shudder.

Some of his agony must have filtered through their bond, as Asyl glanced up at him. His Fated gave him a warm smile, as if he was promising that everything would be all right. Kende knew better, but he allowed himself to indulge and believe he'd made the best choice. He pushed love and reassurance through the bond and smiled at feeling Asyl return his affection.

For now, he wouldn't tell Asyl what Siora saw. The best thing for him at this moment was to take care of Olire and get the boy's confidence back up after being disowned. He deserved to know he had somewhere safe to go and had adults who cared for him.

With that thought, Kende beckoned Lanil over and requested that she figure out what apartment buildings could be purchased, and failing that, what buildings were available and could be renovated. He couldn't house a good number of Void children here, as there weren't a ton of spare rooms. Many of his siblings still laid claims to their old rooms when they visited for whatever reason, which greatly limited his space.

There were only two guest rooms after taking in Olire. No, they needed somewhere where the kids could live safely that wasn't the streets. Even still, they were kids. He should have a cafeteria to ensure they ate, and possibly a few caretakers to make sure they got their homework done and got to school all right. If they had any issues, they would hopefully go to the caretaker to get them settled.

That would make it a lot easier to help any children that were kicked out without panicking because he had no more room in the manor. Unless he could get his siblings to agree to give up their rooms. It wasn't as if they really ever stayed over anymore.

But what about Void adults? Asyl had been very lucky, managing to find Naias again after running from his savior. Past him and Rojir, how many more were on the streets? He didn't really want to house the adults and children together, so maybe he could look into two different places. Truly, no one deserved to be homeless. Perhaps once these were established, he could get a third building for Craft Blessed who found themselves in hard times. That wasn't a priority, though. The abandoned Void children were.

Kende sat at his desk, outlining two new charity events: one for the acquisition and renovation of a building, and another for employing the staff necessary to run the place. As much as he wanted to, he didn't have the funds to handle this project on his own. His father and cousin most certainly had enough, but he doubted his father would be willing to open the coffers for this. The duke had plenty of feelings about Voids, and helping them wasn't one he was interested in.

Hopefully after Asyl's introduction gala, he'd feel differently.

His focus landed back on the letter that Birgir had given him. Yolotzin's handwriting was neat and prone to unnecessary embellishments. Addressing the letter to Kende had taken up most of the envelope. Rolling his eyes at his cousin, Kende sliced open the letter and removed the papers inside. Luckily for him, it appeared that Yolotzin had dictated his message to his secretary, and Kajaan's handwriting was much more legible.

> *My Dearest Cousin,*
>
> *Kajie and I are leaving Bhyvine tomorrow to head home. King Cossus has expressed interest in trading rice for wool, so maybe father wasn't totally wrong in having me travel around and visit the other kingdoms to improve relationships. Except for Nabene. They're terrifying. If you travel with your Fated, don't go there. They're no fun anyways. No sense of humor, and the dances are incredibly dull. My poor Kajie couldn't even get a good conversation out of the carriage drivers there!*
>
> *What I do want to tell you is that I found something out about Voids that you might find infinitely fascinating. While we were visiting Duke Vitalis—who's also a Void and a delightful man—he asked if Averia would ever value their Voids as the essential Craft Blessed that they are. I told him that when I was crowned king, I'd work on the misconception that Voids are inherently evil and openly support any charities for them you and your Fated might dream up, but I didn't regard them as being Craft Blessed.*
>
> *Duke Vitalis told me that Voids had a unique role in our world and that they should be considered Blessed, even if they don't have a fancy mark on their foreheads. He called himself and the other Voids empty vessels,*

though he didn't mean it as an insult. I can't really figure out a way to explain it that won't get too convoluted or confusing, and a physical demonstration with your beloved might be easier.

Something about white energy that exists inside our Craft that can empower Voids when they draw upon it. Kajaan and I will discuss what he told us during our ride home and see if we can put it into better words. Maybe your Fated will understand it instinctively and know what Duke Vitalis was talking about so he can tell us.

We both look forward to meeting your heart's twin during the gala. Give Maielle a hug for me when you see her next.

All my love,
Yolotzin

Kende resisted frowning down at the letter. He hadn't even considered the possibility that other kingdoms would look into Voids and research why their Awakenings "failed," uncovering this white energy phenomenon. Why wasn't that knowledge shared with Averia and her citizens? Unless…. Did King Tonalli not want his subjects to know?

That was an uncomfortable thought. Kende looked over at his Fated, who had Olire in his arms, hugging the child while one hand carded through his coarse red curls. At some point, the young teenager had fallen asleep. The open affection on Asyl's face convinced Kende that his lover would make a wonderful father.

Someday.

CHAPTER 12

SOMEHOW, ASYL had acquired a bodyguard. Neither Kende, Lanil, or Siora had said anything to him about it, and the huge Gaian man was pleasant enough. He was older and worked quietly with Asyl, moving boxes and double-checking his inventory numbers. What had changed, Asyl wasn't sure. Kende didn't have a visible guard of his own that Asyl could figure out, so why was he assigned one?

Did Kende not trust him to stay safe? Did he think that Asyl would run away again?

That wasn't fair.

The only thing Kende was concerned about was his well-being and trying to head off any problems. Asyl could suffer with an assistant and bodyguard. At least the Gaian had the quietest demeanor and a kind smile. He didn't seem to mind taking directions from a Void and didn't complain whatsoever. The man had insisted he handle the heavier boxes since he had the strength, either waving Asyl away or gently steering him toward the sacks of herbs. Asyl did his best to not feel too emasculated by that.

Only a week after sealing his Fated bond with Kende, his living quarters were completely packed up. The battered furniture had been removed and donated to any shelters that could use it after letting Rojir take what he wanted or needed. He knew that Rojir was exchanging letters with Kende about his idea of renovating the temple into a safe place for Voids. What his dad wasn't telling him was whether he had agreed to help run the events.

He vaguely hated that Rojir wouldn't discuss the project with him, always telling him to talk to Kende if he wanted the information. Asyl didn't know why, since he had come up with the idea of contacting his father about the produce and suggested the idea to see if tailors and cobblers would be willing to donate their apprentices' works. Instead, Asyl had to get home to ask Kende about the temple's progress.

Home.

If Asyl thought about it, calling Ruvyn manor home was dizzying. The house itself still unnerved him with its size and implications, but as long as he was with Kende, he was happy. He still got to have quiet nights alone with Kende before retiring to bed, curled up in his arms. Asyl hadn't had a nightmare for the entire week he'd been working on his move. Bringing Olire into their household just brightened his days even further.

Olire's return to school was met with mixed emotions, as he lost quite a few friends and gained some others. Kende had sent a letter with the redhead to give to the principal explaining that he was there under Kende's direction, guidance, and protection. A large Gale man had accompanied the teenager, aware of the situation and ready to defend Olire. At the end of his school day, Toemi would pick up Olire and ferry him to Enchanted Waters to help Asyl pack his supplies and herbs until the store was ready to close for good.

The last thing to do was to move his Ignis Plates. Keyna met with Asyl and Olire along with her burly Ignis coworker. The two crouched down and got to work uninstalling the three plates while the two Voids relaxed and took a break from moving the last of the furniture. Asyl hadn't realized how heavy his work desk was. Keyna hummed and frowned, looking at the Plate she was uninstalling from the floor.

"Everything all right?" Asyl asked, capping his waterskin.

"Yeah. It's just fighting me," Keyna told him, glancing in his direction.

Asyl tilted his head at that but shrugged. He turned to Olire and instead asked him about his day. The teenager bounced as he regaled Asyl about his lab work for the day, a bright grin on his face. He pulled out his latest test, proud of the high marks he'd gotten. His chatter seemed to bring the two Ignians amusement, Asyl catching their glances and smiles toward each other.

Once the plates were up, his bodyguard and the Ignis man took them out to the cart for transport. Olire followed to "keep watch," though Asyl wondered if he was more fascinated with the Ignis. Keyna eyed his old Plates stacked in the corner. Asyl had no idea what he was going to do with them and had even debated abandoning them. He had no use for them now that he had his fancy new Plates, and he had no idea how to sell them.

Without a word, she walked over to the plates and studied them with a small hum. She picked up the smaller one, her toned arms flexing under the weight. Sure, they were designed to be portable, but the things still weighed about fifty pounds. Keyna hefted it like it was nothing, examining it as she rotated it in her hands before looking at him.

"Can I take these?" she asked.

Asyl blinked. "You weren't interested in them before."

She shrugged, "I want to try out a new project."

"Yeah, go for it. It's just metal to me," Asyl said with a small smile. "Don't really think they're worth trying to refurbish or repair."

At that, Keyna nodded, though Asyl questioned again why she wanted to take them. She trotted out of the building, and a minute later, her companion came in to grab the second plate. Olire had stayed outside, likely enjoying the rare early winter sun. Lanil looked at him as Asyl turned in the workroom, making sure they got everything. He did one final sweep of the living quarters upstairs and the front room.

It was as bare as the day Naias purchased it. A lump formed in his throat, and Asyl blinked back tears pricking at his eyes. He'd done a lot of recovery here after he wasn't completely paralyzed with fear. Living above Enchanted Waters gave him a freedom that staying with Naias hadn't, and he'd had to relearn how to live with himself. How to not blame himself for what happened.

All his hours spent bent over books and studying the hell out of any medical tome he could get his grubby hands on. His piles of notes, hastily bound together by the same twine he labeled his medicines with. Days upon days of standing over boiling cauldrons, sweating right through his tunic, anxious to know if he'd gotten his recipe right.

Goddess, this was really it. Asyl made sure the back door was locked before heading out the front after Lanil. Closing the original location was bittersweet. Asyl stood in front of the building, staring up at it. They already had a buyer for the building. It would be renovated into a small grocery, which would be helpful in its own way.

"Ready?" Lanil asked kindly.

Asyl took a deep breath and nodded. The sale had been finalized, and Enchanted Waters was now officially moving. Most of the money went back to Naias, for the original amount that she'd purchased the building for and a good amount of the taxes they'd paid in the last four years. She deserved the extra funds for her use and her dowry. Whomever her intended was, they wouldn't be hurting for money and might even have a nice luxurious life depending on what her partner brought to the table.

They would still have quite a lot of money left over to help supply the new location, which Naias was absolutely delighted about. She'd helped set up the front room in the first building, so it was only fair she be included in the second. While she was tasked with putting it together, Asyl had most of his brewing room set up. As soon as the Plates were installed, he would be able to start in on potions. Salves and tinctures were easy to make without his cauldrons, and he had enough of those right now.

To keep Olire busy once he was done with his studies, Kende had him help Asyl. It only took a few tries for the redhead to understand the recipe, and he took to the physical mixing quickly. When he was older, Asyl might have him help with the potions, once he could ensure the teenager wouldn't burn himself. After swinging up into the back of the cart, Asyl sat next to the Plates while Lanil guided the horses back to the new building.

"What do you think Lady Elrel has done in the front room?" Olire asked with a smile.

Asyl grinned. "Not sure. She's got a great eye, so I'm excited to see what she does with it."

The rest of the ride was in silence, Asyl trying to soak in as much of the pale winter sun as he could. Keyna and her associate followed their carriage to install the Plates once they arrived. Naias was a hive of activity when they pulled to a stop at the large open doors, humming happily and digging through the packed boxes of their finished product to fill out the displays. She'd set a few up, take a step back, hum, and either leave it alone or fiddle with it some more. Asyl planned to stay firmly out of her way.

Smiling at her, Asyl quietly slipped through the front, carrying some of the last few boxes of herbs that were solely for potions. Once again, he glanced over at the hanging cloth that closed off at least a third of his workspace. Kende had told him not to peek, and so far, Asyl had been good and listened despite his fingers itching to disobey. He knew it was another surprise gift from his Fated, and as much as he wanted to spoil it out of curiosity, Asyl kept his hands to himself.

Except today Kende was standing in front of the curtain, smiling. Asyl jumped, startled, even as his grin deepened. He hadn't realized that Kende had moved away from the manor at some point during the day. His sneaky Fated was even concealing his emotions, though Asyl could see the nervous anxiety on his face plain as day.

"What are you up to?" Asyl teased, hefting the box onto the growing pile. "You've got your plotting expression on."

"I would never plot against you," Kende replied with feigned horror.

"You absolutely would, though always in the context of kindness," Asyl said. "You're a sneaky one, Lord Ruvyn."

"Sneaky Lord Ruvyn sounds good," Kende said and smiled. "Maybe I should start introducing myself like that."

Asyl let out a bark of laughter and shook his head, carefully beginning to unpack the herbs onto the gorgeous and expansive work desk Kende had commissioned for him. Asshole. Though Asyl really truly enjoyed the way Kende was so adamantly taking care of him. The few days of uncertainty were gone, especially after Asyl had told him how much he appreciated the way Kende spoiled him.

While he likely would never be able to pay Kende back, he could at least show how much the consideration meant to him. That would be a lifetime project Asyl was more than willing to work on every day.

"Is your secret project finished?" Asyl asked. "Did you make another five work desks back there?"

"Sort of," Kende said and grinned.

Surprised, Asyl stopped what he was doing and turned around to look at his Fated. Kende reached up and pulled the curtains back on the rod they'd been affixed to at the top of the ceiling. Asyl's breath caught in his throat as he stared at the rows of shelving.

He could compare it to Kende's fancy library, with a sliding ladder that gave him quick and easy access to everything. The shelves themselves were mostly thin, deep enough for only one or two boxes. Some had baskets built into them, able to slide out as if they were drawers.

"Kende," Asyl said softly, taking a few steps closer, "what?"

"I thought instead of piling your boxes on the ground, you could store them here. Maybe unpack one or two so you can have a better visual at what you have, or however you want to keep your containers. I thought you could use the baskets for the berries and smaller ingredients, and over here, I was assured that these racks would be great for hanging herbs. Of course, if you want to use it for something else—"

Asyl strode over the last few steps and grabbed Kende's vest, yanking him down and accidentally smashing their lips together hard enough that they split. The coppery tang of blood accompanied Kende's usual taste, and Asyl couldn't help but whimper and step closer. He felt Kende's hands rest on his hips, embracing him.

This was how Asyl knew that Kende listened to him and his fears. He always did his best to make sure Asyl didn't feel pressured to have his workspace set up in a specific way, just quietly supporting him, from spreading awareness of his products to making sure Asyl had the best tools for his work.

Someone whistled appreciatively behind them, and Kende slowly let Asyl go, both of them breathing heavily. Kende smiled and chuckled faintly.

"I take it you approve," he said softly.

"Goddess, yes," Asyl said. "I don't understand how you can anticipate what I want or need, but I adore you for always seeming to know when to not overstep."

Kende's smile widened, and he leaned in, pressing their foreheads together.

"Asyl, where do you want these Plates?"

Well, he'd have plenty of time later to cuddle up to Kende and tell him thank you over and over again. If he could take Enchanted Waters even further, perhaps that would be the best thanks he could ever give him. Besides, Asyl truly loved brewing and helping others. It gave him a peace he hadn't known he needed.

With a heavy sigh, Asyl stepped away from his Fated and showed Keyna where he wanted the installation. Knowing he'd have three cauldrons likely brewing full force, Asyl wanted a permanent workspace between each one: two cauldrons with a bench for each set perpendicular between them. The bench legs were made of wrought iron to avoid a fire hazard, though the top was still wood. His distillery was now permanently set up on his old worktable, with his research books and recipe journals stored on the new one.

Some new books were mixed among his old ones that weren't there before. They looked to be books that only Healers could get their hands on. Asyl couldn't wait to read through to see what they were and try to figure out new potions, tinctures, or salves to make and sell.

Maybe he could have Kende help him test his bone-growth potion. If he could work with a select clinic or two for trial runs with patient approval and confidentiality, then that would speed up his testing quite a lot. He could even work on improving his recipes and try to make them even more potent.

While the two Ignians installed the Plates, Kende and Olire unpacked the boxes of herbs and ingredients to Asyl's instructions. Both his and the redhead's bodyguards moved the supplies to where Asyl wanted them to go without complaint. Over the next moonturn, he would likely make changes, but right now the setup was nice.

Instead of throwing away the packing boxes, Asyl stacked them in a very specific pattern along the wall. It was hidden from most places in the room. When Kende asked him about it, Asyl simply shrugged and mentioned using them to transport products in for their community days. He wasn't sure if Kende believed him, but he didn't press further.

Finally, his workroom was complete.

Asyl couldn't help the grin on his face as he moved around the new space, absentmindedly grabbing the ingredients he needed for a batch of full-strength healing potions. There was a well in the corner that Naias could draw pure water from and place it into a large vat for Asyl's use. Right now, it was empty. Tomorrow morning, Naias would draw as much as she could from the well, and he'd begin making potions again.

He waved farewell to Keyna and the Ignian man. Neither of them was staying long, and Keyna kept getting a pensive look on her face whenever she regarded the Plates she had been installing. Olire was starting to snap a little and get huffy, so Kende sent him home where he could get a snack before dinner. The Gale left with him.

Naias sighed happily at the workroom and twirled in the open space.

"It's not very homey yet, but it's clean," she remarked.

"Are you saying my old workspace was dirty?" Asyl asked, faking being appalled.

Naias laughed. "Yes. You never swept! So many complaints about the floor hurting your feet when you didn't have shoes that one moonturn."

"It's not my fault I didn't have my shoes," Asyl said.

"Not mine either," Kende cut in, smiling. "You ran off before I could give them to you."

His best friend snorted and grinned at the two of them. "I can't wait to see how you decorate this space in the next few moonturns. I'm going to bet by next spring you'll have herbs hanging from the ceiling and walls again. Plants. Ivy."

"I've got decorative flowers," Asyl said, pointing at the fresh bouquet that had been delivered at some point that morning.

"Maybe a cat or two?" Naias asked.

"I'm not risking the quality of my potions from a cat deciding to drink from the water you draw," Asyl said flatly.

"But think of the hours you can spend with a sweet feline on your lap while you study," Naias cooed.

Asyl wrinkled his nose. "And get stabbed millions of times with their claws while people promise me that they're doing so because they're happy? No thanks."

"Kende," Naias said, looking at him, "you don't think a store cat would be nice?"

"Don't tell me you've got one already!" Asyl said, standing up straight. "Naias, please, the glass won't survive a cat knocking it off a shelf!"

Naias gave a put-upon sigh and pouted at him. "No. But Yona's cat is having kittens, and I thought we could adopt one or two."

"*You* can adopt one or two. They just stay in your home," Asyl said.

"It's been a while since we've had a cat at the manor," Kende said slowly.

"No," Asyl groaned. "I don't heal like you two do! I'll end up looking like a pincushion!"

Asyl glared at his best friend when she giggled at the predicament.

"A kitten would be fun to have around," Kende said with a crooked smile.

"Kende," Asyl groaned.

"Imagine how much Birgir would hate it."

Asyl stopped and stared at his Fated. A slow smile spread across his face, and Naias laughed at Asyl's reaction.

"That is a good point. But do we really want a kitten just to annoy Birgir?" Asyl asked.

Kende shrugged, smiling. "I would love to have pets in the house again, but it's up to you."

Naias bounced forward and grabbed Asyl's head. She pulled him down the few inches he had on her and kissed his cheek noisily.

"Well, you've still got about a moonturn to decide," she said with a smile. "For now, I'll leave you be. I'll be back tomorrow to get everything organized."

Asyl grabbed her in a tight hug before she scurried away. He squeezed, getting a squeak from her and a breathless laugh. Naias gave Kende a wave and left the two of them. The two assistants and the large Gaian remained, loitering in the main room.

"Stay here," Asyl told his Fated.

Kende raised an eyebrow but stayed put. Asyl slipped to the front room and wandered over to Lanil. She took a step back from admiring the shelving and smiled at him.

"Can you take Siora and... um...." Asyl glanced helplessly at the bodyguard.

"Tsela," Lanil whispered.

Asyl smiled. "And Tsela back to the manor? Take Toemi's carriage. Kende can get us back with the Craft vehicle."

Lanil raised an eyebrow and smiled knowingly. "Sure. Have fun."

He blushed and smiled at her. Lanil walked over to Siora and placed a hand on her shoulder, whispering in her ear. The other woman laughed and nodded, beckoning for Tsela to join them. He glanced at Asyl for a moment before following. Asyl shut the workroom door solidly behind him and looked at his Fated.

Now that his secret had been revealed, Kende had reopened himself to their bond. He was happy and content. Asyl walked over to where he was sitting at the brand-new desk and grabbed his Fated's hand, hauling him to his feet.

"What?" Kende asked, laughing.

"Shush. Come with me," Asyl told him.

The man smiled at him, following without any complaint. Asyl led him over to the boxes and turned around. Kende regarded him with a cocked eyebrow and a smile. Humming happily, Asyl pushed Kende back until his knees hit the lip of the boxes and he fell back. The man blinked up at him and laughed.

"Of course, it's a chair," he said.

"That it is," Asyl replied, nodding and smiling. He clambered onto the boxes, straddling his Fated's lap. Kende let out a slow sigh, resting his hands on Asyl's hips. Asyl leaned in and placed a small kiss on his lips. "I can't ever repay you for everything you've done."

"I don't need repayment," Kende said. "I just want you to be happy."

"I know," Asyl said and smiled, kissing him again. He pulled away before Kende could deepen the kiss, laughing at his groan. "Just stay still."

Kende tilted his head but nodded. Asyl scooted back and off his Fated's lap, kneeling in front of him. He heard Kende's sharp intake of breath and felt the spike of nervous excitement through their bond as he placed his hands to either side of his hips. Asyl reached up and slid the buttons of the man's slacks free. He sat back and tugged on the underside of his knees, drawing Kende closer to the edge.

"You don't need to do this to show thanks," Kende said softly.

"I know," Asyl said, smiling up at him. "I want to, though."

Kende reached down and cupped his jaw. He tilted Asyl's head up and bent over, brushing their lips together. The splits on their lips were a little rough, but neither of them reopened. Asyl briefly wondered why Kende hadn't healed himself but didn't care to ask at the moment. As soon as Kende released him, he parted his Fated's pants, pushing aside all the excess cloth. The man was half hard. Asyl could work with that.

He nudged Kende's legs wider, and his lover easily obliged. Asyl leaned in, grasping his lover's prick and feeling a surge of excitement. He licked him from root to tip, drawing in his love's taste. Kende groaned as he leaned back, giving Asyl complete control. It had been so long since the last time he put his mouth anywhere near another penis, but he didn't remember it tasting so good. Salt and earthy musk.

Dipping his head, Asyl drew his love's balls into his mouth, laving them thoroughly. He slowly pumped Kende's dick as he did so, delighted to feel him thicken to full hardness. Asyl dragged his tongue over his whole length again, kissing the slit and the bead of precum that sat there. He let out a small noise from the back of his throat and tilted his head to ever so gently nip and kiss down his length.

Kende moaned heartily as Asyl moved his mouth back up to the crown, swirling his tongue around the tip. He looked up at his Fated, who was watching him with half-lidded eyes, and grinned. Kende barely smiled back before Asyl swallowed him whole, reveling in the heavy weight on his tongue. He felt Kende's hand come up as he gave a choked cry. Asyl was pleasantly surprised when Kende didn't start tugging his hair.

He reached out for his Fated's hand and moved it to the back of his skull. Kende slowly slid his hand into Asyl's hair, tangling his fingers thoroughly. Asyl anticipated Kende taking over, tugging him wherever he wanted him to chase his own pleasure. Instead, Kende simply scratched at his scalp, carefully flexing his hand whenever Asyl opened his throat to have his love's cock tap the back of his throat.

"Oh Goddess," Kende groaned.

Asyl held his position, keeping Kende's prick completely in his mouth, cutting off his air for several seconds. He backed off, gasping, pumping Kende furiously while he panted. As soon as he felt like he could breathe again, Asyl dove right back in, moaning around his love's cock. He parted his legs, realizing how tight his pants were, and untied his placket to give him some more room. Asyl took himself in hand, lazily stroking his dick.

"Sweetheart," Kende gasped, "I'm going to cum."

All it took was for Asyl to hum his acknowledgment for Kende to spill down his throat, groaning. Asyl gagged briefly, unused to the feeling, before he swallowed everything Kende gave him. He pulled off, cleaning Kende's length with quick little licks and looking up at him. Kende was slumped against the wall, his head tilted back as he worked on catching his breath.

Asyl sat back on his haunches, closed his eyes, and began stroking himself.

"Stop," Kende said, his voice thick.

"What?" Asyl said, blinking a few times to look up at him.

"My turn," Kende told him, a crooked grin on his face. Before Asyl could parse what he meant, his love grabbed him under his arms and hauled him up. He squeaked as Kende swapped their positions and stared up at him in surprise. "What? Did you think I'd just let you rub yourself off after that?"

Asyl didn't have to voice his reply as he flushed. Kende simply kissed the tip of his nose and slid to his knees in front of him. Kende's hand wrapped around his prick, pumping slowly. Asyl fought to keep his eyes open as he whimpered, pressing his hand to his mouth to stifle the sounds flowing from him. His lover grinned up at him and kissed the tip of his dick.

Wet heat engulfed him, and Asyl gasped, unable to help himself from bucking up into his Fated's mouth. Kende ran his hands up and down Asyl's thighs, one dipping down to fondle Asyl's balls as he bobbed his head. He didn't seem bothered by Asyl squirming underneath him, spasming from pleasure.

Trying to breathe was hard. Asyl found his hand curling in Kende's hair, holding him tight and bucking when he felt a flash of teeth on his crown. The pain was barely there, more pleasure than anything. Kende wrapped one arm around Asyl's hips, pulling him closer, rolling Asyl's balls in his other hand.

"Kende," Asyl whined.

His lover raised his eyes to meet his, and Asyl hoped that Kende couldn't see the vulnerability in his expression. Kende pulled off, licked his slit, and engulfed him again. Asyl shouted and spent down his Fated's throat, gasping in harsh breaths. He watched his dick slide from Kende's lips with half-lidded eyes, feeling boneless and exhausted.

Kende leaned up and kissed him sweetly. Asyl easily opened his mouth, tasting himself on his love's lips. He wondered if Kende didn't mind the salty sweetness they shared with each other. Asyl sighed softly, blinking slowly up at him.

"All right?" Kende asked.

Asyl smiled and hummed quietly. His lover chuckled, redoing the placket ties and buttoning himself back up. He gathered Asyl up, turned around, and sat down, cradling Asyl in his arms. They sat there for a while together, their bodies cooling in the evening chill.

For once today, his mind was quiet. Asyl closed his eyes, nestling into Kende's chest and wrapping an arm around his lover's neck. Kende hugged Asyl close to him, pressing a kiss to the top of his head. How did he get so lucky? Asyl stretched in Kende's arms, sighing happily. He tilted his head back and kissed Kende's neck.

He was happy. Content. As was Kende, according to their bond. Asyl hadn't thought he'd ever feel safe in someone else's arms, that he'd be someone else's priority. With Kende, he had no doubts. The man would love him wholly—did love him wholly. Even though they hadn't said any words to each other, Asyl knew how Kende felt about him.

Asyl just hoped that he could be worthy of the man's love.

CHAPTER 13

WATCHING ASYL conduct his research was most definitely a joy. He got lost in reading, scribbling notes on his papers without even really looking at them, comparing information between tomes, finding small nuggets of knowledge that were hard or impossible to puzzle together without multiple sources. Asyl was quick at it, too, getting the information he needed simply by scanning.

He would be invaluable to the scribes who pored through history's archives to try and get a clear look at past events. Family lineage, wars, births, deaths, marriages. Anything they could get their hands on, really. They'd just have to try and pry Asyl away from his beloved alchemy, which wouldn't happen as long as Asyl breathed.

Kende just loved watching him, the tip of Asyl's tongue caught between his teeth. Usually his Fated didn't even know he was there with how hard he concentrated on his work. Asyl would finally surface when Olire bounded through the workroom door, excited about one thing or another that happened during school.

That usually got Kende a sheepish smile and a few chaste kisses before Kende shared a late lunch with him. He really didn't mind and enjoyed the break from his own duties. Trying to juggle the acquisition of several buildings and getting them up to code along with planning Asyl's introduction gala, Marielle's summer party, and working with Rojir about the temple…. It was a lot.

Returning home after that was always hard to do, but the events wouldn't wait, and Siora most definitely was doing her best to keep him on track. She would glower at him whenever he slipped back into the manor, always doing his best to sneak away so that he and Asyl could be alone. Yet he still always managed to get away every day, much to her exasperation.

Even if Asyl spent half of his days researching, it didn't stop him from coming home and devouring leisure books after dinner, curled up next to Kende. Their nights were spent by the fire in his suite, often with a hot mug of tea or cocoa. Asyl was perfectly content, his happiness and love strong through their bond. Kende wanted to tell him those three little words if he knew it wouldn't make his love anxious.

Reading together was something Kende thoroughly enjoyed. While their tastes ran differently, if a passage was amusing, they'd read it out to each other. Or in Asyl's case, he'd complain about the protagonist doing something stupid and how the situation could be handled better. Usually, Kende would just laugh and kiss the top of his head while Asyl nestled deeper into his side.

Even if they weren't Fated, Kende would have been hard-pressed to not fall in love with Asyl. He looked forward to their time cuddling all day and wished they never had to get up in the morning. Every night he got to sleep with Asyl in his arms, holding him close to his chest. For the nights when Asyl was feeling frisky, Kende would let him dictate what he wanted. Usually, they'd grind up against each other until they spent and fell asleep, sated and content.

Time could stand still, and he'd be the happiest man alive.

THE GALA was next week, and Kende hadn't done much in making sure Asyl could dance. Maerie had finished both of their outfits, and Asyl's was closer to a gown than a suit. His Fated adored fabric swishing around him when he moved, which showed in his insistence to wear slightly too large tunics. If Asyl didn't take great joy in the clothing, Kende would wonder if he wore them to hide his body. Maybe he did.

When Asyl came home from Enchanted Waters that night, tired and smelling of smoke, Kende urged his Fated to take a quick bath. It took Lanil about a half hour afterward to persuade her charge to come back downstairs into the ballroom where Kende waited for him. The last two days, he'd had his servants do a deep clean of the room. In a few days, they'd polish the floor until it was nearly a mirror, and then the night before they'd draw elaborate chalk designs.

Lanil and Siora sat together on the low bench, comparing notes and schedules, probably making sure they were getting last-minute plans sorted out and ensuring that the companies they hired would be able to deliver on time. Kende had delegated such tasks to Siora once he got the deed to the abandoned temple. Tsela stood on the opposite side of the room, near the garden windows, his face unreadable.

Asyl was already tugging at the hem of his tunic as he walked over to Kende, apprehension in his eyes.

"We've put this off long enough," Kende said softly. "Ready?"

"Sure," Asyl said, tugging once more on the hem before jerking his hands away.

"Remember, don't look at your feet," Kende said, kissing Asyl's scarred fingers.

Asyl smiled faintly and stepped close to Kende. He moved one of Asyl's hands, guiding his Fated to hold on to his shoulder as he rested his own on Asyl's hip. Slowly, they moved through the standard waltz together, Asyl frowning when he tripped a few times, his frustration flaring. Each time, Kende dipped down and gave Asyl a gentle kiss to distract his Fated and fortify his resolve.

After about an hour, they were able to make it fully through the formal dance with no tripping or treading on toes. Another half hour saw them moving easier, and a smile finally formed on Asyl's face. Kende quietly guided Asyl into more intermediate dances and moves, twirling and spinning his Fated. These steps likely had never been taught to him, and Asyl took to them easily.

They were both smiling now with the joy of dancing with each other. Kende could no longer feel any frustration or irritation from Asyl as he fought to relearn the waltz in a different position than what he was taught. Asyl was fine with being spun, dipped, or even lifted off his feet, though those had the added bonus of getting some giggles.

Once they started deviating from the expected waltz, Asyl began to show Kende some of the dances that he'd been taught on the streets. It involved quite a bit more hip-swinging action, and Kende quickly found himself entranced. He'd never heard of bachata until now, but he found himself loving it. Asyl eagerly taught him how to lead, a thin sheen of sweat making him glow.

It was several hours later before Asyl moved back into Kende's arms and wrapped his own around Kende's neck, pressing in close and just swaying together. They were both slightly out of breath, but there was no mistaking the look in Asyl's eyes.

He didn't even need to consult their bond for Kende to know how happy and delighted his love was. Just the light in his eyes and the smile on his face was enough. Kende kissed Asyl's forehead, letting his lips linger as they swayed back and forth together, letting their muscles rest and cool.

"Kende," Asyl said softly. Moving his hands to Asyl's hips, he looked down at his Fated, unable to stop himself from smiling. Asyl tilted his head back and Kende gave him a gentle kiss at the silent request. His Fated was nervous, unable to keep eye contact and biting his lower lip as he worked up the courage to say what he wanted to. Finally, Asyl drew in a deep breath and locked their gazes together. "I love you."

Kende couldn't stop the smile that spread across his lips if he tried. His heart swelled at hearing those three simple words from his Fated. From the man who'd suffered so much and had been so closed off when they first met. The amount of trust that Asyl was giving him wasn't lost on him, nor did he discount how much it took for Asyl to tell him how he felt even with the knowledge of what came through their bond.

"I love you too," Kende murmured, resting his forehead on Asyl's, "I think I fell in love the moment you flipped me off and then ran across the city barefoot to keep yourself safe."

Asyl snickered. "You're never going to let me live that down, are you."

"Never," Kende teased.

He heard rustling and the quiet click of the door. They were alone. Asyl pushed up on his toes and pressed their lips together, one of his hands tangling into Kende's hair. Before, Asyl had always been a bit tentative before they deepened the kiss. This time, the kiss made his head spin with the anticipation of what could follow, though he made sure to be careful of the healing cut on Asyl's lip. Kende moved one hand to cup the back of Asyl's head as he eagerly took possession of his Fated's mouth.

Asyl's other hand slipped from over his shoulder to rest on his chest, just above his pec. The small, steady whimpers he got from his love fueled Kende's desire, and his trousers grew tight. He didn't want to pressure Asyl into anything further, but his body moved on instinct, slipping one leg between his Fated's. There, he got a small surprise. Instead of shying away or freezing at the intimate contact outside of their bedroom, Asyl arched into him instead.

Kende broke the kiss, both of them gasping for air. He shifted his leg, pleased to feel an answering hardness against his hip. Asyl's eyes were slightly glazed over, his pupils enlarged. His grip on Kende's arm tightened, and Asyl pushed his hips forward, moaning quietly. Oh, he was most definitely wanting. Kende would be so happy to provide that to him.

"Tell me what you want," Kende whispered.

Asyl pressed his face into his neck before mumbling, "Make me yours."

"You're already mine," Kende assured him, kissing the curve of Asyl's neck and nuzzling the side of his face, "but I will absolutely make love to you."

"Please," Asyl pleaded.

Despite Asyl only being a few inches shorter than him, Kende knelt and picked him up easily. His Fated immediately wrapped his legs around Kende's waist, holding on tight. Nudging the ballroom door open, Kende spotted Birgir down the hallway, waiting for them. The man opened his mouth and started to walk toward them. Oh hell no. He would ruin the mood and Asyl would pull away again. Before he could snap at his butler, Siora intercepted him and pulled the man into the library.

She absolutely deserved a raise.

Kende walked up the stairs, careful with his precious cargo. Asyl nuzzled into his neck, his hips rocking slightly, tempting him to just put his Fated down on the steps and take him right there. In response, Kende lightly traced circles in the small of his lover's back with his nails. He didn't see any of his staff on his way to his bedroom, and his door was even slightly ajar. Their assistants absolutely knew what was going to happen. The thought made Kende smile faintly.

He kicked the door shut and walked over to the bed, then gently deposited his lover on the sheets.

"Do you need to lock the door?" Asyl asked as he blushed.

Kende smiled and shook his head. "If I'm right, both Siora and Lanil are running interference. We won't be disturbed."

Asyl smiled sheepishly and nodded. At Kende's direction, he toed off his shoes and scooted firmly onto the bed, Asyl's head resting on the pillows. He put one knee in between his Fated's, and Asyl spread his legs easily. Kende rested some of his weight on top of his lover, bracketing Asyl's head with his arms, and dipped down to kiss him again.

Apparently that hadn't been what Asyl thought he would do, though this position wasn't new to either of them. Beneath him, his Fated's body relaxed, and he felt Asyl's heels rest gently against his ass. Kende teased his lips open, and as soon as he heard another small whimper, he broke away from his mouth, instead trailing kisses up his jaw to his ear. Asyl gasped when Kende nipped his earlobe, his hands coming up to grip his forearms. His nails dug in, and his hips bucked as Kende licked the skin behind his ear.

Enjoying his reaction, Kende repeated the motion with agonizing slowness, gently nibbling a few times. Asyl groaned, his legs tightening around Kende's hips. Hearing and seeing his lover so responsive made excitement pour through Kende as he nibbled down Asyl's neck to his collarbone. He shifted his weight onto one arm and slid the other up Asyl's tunic, tracing his way up to his nipple. Asyl gave a small squeak when Kende plucked at it, nipping his collarbone at the same time, his hips jerking into Kende's clumsily.

Asyl dropped his head back, eyes closed, and his breath came quickly. He tugged at Kende's shirt, his fingers deftly pushing the buttons through. In less than a minute, his shirt hung open and Asyl pressed his hands to his broad chest. Asyl curled his fingers through his body hair, tugging gently at the fuzz that spread across his pecs.

"Feels so nice," Asyl murmured.

"So do you," Kende replied, equally soft.

He pushed Asyl's tunic up to his throat and nuzzled the smooth skin before seeking out one nipple and clamping on to it. His hand found the other one, and he rolled that one with his fingers even as he licked and nipped at the other small bud. Asyl's nails dug into his chest, lightly scratching him as he moaned, pushing his chest up toward his mouth. Kende swapped places after a couple of minutes, lavishing both sides of his chest equally.

Releasing the small targets, Kende kissed down the center of his chest to his belly button, where he nipped the top and let his tongue dart into the small recess. Asyl giggled, squirming and sinking his hands into Kende's hair, gently scratching at his scalp. Kende glanced up at his Fated's flushed face and smiled, kissing right above the waistband of his breeches.

Asyl sat up, whipping his tunic off somewhere. He tugged Kende's shirt off his arms, and that too went flying off the bed. Asyl's fingers quickly slid back into Kende's hair as he surged forward, their lips crashing together even as they tumbled back to the mattress. The kiss dissolved quickly as Kende untied Asyl's breeches and loosened the straps. Asyl went very still, and Kende studied him carefully.

"Are you all right?" Kende asked softly. "We can stop."

"I want this," Asyl said. "I've always associated sex with pain. We.... The stuff we've done before has helped but...."

"Promise me that if it gets too much, you'll tell me," Kende urged him. "I'll stop, and we can either do something else or just go to sleep."

Asyl took a deep breath and nodded. "I promise."

Kende waited for a minute, watching his Fated's face and consulting their bond for any sign of fear. When he didn't feel any, he gave Asyl a gentle kiss and slowly tugged his pants down to his thighs. Kende sat back on his heels, undoing his own trousers and letting them fall to his knees. He kicked off the last of his clothing before gently sliding Asyl's off.

So many times he'd seen his lover's body, and every time it felt like a gift. This time, like all the other times, Kende's mouth watered, and he smiled up at his blushing Fated. Kende scooted back before kneeling over and grasping the uncut cock in his hand. He pumped a few times, glad to see that even with Asyl's nerves he was still plenty hard.

Kende dipped his head and licked from the base all the way to his crown, flicking his tongue over the slit. Asyl gasped as his head fell back, and he pulled his legs up toward his chest. Kende gently grabbed the backs of his thighs, holding them there as he sucked the head between his lips. A moan escaped from Asyl, and his hips jerked.

He slapped his hands over his mouth and whimpered as Kende slid down his length. Kende caught Asyl's eye as he looked up and smiled as best as he could. His Fated's face was nearly completely red, his eyes glazed over in pleasure. Relaxing his throat, Kende engulfed him entirely, burying his nose in Asyl's curls.

Bobbing his head, Kende slipped one hand from Asyl's leg to play with one of his nipples. One hand shot down, grabbing Kende's hair and holding him tight. He slowly pulled off, licking and nipping gently down to his balls. He sucked one into his mouth, rolling it with his tongue.

"Oh *Goddess*," Asyl gasped. "Kende, please!"

Kende took the skin of his sac between his teeth and pulled very gently. His Fated moaned heartily, and Kende grabbed the back of his thigh again, pushing Asyl's hips off the mattress. He licked his perineum and blew a hot breath over the pink pucker. Asyl squeaked, his hand flexing, tugging sharply on Kende's hair. Smiling, Kende dragged his tongue over his hole, loving the sharp musk playing on his taste buds.

He licked a few times, letting Asyl get used to the sensation of being rimmed before teasing his entrance with the tip of his tongue, breaching him. Above him, Asyl shouted, and his body went rigid as he coated his stomach with pearly white release. His muscles relaxed even as he shuddered, and Kende slid his tongue farther inside Asyl's passage, stretching him. Asyl moaned with nearly every exhale, his hand shaking as he ran his fingers through Kende's hair.

Once Asyl's hole was basically dripping with saliva, Kende sat back and looked down at his lover. His face was flushed, eyes half closed and pupils blown. Hair tangled and spread out over the pillows, legs slowly falling open now that Kende wasn't holding him in place, and a belly decorated in white splatters. Leaning down, Kende licked up Asyl's release, lightly grasping his Fated's cock.

Asyl didn't seem overly sensitized, so he slowly began pumping his length. If he could get Asyl hard again, he would absolutely do his best to get his lover to cum twice. Asyl whimpered at the stimulation and reached out. Kende eagerly went into the man's arms, kissing him. His Fated made a small noise, and Kende pulled away just slightly.

"Tastes weird," Asyl admitted with a shy smile.

"Good weird?" Kende asked, delighted to feel Asyl begin to harden again.

"I'm not sure. I've never tongued someone like that before," Asyl said, blinking a few times. "They were always focused on having a cock in my mouth instead."

"Well, I'm delighted to be the first to rim you," Kende replied, his voice growing rough.

Asyl hummed and smiled sleepily. Kende kissed him lightly again before leaning over and pulling some slick from his nightstand. His Fated was watching him curiously, blinking at the small vial.

"What's that?" Asyl asked.

"Slick. It'll make things easier," Kende said.

The fact that Asyl had no idea what it was gave Kende a small twinge of sadness. The least anyone could have done was make it less painful for his Fated. He supposed they hadn't cared enough. Uncorking the vial, Kende poured some on his fingers and slipped them between Asyl's legs. His rimming had already loosened him up, and Kende's finger slid inside without much resistance at all. Asyl grunted, scrunching his nose.

"All right?" Kende asked.

"Yeah. Haven't done anything like this in four years," Asyl said with a lopsided smile.

"I'm not just fucking you," Kende chastised. "We're making love, sweetheart. There's a difference."

Asyl flushed and smiled, nodding. Kende slid his finger in deep and easily found the sensitive nub, making Asyl's muscles contract, and his Fated moaned. He added a second finger, patiently working the tight guardian muscle until it accepted him without resistance. Kende rubbed his sweet spot, moving with Asyl's rolling hips, enjoying the whimpers his Fated made.

As soon as his Fated shuddered and pushed down on Kende's fingers to take them deeper, he grinned and removed them. Asyl whined, and Kende chuckled. He leaned over and crooned at him, lightly kissing his lips as he slicked his aching cock. Pressing the head of his cock to his love's entrance, he pushed in. Asyl closed his eyes and moaned, pulling his eyebrows together. The edges of his mouth twisted into a grimace.

"Open your eyes," Kende murmured. "Know that it's me."

The expression faded, and Asyl opened his eyes, his dark pupils locking on to Kende's. There was only a thin ring of pale blue left. Kende grabbed Asyl's hips with one hand, resting his other arm on the pillow next to his love's head. He dropped another light kiss on the man's lips and slowly thrust a few more inches into the intensely tight heat. Asyl bit his lower lip and wrapped his arms around Kende's neck, his breath coming faster.

Kende rocked his hips, sinking an inch or so at a time. His lover breathed out, blinking slowly as he arched his hips in tune with Kende's thrusts. It took a little while until Kende was fully seated, hips pressing to Asyl's sweet ass. Small tremors ran through his love's body as he adjusted to his girth.

At a small nod from Asyl, Kende slowly pulled out and pushed back in. Moaning, Asyl dropped his head back, and Kende grinned, watching him. He rocked his hips back and forth, dropping his head to rest his forehead against his lover's. Kende shifted, rolling Asyl's hips up a bit higher. His next thrust with the angle change got Asyl to buck, gasping.

"Feels," Asyl panted, his eyes rolling back before they closed, "so good."

Kende grinned at that. "You do, sweetheart."

Asyl mewled and tilted his head, kissing him. Moaning, Kende returned the kiss, slowly rolling his hips to drive his Fated even higher. He tilted his head, kissing along Asyl's jawline before proceeding down his neck, teasing the curve of his neck with his tongue and lips. Asyl dropped his hands to either side of his head, and Kende covered one with his, interlacing their fingers. His lover squeezed and moaned when Kende buried himself again and again, arching to meet each thrust.

Goddess, he loved how vocal his Fated was. Kende latched on to Asyl's neck, sucking up a bruise before nipping the area. Asyl's legs clamped around his hips, urging him to thrust harder. He was close, feeling the tingle at the base of his spine intensify. Lifting himself slightly, Kende fished between their bodies to wrap his hand around Asyl's cock. The moment he touched it, Asyl bucked and whimpered, his muscles squeezing Kende's length.

"Cum with me," Kende murmured.

As if the words were a command, Asyl gave a choked sob as he spilled a small load onto his stomach. He spasmed a few times and his head fell to the side, breathing hard with glazed-over eyes. Kende grunted, losing his rhythm for a minute before pouring his seed deep into his Fated. He held himself carefully as he caught his breath. All the energy that he'd been alive with just seconds ago seemed to desert him.

Kende carefully slid out and lay down on top of Asyl, nuzzling into his lover's hair, squeezing his hand and sliding his other arm underneath Asyl's body to hug him tight. His Fated was still panting, though he seemed a bit more alert than he'd been a couple of minutes ago. There was no undercurrent of fear, disgust, or shame that Kende could feel. Just contented exhaustion.

"Is it always like that?" Asyl whispered.

"Not as intense, but yes," Kende replied, just as softly. "It's supposed to feel good."

Maybe he shouldn't have been surprised to see the tears forming in Asyl's eyes, but a jolt went through him, seeing his Fated try to blink them away.

"I've missed having this for so long. It could have been so much better," he said, his voice breaking.

Kende gently hushed him, kissing his temple and squeezing him to try and give him some sense of comfort.

"You're here now," Kende tried reassuring him. "That's all that matters."

Asyl looked at him, tears flowing freely down his face toward his ears. His eyes closed when Kende dipped down, kissed his eyelids, and rolled them onto their sides to curl up together. Hearing his Fated mourn over what he'd suffered tore at his heart, but Kende knew this was essential to his healing. That being said, if Kende ever ran into Tillet, the man would have quite a lot to answer for.

"I hate this," Asyl grumped, pressing his forehead into Kende's chest.

"Hate what?" Kende asked softly, running his fingers through Asyl's hair.

"That everything was so awful that it's euphoric when I'm with someone who cares," Asyl replied. "That I keep crying over it."

Kende pressed a kiss to the top of his head, squeezing Asyl briefly, "I'd like to think it's a compliment that you're so overwhelmed when you cum that you cry."

Asyl let out a shaky laugh, and his slim arms wrapped around Kende's chest. "I much prefer that explanation."

Eventually, Asyl's tears dried, and his body went lax in Kende's arms, his breathing evening out. A quick check told him that Asyl had simply fallen asleep. Smiling, Kende slipped away to grab a damp cloth and clean them up before crawling back into bed.

His lover didn't even wake as he snuggled in close, Asyl's arms making their way around his neck to hold him. There was no question whatsoever in Kende's mind.

Asyl owned his heart completely.

CHAPTER 14

"I CAN'T do this," Asyl said in a near panic after seeing another carriage drop off an exquisitely dressed lord with his lady.

He darted away from the window and right into Naias's arms. His best friend had decided she was going to come early to make sure he was ready and to provide support. In that moment, he was both absolutely overjoyed that she was there for him and hated her for being excited about the gala. What made him think he could do this? It had been nearly fourteen years since he'd been abandoned by his parents. He wasn't gentry anymore. He was a Void.

"It'll be all right," Naias cooed. "Kende or I will be at your side all night tonight. And if we're not there, then Siora or Lanil will be nearby. Or Olire, Tsela, Rojir… or any of your other friends. Aren't Maerie and Heina coming too? You'll have plenty of support here."

"What about your parents? They hate Voids. So does my mom," Asyl said, feeling panic begin to grip him.

"Kende specifically asked your father to leave his wife at home. You might see your twin brothers, though," Naias said with a smile.

A thought struck him. Had Naias known about his siblings? Maybe she just never told him. Asyl still wasn't sure what to make of the fact that he had nearly six siblings, with another on the way. He wished dearly he could have been the big brother that he wanted to be when he was a kid, before his Awakening failed. A shudder ripped through him, and Asyl shook his head, dropping his face into Naias's shoulder.

"I can't do this," he repeated.

"Yes, you can," Naias said. "Kende will be here in a minute. Take a breath."

Asyl nodded and took a step back, looking out the window again. Maybe hiding in Kende's study wasn't proper, but he felt safe in here. No one was allowed inside except for those his Fated personally invited, and it was a short list. It had begun to snow at some point while the celebrants had begun arriving. The carriage wheels left a thin trail of stark gray stone against the white snow.

Birgir met a finely dressed couple and welcomed them into the manor, and the two disappeared past the portico to where Asyl could see through the window. Their carriage moved on, and another driver brought up their charge. Just how many people did Kende invite?

Tears pricked at his eyes as his anxiety spiked, and Asyl tried to take a deep breath, hating that it hitched halfway through. Naias gently rubbed his back, guiding him away from the window.

"They're all so perfect," Asyl whispered, "and I'm nothing."

"The gentry are the farthest things from being perfect. They regularly disown their children for being Voids, and they're too concerned about making sure they live well rather than helping the neediest of our fellows. Look past the clothes and made-up masks. I know you're a good judge of character," Naias said with a smile. "Besides, you're absolutely beautiful. Maerie outdid herself."

Asyl looked down at his clothes. He was wearing a sleeveless baby blue knee-length tunic underneath a long-sleeved knitted black cardigan that fell to his calves. While the tunic was more form-fitting around his chest, it loosened considerably past his waist. The pair of brown breeches he wore were almost a second skin, tucking into thin black boots.

As for jewelry, Kende had gotten him a matching light silver bracelet and necklace. The necklace had a small pearl that nestled in the hollow of his throat, matching his pearl stud earrings. This time, he wasn't wearing a circlet to hide his Void status. Asyl hadn't been entirely sure about Kende's decision to forgo the circlet this morning, but he knew his Fated truly didn't care what he was.

Knowing that Kende would proudly stand at his side made him breathe a bit easier. Whatever happened, they would face it together. Nothing could break their bond. Like Kende said, everything else was just details.

The door to the study opened and Kende slipped inside. He was dressed in his classic long-sleeved white button-up, with a baby-blue vest to match Asyl's tunic. Over that he wore a black blazer and breeches. While Kende didn't wear any jewelry, the man truly didn't need it. He was beautiful, the lamplight making his blond hair shine. Goddess, could he love this man any more?

Kende smiled, seeing him, and crossed over to gently take his hands. Naias murmured a farewell and left the study to take her place at the gala.

"Everyone's here," Kende said. Asyl shuddered, and his Fated just gave him a soft smile. "You can do this."

Asyl nodded, slowly wrangling in his anxiety, and smiled weakly up at the man. He felt Kende push affection and pride through their bond. Asyl lifted onto his toes and claimed a kiss from his lover.

"I love you," Asyl said.

A sweet smile broke out on Kende's lips, and he bent over to kiss him gently. "I love you too."

He would never get tired of hearing that. Twining their fingers together, Kende led Asyl from the study toward the ballroom doors. After their spectacular dancing lesson last week that ended with them in bed, the two had taken to dancing with each other for at least a little bit every evening. It was a great way to wind down for the night, and a great way for Asyl to flirt suggestively.

The memory of their lovemaking this morning warmed Asyl, and he smiled faintly, glancing at his Fated. Kende had painstakingly taken his time to keep Asyl at the edge of his orgasm for an hour. He'd been so wrung out until lunch that Asyl hadn't had the energy to worry about the gala tonight. Maybe that had been Kende's intentions all along, and if it was, Asyl had to admit it was pretty effective.

Besides, he enjoyed all of their couplings. Asyl had worried that he'd hate Kende for having sex at the end of the day before going to bed. In fact, it was the complete opposite. Now that he knew how good Kende made him feel, it took nearly all Asyl's willpower to not jump his Fated at every opportunity he could.

Maybe this was why so many new heterosexual Fated couples ended up with children ten moonturns after meeting for the first time.

"Ready?" Kende asked softly.

Asyl nodded weakly. He really wasn't, but he was with his lover. He could stand tall. After this, the gentry would know him as Kende's Fated, and the next gathering would be easier. Hopefully. He was sure that there'd still be whispers and sneers wherever they went for a long time. Just because he was with Kende wouldn't automatically change their minds. It would be an uphill battle for a while.

One of the footmen opened the ballroom doors as they approached. All of the guests were standing around the edges of the ballroom, keeping the main dancing floor clear. The wood positively gleamed in the lamplight, shining through the intricate floral chalk designs. The page announced them over the gentle music.

"Lord Kende Ruvyn and his Fated, Asyl."

If the lack of a last name hadn't been a giveaway, his bare forehead certainly was. For a moment, there was a shocked silence before the frantic whispers started. Asyl did his best to keep his expression neutral, drawing on Kende's reassurance through their bond. He could see several glares from the older families and tried not to shrink away from their gazes.

Asyl wasn't sure if he couldn't move. His legs felt as if they were made of lead. The tension intensified when Naias strolled up and curtsied to Kende. Those with whispering sneers fell silent, watching avidly.

"Lady Elrel," Kende acknowledged.

"It's an honor to meet you and your Fated, my lord," Naias said.

It was a little weird, pretending Asyl hadn't seen Naias since his failed Awakening, and Kende not at all. Their words carried over the rest of the stunned gentry, and Kende inclined his head toward their friend. Naias smiled and held out her hand to Asyl. Manners that had been drilled into him since he was a babe took over and Asyl bowed over her hand, kissing the back of it.

"Pleasure to make your acquaintance, Lady Elrel," Asyl said clearly, projecting his voice.

With that, his proper wording tested and breeding appraised, the whispers stopped, and the pall broke. Naias backed off, and Kende guided Asyl around the ballroom to meet the clustered gentry by family. They got a variety of reactions, from enthused acceptance to overt disdain. Those, Asyl knew, would be getting a strongly worded letter in the next few days. Either Kende or Siora were surely taking notes on their reception.

At least Kende was still pushing calm and affection through their bond. Otherwise Asyl would have probably bolted. Asyl recognized many of the gentry from when he was a child and his parents hosted parties. Names and titles swirled around him, and he did his best to remember everyone. He didn't want to accidentally insult anyone and fracture their tenuous relationship.

Not once did Kende let his hand go.

Asyl officially got acquainted with Jaclyn and Macik. Kende's sister seemed annoyed at both of them and snidely told Kende she'd visit later in the week to discuss his actions. At her tone, Kende simply raised their clasped hands and kissed the back of Asyl's, right on his mole. Her disgusted expression had been delightful, and Asyl couldn't stop himself from giggling once she turned away. Macik looked over his shoulder and winked at the two of them with a lopsided smile.

Kende had a frustratingly large family. Four sisters and five brothers, rounding out at ten children in total. As much as he tried, Asyl couldn't recall their names after he'd been introduced. His mind was already spinning by the time they got to Kende's relatives. He hoped they wouldn't be too offended when they came back together for the family dinner.

Maielle was the last sibling they greeted, with a handsome man on her arm. She introduced her Fated and gave Asyl a tight hug, which he returned happily. Whenever she visited during these last few weeks, she'd always been a delight to have around. Her wicked sense of humor kept both him and Kende on their toes, and Asyl firmly enjoyed her presence. Asyl had a stray thought that he should introduce her to Naias.

Then they approached a couple that were obviously Kende's parents.

Following his Fated's movements, the two bowed to Duke and Duchess Ruvyn. Kende's father was an Ignis and his mother a Gaian. Duchess Ruvyn was a tiny and stern-looking woman, her thin lips pressed tight together as if she'd just bit into a lemon. She shared Kende's golden hair and almond eye shape, standing just slightly shorter than Asyl. Her dress looked uncomfortable, thick red brocade that buttoned all the way up to her chin.

Asyl retreated behind Kende, glancing between the two men, who seemed to be preparing for a fight. The duke was terrifying, with a dour expression on his saturnine face, and his piercing green eyes were cold and calculating. And completely focused on him.

"That's quite a proclamation you made," the duke said. "I assume this Void is the reason you're skipping the dinner."

"Yes. I didn't want you to terrify Asyl the first time you met him. Figured this was a more even playing field," Kende replied with a smile.

"What does he have over you? There's no reason to go along with this farce," he said.

"No farce, Father. He truly is my Fated," Kende said, his spine growing rigid. "I found him in an abandoned church."

"Anyone could have wandered into a church," the duke said with a scowl.

"He was unconscious at Ilyphari's feet in the sanctuary," Kende replied, frowning at his father.

Asyl blinked and looked up at him. He found him where?

"Is that not where you were?" the duchess asked, apparently not missing his confusion.

"I thought I lost consciousness outside," Asyl said softly, turning toward her.

He blinked when Kende kissed the top of his head. When Asyl looked up at his Fated, Kende smiled and lightly kissed his lips. The duchess sighed softly and hummed in approval. Apparently it didn't take much to get her approval, despite her severe expression.

"And he accepted being your Fated right away?" she asked.

"Goddess, no." Kende chuckled. "It took a bit of doing. Lots of trust."

"Voids aren't capable of having Fated," the duke snapped.

"Oh, come now. Just last week you were asking me to take Kende on an extended trip to try and find his Fated. Now that he's found his heart's twin, you're upset? Make up your mind, Uncle Kiyiya," a joyous voice said, tinged with laughter.

Asyl looked toward the newcomer and went stock-still, staring wide-eyed at the tall brunet approaching them. He was even taller than Kende and had warm, kind brown eyes. His Mark identified him as a Sympathetic, which had always seemed like such an odd blessing for the prince of Averia.

Asyl felt his throat close up, and he pressed into Kende's side, subtly trying to hide himself. His Fated glanced at him and began rubbing the back of his hand with his thumb.

"It's okay, sweetheart. Yolotzin is my cousin, remember?" Kende said gently. "Speaking of, I thought Uncle Tonalli sent you up north to Pemalia."

"I got word that my favorite cousin had set a date for his introduction gala," the prince said with a grin. "No way was I going to miss this."

During the planning, had Siora or even Maielle reached out to the prince to summon him home? Did they know he would hurry back to attend? Kende's father scowled at the prince before sighing and leading the duchess away. Snapping his gaze back to the prince, Asyl noticed the man was smiling at him. He had a lovely smile, and Asyl noticed a bit of a golden sheen to his hair. Fascinating.

"Asyl, my cousin Yolotzin," Kende said, gently pulling him out from his hiding spot, "supposedly traveling until spring."

"Better things to do," the prince replied, shrugging. The man reached out and clasped Kende's shoulder. "I'm quite happy for you. I'm hoping Father won't use this as an excuse to get me married without finding my Fated."

Even as he said so, Prince Yolotzin's eyes slid away from Kende's and scanned the crowd around them. Apparently, he didn't find what he was looking for, as his attention snapped back to his hosts.

"Are any of your other family here?" Kende asked, a wariness in his tone.

The prince shook his head. "My sisters are busy with their families, Father's too good to show up to support his nephew, and Mother is still… quiet."

Asyl felt a shock of sadness come through his bond. He glanced up at his Fated and the prince. There'd been rumors on the streets that the queen's strength was failing. That she usually lay abed all day and rarely spoke to anyone. He tried pushing reassurance to Kende and smiled when his lover glanced down at him.

"Let me know if there's anything I can do for Auntie," Kende said, real worry in his voice.

"Of course. You and Gojko will be the first two we contact if we think she needs healing," Prince Yolotzin confirmed, nodding, "Though I do wonder if it's more mental than physical these days."

"With how Uncle Tonalli acts some days—"

"There you are," another cheerful voice called out, cutting Kende off.

The prince grinned and held out his hand. Another man sauntered over and placed a flute of champagne in his hand. Prince Yolotzin easily transferred the drink to his other hand and wrapped his arm over the newcomer's shoulders. Asyl blinked at him, recognition pinging at a faint memory. He couldn't place it, and Asyl looked up at his Fated.

"Hey, Kaj. Figured you'd be here too," Kende said with a laugh.

"Never far from my prince, Lord Kende," the redhead replied, a twinkle in his green eyes.

Kaj, an Aquan, caught Asyl's eye, and he tilted his head, eyes narrowing as if he also knew him. Where? Where did he know him from?

A deep-rooted sense of danger began forming in his gut, and Asyl slowly moved behind Kende once more. He felt vulnerable. Exposed.

"I'm so delighted you finally found your Fated," the prince said before briefly looking around. "One of these days, I'll have to visit and hear the whole romantic story."

"Thank you. You know you're always welcome here. Just drop by whenever you want to come chat," Kende replied, grinning.

Prince Yolotzin nodded absently. "Before the week is out, I would like to talk to the two of you about what I wrote to you last moonturn. Kajie and I still don't quite understand, but Duke Vitalis wrote his own letter to your sweetheart, trying to explain as well as he could from one Void to another...."

Despite being curious about what the prince would want to talk to him about, Asyl couldn't concentrate on what he was saying. He shuffled his feet, managing to resist the urge to tug on his tunic as the noise in the room rose even though he couldn't understand a word. His heart beat rapidly, and he broke out in a cold sweat.

Kende glanced down at Asyl, his grin fading when he noticed Asyl's discomfort. Smiling weakly up at the three men, Asyl did his best to not give in to the urge to run away and hide. He wasn't sure how much anxiety was leaking through his body language or their bond, but he could feel his Fated tense next to him.

Asyl kept a careful eye on the other man as the prince asked Kende about his recent charities. Kende hesitated for a moment before detailing his clinic charity and how successful it was, omitting the fight they'd had. Kende mentioned the project he and Asyl were sketching out to help the homeless Void community, and Prince Yolotzin made approving noises.

The entire time, the redhead's eyes never left Asyl's face.

Maybe his anxiety peaked enough that Kende could no longer ignore the silent staring contest. He eyed Kaj warily and gently shuffled Asyl behind him a little more firmly. Having his lover physically between them was a bit of a relief, and Asyl finally averted his eyes from Kaj's, staring down at the floor instead. By that time, the prince had fallen silent as well.

"Kajaan, what is it?" the prince asked.

"Don't I know you?" Kajaan asked Asyl, and his head snapped up.

"Have you been to the apothecary market recently? Or at Maerie's?" Asyl asked.

Kajaan shook his head slowly, glancing at the prince. "No, I don't really go shopping. Usually, one of the servants does that instead."

"Then it would have been at least four years ago," Asyl said and shrugged. "I don't really get out much these days."

"Four years," Kajaan murmured and frowned.

"Is that meaningful to you?" Kende asked, his voice gaining an edge to it.

Of course, Kende knew why that would be significant. The chatter and music around them faded as Asyl did his best to stamp down the panic rising in him. He knew the Aquan before him wasn't someone he'd run into after Tillet's. If this man had attended one of his parties, he'd seen Asyl at his worst.

If Kajaan told everyone he'd lived as a sex worker, it would tear his weak reputation apart. Not to mention his father's and siblings'. It would be an utter disaster. Granted, plenty of the gentry knew that Asyl had been on the streets, but to have a firsthand account.... Hopefully the prince would be kind enough to force Kajaan's silence, but Asyl had no idea if he would.

"Do you know Tillet?" Kajaan asked.

Kende inhaled sharply and fully put himself between him and Asyl as a chill gripped his spine. His Fated's face was dark and his lips set into a sneer. Asyl could feel the deep-seated anger from his lover, and he staggered backward, his body going taut. Only Kende's grip on his hand stopped him from fleeing the ballroom and running to hide at Enchanted Waters.

"How do you know that name?" Kende spat out.

Prince Yolotzin took a step back, looking between Kende and his friend. His face was studiously blank as he regarded the two carefully. He could likely feel the overwhelming gamut of emotions from the three of them. Or at least the intense protective urge Kende was giving out and the overwhelming need to flee from Asyl. The prince frowned.

"I thought you were better than that," Kende snarled. "We grew up together. How could you get involved with someone like Tillet?"

"Mind explaining, Kaj?" the prince asked sharply.

Kajaan blinked a few times, ripping his eyes away from Asyl to look at Kende. He smiled faintly and fiddled with the flute in his hand as if he was nervous. Clearly this hadn't been something he'd expected to run into tonight. Or maybe ever.

"I was invited to a party hosted by Tillet almost five years ago. I never told you about it because I figured he was a bottom-feeder social climber, and I wanted to check it and him out first. Make sure he and his Fated were decent people," Kajaan said, looking at the prince. His face darkened, and the redhead growled out, "But what I saw…."

His expression cleared, and he glanced at Asyl before giving Kende an embarrassed look. Presumably he wasn't sure about how much he should say about what he'd seen and bit at his lower lip. Kende took a deep breath and squeezed Asyl's hand, reining in his anger with an effort. The rage boiling through their bond settled to a pulsing ember.

"I know about Asyl's history. Not all of the intimate details, but I'm largely aware of what he's been through," Kende said.

Kajaan sighed, his shoulders relaxing at that. Asyl gave him a bit of grudging respect for not blurting everything out and potentially destroying his and Kende's relationship. The Aquan looked down at the champagne flute in his hands and took a sip of the bubbling liquid before seemingly coming to a conclusion in his mind. Kajaan looked at Prince Yolotzin.

"It was a sex party," Kajaan said, his face flushing. "There was no indication of that in the invite, even when I examined it when I got home, and when I arrived it was… already in full swing. Tillet told me that the person in his spare room was up for anything. I took one look inside and knew that he was lying."

"How?" the prince said sharply.

Kajaan gave Asyl a pained look. Swallowing hard, Asyl tugged on Kende's blazer to quietly signal him to back off. The man seemed pretty sincere in his retelling, and the pain in his expression was genuine. After a tense moment, Kende stepped back, tucking Asyl tight to his side. His eyes didn't leave Kajaan's face.

"I was tied down," Asyl interjected softly.

The prince's focus snapped to him, and bare anger twisted his features. If that fury had been directed toward him, Asyl would have bolted. Instead, he lowered his eyes and pressed his face into his Fated's chest.

"It wasn't just that. I could count your ribs, your hair was unkempt, and there were too many marks on your skin that couldn't be explained away from only a few hours of play. If Tillet hadn't lied, I would have just left and ignored any other invitations from him. But I couldn't... I wasn't going to walk away from someone in need.

"So I changed the alcohol content of what was being offered in hopes that it would get everyone to pass out. But it was taking too long and... the laughing was too much. So I added a strong sedative and handed out new cups. As soon as everyone had passed out, I found the padlock keys, bundled him in a blanket, and ran," Kajaan explained.

"How do I know it was you? You could have garnered this information from Tillet afterwards, and you were an active participant," Kende accused with a sneer.

Kajaan looked crushed. He looked at the prince before directly catching Asyl's eye. His gaze was soft, and he gave him a gentle smile.

"I took you to one of Tzin's townhomes, though you weren't exactly coherent. I cleaned you up, took care of any open wounds you had, and dressed you in green pajamas," Kajaan said fondly. As he spoke of what he did to help, Asyl felt himself relax. How would Tillet have known what color clothes he'd been dressed in? "I helped feed you a hearty bone broth and tucked you into my bed. I slept on the couch, but when I woke up, you were gone. I looked for you for moonturns, but I could never find you."

"I ran into Lady Elrel, and she took me in," Asyl said quietly. "I thought it was weird that I found her, but if you took me in, then I was in the gentry neighborhoods, and that increased my chances to find her."

"Why would Lady Elrel take you in? I mean no insult by my question," the prince asked, "just trying to understand relations."

"Naias was my best friend up until my Awakening failed. She smuggled me into her family home, and I stayed there until she nursed me back to health and I got my apothecary up and running," Asyl said. "She's been wonderful."

"Good to know you have a habit of running away when waking up in Good Samaritans' houses," Kende teased ever so gently.

Asyl snorted and smiled up at his Fated. He could feel the tension leaving his body, his energy going with it and making him tired as he leaned into his lover. Kende's anger was gone now as well, though Asyl thought he could detect a bit of shame amongst his relief.

"You have an apothecary?" Kajaan asked, his shoulders relaxing and a true smile spreading across his face.

"Enchanted Waters," Kende said, the pride in his voice unmistakable. "He donated a hefty number of potions to the clinic charity earlier this year."

Prince Yolotzin grinned. "Those were yours? Absolutely amazing. Even Jeryit has praised them, and it's practically impossible for him to have a positive word about anything."

The warmth in his tone made Asyl blush, and he smiled shyly at the prince, finally feeling himself fully relax for the first time that day. Kende bent and kissed the top of his head again and Asyl sighed, nestling into his Fated.

"I'm sorry for doubting you, Kaj," Kende said with a hint of agony. "I just can't stand the idea of… what he did to my Fated."

"I understand, Lord Kende. I'm so glad you're all right, Asyl," Kajaan said. "I know Lord Kende will treat you right."

"Stop with the honorifics. You know you don't need to use them," Kende admonished.

A wry smile tugged at Kajaan's lips. "Anything you say, Lord Kende."

"Why didn't you go to the police?" Kende asked with a shake of the head. No doubt he'd given up on correcting Kajaan's vernacular. "Could Tillet be hurting another Void?"

Kajaan sighed softly, "I truly hope not. Without Asyl, there wouldn't be a case. Tillet could claim that he'd hired a sex worker for the party, and no witness to contradict him. None of his friends and regular guests would dare testify against him, even if they knew that Asyl hadn't been willing."

"Talk to Macik," Asyl said, rolling his shoulders back and standing straight, trying to be strong even as his stomach clenched. "He knows about Tillet. If you think we can build a case, let's do it. You at least know where he lived four years ago. Maybe you can help find him."

Kajaan nodded and looked around the ballroom. He must have located the Sympathetic, for he bowed in farewell and quickly slipped through the crowds. Prince Yolotzin stared after him for a minute, a gentleness in his expression Asyl thought was only reserved for lovers. Shaking himself, the prince smiled at the two of them, though his eyes started darting from person to person again.

"I believe your family and the Voids you invited haven't said hello," Kende said, breaking through the gloomy mood that had befallen them. "Shall we go accost them before our first dance?"

Asyl nodded and squeezed Kende's hand. Prince Yolotzin stepped close and kissed Kende's cheek before doing the same to Asyl, prompting his face to flush before the prince wandered away. He didn't quite seem fully present, and when Asyl looked up at his Fated, Kende was smiling.

"He's feeling the tug," Kende murmured. "Apparently his Fated is here."

At that, Asyl grinned and smiled. "I hope he finds them soon."

"Me too," Kende said warmly.

"What is his relationship with Kajaan?" Asyl asked.

"It's complicated," Kende replied, sighing softly. "Yolotzin finding his Fated will only twist it further. Especially since it doesn't seem like it's Kaj."

With that, Kende began tugging Asyl toward the quiet pair of men standing apart from the gentry. While his Void guests were dressed nicely, they were clearly uncomfortable. Once they got closer, Asyl stepped forward and pulled Kende with him to excitedly greet them. He got to introduce his Fated to Rojir and Mato, who both cut handsome figures in their suits.

"Good to finally meet you, Rojir," Kende said, shaking the man's hand.

Rojir gave a lopsided smile and nodded. "Good to be able to speak with you in person. Your house is… impressive."

"I feel vaguely insulted," Kende replied, laughing. "Unfortunately, one of us brats needs to take care of it, and the duty fell to me as a bachelor."

"Not a bachelor anymore," Mato said, eyeing Asyl with a smile.

Asyl got on his toes and eagerly accepted a hug from the massive man. He remembered many nights curled up in Mato's arms, reveling in the man's sheer bulk. He was about the same height as the prince, though probably twice the width. All that casual strength was used for protection and physical labor. Asyl had never heard of Mato hurting someone.

Rojir got a hug as well, and the man placed a kiss on his temple.

"I'm glad you came, Dad," Asyl said.

"Wouldn't miss it for the world, son," Rojir replied.

"You told him," Mato said fondly.

Asyl watched Rojir flush and wondered once again why Rojir and Mato had broken up. When he'd been abducted nine years ago, the two of them had been as thick as… well… thieves. A small pang of worry hit him that his disappearance had been the reason for their parting. He hoped not.

"Well," Rojir said, clearing his throat, "mostly to help him get his head out of his ass."

"To which I thank you," Kende said, smiling. "I don't know how much longer I could have held on otherwise."

Olire joined the small group and smiled up at the two older men. Apparently, they knew each other, though Asyl wasn't quite sure how. Mato immediately inquired about the redhead's schooling, and Olire launched into what his science class had taught him a few days ago. As they talked, Kende stood behind Asyl, wrapping him up in a hug as the two of them engaged in the conversation.

It was maybe about a half hour later when two boys ran up to him. One of them was marked as an Illusionist, and the other a Healer. Asyl vaguely recognized them. It was more like looking at his reflection through a muddy pond. He could see several features that he shared with them, and those that resembled one of his parents.

"Arik, Alyn, good to see you two," Kende said warmly.

Olire whipped around and grinned, bouncing on his toes. "Hey!"

His brothers. Asyl drew in a deep breath looking at them as a stab of jealousy ran through him. Why did his brothers get to be blessed with Crafts, but he was denied one? He tensed in Kende's arms for a second before he forced himself to relax. It wasn't their fault, and he couldn't blame them whatsoever. Asyl smiled weakly at the twins, who were chatting away excitedly about their recent lessons.

Asyl jumped when each twin grabbed one of his hands and pulled him away from Kende and the three Voids. He stumbled after them, flushing when he heard Kende, Rojir, and Mato laughing behind him. The twins brought him to their father, who was looking at him with a sad smile.

"I'm glad you're all right," his father said, "Sorry for ambushing you at the charity."

Clearing his throat, Asyl looked at the boys at his side before finally nodding. "Yes. I apologize for yelling at you."

"Don't be concerned about it. I more than deserve your ire," Lairne said. "Kende was kind enough to let me know that you two reconciled and that it was your decision to include me in your introduction gala."

"I... I wanted to know my siblings. Rojir told me that he'd petitioned you a few times while I was on the streets to help take care of me," Asyl said.

"Yes," Lairne all but whispered. "I wish I'd been able to get Ilfa to see reason, but.... She's always been a stubborn woman."

"Oh, I remember," Asyl said. A small giggle escaped him. "I remember she insisted I continued to learn how to ride even after I'd been bucked off of a pony and refused to get back into the saddle."

"The fights we had about that," Lairne said and laughed. "She only backed down once I told her that she was putting you at risk of injury."

Asyl's smile faded. "I don't understand why she hates me so much."

"I don't either," Lairne replied. "I've been trying to work on her hatred for the last decade. Nothing's worked. Not even the twins' Awakenings."

Asyl looked down at his brothers, who had been watching him carefully. Probably worried that he'd blow up again and start yelling. His heart ached. That hadn't been a good first impression at all. Biting his lower lip, Asyl held out his arms, relieved when the two didn't hesitate in hugging him tight. He felt Lairne's hand heavy on his shoulder and looked up at the man.

Lairne's smile was sad, though he didn't push for anything more. The twins seemed to realize that there'd been some sort of shift in their relationship as the two pulled back. Arik and Alyn, Kende had said. Asyl was hopeless in trying to remember which was which. He just hoped he'd figure out some sort of clue as to the identities of his brothers. After that, their Marks would make identification much easier.

They began asking rapid-fire questions about his clothes, what it was like living with Lord Kende, and what Asyl did for work. He flushed and did his best to answer as many questions as he could, slowly relaxing under the twins' attention. He found himself truly wanting to know the boys and any of his other siblings that would be interested in having him.

A soft hand pressed at the small of his back, and Asyl looked over his shoulder to see Kende. His Fated smiled softly, and after promising Arik and Alyn a tour of the new Enchanted Waters workroom, the boys let him go. Kende cupped Asyl's face and pressed a kiss on his bare forehead. Asyl gripped Kende's wrists, looking up at him with a soft smile.

"It's time for the dance," Kende murmured. "Are you ready?"

"No," Asyl replied, smiling weakly.

"Just focus on me and block everything else out. Details," Kende assured him.

Asyl couldn't stop the smile that curled his lips if he tried. He could feel his Fated push reassurance and love through their bond.

"Details," Asyl repeated with a weak smile.

Kende dipped down and kissed his lips before letting go. He snatched one of Asyl's hands, twining their fingers together. The music died down, and Kende guided Asyl to the middle of the dance floor. They were the first ones to smudge the chalk, which made Asyl feel slightly guilty. Wasting beautiful art like this wasn't something he'd understand.

Taking a deep breath, Asyl smiled up at his Fated, doing his best to ignore the people watching them. They didn't matter. The only person who mattered was the one in his arms. Details. Holding that firmly in his mind, Asyl put his hand on Kende's shoulder as his lover held his waist. The music picked up, and after the first step, instinct took over.

His smile grew as they danced through the song together, adding some fun steps from his street-learned bachata into the traditional introduction waltz. Neither of them cared that they were adding to or slightly changing tradition. In fact, Kende had encouraged it. Mostly to help boost Asyl's confidence, but still.

Nothing about their relationship had precedence. They were the first Craft and Void Fated relationship, at least within the gentry. After the notes of the first song died away, there was a round of scattered applause, and other couples moved onto the floor with their partners. Asyl excitedly shimmied back to Kende, grinning up at him. No more stuffy dancing if he wanted. He was pretty sure he could even get Rojir or Mato to dance with him.

Kende kissed him lightly, taking his hand and starting up one of their more energetic bachata routines. During one swing, Asyl stopped and laughed to himself. He nudged Kende's hip with his own and nodded over to the pair he'd spotted.

The prince and Naias were dancing together, looking at each other with a starstruck expression. Kende wrapped Asyl in his arms, and when he chuckled, Asyl figured he saw the couple. His Fated hugged him to his chest, tilting his head and kissing his temple, gently rocking him from side to side.

"Well now. You and Naias will officially be family," Kende murmured in his ear.

Smiling, Asyl turned and grabbed Kende's hands into his. The two finished out the song, much to his Fated's delight when Asyl pressed up to him. They exchanged another kiss, and Kende led him off the floor toward the bar. With a smile, Asyl ditched his Fated and slipped through the crowd to locate Rojir.

The two Voids hadn't moved from their corner, though Olire was nowhere to be seen. Asyl knew that the redhead's parents were present, despite their lower status. Kende had wanted them to see that Voids could be accepted within the gentry. If they'd only try to change. It was a long shot to try and get Olire back with his family, but they both agreed the risk would be worth it if they were successful.

Asyl bounded up to his unofficial adoptive father and stuck out his hand. Rojir took it and bent over, kissing the back of his hand, right on the mole. Shaking his head, Asyl grabbed his hand and turned to drag him out to the dance floor. He could hear Rojir's weak protests under Mato's hearty laugh and grinned.

"Let's show these prudes how fun dancing can be," Asyl said.

At that, Rojir snorted but grinned, nodding. He bowed formally to Asyl, then took his hands and cocked an eyebrow at him. The dance Rojir led him through was a blend between bachata and salsa. Plenty of spinning, hip wiggling, and energetic flourishes caught the eyes of the gentry around them. Asyl ignored them all, just having fun with Rojir.

Funny how his life had changed in so short a time. He never would have thought he'd dance like this with Rojir again. Too busy taking care of the apothecary. Too apathetic to break from his routine and find what he needed. He'd needed the companionship and love that Kende gave him. Needed it like a drowning man needed air. He could feel Kende's amusement and slight arousal through their bond and knew without a doubt his Fated had been watching them.

It took Rojir a few songs to finally convince Asyl he'd had enough. The man retreated to Mato with claims of age and tiredness. Maybe he could teach Olire the dance. Or Kende, if he wanted to. Though that might turn a bit obscene with how form-fitting both of their pants were. Asyl knew he'd dance closer and more provocatively with his Fated.

Best not. Asyl slipped back through the crowds to join Kende near the refreshments. His Fated greeted him with a glass of water and a heated gaze.

"You haven't danced like that with me," Kende said, a bit of a pout on his lips.

Asyl got to his toes and kissed his Fated lightly, grinning up at him. "Now that you're not so worried about the gala, I can teach you more. Might not want Siora, Lanil, or Tsela present, though."

Kende let out a low groan and cupped Asyl's face as he returned his attention to the water. He drained the glass fairly quickly and handed it to a servant who came up to them. That was still something he was getting used to again. Asyl concentrated on his breathing, trying to help return his heart to a normal pace. Kende's fond smile wasn't helping.

Duke Ruvyn wandered over toward them without his wife. Spotting him before his Fated did, Asyl spun to his love and gave Kende a quick kiss.

"I'm going to go cool down," he said with a smile.

"Make sure Lanil or Tsela knows where you're heading," Kende told him.

Nodding, Asyl scampered away, hoping that he wasn't causing more trouble by avoiding the duke. Telling his assistant and bodyguard seemed like a waste considering Kende knew where he was at any given time. Asyl didn't have the pinpoint accuracy that his lover did, which was a bit of a shame. It gave Kende leeway for being a sneaky bastard. Loveable, though.

He slipped through the garden door, enjoying the sudden rush of cold air. His cardigan wasn't overly thick, but he'd be comfortable for a bit of time out here. Trotting away from the building, Asyl made his way to the gazebo where he'd spent hours with his Fated this past moonturn. Snow clung to his hair and eyelashes, little white pinpoints amongst his black hair. He'd forgotten how much he loved the snow, though he was grateful he didn't have to work outside anymore.

The heater in the gazebo had been turned on, and Asyl warmed his fingers and face for a few minutes. The snow was peaceful and quiet, giving him plenty of time for reflection. He could hear the orchestral music drifting over from the ballroom, the large windows letting him see the scandalized gentry. Most of them must have ended up not caring about what Asyl was, as many of the brightly colored popinjays were enjoying themselves. Or they just wanted free food.

An odd sense of loss washed over him, and Asyl clamped down on his bond with Kende, not wanting the man to worry about him. The last time there'd been a party with him as the focus, he'd been disowned. That wasn't a remote possibility here, yet an uneasiness settled beside his heart. He needed to walk off his darkening mood. In the peaceful silence of the snow, Asyl found himself wandering deeper into the gardens.

He was out of sight of the manor when Asyl realized his mistake.

Snow crunched behind him, and Asyl paused, turning to see who was approaching him. His breath caught in his throat, eyes fixed on the woman who had abandoned him so easily. Her belly was swollen in an obvious sign of her pregnancy. She was dressed in several layers, all black, and her cold brown eyes were fixed on him.

She appeared to be unarmed, but that didn't mean anything to a Harvester. There were plenty of plants within range that she could manipulate. He'd come out here without anything to defend himself. No weaponry, no Craft, no bodyguard.... Asyl shivered, though it had nothing to do with the cold.

"Son," Ilfa said flatly.

"You don't get to call me that," Asyl snapped.

He could make concessions for his father, but nothing could make him forgive his birth mother. Not since she continued to refuse him, and according to Rojir, was advocating against protections for Voids. The exact opposite, from what Kende had told him.

"Don't talk to your mother that way," a man's voice chided him, and Asyl froze, fear turning his blood to ice.

"You remember Mr. Gaten, don't you?" Ilfa said innocently, a smile forming on her lips. Asyl turned his head to look at the brunet approaching him. In his hand was an iron rod, similar to the ones that he'd been beaten with moonturns ago. The man leered at him, grinning. "Don't make a fuss. Just go with him and disappear again. Stop poisoning the gentry with your false claims of being Fated."

Asyl flicked his eyes toward the woman, keeping his attention on Tillet. "I refuse to be tied down and raped repeatedly again."

"You won't be in any position to argue," Tillet said.

The brunet rushed forward, swinging the rod as Ilfa called to the nearby plants, sending vines to grab and restrain him.

CHAPTER 15

"I SEE the fraud has fled," Father said acerbically.

Sighing heavily, Kende folded his arms and cocked an eyebrow at the duke. "Or perhaps you terrify him, Father. He's naturally nervous, and being accused so vehemently unsettles him."

"Do you truly believe he's yours?" the duke asked.

"Yes," Kende said immediately. "I never would have found him in the church, let alone heard him humming while he brewed."

His father frowned faintly and sighed, his posture finally relaxing. He looked toward the door that Asyl had fled through and shook his head, seemingly coming to a conclusion in his mind.

"A Void as your Fated. You truly defy every expectation in this family," the man said.

"Gay, non-elemental Craft, no true career, unattached until now…," Kende said, ticking off the major flaws in his father's eyes. "Asyl is a wonderful man. Just get to know him."

"I will, during the dinner that you will be hosting before your engagement ball," the duke said firmly.

Kende couldn't help but chuckle. He resisted the urge to tell his father that he'd been toying with the idea of Asyl's introduction gala also being their engagement ball. Maerie was a wonder with clothes, and Kende wanted to see what she came up with for each event. He briefly consulted their bond, able to feel the slight chill of winter, and knew that Asyl was near the gazebo.

"I will. Tomorrow I will talk with my chef to see when we can accommodate the family and what we need to get," Kende said. "It'll be within a week, I'm sure."

"Will his parents be attending?" his father asked.

"His father, potentially," Kende replied. "He was disowned when his Awakening failed, so technically he doesn't have any family to sit with him." Something that looked like sadness crossed his father's face, and the man looked toward the garden door again. "Father, he was on the streets for years until he was imprisoned by another for several more.

He's been standing on his own for four years now. He's not a project or someone I'm taking pity on."

The duke smiled at him. "No. You have a kind soul, but you don't open your doors to just anyone. You're a better judge of character than that."

The faint praise surprised him. Kende blinked at his father and smiled. A small commotion at the door leading to the entrance hall grabbed both of their attention. A familiar redhead rushed over to them and sketched out a hasty curtsy. She'd clearly just come from her workroom, as there were spots of grease and soot on her clothes, and a streak of something dark across her forehead.

"Duke Ruvyn, Lord Ruvyn," Keyna said, standing back up. Her face was flushed, spots of color high on her cheeks. Something was upsetting her pretty heavily if she'd gone against every social nicety and barged in. She wrung her hands nervously as her eyes darted around the ballroom. Siora came up behind her, scowling. "I must talk with you, my lord."

"Does it have to be now?" Kende asked.

"Yes," Keyna said urgently, "especially seeing so much anti-Void sentiment on the streets these days. It concerns your Fated. I think he's in danger."

Kende glanced at his father, who gestured for him to follow the Ignian to a quiet corner. Siora joined them, pulling out her notebook from her book holster to take notes. Behind him, Kende could hear his father's long familiar sigh.

"What is it?" Kende asked her.

The woman took a few deep breaths, her complexion returning to normal, and she nodded. "Okay. I thought something was odd when we moved the permanent Ignis Plates for Enchanted Waters from one building to the other. Their reservoirs were far lower than I would have expected. Almost as if they'd been running continuously for a year straight."

"He does use the plates fairly heavily," Kende said, frowning. "It's almost a guarantee that if he's in Enchanted Waters, he's brewing."

Keyna shook her head. "No, that's not what I meant. The usage would have been if he'd had the Plate burning at full strength for an entire *year*. He's only had them for a few moonturns. It's *impossible* for them to be as drained as they are!"

"So, what are you saying?" Siora demanded.

The redhead glanced at her and shoved her shaking hands into the pockets of her sooty overalls. "I looked at the old Plates that we'd replaced with the new ones. They were completely drained. There was no trace of any Craft in them. It's a wonder they even still worked. But they truly weren't that old when I inspected them. They shouldn't have been so worn out and should have been good for another four years."

"They're being drained faster than expected?" Kende asked, frowning.

Keyna nodded emphatically. "Yes. Bresk and I charged up the plates we got from Asyl, and it took far more power than we anticipated. But just doing that doesn't mean much. So we found a Void willing to help with our research."

"What kind of research?" Siora asked.

"Bresk played around with one plate for several hours, and we checked the levels. It was drained for the expected amount. Then with supervision, we had a child play around the Plate after we refilled it. It too had been drained normally. But when the Void played with the Plate...." Keyna paused and her face paled, looking intently at Kende. "The plate was drained at twice the rate."

Siora gasped, turning to look at Kende. Kende blinked a few times and frowned. Duke Ruvyn stepped up to his side, a similar frown on his face. Keyna's eyes flicked toward the man but settled quickly back onto Kende.

"All right, but what does that mean?" Kende asked.

"What if the fears of Voids being able to drain Crafts isn't exactly unfounded, but at the same time, inaccurate?" Keyna said. "What if Voids inherently absorb Craft abilities? I asked the woman to hold my hands, and I began exuding copious amounts of heat. Not once did she complain, nor did she get burned. When I held out my hand to the child, he couldn't grab it, yet the Void held on to it just fine."

"So, Voids can't be touched by Craft?" Duke Ruvyn asked. "Do they absorb it instead? For what purpose?"

Keyna shrugged. "I don't know. All I know is what I experimented with. But if Voids aren't affected by Crafts, then what kind of experiments would those anti-Void fanatics do to them under the guise of research?"

"Perhaps that's why potions don't work on them. They're imbued with Craft, so perhaps their bodies absorb it instead," Siora trailed off.

"Why couldn't this wait until tomorrow?" Duke Ruvyn asked as he folded his arms over his chest. "Such a revelation and theory is hardly cause to interrupt tonight's gala."

The Ignis swallowed hard, rubbing her hands together, sending some soot to the floor. "Because the Void who was working with us cut her hand on one of the Plates. Usually we just use our Craft to burn blood away and sanitize the area, but it didn't work! The area around the blood was warm, but the blood itself was untouched! As soon as Bresk and I realized that their blood is impervious to Craft too, I *knew* I had to come tell you."

"The exsanguinated Voids that the police have been finding," Siora said.

Worried, Kende consulted his bond, only to find it shut tight. Not absent, just suppressed. He couldn't quite make out where his Fated was. Outside, he thought. Why was their bond suddenly fuzzy? Had Asyl been knocked unconscious again?

"Where's Asyl?" Kende asked. He located Mato and Rojir amongst the rest of the gentry. They were safe enough and had started mingling with the other guests. "I don't see him."

"Did he not tell you?" Siora asked.

"He said he was going to go cool down," Kende said, fear starting to gnaw at his gut. "Last I felt, he'd gone outside and was by the gazebo. I thought he'd be back by now."

"Excuse me, Lord Kende," someone hailed.

Kende turned to see a man with long black hair and piercing green eyes. He didn't look entirely friendly and was bundled up in several thick layers. Snow slowly melted off his heavy cloak. Had he just come inside? If he'd walked through the entry hall, he likely would have dried off by now. Or at least all the snow would have melted from him.

Something about him gave Kende pause, a quiet warning bell going off in the back of his mind. Black hair, green eyes. Why couldn't he recall anything now? His heart rate spiked, and he started to feel some panic come through their bond. Kende swallowed it and faced the man.

"Do I know you?" Kende asked.

The man just smiled and took a step forward. He was uncomfortably close, and Kende took a step back. The smile unnerved him, though Kende couldn't quite discern why.

"Excuse me," Siora snapped as she visibly bristled. "Back away."

"You need to leave," his father growled.

Duke Ruvyn wasn't a small man and was generally used to people obeying him out of fear. It seemed like that tactic wasn't going to work this time. The man's smile grew, and he lunged forward. Kende caught a flash of steel coated in a reddish-brown substance before pain exploded in his side. He grunted, staggering back as Keyna screamed.

The man turned to flee, though he underestimated Siora. His assistant grabbed the back of the man's coat and yanked him to the ground, kicking him squarely in the face. The duke quickly pinned him, a murderous look on his face. Guards ran over as Kende collapsed, gasping for air.

He felt weak, like his body was recovering from a prolonged fever. Someone cradled his head, and Gojko dropped to his knees beside him.

"Just a bit of pain so we can remove the blade," Gojko said kindly. "Breathe through it."

Kende nodded and tried to relax into whomever was holding him. His mentor reached out and pulled out the blade, his hand glowing with his Craft. Blood soaked his shirt and vest, and the Healer cursed lightly. He tore open Kende's clothing to reveal the wound. Dark red lines spread from it, ugly and harsh against his tanned skin.

He could feel Gojko trying to heal him with his Craft. The energy filled his body before dissipating without any effect. Kende could feel himself growing weaker even as his mentor pushed in more energy.

"It's not working," Gojko said, a hint of panic in his voice.

"What was on your weapon?" Siora demanded of the man.

The black-haired man began laughing. "How does it feel to have your Craft stolen from you? You're a disgrace to the Craft Blessed, claiming a Void as your Fated."

"Shut him up!" Gojko snapped. "The only words I want out of him is what was on the blade."

"Allow me," the duke said, kneeling in front of the man.

He held up a finger, and a pure white flame ignited above his skin. Soon, the black-haired man screamed in agony as the fire seared into his skin. Yet even in agony, he didn't reveal the poison that Gojko couldn't neutralize.

"Let's see if we need to wash the wound," Naias said, dropping to her knees beside Gojko.

She extended her hand and drew upon the moisture in the air to pour water onto him. The water rolled down his skin, though as soon as it came into contact with his open wound, it evaporated. Keyna gasped, slapping her hands to her mouth.

"Void blood," she whispered. "The weapon was coated in Void blood."

Rojir walked up behind Naias and handed her a few absorbent cloths, worry clear on his face.

"Clean the wounds with this. See if there's any residue that needs to be cleaned out. If your Craft isn't healing him, then we need to use mundane techniques. Get his blood pure again," the man said.

"How do you know that'll work?" Naias asked, even though she took the offered cloth.

"I don't," the Void said, "but we might as well try instead of letting him bleed out."

Gojko took one from Naias and pressed it to Kende's wound. He shouted from the pain that seared up his side, dropping his head back. Yolotzin was holding him, his face set in a stony expression, jaw clenched tight. His cousin was pissed. Beyond pissed. Kende closed his eyes, gritting his teeth as it felt like Gojko was scraping his insides with a serrated knife. He couldn't stop the tears forming in the corners of his eyes, even as he desperately wished Asyl was here with him.

Warmth from Gojko's healing flooded his body, except for the area where he'd been stabbed. The wound stayed ice cold, the chill slowly seeping into the warm healing. He began to shiver, and Kende looked up at Yolotzin and the concerned faces of his family. It seemed as if a good chunk of the gentry had been ushered away. Maielle had her hands over her mouth and nose, tears flowing freely from her eyes.

"Just breathe, cousin," Yolotzin said softly. "Breathe."

"Asyl," Kende gasped. "Where?"

"We'll find him," Macik promised him.

Kende nodded and closed his eyes as the world dimmed at the edges of his vision. He floated away on the next wave of pain.

CHAPTER 16

ASYL JUMPED away from Tillet, tripping over one of the vines Ilfa shot at him. He stumbled and fell backward into the snow with a painful thud. Rolling to his side, Asyl grabbed the vine squeezing his ankle, trying to rip it from his body. As soon as his hands touched the plant, it withered at an alarming rate, becoming brittle and snapping easily.

He scrambled to his feet, swinging his arm up to block the rod from cracking his head open. The pain in his arm would be nothing compared to getting a concussion. A concussion could mean the immediate end to the fight and his abduction. Tillet pushed forward, trying to keep Asyl off balance as he swung again. Vines wrapped around his waist this time, and Asyl frantically pulled at them, trying to free himself to get away.

The next blow to his arm was almost at the same spot the first was, and Asyl couldn't stop his cry of pain. Tears flooded his eyes as he broke through the withered plants, trying to run back toward the manor. He couldn't block the hit to the back of his knee, and Asyl screamed in agony as he pitched forward into the snow. Thorny vines wrapped around his wrists, chest, and hips to pin him to the ground. He was helpless to stop Tillet.

Squirming as best he could, Asyl felt the man kneel astride his hips, his hand sinking into his hair. Tillet yanked his head back as much as he could with the thorns digging into his body.

"This time, slut, I won't let you get away. Your Fated will be taken care of soon, so he won't be looking for you," Tillet whispered in his ear.

"Macik knows about you," Asyl snapped. "So does Prince Yolotzin and his friend Kajaan. The first thing they'll do is track you down!"

"Then I suppose I'll just leave Averia," Tillet said with a sigh. "I'm sure we can start somewhere new. You're still cute. You can make me money for a few more years. But first things first...."

Asyl felt the vines tighten around him, and Tillet pushed Asyl's face into the snow, his weight shifting. He tensed, preparing for a strike to the back of his head when he heard a scream. Tillet's weight disappeared from his back, and Asyl frantically tugged at the thorns, managing to get one hand on the plant. By the time he freed himself enough to roll on his back, Tillet had gotten back to his feet.

Olire stood between them, glaring at Tillet and Ilfa. He had somehow wrested the brunet's rod from him and held it tight in his hands.

"You stay away from Asyl!" Olire shouted.

"Who is this brat?" Tillet asked.

Ilfa sniffed derisively. "Some Void trash that Kende took in, the bleeding heart."

"Another one? Well now. I can take him too. Red hair can be one hell of a draw for some clients," Tillet said with a laugh.

Asyl's eyes widened as the severity of Tillet's words struck him. He got to his feet, yanking free of the last thorny vine.

"Don't you dare touch him," Asyl snarled.

Tillet laughed and tilted his head. "And what are you going to do? You're a powerless Void. There's nothing you can do to stop us!"

Tillet snapped his hand out, and fire exploded from his palm. Asyl grabbed Olire and threw the boy behind him, ready to feel the agony from burns searing his skin. Warmth surrounded him and died away, leaving him shivering in the winter air. At his feet was a puddle of near-freezing water.

Tillet and Ilfa stared at him, and Asyl looked at his hands. He was unharmed, though he felt energized. His body thrummed with power he'd never felt before. Was this how the Craft Blessed felt? Asyl looked at the two and blinked a few times.

Tillet had a red glow emanating from his core, whereas his mother had a light green one. Asyl turned and looked at Olire. He had a black core, his forehead no longer naked, but displaying a vortex. Void. What in the world? He'd never seen anything like this before.

"You *freak*," Ilfa snapped out.

"Fuck you!" Asyl shouted, kicking up the slowly freezing water toward their faces.

Whatever excitement he might have been experiencing died when the undercurrent of calm that he felt from Kende vanished. Asyl gasped in a breath as his chest clenched, and he looked toward the manor. Something was wrong. Very wrong. What had Tillet said? Kende was being taken care of? *Oh Goddess, don't let him be dead!*

He turned back to Tillet right as the man charged him, fists clenched. Apparently he decided that he could handle a teenager who'd stolen his baton and a skinny alchemist. His fists were hot enough, steaming as snowflakes hit his skin and evaporated immediately. Yet whenever Asyl blocked his attack, he didn't feel any sort of heat or pain.

Somehow, the two of them were holding their own, even with Ilfa's attempts to yank them off their feet or try to make them lose their balance. Asyl was moving faster than he should have with his injured knee, surprising both himself and Tillet.

Asyl swung at Tillet, and the man ducked, spinning to avoid the swing from Olire. He stumbled back, and Asyl rushed forward to kick at the Ignian's knee. Let him know how much it hurts! Asyl's leg was pulled back to the ground with a vine, forcing him to duck and grab at the dark green plant. Tillet slammed his fist downward, only to have the rod intercept and crack his knuckles.

Fire erupted from Tillet's other hand as he fell to the snow-covered ground. The embers warmed Asyl's face before they died harmlessly. Breaking the now dead vine, Asyl launched himself at Tillet, who'd just gotten back up. He buried his shoulder in the man's gut, taking him down once more.

Olire ran forward and caught Tillet on the side of his jaw with a well-aimed swing. A sickening crack echoed through the night, and Ilfa screamed. Vines wrapped around them both, completely restraining them, carefully not touching any bare skin.

"What have you done?" Ilfa snarled at them.

Thick slabs of earth shot up from around her, entombing her from the neck down. She screeched in rage, hatred pouring from her lips. Who?

"Asyl!"

His bodyguard had located them. Sighing in relief, he waited until the large man knelt next to him and ripped the thorny vines from his skin. Asyl lunged to Olire and touched his restraints, freeing him in a few short tugs.

"I need to go," Asyl said, getting to his feet. "Kende's hurt."

"Go," Tsela said, "I'll restrain Lady Seni and this man. Olire can help me."

Asyl gave him a curt nod before rushing toward the manor. His knee began twinging in pain, and his arms ached from the blows he'd sustained. His forearm was probably fractured at minimum. At least the cold air was keeping it somewhat iced, encouraging the swelling to be minimal. He could see the manor. Through the windows. The ballroom was nearly empty. Only a small group remained....

After crashing through the door, Asyl quickly limped over to the remaining group. On the outskirts were a blend of his and Kende's family. He couldn't see Rojir or Mato. Were they okay? Panic welled inside of him. He needed to locate his Fated!

Asyl squirmed past his father and Jaclyn to see Kende, pale on the ground with his head in the prince's lap. His chest was exposed, a vile wound on his abdomen with dark red veins stretching out toward his belly and neck. Gojko and Rojir knelt next to him, pushing along those baneful veins toward the wound and wiping away the disturbingly unusual dark red blood. It wasn't stopping. Wasn't coagulating.

Asyl dropped to his knees next to Kende's head and hesitantly reached out to cup his face. His trembling fingers stopped just before he made contact with his love's skin. Kende was barely breathing, his face completely ashen. This couldn't be happening. He'd had Kende for less than half a year. He wasn't ready to let go!

"What happened?" Asyl gasped out.

"The bastard over there stabbed him," the prince sneered, jerking his chin toward another prone figure.

Looking over at the man, Asyl gasped. His body ached as he got to his feet and stumbled toward Kende's attacker, who was pinned quite thoroughly to the ground by Mato. Oh yes, Asyl knew this man. Hard to forget someone who'd nearly beaten him to death, even if it was quite a few moonturns past. An overwhelming rage burned in his gut, and he clenched his hands into fists.

"*You*," Asyl snapped and darted toward him. Two large arms wrapped around his chest, yanking him off his feet. "You utter *bastard*! Let me go! I'm going to kick his stupid face in!"

"Asyl, breathe," Lord Seni said, holding on to him.

"You can't do much else to him. He'll be facing the executioner's axe soon enough for attacking Kende," the duke said flatly.

There was an odd look on his face that Asyl couldn't make out. Fury, yes, Asyl could identify that easily. Regret? Asyl found he couldn't care enough to try and figure out the puzzle that was the duke.

"Then he won't have to worry about having a bloody nose for too long," Asyl spat.

"Do you really think that'll make you feel better?" his father asked softly. "Your energy will be spent better elsewhere."

"Like defending myself from your wife trying to kill me?" Asyl snarled at him.

His father's arms relaxed, and Asyl winced as his feet hit the ground and his knee shot pain up his leg. Gasping, Asyl staggered forward, glaring at the man who had assaulted him so many moonturns ago. The man was panting, wincing from waves of pain, his arms and legs covered in small burn marks that were seeping plasma. Mato looked up at Asyl, his face studiously blank, with his knee planted firmly in the attacker's back.

Maielle held out her arm, and Asyl gratefully took it to lean on. Now that he had leverage, Asyl shifted his weight onto his injured leg. She held his arm while he regained his balance and said nothing, glaring down at the intruder. His best ally….

Before any of Kende's other siblings could intervene, Asyl drew his uninjured leg back and slammed his foot into his attacker's face. A satisfying crunch and a howl of pain from the man made Asyl smile despite Mato shaking his head, clearly not approving. Beside him, he could have sworn he heard Maielle snicker. Blood and snot ran down the man's face, and Asyl limped away, leaning heavier against his future sister-in-law.

She led him to Kende's side, and Asyl knelt next to his Fated. His injured knee buckled, and he would have fallen if Prince Yolotzin hadn't grabbed his arm. With the prince's help, he knelt properly beside his lover, trying to hold back the panic brewing inside him.

The lines on Kende's stomach were fading, though he was still bleeding far more than Asyl liked. Rojir didn't seem too concerned just yet, so Asyl did his best to not worry, which was a battle he was sorely losing. Out of all the Voids he knew, Rojir had the most mundane medical knowledge. Except for maybe Mato.

"How is it?" Asyl asked him.

Rojir shook his head. "He's bleeding a lot, but it's getting better. Gojko is starting to get Lord Kende's Craft to respond."

Nodding, Asyl shifted to his hip to get pressure off his knee and cupped his Fated's cheek. He felt a dizzying sense of the world around him falling away. His mind's eye filled with what he could only understand as a visual list of what was in danger. Low blood pressure.

Failing kidneys. Nicked lung. Cracked rib. Dangerously low reservoir. Poison in the bloodstream. Infection starting to set in.

With a gasp, Asyl yanked his hand away and fell back on his ass. What was that?

"What did you do?" Gojko demanded, looking up at him.

"I don't know!" Asyl said, breathing hard.

"You pushed me out of trying to heal him," Gojko said, his voice in a near snarl.

"I... what?" Asyl asked, blinking a few times.

"What happened?" Rojir asked calmly.

It was easier to look at his adoptive dad, shivering underneath the weight of Gojko's glare.

"I don't know," Asyl repeated, hating the frightened whine in his voice. "I just touched him and got the sense of his injuries."

"Impossible!" Jaclyn snapped behind him.

"List them," Gojko said. When Asyl repeated them, the Healer just stared at him. "Fascinating. It sounds as if you dove inside him to try and heal him."

"Research later!" Duke Ruvyn shouted.

Asyl flinched, yelping when his knee smacked against the floor. Gojko's head bent back to Kende's body, and he placed his hands around the bloody wound again.

"What does it mean if his reservoir is empty?" Asyl asked the crowd at large.

"He'll die," Marielle said softly. "Our Craft is tied to our souls. If it's gone, then a part of him dies, and his mundane body will follow."

Asyl stared up at her for a minute, horror choking his throat. His left palm began itching, and he rubbed it against his breeches without thinking too much about it. Was this it? Was Gojko fighting a losing battle? He couldn't... wouldn't accept that answer.

Feed him your energy.

His energy? Asyl shook his head, the tears that had been forming in his eyes spilling to his cheeks. He felt someone kneel behind him, and his father's hand gripped his shoulder. He was just a Void! He couldn't do anything. This was something for Craft Blessed to deal with. And if Gojko couldn't.... Duchess Ruvyn was already letting out gasped sobs, as if Kende's death was inevitable.

Fill his reservoir.

That hadn't been his thought. A woman's voice? Asyl scrambled to his knees again, ignoring the jolt of pain that spasmed through his leg. He placed his hands on Kende's chest, disregarding Gojko's angry shout.

Push!

Wispy white energy rose from inside him. He had no idea where it had come from, and he knew the fog hadn't been there before the gala. Asyl imagined the energy flowing from his core, down his arms, through his fingers, and into Kende's body… to the reservoir that he had no idea even existed until a few moments ago. He pushed all the white energy from him, getting some sort of feedback.

The list of Kende's injuries hadn't changed, yet the bright, loud warning about his depleted Craft was starting to fade. It wasn't enough. What he had wouldn't get Kende out of danger. Maybe give him another couple of hours. But…. Yes. He could feel another energy source.

This energy was a slippery soft yellowish white, like a sunbeam through a break in the clouds. Leaves dancing in a spring breeze. Asyl frantically grabbed at it, stripping it down to the wispy white energy he was familiar with, and poured it into Kende as well. The connection broke suddenly, a shout of surprise coming from behind him.

"What was that?" his father demanded.

Asyl's shoulders sagged. No, he still needed more! A keening noise escaped him. He could do this! He just needed more. Asyl crumpled, his forehead dropping to Kende's collarbone as his tears started flowing stronger. He'd failed. He couldn't call up the health report anymore. Couldn't tell if Kende was out of danger or not.

A gentle touch on his jaw brought his head up. Prince Yolotzin was looking at him curiously, though he tightened his grip on Asyl's jaw. Something must have occurred to him, as his eyes widened and he gasped.

"Take mine," he said. It didn't make sense. Take what? Asyl started to shake his head. "Asyl. Take some of my Craft. If you can use it to help Kende, then do it."

"What are you talking about?" Duke Ruvyn demanded.

Prince Yolotzin's eyes didn't leave Asyl's as he answered his uncle's question. "I've traveled extensively over the last ten years, and seen plenty. Voids can utilize Craft energy and transfer it between hosts."

"I don't know what you're talking about," Asyl said.

"You do. You just don't understand," the prince said kindly.

Warmth. Calm. The energy filling him was like molasses, comforting and sweet. It made Asyl want to curl up with some cocoa and a good book. Lean into Kende and have a quiet evening. His eyes slowly closed, and Asyl grabbed at the energy inside him. He could extract the white he was so used to and send it on to where it needed to be. The reservoir wasn't in as much danger anymore. He pushed toward the poison coursing through Kende's veins.

He could feel Kende's breathing grow stronger.

"Goddess."

The warm energy left him, and Asyl wavered slightly on his knees.

"… someone strong," he heard the prince say.

Another hand touched him, cupping the back of his neck. This source was bright and flickered as Asyl tried to reach out for it. As if it was a bonfire, Asyl could almost hear the crackling and popping of the wood. This time, the white energy leaped eagerly to his touch. Asyl fed it directly into Kende, pushing the poison back toward the break in his skin.

Until it was gone.

"It's done," Gojko's voice came distantly.

The bonfire left, leaving Asyl's head spinning and his stomach rolling. He couldn't feel Kende's injuries anymore, didn't know if his reservoir was drained or if it would recover naturally. Asyl forced his eyes open to look down at Kende. His Fated was watching him, bags under his eyes. How long had he been conscious?

Asyl's strength failed him. He collapsed onto Kende, his arm and knee suddenly throbbing, radiating pain up his spine to the point where he could barely think. His breath came in great gasps, his forehead breaking out into a cold sweat. A hand slid into his hair while another grasped his thigh and squeezed gently, pulling a whimper from him.

"Careful," he heard the prince whisper, "his leg's been injured."

The grip on his leg turned into a slow, gentle caress. Slowly, Asyl could feel their bond returning. Tired. Drained. Hurting. But there. Love. So much love and affection. Asyl could only sob in response, pressing his face into Kende's chest. His world narrowed to the man under him, with his beating heart. The faintest whisper of a woman's voice echoed through his mind.

He's safe. Sleep.

Dizzy with relief and safely surrounded by family, Asyl allowed his body and mind to rest.

EPILOGUE

"HOW ARE the gloves working?" Keyna asked.

Asyl turned to look at his friend and smiled. It had been an interesting two moonturns, and he'd grown close to the Ignian woman. Learning that he absorbed Craft was fascinating, but not as much as the fact he could either enhance his own natural abilities or give that energy to another Craft Blessed. Prince Yolotzin had been invaluable there, helping Asyl understand what he was doing even though he was half out of his mind with pain and worry.

At least it finally made sense why his pain had faded away to almost nothing and he'd moved faster when he and Olire were attacked by Tillet. Why the man's fire never hurt him and Ilfa's plants died at a touch. The sling supporting his arm and the brace on his knee was a constant reminder of Tillet's attack and how slowly his body healed compared to a Craft Blessed.

Tillet, Ilfa, and the man who had attacked Kende were all in perfect health. Even Kende was back to full health, though he tired easily right now. Gojko assured him that Kende's energy would return to normal in a few moonturns. He just needed to take it easy and let his Craft replenish.

Only Asyl bore the physical injuries of the night of his introduction gala. Olire, luckily, hadn't been hurt during the fight. That left Asyl to try and maintain his pain levels with mundane medication. At least his salves and ointments were fantastic quality and highly potent. Gojko had tried, bless him, but he only ended up filling Asyl with that white energy.

No matter how much he'd tried to push that energy into his wounds, he simply couldn't heal, not even with Gojko trying to guide him in how to use it. Eventually Asyl returned Gojko's energy to him, baffling the Healer even further. He'd resigned himself to healing the natural way, even though he'd be in this infuriating brace for several more moonturns. Apparently torn ligaments in his knee and a nearly broken arm weren't something to mess around with.

Out of all the things that came out of the interrupted gala, one of the few good things was his growing relationship with his father. His father had turned his back fully on his wife, not forgiving her for teaming up with Tillet and trying to kill his son. Asyl had gotten to meet all his siblings while he was laid up, much to his delight. Arik and Alyn were a wonder, and both were more than excited to practice their Craft around him.

Though Asyl was always careful to not take any of their Craft from them. At least Arik could put on an entertaining show of colors and images for him as the three nestled in the large bed together. Sleeping had been crucial that first fortnight, and if it hadn't been for his brothers and Kende practically sitting on him to keep him in bed, Asyl could have very likely reinjured himself with his restlessness.

He'd finally convinced Kende to let him go back to work at Enchanted Waters. Kende had only agreed so long as Toemi took him and stayed with him the entire day. Tsela was accompanying him as well, and though Asyl would never admit it, the bodyguard helped him quite a bit during the day. He'd gone back to not saying a word, but Asyl found he didn't mind.

"I'm definitely more tired at the end of the day," Asyl told Keyna. "Not absorbing the Craft from the Ignis Plates has cut down on my productive hours. I don't have the energy I used to."

Or maybe it was him simply recovering from his injuries, but Asyl didn't think that was the answer. He'd always felt energized at the end of a day's work when he'd been brewing. That was just gone now that he was using the special gloves Keyna made for him.

Keyna hummed. "That's good to know. Has it negatively impacted anything?"

"Other than not being able to dance with Kende every night?" Asyl teased with a soft smile. "No. I just hope I'm not taking any of his Craft when he needs it more than I do."

Keyna shook her head. "No. According to the prince, energy transfers are deliberate. You've either got to be searching for it, or he has to give it to you. Inanimate objects are different, since they constantly put out Craft energy."

Asyl nodded. It was good to know he wasn't unconsciously taking anything from Kende and delaying or preventing his healing. As soon as his Fated was back to full strength, they would host the introduction dinner with the rest of the Ruvyn family. Naias was kind enough to agree to come as Asyl's family, along with Rojir.

The two turned as Olire burst through the back door, a grin on his winter-flushed face. He rushed to Asyl and nearly bowled him over in a tight hug. Ever since Olire all but saved Asyl from Tillet, the boy had spent as much time as he could with Asyl.

"What is it?" Asyl asked, laughing.

"My mom wrote to Lord Kende. She wants me to come home!" Olire said, bouncing in his excitement.

Asyl smiled wide and hugged Olire tight. "That's wonderful! I'm so happy for you."

"I'm going to run to Lord Kende's manor and let him know," Olire said. "Mom is picking me up tonight. But… can I keep working here? I really like distilling herbs."

"Of course you can," Asyl reassured the boy.

Grinning, Olire gave him a tight hug before running out of the workroom again. Keyna began laughing, and she looked at Asyl once the outside door slammed shut.

"Well now. Times are most certainly changing," Keyna said. "Freyiane, the Void woman who's helping me with research, has been accepted into stores and restaurants she hadn't been able to go into before. You and Lord Kende are setting a wonderful precedent."

Asyl flushed and smiled. His Fated was openly advocating for Voids, and his work on opening a center for disowned youth was proceeding well. Just recently, the priests signed over the abandoned temple to Kende for his community work. Marielle had decided she was going to help set the center up, and with Rojir's help, the renovations were proceeding quickly.

One of the odd changes to the former temple had been the decision to keep the statue of the Goddess Ilyphari with her kneeling as if in supplication. Even the former priests had shrugged when asked about the odd choice of posture. Not that it mattered to those the new center would help, who decorated her with sheer fabrics and flowers hanging from her shoulders. Tributes to the goddess were placed in her cupped hands, often in the form of tree fruit and copper.

It helped that a lot of the gentry were eager to assist to show they didn't share Lady Seni's sentiments about Voids. Once word had gotten out that she'd tried to kill not only her own son, but Kende's Fated, nearly all her support vanished. As for his mother… she was facing trial and incarceration. After she gave birth, she'd be moved from the infirmary ward into a proper cell.

"What else can I do for you?" Asyl asked Keyna with a smile.

"That's it for now. Keep using the gloves so you don't wear out the Plates. I'm sure Kende will gladly pay for servicing, but let's try to delay it as much as we can," Keyna replied, grinning.

A gentle hand tapped Asyl's shoulder, and he looked behind him to see the massive Gaian. He smiled up at the bodyguard and looked back at Keyna. She waved farewell at him and left the workroom.

"Potion ready?" Asyl asked. Tsela nodded. "All right. Let's start decanting and get a chunk of the private orders filled. The storefront is a little sparse, but whatever's left over can go to the shelves."

Tsela followed him to the cauldrons. He was the first Craft Blessed who didn't seem terrified to help him with his alchemy. Well, outside of Kende. Asyl smiled fondly as he filled the bottles with the modified ladle that he could use easily with one hand, remembering when Kende worked with him after he'd burned his hand.

He checked his bond with his love. It was dull, but Asyl didn't panic. Kende was likely asleep again, needing a nap in the middle of the day to be awake when Asyl got home. Just a few more hours. Once he was done decanting with Tsela and got the man to help mix up a frost burn ointment, it would be time to go home.

Just a few more hours….

BIRGIR GAVE Asyl a scowl as he got out of the carriage and sank into the deep snow that hadn't been cleared in front of the portico. The steward sniffed, his lip curling into a sneer, though he opened the front door without saying anything else. Tsela, the tall bastard, hooked his hands underneath Asyl's arms and helped him get to the stairs.

Waving farewell to Toemi, Asyl trotted inside, stamping his feet on the runner to knock off as much snow as he could. Kende wasn't in his study, and the bond told him his love was awake, so Asyl entered the library. His Fated was sitting on the couch next to the fireplace, a book in hand. He was still slightly pale and had lost weight, but he was looking far better than he had even last week.

"Hey, sweetheart," Kende said, looking up from his book. Asyl sat down on the couch next to his Fated and tucked his legs under him, ignoring the twinge of pain from his knee. He leaned into his lover and nestled into him, sighing contentedly. "Good day?"

"Yeah," Asyl replied. "I was able to fill a couple orders for the police to have generic healing potions on hand, and one of the clinics agreed to test my bone-growth potion with patients that sign a waiver. I wasn't able to research more on the eye restoration, but I'll probably have time later this week."

"My little workaholic," Kende murmured, kissing the top of his head. "You should hire another alchemist to help you out so you can focus on your research. It's great you got Naias to help for the front room, but you deserve it too."

"I got Naias to help because she's involved with Prince Yolotzin," Asyl said and laughed. "At least the other Aquan lady is really nice and completely fine with drawing water for me."

That had been a wonderful announcement following his introduction gala. Prince Yolotzin and Lady Naias Elrel were a Fated couple. Her parents were over the moon that she'd be marrying into the royal family. Naias was just excited to have finally met her Fated, and with a man who was down to give her all the children she wanted.

Asyl had cheerfully resigned himself to being the unofficial uncle to her kids, though he would legally be their cousin. If Naias got her way, he'd be their godfather too. He wouldn't be free of children for the foreseeable future, and Asyl couldn't be more pleased.

Kende hummed, set his book down, and drew Asyl into his lap. They exchanged a languid kiss, and when they broke apart, Asyl inhaled deeply to take in his love's scent.

"I've been taking it easy today," Kende said slowly.

"Mmhmm?"

"I think I'm up for some vigorous activity," his lover said with a racy smile.

Asyl snickered and got out of Kende's lap, holding out his hand to help the man up. He couldn't help but smile as they made their way up to their bedroom. He wasn't anything special and he didn't have a Craft, but he was most definitely blessed.

WHO'S WHO

Asyl—Void, 26—Formerly Lord Asyl Seni. Disowned at thirteen, Asyl did what he could to survive until four years ago when he found Naias once more. He became fascinated with alchemy and opened his own shop, Enchanted Waters, with his best friend. Alchemist and researcher, Asyl strives to keep his medicines as cheap as possible to help those in need. Fated to Kende Ruvyn.

Kende Ruvyn—Healer, 32—The youngest son of Duke Kiyiya Ruvyn. Known to his family and the higher gentry as the one to go to for planning parties, though he runs charities and benefits consistently to try and get the gentry to help the city. He wants what's best for the destitute of Alenzon and works hard to keep the city in good health. Fated to Asyl.

Naias Elrel—Aquan, 27—Asyl's best friend and unofficial caretaker. She owns the building that Enchanted Waters operates out of and helps run the front of the store. Naias wants the best for her friend, even if it means smacking him when he's being obtuse. She dreams of traveling and having a large family. Fated to Yolotzin Navarre-Hamonn.

Siora Thelee—Seer, 38—Kende's personal assistant and highly loyal to him. She's got a stubborn personality and is slow to let newcomers in. Always prepared, with a mind like a steel trap, Siora is always ready to help Kende, even if she disagrees with him. Married to her Fated, she lives in the servant's hall at Ruvyn manor.

Gojko Laltine—Healer, 58—Despite being renowned throughout Averia as a surgeon of skill, Gojko quietly retired to become the Ruvyn family's personal physician. He took Kende under his wing and helped train him to be a proper Healer and to have an open mind. His two daughters, one a Healer and the other a Void, left Averia and traveled to Zothua. Lives in the servant's hall at Ruvyn manor.

Rojir—Void, 46—Rojir has lived on the streets of Alenzon for nearly three decades after his aunt kicked him out. He takes in newly disowned children and teenagers and tries to help guide them to have an easier future. Rojir acts as a central hub to those on the streets as a protector, mediator, and father figure. He took a particular shine to Asyl and would have gladly adopted him if it had been possible.

Birgir Cyncas—Gale, 67—The surly and pompous steward at Ruvyn manor. He keeps the household running smoothly, even if the occupants don't understand how. Deeply distrustful of Voids due to his theological upbringing. Reports to Duke Ruvyn on Kende's activity under the guise of keeping Kende safe.

Tillet Gaten—Ignis, 36—Kidnapper and abuser of Asyl and potentially other Voids, Tillet's life goal is to make Voids suffer. He's needlessly cruel and gladly allied himself with Ilfa once he heard of her widespread hatred. It's unknown if he knew of the familial ties between Asyl and Ilfa at the time, though he was aware at Asyl's introduction gala. His ultimate plans are unknown.

Olire Ebornzaine—Void, 13—A timid young man who was disowned once his Awakening failed. He's academically smart and picks up alchemy quickly. He's fierce when it comes to protecting those he cares about. Olire tries to stay hopeful about the future, though he gets overwhelmed fairly easily. He views Asyl like a big brother and looks up to Kende for what he did to help him.

Jaclyn Pellize—Ignis, 42—Kende's eldest sister. She's a no-nonsense woman and often thinks her work and opinions should be what everyone else believes. Those with non-elemental Crafts are beneath her and aren't to be acknowledged. Fated to Macik Pellize.

Macik Pellize—Sympathetic, 44—Detective within the Alenzon police force. Raised to be open-minded, Macik believes Voids should have the same protections as all other Craft Blessed. Though Macik is usually amicable, those who threaten or injure his family are treated with open hostility. Fated to Jaclyn Pellize.

Maielle Duotas—Gaian, 34—Kende's youngest sister and strongest advocate. Anything that makes him happy makes her happy. She refuses to let life get her down, doing her best to stay cheerful and kind. Though she will take her revenge however she can, even or especially if it's petty.

Lairne Seni—Gale, 46—Head of the household, Lairne controls the imports of produce into Alenzon. While he chose to disown Asyl, he regretted his decision within a moonturn. He does his best to pacify his wife, though he doesn't share her views on Voids. Lairne wants what's best for his children and to see them happy. Fated to Ilfa Seni.

Ilfa Seni—Harvester, 45—Twisted in her hatred of Voids, Ilfa joined forces with Tillet to try and arrest every Void while trying to convince the gentry that Voids are no better than animals. It's unknown if she was aware of Tillet's role in Asyl's life before the gala. While she's had many other children after Asyl, she holds them at a distance, not wanting to love another child that becomes a Void. Fated to Lairne Seni.

Alyn Seni—Healer, 13—Heir to the Seni household, Alyn learned quickly from watching his mother to stay quiet and observe rather than act rashly. He's rather reserved, though endlessly curious and wants to know all about his older brother, whom he would have loved to grow up with.

Arik Seni—Illusionist, 13—Energetic and prone to emotional outbursts, Arik often takes the back seat in tense situations. Unlike his twin, Arik acts without thinking, though it hasn't gotten him in trouble yet. What he lacks in forethought, he makes up for with enthusiasm.

Airol Seni—Unawakened, 5—The youngest girl in the Seni household. Curious and joyful, she tries to get her big brothers to play with her even though they'd rather not play with dollies. Apparently resembles Asyl, according to Alyn.

Keyna Wypsei—Ignis, 28—One of the few redheads in Alenzon, Keyna quickly made a name for herself at 18 when she learned how to store latent Ignis energy into constructs, such as the Ignis Plates. She continually works to better her invention in hopes it'll use less energy and power, and is highly curious on how Voids interact with Craft-worked items.

Toemi Pintox—Aquan, 30—Kende's faithful carriage driver. He's a reclusive man, preferring the company of his horses rather than his fellows. Whenever he's waiting after driving Kende to wherever, he'll curl up with a book after seeing to his horses. He's ambivalent about Voids, though he enjoys Asyl's company well enough.

Lanil Shuman—Seer, 24—Asyl's personal assistant, Lanil is a brilliant young woman who has a mind like a steel trap. She's fast at organization, which is something Asyl greatly appreciates. Lanil is a kind woman, and though she wasn't raised one way or the other about Voids, she doesn't believe the stigma surrounding them. All she cares about is seeing her employer happy, though she's still a bit shy around Kende.

Tsela Koi—Gaian, 40—Unable to speak due to massive anxiety unless in extreme situations, Tsela shied away from any professions that would put him in a leadership role. Despite his Craft being fairly powerful, he's much more comfortable as a silent bodyguard where he doesn't need to use his Craft very much at all. He appreciates Kende and Asyl's willingness to be patient with his pantomiming rather than forcing him to speak.

Maerie Sceite—Illusionist, 61—Maerie's first and only love has been clothing. It's her dream to see Alenzon full of beautiful people wearing beautiful clothes. Craft doesn't matter to her. Though she does judge if someone comes into her shop with ill-fitting or colored clothing.

Heina Nsich—Harvester, 45—Prideful of her plants, Heina strives to make her herbs the healthiest and most potent of all Averia. She's often joyful and sees the best in others, though still a shrewd businesswoman. And according to Asyl, far too observant for her own good.

Mato—Void, 44—Mato was already on the streets when Rojir was kicked out. They quickly struck up a friendship, and then a relationship shortly after. Together, they pulled the shattered Void community together to make it into a refuge despite the conditions they live in. Mato walked away from Rojir after Asyl was abducted, too grief-stricken to continue their work.

Kiyiya Ruvyn—Ignis, 62—Younger brother to Tonalli, Kiyiya inherited the title of duke. He's a severe, suspicious man who seemingly valued strength over any other trait. Due to this, he treated Kende poorly while he was a boy and disagrees with his line of work. Even still, he's loyal to his family and will put his mistrust aside to protect them. Fated to Liluya Ruvyn.

Liluya Ruvyn—Gaian, 61—Raised in a strict household, Liluya's only escape was through the romance novels she hid under her bed. She's a romantic at heart, though she does her best to hide it to varying degrees. All she wants is for her children to be happy, though she won't contradict her husband, always wanting to put out a united front. Fated to Kiyiya Ruvyn.

Yolotzin Navarre-Hamonn—Sympathetic, 30—The crown prince of Averia, Yolotzin is a kind soul who waits for as much information to present itself before he reacts. He's frequently ruled by his heart when it comes to those he loves, even if that means he doesn't see their flaws. Lover to Kajaan Pernoac. Fated to Naias Elrel.

Kajaan Pernoac—Aquan, 30—Raised in the castle alongside Yolotzin after his mother's death, he and the prince grew up together. As such, he fell into the role of Yolotzin's personal secretary and handles almost all of the prince's correspondence and traveling details. He's friendly, though reserved, and can't abide seeing someone hurt. Lover to Yolotzin Navarre-Hamonn.

Tonalli Navarre-Hamonn—Ignis, 66—King of Averia and Kiyiya's elder brother. It's said at one point, he loved his children dearly and ruled the kingdom kindly. Somewhere within the last twenty years, that changed, and Averia's laws have gotten tighter. The reason for his change of heart is unknown, as is the reason why his wife has been absent for the same amount of time.

WHAT'S WHAT

(And other worldbuilding info)

CONCERNING CRAFTS:

Awakening—Upon a child's thirteenth birthday, at the exact second they first drew breath, their Craft becomes accessible to them. There's no real explanation as to why the child doesn't have access to their Craft beforehand. Many kingdoms treat the occasion as a ceremony, often resulting in a several-hour party. Traditionally, the child will tilt their face to the heavens to receive their Craft, though it isn't necessary.

Fated—Believed to be two halves of a whole; Fated soulmates. The tug that many describe only occurs when the two are ready to meet, even if they already know each other. This tug can expand over several miles. Once established, the two share a connection, able to locate their Fated many miles away and can feel their current emotions. The strength of the bond depends on the cumulative strength of the individual. In very rare circumstances, the bond can be rejected. If done so by both parties, the break is clean. Otherwise, the one rejecting their Fated is subjected to heartache.

Craft Mark—Upon Awakening, the Mark appears in the center of the forehead. It is a simple symbol, easily recognizable at a glance. For the most part, the mark is slightly darker than the skin, like a mole or blemish. For those with darker skin, the Mark is a few shades lighter. Some cultures paint their Craft Mark to match what they're wearing for the day.

Craft Blessed—References anyone who has gone through their Awakening. Some religious sects claim that Voids aren't a part of the blessed and preach against them. Most believe that the Craft given to an individual is predetermined, while very few insist that it's based on their actions as a child and potential or intent.

Aquan—Someone who can manipulate not only water, but all liquids. They're able to locate water sources deep underground and even pull moisture from the air. A more uncommon talent is being able to breathe underwater. One of the rarest abilities is to be able to manipulate liquids on a molecular level.

Gale—Manipulators of air and other gases. They're often guardians of the sky and will be the "canary" when it comes to mining expeditions. Rarer talents run toward being able to manipulate the air around to make people and objects fly. Even rarer is being able to use their Craft to manipulate the weather, though those individuals are heavily regulated.

Gaian—Movers of earth and metals. Gaians can form the earth beneath their feet at a whim, and the stronger individuals are able to manipulate the hardest metals. Some Gaians are able to identify the composition of an area immediately to know where to plant to yield the best crops without the aid of a Harvester.

Harvester—Attuned to all plant life, Harvesters are able to coax plants to grow without blight and on minimal resources. Many tend to stay within the agricultural professions and take pride in sustaining their communities. Strong Harvesters can grow a plant from a seed with just a whisper, though it's rare to be able to do so.

Healer—The one Craft that is bound together by a guild. Healers are only able to go into some form of healthcare, whether that's general or private practice, alchemy, or research, with very few exceptions. They're enrolled in school from the moment they Awaken to learn anatomy and psychology. Their Craft allows them to "dive" into a Craft Blessed patient to get an itemized list of ailments to then invoke healing. Children and Voids are unable to be healed this way and must rely on mundane medicines. While children are completely unaffected by healing, Voids absorb whatever the Healer pours into them, though to no effect.

Ignis/Ignian—Tamers of fire and energy. Ignians can call flame from nothing via their Craft, though trying to burn something that's not flammable is a greater energy drain. Some Ignians have figured out how to use their Craft to heat or cool the air around them. A very few Ignians are fireproof and have been rumored to be able to alter lava flow.

Illusionist—Often viewed as the most useless Craft, Illusionists are able to create images of varying detail that hang in the air. Some use their Craft as a substitute for fireworks during burn bans. A few Illusionists can create lifelike illusions that can move in a realistic way. The talent to be able to conjure sound with their illusion is almost unheard of.

Seer—Depending on the person, Seers can be the most annoying Craft Blessed solely based on the unpredictability of their Craft. Their abilities range far from seeing multiple futures but being unable to act upon any of them, to seeing one single critical point, but not knowing the circumstances around it. Most of the time, Seers are awake and are taken to a fugue state where they have their Vision and are released. Some have their Visions as dreams instead.

Sympathetic—Always able to feel the emotions around them, Sympathetics are nearly impossible to lie to. They're eerily good at reading people and drawing out their true intentions. To some, emotions are a specific color aura or shape, whereas others describe it as a type of scent or tone. Very few Sympathetics can read thoughts at the base level, though that tends to be draining.

Void—The unofficial tenth Craft. Voids are unique, as they have no well to replenish their reservoir. Instead, they must rely on outside Craft Blessed to give them energy to manipulate. Voids can either take the energy as is from the individual or strip it down to its pure form. They can use this energy to either enhance their own bodies to give them better strength, speed, or senses, or they can transfer it into another Craft Blessed. In an energy transfer, the receiver either must be the same Craft as the donor, or the Void needs to strip it to pure energy.

Reservoir—An innate pool of ready-to-use power by the Craft Blessed. Larger reservoirs usually denote stronger individuals who can either use that energy in a single strong burst or sustain a smaller effect for longer. Smaller reservoirs hold less and therefore tend to leave their hosts in a weaker capacity. Continual training after Awakening until about twenty is essential to maximize the size of a reservoir, though some claim the size is predetermined.

Well—The size of the well determines how fast the reservoir is refilled. Larger wells naturally hold more and can produce energy faster than a thinner one. Voids are the only adults who don't have a well and have no natural energy regeneration. If a Craft Blessed drains their Craft well all the way down to their core, they run the risk of stripping their souls and ending their life.

KINGDOMS:

Averia—The southwestern most kingdom. Stretches further north and south than it does east to west. The eastern border pushes up to the Reidden mountain range. The western and southern edges of the kingdom lead to the Duparthon Sea. To the north is the kingdom of Pemalia. Unfriendly toward Voids. Claims more Seers than any other kingdom. The king lives in Castle Avitou, located at the center of Alenzon. Her king is Tonalli Navarre-Hamonn.

Zothua—A massive desert kingdom that stretches across most of the continent. A large chunk of the kingdom is claimed by the Laiyi desert. To the east is Nabene, southeast Bhyvine, north Pemalia, and west Averia. Claims more Aquans than other kingdoms. The kingdom's capital is Sestella, home to Paelfjord Castle. King Cadeyrn Greatblaze is her current ruler.

Pemalia—A harsh, landlocked barren kingdom. From the western to eastern border is Valvinte, south Zothua, southwest Averia, and southeast Nabene. Filled with arid hills and fallow plains, Pemalia doesn't have much to boast about, except for the pride of her people. Claims more Ignians than other kingdoms. The Royal city of Cleroux encompasses Parandor Castle. Ruled by Queen Linriyo Dallae.

Valvinte—A kingdom to the far north, frigid and covered in snow and expansive forests. North, east, and western borders lead to the icy, perilous Cresok ocean. To the south is Pemalia. Produces the most Harvesters. Droskyn Castle is nestled inside the city of Evigoza, which is built into the Okapi Forest. Currently ruled by Queen Terenna.

Bhyvine—Northwest border leads to Zothua and east to Nabene. The rest of the western and southern border leads to the Duparthon Sea. Most of Bhyvine alternates between plains and marshland. Produces a large amount of Gaians. The capital is Khathen, home to Ichepi Castle. Ruled by King Cossus Verulus.

Nabene—A far eastern kingdom. Northwestern border leads to Zothua and southwest to Bhyvine. North border leads to Pemalia. East leads to the expansive Haeftanne Sea. Fairly flat, Nabene raises a variety of animals and is known as a pastoral kingdom. Unfriendly toward queer couples. Produces the most Gales. The capital is Oviedura, home to Draris Castle. Ruled by King Henrik Gyula.

Ilyphari—Goddess of all Craft Blessed. Her priests usually preach about kindness, love, and acceptance, except in Averia, where Voids are shunned. She's always depicted as a mother and never has had a Craft Mark placed on her forehead.

Tratane—Intravenous drug, upper. Offers the user a euphoric release while potentially causing hallucinations. Highly addictive and popular amongst those who live in squalor. It's also an appetite suppressant, often causing the user to rapidly lose weight. The effects of a dose can last anywhere from three to eight hours depending on quality, quantity, and the person's metabolism. No restrictions on those it can affect.

Keep reading for an excerpt from
The Guardian of Machu Llaqta
by Ariel Tachna!

Deep in the rainforest, in a land time passed by, dwelled a forgotten people known only as the Lost Ones, if they were known at all. They lived as they always had, simply and in harmony with the land. From time to time, one of them would wander the wider world to see what had been learned in their absence and, if the wanderer deemed it worthy of the goddess, bring it back to aid the Lost Ones. In time the goddess blessed them for their faithfulness, bestowing on them Chapaqpuma, a guardian who would ensure no harm came to them from outside, for everyone knew outsiders meant trouble—disease, famine, war, and death followed wherever they trod.

The role and gifts of Chapaqpuma passed down from generation to generation, parent to child to grandchild and beyond, for the need of the goddess's protection never waned. The gifts of the goddess were bountiful, but the price was high, and Chapaqpuma could not walk that path alone. Instinct pushed Chapaqpuma to find a mate, a partner in whom to balance the senses so that the guardian could always return to the valley in proper form, yet few were they who could meet all of a guardian's needs. Thus it became the way of the Lost Ones for Chapaqpuma to take not one but two mates, a balance to each other as much as to the guardian, so that when calamity came, Chapaqpuma had the strength to ward it off and the humanity to return home after.

Thus was the way of the Lost Ones.

Thus is our way now.

DR. VICTOR Itoua stopped outside the anthropology department chair's door, glanced down at the grant recipient notice in his hand for courage, and rapped sharply on the thick wood.

"Come," Dr. Fowler called from inside.

Victor opened the door and walked in. "Do you have a minute, sir?"

"One, maybe. What do you need?" Victor might be accustomed to Fowler's curt tone and short, blunt ripostes, but they never failed to leave him on edge. At least Fowler spoke to everyone that way.

"I've come to submit notice for a sabbatical for the summer and fall semesters. The grant I was hoping for came through, and I'll need at least six months in the field to do it justice." Victor handed the dossier to Fowler and braced himself for the response.

"Really, Itoua?" Fowler frowned. "I thought we'd agreed you would stop this nonsense with the Philli-philli. Next you're going to tell me you're going to search for Sasquatch."

Victor suppressed a sigh with the same blank stare he'd learned to maintain in the face of any criticism. They looked at him askance because he was foreign, because he was Black, because he approached things differently from most in the establishment. He didn't let it stop him, but some days it got old. "If you look closely, sir, the grant is to research the origin and evolution of the Philli-philli legend among the Indigenous peoples of the Andes and upper Amazon, not to prove or disprove the existence of such a creature. The legend exists and is a valid subject of study regardless of its veracity."

"Fine." Fowler tossed the dossier on his desk. "But you better get the best damned paper in the world out of this—and not one hint of any of your crazy ideas about whether there's such a thing as a half man, half beast running around South America—or you'll be looking for another job."

"Understood, sir." Victor gathered his papers and turned to leave.

"And take Harris with you," Fowler ordered. "He's the only one crazy enough to put up with your theories for that long."

"Yes, sir."

Victor had already planned on asking Jordan Harris, the department's best—in Victor's opinion—research and teaching assistant, if he would be interested in the project. Every time Harris had gone into the field with him, his help had been invaluable, as Victor had known it would be from the first time they met, on a joint field expedition he'd done in the Yucatan with Harris's supervising professor during his undergraduate years. He would still ask, not demand, but now he'd have Dr. Fowler's prior approval to add to the discussion.

And if it meant he had six months or more to spend with the object of his unrequited, unethical, and impossible crush, eh bien, he'd survived worse.

He glanced at his watch. At this time of day, Harris would be finishing up his last section of Intro to Anthropology. Victor could catch him outside his class, suggest a cup of coffee in his office, and talk to him in private.

Harris was finishing his lecture when Victor arrived at the classroom, giving Victor a moment to just look at him. It was unprofessional, not to mention unethical given Victor's role as supervisor to the department's teaching assistants, a position Victor had fortunately not held when Harris was hired. If he had, he would never have been able to suggest Harris apply to the department's combined master's/doctoral program when he realized Harris would be finishing his gap year internship in a matter of months and was looking for an advanced degree program and a job to go with it. Victor would never act on it, of course. If he thought he had a shadow of a chance, he might feel differently, might look harder for a way around the issues, but Victor wasn't blind. He'd seen the kind of men Harris went out with. Young, beautiful, flashy. All the things Victor wasn't. No, he knew where he fit in Harris's life—as a mentor, maybe a friend, but it would never go beyond that. Harris could have anyone he wanted. Why should he settle for Victor?

Even knowing all that, though, he couldn't seem to stop himself from looking. Harris wasn't what Victor would call classically handsome, even with his blue-gray eyes and sandy blond hair. His nose had been broken at least once, possibly more, but paired with his crooked smile, it gave him a seductive air more than a dangerous one. The same went for the scar on his jawline, barely visible unless he started letting his beard grow out. Then the lack of stubble drew the eye like a magnet. And that didn't even take into account the calluses on his hands. Victor had never asked him where he worked out or what kind of martial arts he did, but Harris had to be maintaining his skills somewhere. Victor might not have kept up with all the skills he'd learned during his mandatory military service in France, but being a decent shot had come in handy more than once on field expeditions too, for hunting and for defending himself from anything—human or animal—that might think any of his team would make easy prey.

Harris hid his rough edges well enough to pass muster at the university, but Victor was a past master at seeing beyond the obvious. He had to be if he was going to make it as an anthropologist. Harris always wore a sports jacket and dress shirt when he was teaching, but Victor had seen him switch them out for a T-shirt—usually one with a punny Lord of the Rings quote on it—as soon as his classes were over, topped by a beat-up leather bomber jacket when the weather was cool enough to justify it.

Harris dismissed class, Victor's cue to step inside.

"Do you have a few minutes, Mr. Harris?" Victor asked as the students filed out.

"For you, sir? Sure."

Victor tamped down his instinctive desire to preen at Harris's reply. He was never impolite to any of the professors, but his response to Victor was always a touch warmer than his interactions with anyone else. Victor told himself it was the camaraderie of time spent together on field expeditions, nothing more, which did absolutely nothing to stop the feeling. No other reason for Harris to be nicer to his graying, fortysomething supervisor.

"Good. I'll put on a pot of coffee."

Harris's smile widened. "If you're offering coffee, I might even have more than a few minutes."

Which was exactly why Victor made sure to have a fresh pot brewed whenever he had a meeting with Harris.

He didn't let that show, though, rolling his eyes instead. "Meet me in my office."

"Sir, yes, sir." Harris threw him a half-assed salute.

Victor turned away so Harris wouldn't see the smile he couldn't quite hide, although knowing how good Harris's observational skills were, he probably saw it anyway. The man had been a Marine sniper, the best of the best to hear him tell it. Then again, Victor had seen him shoot in the field. He'd never seen Harris miss, so maybe his tales weren't all tall.

Victor went back to his office and started the coffee brewing by rote, his mind racing as he went over plans for the upcoming trip. Most of his research was at his apartment rather than in his office, but he'd spent enough hours staring at it that he didn't need the maps in front of him now to start thinking about where they would need to visit. Rumored sightings of Philli-philli ranged from Quito, Ecuador, all the way down the coast to Santiago, Chile, far too great a distance for even a mythical creature to cover, but the majority of the sightings were in Peru between Lake Titicaca and the ruins of Huánuco Pampa. He flipped his atlas open to Peru and started marking places on the map: Cusco, Pisac, Urubamba, Ollantaytambo, of course, but anything they heard there would be tainted by modern influences. They'd still start there, if only to see if there had been any new sightings or rumors, but ultimately they'd have to head into the mountains and possibly the Amazon headwaters to get closer to the original legends. Victor might hope they would find more than just legends, but he'd keep that to himself.

He looked up when Harris rapped on his open door. He'd unbuttoned his dress shirt, revealing a Mordor Fun Run T-shirt. He had his leather jacket hooked over his shoulder and looked good enough to eat. Not that Victor was looking.

"Hey, boss. Is that coffee ready?"

Victor inhaled the rich, dark aroma of brewing coffee and glanced at the nearly full carafe. "It should be. Pour yourself a cup and have a seat."

Harris froze on his way to the coffee pot. "Is this a good seat or a bad seat?"

"I suppose that depends on whether you're interested in going in the field with me again." Victor kept his tone even by force of will. He'd learned as far back as the first joint expedition that Harris had a whole host of abandonment and authority issues and that the best way to address them was to be as honest and steady as he could be.

Harris spun to look at him. "You got the grant?"

"Coffee first. Then we'll talk," Victor said with a chuckle.

Harris shot him a disgruntled look but poured two cups of coffee and doctored them both with cream and sugar. When Victor took a sip of the mug Harris handed him, the coffee was exactly the way he would have made it for himself.

Another sign of just how observant Harris was. Another sign of just how gone Victor was on him. Get it together. No lusting after your subordinates.

"Okay, I have coffee. Now spill. Did you get the grant?"

Victor allowed himself one moment of internal glee before pulling his professional façade back into place. "I got the grant."

Harris's eyes, always sharp and focused, brightened, and he leaned forward. "When do we leave?"

Any other time, the slight breathlessness in Harris's voice would have set Victor's imagination racing, but he was too excited about the grant for it to register as more than shared enthusiasm. That said, it was one thing to gamble with his own career. Gambling with Harris's was something else entirely. "Harris… Jordan, have you thought about this? You know as well as I do how the academic community views Philliphilli. You'll get about as much respect for whatever we accomplish in Peru as you would for chasing Sasquatch or Nessie."

Harris's expression didn't change a bit. "I know, sir. I've listened to people talk smack about you for it since I got here, but that's their problem. I'm never gonna be in the big leagues. Eventually I'd like to be an assistant teaching professor instead of just a TA, but that's really a matter of getting off my ass, finishing my thesis, and applying somewhere as opposed to needing publications or shit like that. And honestly, the only reason I want that is for the salary. I like what I'm doing here. I like the teaching, I like the students, and I like the opportunities to do research with you. And anyone else who has ongoing projects."

A shiver of delight ran up Victor's spine at the notion that the last sentence was tacked on as an afterthought, but believing that would be self-delusion. He wouldn't allow himself to imagine such a thing with Harris sitting across the desk from him. He wasn't anything special, just a boring associate professor whose obsession meant most of his colleagues kept him at arm's length.

"If you're sure, then we leave as soon as the semester is over. Dr. Fowler has approved a sabbatical through the end of fall semester. That gives us seven months to see what we can find. Of course we can petition to extend if we need it, but it's a good chunk of time to start."

"Good thing my passport is up-to-date. A month isn't a whole lot of time to prepare," Harris replied.

"Do you need help getting things set?" Victor asked before he could stop the words from escaping. "Subletting your apartment or anything like that?"

"Nah, I got it covered. I usually go on field expeditions in the summer anyway, or travel if I can't find one, so I have someone lined up for the first three months already, and I'll figure something out for the fall. Or ask my neighbors to keep an eye on things if I have to. It wouldn't be the first time."

Harris's predilection for joining every possible expedition had made him invaluable as a research assistant, but it had slowed down his doctoral program. Of course that meant more time for Victor to spend with him, both in the field and at the university, so he wasn't going to complain.

"In that case, here's what I was thinking…."

JORDAN HARRIS let himself into his crappy studio apartment, tossed his jacket on the back of his pullout couch, and flopped onto the lumpy cushions.

Peru. Incan ruins. Legends of Philli-philli. And Dr. Victor Itoua. Months and months of close proximity to Dr. Itoua, watching him be all sophisticated and shit as he asked people all the subtle questions that drew out information they didn't even know they had with a finesse that no one else, in Jordan's experience, could match. He'd probably be all casual too, instead of in his usual suits, meaning Jordan would have to suffer through glimpses of strong forearms and broad shoulders not hidden beneath tailored suit coats. Oh, and no tie. That was practically naked by Dr. Itoua's standards, which would leave Jordan perpetually horny. And he'd have to do it all without giving away how hot he thought his boss was. Even if they weren't at the university, it was university-approved field research, and while Dr. Itoua might unbend enough to lose the formal attire, he'd never unbend enough to forget who they were or why they were there. And even if he did (he wouldn't, but even if he did), he took his role as Jordan's supervisor too seriously to abuse his power. Never mind that it wouldn't be an abuse of power at all since Jordan had been head over ass for the guy since they first met. Since Dr. Itoua had looked at him and seen someone worth working with rather than someone with good aim and a bad attitude, a kid with a GED and nothing going for him but enough time in the Marines for the GI Bill to pay for his education. No, Dr. Itoua was too goddamned honorable to take what Jordan would give him willingly.

Not that Jordan blamed him. He knew his own worth all too well, and while he made a decent teaching assistant, the rest of his life was pretty much the definition of fuckup. Witness the crappy apartment, secondhand couch, and lumpy cushions. He could take notes, catalog information, and teach classes, but he'd never have Dr. Itoua's ability to slip in and out of whatever culture they were studying or find the connection between random facts that everyone else missed. Dr. Itoua would say he had his grandparents and the summers he'd spent with them in the Republic of Congo to thank for that, but Jordan had always thought it was more than that.

Jordan himself, on the other hand, was too brash, the veneer of civilized society sitting on him like an ill-fitting jacket, something he had to force into place when he was dealing with the faculty bigwigs, rather than something that came to him naturally. At this point he only even asked for details ahead of time out of sheer stubborn fuckery—and the desire to impress Dr. Itoua with his interest. He definitely didn't want to lose out on a chance to work with the guy because he thought Jordan didn't care about his projects. Even his longstanding obsession with Philli-philli.

Jordan grabbed his cell and texted his best friend, Nandini Rakkar, who he'd met in the Marines and who'd gotten a job with Interpol straight out of the service. With Nan, he didn't have to pretend. She was as foulmouthed and cocky as he was. More now since she was still in an environment where she could get away with it and he had to keep it under wraps around anyone except her. And sometimes Dr. Itoua.

I'm so fucked.

The phone buzzed back almost immediately.

When aren't you?

Fuck you too. Seven months of field research, just me and Dr. Itoua, in the Andes. Kill me now.

Nandini didn't reply for so long Jordan thought she'd given up on him (or was coming to actually kill him—he never knew with her) when the phone buzzed again.

The Philli-philli? Watch your back.

WTF, Nan? Not you too.

Watch Itoua's back if you won't watch your own. His back, Harris, not his ass.

Jordan's cheeks burned at the jab. He'd watch Dr. Itoua's ass all day any day if he could get away with it, but still…. I know my job, Rakkar.

Then do it, because there've been reports of renewed criminal activity in the Amazon basin. Too soon to tell what kind exactly, but enough to be taken seriously.

Jordan tossed his phone into his bag and stalked out of the room. Damn sneaky Interpol agents, always thinking they knew everything and only sharing it in cryptic little dribbles designed to drive him fucking crazy.

Fine.

He'd go to Peru and do his job, both as research assistant and as bodyguard—he had no illusions that his military background and ability to shoot everything from a bow and arrow to a sniper rifle added to his value in the field, both for hunting and for protection—and he'd help Dr. Itoua prove once and for fucking all that the Philli-philli legend was a worthy topic of academic pursuit, if only for its prevalence among the Indigenous tribes of the Andes.

VICTOR SET his briefcase by the credenza in the entry to his condo, pulled off his tie, and slipped off his shoes. He'd spent the drive home thinking about the weather in Peru and what he would need to take with him, not the fact that he'd be spending the next seven months with Harris. Arriving in June, they wouldn't have to worry about the rainy season for the first few months, but they would have to take the varying weather into consideration, what with the altitude in some places counteracting the subtropical latitude. If they stayed in the alpine desert and cloud forests, they'd be looking at weather from near freezing to midsixties, but if they ended up in the upper Amazon basin around Manu or farther north, they'd have warmer weather, more humidity, and the rainy season starting in September.

Who was he kidding? He could pack for this kind of fieldwork in his sleep, especially in Peru.

He poured himself two fingers of cognac and slumped into his favorite chair, all pretense gone. Only here in the privacy of his own space could he truly let down his guard, which was what worried him most. He trusted Harris with his field notes, his "crazy" obsession with Philli-philli, and his life, but not with his sanity, and having Harris with him on this research trip was guaranteed to test that. He sighed deeply. He'd dealt with his Harris-inspired obsession for years. It hadn't killed him yet. The next few months wouldn't be any different, even if this would be the first time they would be alone together in the field.

He just needed to grow a pair and deal with it. Yes, he'd probably be sharing lodgings with Harris while in Peru, at least some of the time, but while they were in the outlying villages, they could find a house, cabin, hut, something with separate bedrooms, and if they were out in the rainforest, they could sleep in separate tents. Even if he had to carry his own damn tent. It would take weeks, if not months, to win enough trust to move past simplified stories and get to deeper truths, and even if they managed to get a lead sooner than that, he had no illusions they'd find what they were looking for right away. The Andes were immense, and the rumors had Philli-philli showing up at locations impossible distances apart, even for a supernatural creature of legend.

He'd just have to pull his professionalism around himself so tightly that nothing could get through, not even the sight of Harris's arms in the tight T-shirts he preferred. Or his ass in the cargo pants or jeans he wore most of the time, even when he was teaching. And if they ended up in the rainforest, Harris would replace them with cargo shorts, and then he'd have to deal with Harris's legs instead.

Just the thought was enough to make his cock stir. He banged his head against the headrest of his recliner. He was so fucked.

Scan the QR code below to order

AR BRYANT has frequently been accused of having their head in the clouds, and quite frankly, it's a lot more fun up there! For as long as they can remember, they have loved telling stories. They wrote their first story in the third grade, and it involved the Backstreet Boys going to the moon. AR is a PNW cryptid who loves the rain, windstorms, sandy beaches, and redwood forests.

They currently guard their book hoard alongside their dog while their two cats get annoyed when AR tries to write, reducing their lap time. If they're not reading or writing, AR is likely playing on their Switch, cross-stitching, or playing their ranger-druid in D&D with their friends. Their favorite genre, in basically everything, is fantasy. More dragons please!

While AR finds social media exhausting, they'd be glad to hear from you at atarbryant91@gmail.com!